"Chronic illness and invisible disabilities are rarely addressed, though prevalent in society. These illnesses can often steal one's dreams, but Leon's characters remind the reader that God's plans make it possible to cope with daily battles and still live life to the fullest. The author's personal experiences are evident in the accuracy of details."
—ROMANTIC TIMES, 4½ Stars, *Top Pick*

"This unusual mix of people discover true courage and friendship as they travel cross-country together. Their growing relationships will tug a few tears, and leave you thinking twice about what steals contentment and keeps you from following your dreams. Poignant, funny, and inspiring, *To Dance with Dolphins* is a beautifully authentic tale of trial and triumph from a master storyteller. I loved this story and highly recommend it!"
—CAMILLE EIDE,
Author of *Like There's No Tomorrow* and *Like a Love Song*

"The story of a cross-country trip by RV with people who met in a disabilities support group, Bonnie Leon's *To Dance with Dolphins* was a total surprise to me. What a wonderful, unique novel. While the group from different age groups tries to overcome their physical disabilities, they discovered not all their disabilities *are* physical. The characters are multi-dimensional, and they pulled me straight into the story with them. They faced insurmountable difficulties, and supported each other through it all. I loved the symbolism of the title. The spiritual struggles and growth were powerful, with touches of romances. A truly delightful read. I had a hard time putting the book down."
—LENA NELSON DOOLEY,
Multi-Award-Winning Author of the McKenna's Daughters Series, *8 Weddings and a Miracle,* and *A Texas Christ...*

D0778374

"*To Dance with Dolphins* is a heart-warming story filled with adventure, faith, and friendships. Bonnie Leon's powerful writing transports readers on a cross-country journey—both over the highways and into her character's hearts. Highly recommended!"
—ANN SHOREY,
Author of the Sisters at Heart Series

"Bonnie Leon has crafted an engaging tale of bravery, adventure, and friendship. Readers will root for these unlikely travelers as they trek across the USA, finding strength to overcome their circumstances, and become the heroes of their own stories."
—CATHY ELLIOT,
Author of *A Stitch in Crime*

"Author Bonnie Leon asks some hard questions about suffering in this compassionately written book. Even though we can't know the entire plan God has for us, she points us to trust in He who is greater for the answers and the Peace that passes all understanding. This story touched me in a personal way. I've asked many of those same questions and am on that daily path of submission and faith right along with Claire, Sean, Tom, Willow, and Taylor. This feel-good story will touch your heart and bring you a better comfort and deeper empathy for those suffering from all matter of brokenness—physical and spiritual—leaving you with the Hope that never fails."
—APRIL McGOWAN,
Healing Fiction Author

"Deeply felt and courageously expressed, Leon explores the difficult intersection of faith and pain in her adventurous first foray into contemporary fiction."
—HILLARY MANTON LODGE,
Author of the INSPY-Nominated *A Table by the Window*

TO Dance WITH Dolphins

Bonnie Leon

Ashberry Lane

Published in association with Wendy Lawton of Books & Such Literary Agency.

ISBN 978-1-941720-00-4

Library of Congress Control Number: 2015946444

Cover design by Miller Media Solutions
Photos from www.istockphoto.com
Edited by Andrea Cox, Kristen Johnson, Rachel Lulich, and Amy Smith

FICTION / Women's Fiction / Christian Romance

In Memory
of
My sister Leslie

Dedicated to my courageous daughter Sarah

CHAPTER ONE

Claire Murray headed for the barn, a burst of cold air lifting her long blonde hair and tossing it into her face. Pulling it back into a ponytail, she glanced at a darkening sky, her cane propped against her leg.

Hopefully a powerful spring storm would soon rumble through the rolling countryside of Southern Oregon.

She opened the door and stepped inside. The smell of hay and horse swept out to meet her like a wave of comfort. Drawing the door closed, she hitched it up a notch to make sure it fell into place and couldn't swing open.

In the peak of the rafters, a shadow of an owl moved. A sparrow darted to a place beneath the eaves where a nest was tucked out of sight. Soon there would be chirping fledglings courageously making their first flight.

Claire breathed in the familiar. Did she have the courage to venture out from the place that had been her refuge for the last twenty-two years?

A soft nicker came from the nearest stall.

Cinnamon.

Claire made her way to the horse, grabbing a handful of grain from a bucket as she passed. "Here you go, girl." She slipped her hand through the gate.

The big red horse snuffled the grain out of her palm.

"How are you this morning? Ready for a run, I'll bet." If only she could be the one riding her. "We had some good times, didn't we?" She stroked the horse's heavy neck, the sound of pounding hoof beats resonating in her mind. "I'm going to miss you." Setting her cane against the wall, Claire opened the gate and stepped into the stall. She stood directly in front of the big horse and placed her hands on both sides of the animal's face, drawing in the animal's steadiness.

Like fresh rain, it quieted her nerves.

She ran a hand down the white blaze on the bridge of the horse's nose, then pressed her brow against Cinnamon's forehead. "I'm sorry

1

I haven't been out to see you. It's been a bad week." She patted Cinnamon's neck and then combed out her mane with her fingers. "I'm going to be gone for a while. But I'll be back. I promise."

The horse nudged her as if trying to let Claire know she understood and that it was all right for her to go.

Claire looked into the horse's dark brown eyes. "I hope one day we can go riding again. Maybe things will be better when I get back." She could almost feel the wind in her face and the movement of Cinnamon under her as they galloped across the rolling hills of her parents' ranch.

The sound of a car engine cut into Claire's reverie, and a shiver of apprehension coursed through her. Maybe she should stay.

The barn door grated as someone opened it.

Time to go.

Footsteps crunched on the barn floor and the gate creaked.

She looked around and saw her mother leaning on it. Claire gave the horse another pat. "I'm going to miss her."

"She'll miss you too." Her mom's gaze went to the horse then back to Claire. "It's time to go. Unless you've changed your mind."

Claire swallowed past the lump in her throat. "No. My things are ready." She ran a hand down Cinnamon's face and across the velvet soft nose, then pressed a kiss to her white blaze. "I guess I have to go now. See you soon."

❧ ❧ ❧

Sunlight heated the interior of her mother's Suburban, but Claire was cold. Maybe her parents were right. Maybe it was foolish of her to take off across the country with a band of disabled friends. She breathed deeply, hoping to calm her nerves.

It's going to be a real adventure.

But doubts pummeled her. So many things could go wrong.

Swimming with dolphins? Where had that idea come from? Willow. It had been Willow. Of course it had been her. She was the dreamer in the group. Although the ideals of the '60s had passed, she'd refused to put aside the lifestyle and dreams of her generation.

Maybe we're all just dreamers. Claire clenched and unclenched her hands. This was a chance of a lifetime. If her illness got worse, it might be her only opportunity to do anything special ... ever.

Claire's mother glanced at her, knuckles whitening as she tightened her steely grip on the steering wheel.

Should she listen to her parents? They were right—stress always worsened her symptoms. So did fatigue. Would hours on the road drain what little energy she had? She could end up in the hospital.

But the trip *could* make her stronger. And wasn't it time she faced life on her own? Twenty-two and still living at home?

Her mother and father had spent the last several weeks trying to convince her to stay.

A month ago, her father had paced the gray carpet in the family's front room. "It's too risky." A week ago, he'd nearly walked off the roughness of the patio stones. "You're being foolish." And yesterday, he'd kicked up hay dust in the barn. "What will you do if you get sick?"

Her mom remained stoically silent. But the fear in her eyes and tight set of her lips revealed her anxiety.

Her older sister, Autumn, had understood. "It's a great idea. Don't give in to Mom and Dad. Do what you want. This is your life. Not theirs."

While Claire packed, she'd tried to shut out the negative voices. But each item she added to her suitcase was accompanied by a reason she should stay home.

Her mother shook her head. "Why must you do something so drastic? Why not begin with something easier? Closer to home. Maybe a trip to the coast." Tears welled up. "I've already lost one daughter." She sucked in a breath.

"You didn't lose Melissa. She just moved away." And Claire had to admit she'd been glad to see her go. Melissa's bipolar highs and lows were hard to take and painful to watch.

"I haven't heard a word from her since she left."

"She's never been good at communicating. And I'm not Melissa."

"I know that. But you're not well. And you barely know these people."

"That's not true. I've been meeting with them for months. I probably know them better than anyone else, except for you and Dad and Autumn. A support group shares things with each other that they don't tell anyone else."

Her mother didn't respond. She compressed her lips and stared straight ahead.

"And while we've planned out this trip I've gotten to know them even better." Claire folded her arms over her chest. "I can't let them down. It wouldn't be right."

Her mother's chin quivered. "I feel like I'm losing you. Maybe you won't come back either."

"I'll be back."

A hawk circled high above a gully that fell between two hillsides.

She loved it here. This was home. She would return. "Maybe you should go out to Grand Junction and see Melissa."

"You know she'd hate that. She'd say I'm interfering in her life."

A desolate silence grew inside the car. Her mother slowed as they approached town. Finally she said, "I just never imagined you'd take off like this. Your doctor is here. What if you need medical help?" She pressed fingertips to trembling lips. "Every single one of you is handicapped. How will you manage?"

"Willow used to be a nurse. She'll know what to do. And we're not handicapped. We have challenges, but the point of the trip is to do this on our own. We need to. Every one of us is in a rut. Maybe the trip will help us find a better life. Even Colleen, our group counselor, believes in us. She thinks we can do it." Claire's own words helped bolster her confidence. "If I have a flare-up, there are other doctors, other hospitals." Even though she said the words with assurance, the idea of trusting anyone other than Dr. Reynolds made her insides quake.

And what about Tom? What if he suddenly became ill, or Willow had a flare-up of her fibromyalgia or her back gave out?

And Taylor was a mental pinball machine.

"This isn't reasonable." Her mother swiped at a runaway tear.

"We won't even know where you are."

Claire hated to see her mother anguish over this trip, but it was too important. "Mom, I'm not moving across the galaxy. I have a cell phone and my tablet. I'll keep you up to date on Facebook. I'll post lots of photos so you and Dad can see what I'm up to. And you can send me mail if you want. We'll have postal pickups along the way. I'll let you know in advance where to send things."

Her mother put on her stoic face and stared at the road. "What if something happens when you're out in the middle of nowhere? You'll be on your own."

"We'll handle things like anyone else. We'll call for help." She offered what she hoped was a heartening smile.

"It's not funny. I've watched you when your dysautonomia flares up. You faint without warning and can't keep anything down. Every muscle aches, and your heart—"

"Mom. I know how I feel. You don't have to remind me." Claire turned so she faced her mother. "Please be happy for me. The last nine years have been about being sick. I feel like I'm drowning in my illness. This is a chance to make my life about something else."

No response.

Perfectly groomed lawns flew by.

"You talk about faith, Mom. This will be a chance to trust God with me. I know it's been hard for you all these years."

"I do trust him. But trusting doesn't mean being foolish. He doesn't want us to be careless with the life he's given us." She tugged a Kleenex tissue from the box on the console.

"What if this is all about living out my faith?"

Her mother nodded and gently blew into the tissue. "Okay. But don't tempt God by doing something imprudent and then expecting him to rescue you."

"I'll be careful. I promise."

CHAPTER TWO

They approached Tom Cantrell's house, and her mom pulled to the curb across the street from a large cream-and-gray motor home with dark gray waves rolling along the sides from front to back.

Butterflies took flight in Claire's stomach. It was really happening.

Her mother reached out and caressed Claire's hair. "You're so beautiful … inside and out. I don't know what I'd do if something happened to you."

Claire rested a hand on her mother's arm. "Nothing is going to happen. I'm going to be fine."

Tears rose in her mother's eyes, but her lips edged up in a smile. "Promise me you won't pick up any hitchhikers. You can't trust anyone these days."

"I promise."

Tom Cantrell stood beside the coach. He wasn't an especially tall man, maybe five foot eleven with a slight paunch, but today he looked bigger than usual, and his deeply lined face was tanned and untroubled. His expression was uncharacteristically pleasant. Hopefully everything he'd said about his health and his ability to drive had been true. MS was unpredictable.

Her mom moved to the back of the Suburban and began unloading Claire's things.

Her knees stiff and aching, she tried to hurry out of the vehicle and around to the back so she could help. "I can get that." She set her suitcase upright and slipped on her backpack.

"I hope you brought enough." Her mom lifted out Claire's walker.

"Tom said to pack light." She eyed the wheelchair. "I don't need the chair."

"You're sure?"

"Yes."

"I'd feel better if you had it … just in case."

6

Tom walked toward them, no sign of weakness in his stride. "You look pretty as a daisy," he told Claire with a smile.

Hmm. Tom was rarely, if ever, sweet. "Thank you. You're looking pretty good yourself."

"That's what an adventure will do for you." He turned to her mom. "Good to see you, Mrs. Murray. I'll get the suitcase." He hefted it in a way that contradicted his age and physical health.

"Good morning, Tom. Can you talk some sense into this girl? She really should take her wheelchair."

Tom turned to Claire. "Do you need it?" Deep furrows lined his brow.

"Almost never, just on especially bad days."

"It's up to you."

Claire studied the chair dubiously. "I don't want to take it." She chewed on her lip. "But all right. Just in case."

"Okay then." Tom set the suitcase down and lifted the chair out of the back of the Suburban.

"I can push it." Claire opened the chair and dropped her pack on the seat. She draped her cane over the back.

Her mother carried the walker.

Tom stowed the chair in one of the massive compartments beneath the vehicle. He lifted his glasses off his nose and glanced down the road. "We're all set, just waiting for Willow. Taylor's on board—and manic if you ask me. She has her nose in that computer of hers, charting our route or something. Says she has our route all mapped out. I'm about ready to put a stop to that." He wore a determined grin as he climbed up the steps, dragging Claire's large bag behind him.

"Don't you have GPS?" her mother asked, voice sounding slightly shrill.

"Yeah, but it's on the fritz. I meant to get it fixed."

"You meant to?"

"Don't get your panties in a wad."

Susan's cheeks flamed, and the disapproving set of her lips left no doubt about how she felt about Tom's comment.

"We've got *real* maps and we can always use Google."

7

Claire turned to her mother. "I guess I'd better go. I'll see you in a few months." Now that it was time to say goodbye, it was harder than Claire had imagined.

Eyes shimmering, her mother pulled Claire into her arms. After pressing a kiss to Claire's cheek, she stepped back. "I'm scared … but I'm proud of you."

"You are?"

She gave Claire's arm a squeeze. "So is your dad. You are so brave."

Why couldn't they have said that earlier? "Tell Dad I love him too."

"I will." Her chin trembled. "He knows. And he's sorry he couldn't be here this morning. He had a meeting he couldn't get out of."

"I understand."

She took an envelope out of her purse and pressed it into Claire's hands. "Just a little extra, in case you need it."

Claire looked in the envelope. Hundreds of dollars in twenties? "No. I'm fine, really. I have my own."

"Well, it's never enough … believe me." Her mom gave her another kiss. "See you soon." She turned, crossed the street, and climbed into the Suburban. As she pulled away, she waved at Claire.

Claire watched, suddenly swamped with uncertainty. What was she doing?

"Good morning."

Claire startled and turned to see a middle-aged man with a big friendly face. "Oh. I didn't see you."

"I'm Frank. Just out enjoying the morning air." He glanced at the RV. "Tom's had that rig parked since his wife, Doris, died. About time he took it out of mothballs."

"Should be fun."

"Morning, Frank." Tom turned to Claire. "Do you need the walker often?"

"No. The cane is usually enough."

"Okay. We'll stow it. You have your meds handy?"

"They're in my pack."

Tom glanced down the road, then at his watch. He frowned. "Willow ought to be here. Told her we'd be pulling out at eight o'clock sharp." His bright mood faded. He walked around to the other side of the coach.

"Have a great time," Frank said, then strolled down the sidewalk.

Tom stood at the bottom of the steps and motioned for Claire to board. He moved aside and then followed her up the stairs.

Claire stepped into the front room and rested a hand on a dark brown leather recliner that sat just to the right of the entrance. It matched a small sofa in the living space.

Taylor sat at the dining table, her long dark hair falling into her face as she concentrated on her computer screen. She barely glanced up. "Hey," is all she said before turning her attention back to the computer.

Thirty-one and acting like a teenager. Claire forced a smile. "Hi."

Tom squeezed past and walked through the kitchen.

Claire followed him toward the back, past a bathroom and a closet. A bedroom with a walk-around bed and cabinets on one wall looked snug but comfortable. Her suitcase sat on the bed.

"You and Willow can share the bed," Tom said. "I'll sleep on the sofa, and Taylor will have the dining room fold-out bed. She said she doesn't mind sharing the room with an old man." He nodded at a small built-in dresser. "Those cabinets are for you two. When your stuff is put away, I'll give you a hand with this mattress. There's a storage compartment under it—good place for your suitcase." He moved toward the front of the RV.

Claire unpacked her suitcase, placing her clothing in the small bureau. She'd brought just necessities, knowing the coach had limited space. After she finished, she made her way to the front and eased her aching body onto the bench seat, across the table from Taylor and her computer.

Taylor didn't look up.

"What are you working on?"

"Mapping out our trip. I have it worked out. We'll take Highway 138 over the Cascades and then use Highway 70 to cross the Rockies and move out over the Midwest. I'd like to make it to Loretta Lynn's place in Kentucky before May. Willow said something about Savannah, Georgia, so we can head straight there after Kentucky, spend a couple of days, and get moving to Florida and the dolphins." She stopped to take a breath. "Do you have some place you want to go?"

"I'd like to see my sister in Grand Junction, Colorado."

"I'm pretty sure Highway 70 passes through there." She squinted at the computer.

Tom pushed down the screen, closing the computer. "No itinerary. We're taking this one day at a time."

"Hey!" Taylor glared at him. "I've been working on that since two o'clock this morning."

"I don't remember anyone voting you in as tour guide." Tom stared at her, his heavy brows bumping into each other. "You take your meds?"

She cast her gaze away from his. "I always take them." She picked up her guitar, which was leaning against the window. "Okay. So we don't have to use *my* plan. But we need a plan. I can stay connected most of the time." She tapped a small modem on the side of her computer before strumming a few chords. "I have the computer wired with satellite."

"I'm impressed," Tom said, his voice laced with sarcasm. "But why do we need an itinerary?"

Claire nearly groaned. This might be a longer trip than she'd imagined.

A taxi pulled to the curb and the driver unloaded two bags and set them on the sidewalk. The passenger door opened and Willow stepped out. She looked like she did most days—graying hair wavy and free, falling to her shoulders. She wore a colorful ankle-length dress and sandals. Willow hauled two bags out of the backseat. Next, she reached into the car and led out a brown and white boxer.

Tom tromped out of the RV and strode across the street.

Taylor and Claire followed but hung back, making sure to stay out of what promised to be a stormy encounter.

Willow turned and faced Tom, her orange-and-yellow shift

billowing in the breeze.

Tom glowered at Willow. "You're late."

"I had a few last minute stops to make."

"And what's that?" He aimed a sharp nod at the dog.

"*That* is Daisy. My boxer. I couldn't possibly leave her alone for months."

"No dogs."

"You'll love her. She's sweet and intelligent."

"Does she bite?" asked Taylor.

"Oh, no. She's very even-tempered." Willow stroked the dog's short, glossy coat.

Taylor edged toward Daisy.

The dog's stub of a tail beat back and forth like a metronome at high speed.

Taylor rested a hand on the boxer's head, and Daisy looked up at her with a sad expression. "She should go with us," Taylor said, throwing an accusatory look at Tom.

Tom studied the boxer, then turned a determined gaze on Willow. "I said no dogs."

Claire joined Taylor and Willow, and gave Daisy a pat. "I love boxers."

Daisy leaned against Claire's leg.

"Tom, we can't leave her."

Tom blew out a loud breath. "How are we supposed to take care of a dog? She's too big. We'll have to pack food for her—"

"I already did that when we were preparing the RV yesterday. It's all put away—food and bowls." Willow smiled.

"She'll be nothing but trouble."

"If she doesn't go, I don't go." Willow's blue eyes locked with Tom's.

He looked at the dog and rubbed his clean-shaven chin.

"She's a good traveler." Willow glanced at Claire and Taylor. "A watch dog will come in handy."

"Oh yeah, she'll protect us all right. I can see she's vicious." Tom smirked. "I said no dogs, and I meant it."

Willow's gaze took command. "Then I'll just have to go home."

No one responded.

Finally, Tom threw up his hands. "Fine. She can come. But you're completely responsible for her. I'm not feeding her or taking her out to … well, I'm not cleaning up after her. And I'm not doctoring her or making sure she stays out of traffic either."

Wearing a triumphant smile, Willow gave Daisy a pat. "Come on, girl." She moved toward the coach.

Tom picked up the bags she'd left behind and followed. "Let's hit the road. I know a great place for breakfast."

CHAPTER THREE

By late afternoon, they'd crested the Cascade Mountains. The beauty of Mount Bailey, Mount Thielsen, and Diamond Lake called to Claire as they hurried past. Tom was forced to stop to let Daisy out, but after she'd done her duty, they were all back in the RV and on their way to Eastern Oregon.

Claire read to pass the time, returning to a favorite book, *Redeeming Love.*

After breezing through Central Oregon, they'd made their way southeast. Now the coach wound its way over a highway that ran alongside the Ochoco River.

Claire put her book aside and stared at the passing landscape of rocks and sagebrush, throat tight with emotion. Many times through the years, she and her family had camped in this area. There were lots of trails for horseback riding, and it was a good spot for dirt bikes too.

The smell of sage, coming through the open window, transported her to Cinnamon's back and the quiet, leisurely trail rides she'd taken with her family. Whether chatting or silently enjoying the solitude, Claire couldn't think of anything better than the times she'd spent here as a girl. While on horseback they often came upon mule deer, antelope, and small creatures, like ground squirrels and jack rabbits. And even an arid place like the desert offered surprises, like brilliantly colored flowers hiding in crevices and along the occasional creek.

Riding dirt bikes was a different experience altogether. They'd cut across streams, splashing water, and then cranked up the throttles to climb steep banks before hitting open ground. They kicked up dirt and rocks, and dodged pucker bushes as they bounced over the parched wilderness. Her dad was the best rider, but Claire and her younger sister, Melissa, used to give him a run for his money.

The ache inside grew more powerful. These days her life felt empty, unlike the vibrant girl who had challenged this desert all those years ago.

She was still only fourteen when it started with what looked like a spider bite on her arm. The itch was fierce. More red bumps appeared, then her feet became swollen and painful, fatigue set in. Still, she wasn't afraid, thinking she had a virus that would pass. But it got worse—pain that emanated from inside her bones, dizzy spells, and fainting. Finally, Claire went to the first of many doctors.

When a diagnosis was finally made, Dr. Reynolds said she would never be who she'd once been.

If only she could wave a magic wand and have her life back. There had been a time when she'd dreamed about having a career, falling in love, getting married, and having babies. And now ... everything was about managing her illness. Dysautonomia had stolen her dreams.

Willow pushed out of the leather recliner and moved to a side window. "I love it here. It's untamed and the sky seems so big. I feel close to the Father."

Taylor frowned. "Oh yeah, it's awesome." She gave Willow a pathetic look. "There's nothing here but rocks and sagebrush. It's ugly."

Tom slowed the RV, peering at a sign through thick glasses. "Says Sheep Rock. Maybe we'll see a mountain sheep or two." He turned the vehicle onto a dirt road.

Taylor peered through the front window. "Not a good idea. The road's as messed up as my mind."

"We'll be fine."

The RV bounced through a pothole.

Tom gripped the wheel more tightly. "The tour book says there are lava beds up this way. And fossils. There's bound to be good rock hounding too."

Willow moved stiffly to the front and stood behind Tom, her hand gripping the back of his seat.

Daisy, the boxer, pushed herself up from her spot on the floor and stood beside Willow.

"Is rock hunting the reason you wanted to come this way instead of heading south?"

"You don't like rock hounding?"

"That's not the issue. You made this decision because it's what *you* wanted, just like you did with breakfast. You didn't consider what the rest of us might want to do."

"That's right," said Taylor.

Claire didn't really care. "Can't we just enjoy where we are? It might be fun to hunt for special rocks."

Willow let out a big breath. "I might like it. I've never done it before." She leaned against the seat. "But I suppose just being out in nature and strolling through God's splendor and breathing fresh air could be pretty fantastic."

Tom flashed a smile at her over his shoulder. "Figured from here we could drive east to Yellowstone. You been? Lots of God's splendor there too," he quipped.

"I've always wanted to go." Willow acted as if she hadn't heard his mocking tone.

Tom eased the RV along the deserted, dusty road. "Keep your back side in a seat when we're moving."

Willow climbed into the front passenger seat as the coach ground along the rocky road.

"I don't see anything worth looking at," Taylor complained. "Nothing but a bunch of dust and rocks."

The words were barely out of her mouth when a hill shaped like a pyramid came into view. The entire mound was the color of whitewash.

Tom stopped and leaned forward against the steering wheel. He lifted his glasses and rested them on his head. "Will you look at that?"

"I wonder what makes it that color." Willow leaned against the window. "God never ceases to amaze me."

"It's unique all right," Claire said. A white hill looked more peculiar than amazing, but she had to admit God was creative. She just wished he'd spend more time on people's needs than on rocks.

"What's the big deal? It's not God. It's geology. This is one of the Painted Hills. Found it online." Taylor sounded uninterested, but she did look at it through the window.

Hills striped with various shades of green and red rolled across the desert.

15

Tom pulled into a parking area surrounded by tidy lawns, bathroom facilities, and picnic tables that rested beneath shade trees.

"It's so nice," Claire said. "How surprising."

The coach came to a stop, and Tom turned off the engine. He leaned his forehead against the steering wheel. "Everyone out."

"Tom?" Willow leaned toward him. "Are you all right?"

"Yeah. Just give me a minute." He looked pale, and droplets of sweat sprang out on his forehead and rolled down his face.

"Give me a minute, my foot. You're not all right." Willow moved to his side and rested the back of her hand on his face, then took his pulse. "Are you nauseated?"

"Yeah."

"Any chest pain?"

"No. I've got the spins," he said in barely more than a whisper.

"Is there anything we can do?" Claire asked. Vertigo was part of her illness too. It was awful.

"I need to lie down. There's medicine in the cabinet. Meclizine." He opened his eyes, but quickly closed them again. "I'll need help."

"Taylor, give me a hand." Willow positioned her left shoulder under Tom's arm. "Lean on me."

"Willow. No." Claire moved to the front. "The last thing we need is for your back to go out. I'll do it."

Willow nodded. "But wait a minute. I'll get the Meclizine pill." She hurried to the medicine cabinet above the kitchen sink and searched through the bottles. "Ah, here they are. Chewable." She dropped a tablet into her palm, returned the bottle to the shelf, and hurried to the front of the RV. "Here you go, Tom."

Keeping his eyes closed, he held out a hand, and Willow placed the small pill in his palm. He put it in his mouth and chewed. "Thanks."

Claire helped get Tom to his feet, then supported him on one side while Taylor helped him on the other. They made their way to the back of the RV.

"Wait. Stop. I've got to stop." Tom leaned against Claire, breathing hard. Then he took a deep breath and said, "Okay."

When the coach narrowed at the hallway, Taylor stepped aside, and Claire helped while Tom felt his way along, grabbing hold of cabinets and doorway frames as he made his way to the back.

He stopped. "I think I'm gonna be sick."

Willow grabbed a bowl out of a cupboard and passed it to him. "Here you go. Don't worry about it. You just be sick if you need to."

"You're going to be all right." Claire patted his shoulder. Was he going to be okay? She was queasy herself. This was their first day on the road and already something had gone wrong.

"Figure I'll live. Let's go."

"You sure you're all right?"

"Yeah. Just get me to the bed."

Daisy leaped onto the sofa and whined. She seemed to know something was wrong.

When they finally reached the bed, Tom crawled onto the mattress and rolled onto his back in slow motion. Panting, he lay absolutely still, his hands gripping the bedding.

Willow leaned over him. "The medication will help soon." She draped a light blanket over him and removed his glasses.

Tom opened one eye and peered at Willow for a brief moment. "Thanks."

"I wish there was more I could do for you." She set his glasses on the bedstand.

"I've had this before. It'll pass."

"How long till you're better?" Taylor asked.

"Your guess is as good as mine. Sometimes a few minutes. Other times a few days. It can come and go for weeks."

"You liar! You told us you could drive this rig across the country. How you gonna do that if you got the spins?" Taylor strode toward the front of the RV. "We can't stay here for weeks. I knew this was stupid. I told you I didn't want to come." She sounded close to tears.

"Calm down." Willow put on a reassuring smile. "We'll be fine. Everything will work out. God has a plan."

With a huff, Taylor dropped onto the sofa. "Oh sure. Like I believe that."

Willow looked at the road. "Didn't we pass a campground a little ways back?"

"Yeah. I think so," said Claire.

"Well … I can drive this thing, at least to the campground."

"You can?" Claire wrinkled her brow. Was letting Willow drive better than being stranded? "Maybe we ought to wait a while and see if Tom gets better."

"I don't think we should wait. It will be dark soon. And there's a sign that says no overnight camping." Willow moved to the front of the RV. "As a young woman, I lived on a bus. An old school bus. This is a limousine compared to that. One time I had to drive that bus up a winding dirt road, then I parked it in a meadow in the middle of the forest."

"Eons ago," Taylor said without humor. "And you were probably so stoned you imagined it all."

Willow eased into the driver's seat. "I might have been stoned, but I didn't imagine it." She flashed a smile at Taylor.

Daisy climbed between the front seats.

"Aww, that's a good girl, Daisy."

"You used to use drugs?" Claire asked. Apparently there was a lot she didn't know about Willow.

"I was young. It was the sixties." Willow brushed her wild mane of hair off her face. "We'll stay at the campground tonight, and maybe Tom will feel better by morning." Willow looked in the rearview mirror. "Hang on. We're headed back to the highway."

Taylor sat on the sofa, palms pressed between her knees.

Claire stood behind the driver's seat. "You sure you can do this?"

Willow smiled in the rearview mirror at Claire. "We're about to find out." She closed her eyes. "Help me, Jesus." She turned the key, and the engine fired to life. "Thank goodness I don't have to back up."

Claire climbed into the front passenger seat. Maybe another set of eyes would help, in case Jesus was too busy.

Willow pressed the gas pedal, and maneuvered through the parking lot, heading back the way they'd come.

The passenger side front tire rolled up onto a curb, then dropped off, jarring everyone inside plus some of the dishes in the kitchen cupboard.

"What was that?" Tom hollered.

"Nothing. Everything's fine." Willow kept going.

Was it Claire's imagination or had the road gotten rougher? And sprouted more potholes?

When they finally reached the highway, Willow looked at Claire. "You praying?"

"Why do you ask now?" Up until that moment, Claire had started to feel more comfortable about Willow driving.

"Well, a dirt road isn't the same as a state highway." She grinned.

"Be serious," Taylor shouted.

Claire's heart sprinted. She pressed a hand on her chest. Tachycardia was not what she needed right now. She took deep breaths and held each one for a moment, hoping to slow her heart rhythm.

"Are you all right, dear?" Willow asked. "You're sweating."

"Don't worry about me. Just think about driving."

Willow pulled onto the highway and headed west. "Feels like I'm steering a boat."

They hadn't been on the road more than a few minutes when Claire spotted a man hobbling east along the far side of the road.

"I wonder what he's doing all the way out here. Maybe we ought to give him a ride." Willow wasn't going very fast, but now she slowed to a crawl. "He's limping."

"No way!" Taylor said. "He could be an axe murderer or something."

Willow looked at Claire. "What do you think?"

Remembering her mother's warning, she said, "It's probably not a good idea. We don't know anything about him." She studied the man.

He was tall and slender, dark haired, and very good-looking.

"Though he looks nice."

"I'm sure that makes him just fine, then." Taylor's voice dripped with disdain. "Even Ted Bundy looked like a nice guy. Not every criminal looks like Charles Manson."

"It doesn't seem right to leave him out here, injured," said Willow. She turned to Claire. "We're on an adventure, right?" She chuckled, eyes dancing with mischief as she stopped the coach.

Willow leaned out. "Are you all right?"

The man drew close. "Yeah. Me and my bike had a close encounter with an antelope a few miles back. The bike is lying in a gully, totaled, and I'm lucky that I only wrenched my knee."

"Where you from?"

Claire leaned toward Willow to get a better look.

"Monterey, originally."

"It's beautiful there. Where you heading?"

"Colorado."

"You look like you could use a ride."

The stranger looked to be in his mid-twenties. He smiled, and his deep blue eyes locked onto Claire's.

Claire's cheeks heated up, and she quickly looked away.

"I sure could use a ride, but you're going the wrong way."

Claire dared to look again. He seemed harmless.

"We're only going to a campground a couple of miles up the road and then we'll be traveling east."

The stranger didn't say anything.

"You're welcome to ride with us," Willow said.

"Thanks."

"Taylor, open the door for that young man."

Taylor threw a disgusted look at Willow, then opened the door.

The man climbed in, favoring his right leg. "Thanks."

Daisy's hackles were raised, and she woofed at the stranger.

"Hey, girl," he said and held out a hand.

Daisy sniffed his fingers and seemed to relax.

"Nice dog." He stroked the top of her head. His gaze fixed on Claire for a brief moment, then he turned to Willow. "I'm Sean Sullivan. I appreciate the ride."

CHAPTER FOUR

After quick and awkward introductions, Willow returned to driving.

When ignoring the good-looking stranger by watching the road didn't work, Claire instead turned her seat so she could see what was going on in the back. Sean kept chatting with Taylor, who was acting as if she and Sean were old friends. How did she do that? Claire never knew what to say to men.

"Keep an eye out for that campground," Willow said. "I know it has to be coming up." She called behind her, "How you doing, Tom?"

When there was no answer, Sean asked, "Tom? Is he in the back? Is that your husband?"

"No. Absolutely not."

"The girls' father?"

"You've got to be kidding." Taylor shook her head. "No way."

"Tom is our friend," Claire said. "We're all just friends."

"He was driving this rig until he got sick." Taylor stood. "I better check on him." She headed toward the bedroom and nearly lost her balance when Willow negotiated a curve. "Hey, watch it." She disappeared through a doorway. A few moments later, she found her way back to the sofa and plopped down. "He's better. Trying to sleep."

"What's wrong with him?" Sean asked, then shook his head. "I'm sorry. It's none of my business."

Willow glanced at Sean in the mirror. "He's dizzy. Nothing for you to be concerned about."

"Don't worry. He's not contagious. He's got MS," Taylor said.

"Oh. Sorry to hear that." Something flashed in his eyes.

Was it fear? Or revulsion?

"I wasn't worried about him being contagious. Just wondering is all."

Daisy put her paws up on Taylor's lap.

She stroked her head, then pushed her off, and the dog sat at her feet. Taylor turned to Sean. "Willow's driving because Tom can't. He

21

said his MS wouldn't be a problem."

Willow veered toward the center line, then overcorrected, and the RV swayed toward the side of the road. "Sorry," she called over her shoulder. "I'm a little rusty. It's been a while."

Sean leaned toward Taylor and quietly asked, "Does she know how to drive this thing?"

"I heard that." Willow chuckled. "I'll get us to the park in one piece. I promise."

Hopefully Willow could keep that promise.

Sean remained seated and rocked his booted feet back and forth as if he might launch himself out of the coach at any moment. Finally he stood and moved to the front, kneeling between the two captain's seats. "Do you need me to drive? I know how. My dad used to have one of these."

He was too close. And way too good-looking. What would he think of her if he saw her using a cane?

"Thank you, but I'm fine—just out of practice. It's not far now."

In a derisive tone, Taylor corrected her. "She doesn't *really* know how to drive this thing. All she's ever driven is an old hippy bus, and that was back in the sixties."

Willow ignored the comment and told Sean, "Sorry if I scared you."

"You didn't—"

"Oh, there's the camp." Willow took her foot off the gas. "We made it."

Sean remained where he was, his hands on the back of the seats, almost touching Claire.

She turned her seat so it completely faced forward and edged closer to the window. When Willow pulled into the campground, Sean pushed to his feet, and Claire got a whiff of sweat—not entirely unpleasant.

"The camp looks crowded." Willow followed a narrow roadway that wound through camping sites. "Oh dear. There's not much room to maneuver."

The front driver's side tire dropped into a hole, jarring Claire and reminding her how much her body ached.

"I can take over," Sean said.

Willow acted as if she hadn't heard him.

He should move back and sit down—he was entirely too close.

"Oh. There's one. It's perfect." Willow stopped the RV. "Do I need to back in?" She chewed on a nail.

"Yeah." Sean pointed at the hookups. "You need to line up with those, and this isn't a drive-through site."

"Okay. No problem. I can do it." Willow glanced at Claire. "Anyway, I'm going to give it a good try." She lifted one side of her mouth in a half grin.

Sean leaned over Willow's right shoulder. "You sure—"

"I've got it."

In the end, Sean climbed out to offer his guidance, and after a series of jogs Willow finally parked the RV and turned off the engine. "I did it!" She high-fived Claire, then opened the door and climbed out.

Daisy leaped onto the seat and followed her.

"Hallelujah!" Willow did a slow twirl with her arms upraised while Daisy danced around her feet. "We did it—God and me. And of course you, Sean." She laughed and hugged Daisy. "I'd better check on Tom." Willow made her way to the side door, hobbling slightly. "Come on, Daisy."

The dog leaped back into the RV.

Willow filled a glass with water, then moved to the back room. "Tom, how are you feeling?"

Claire followed her.

"Better." Tom opened one eye and looked at her, but quickly closed it again. "But it felt like you nearly killed us. What were you doing to my RV?"

Willow wore a small smile. "Just driving and parking. And doing it quite well, I might add."

"Really? You think so?"

If his sarcasm was back, he must be better. Claire sat on the edge of the bed. "Willow did a good job. I wasn't scared at all."

Willow winked. "Thank you, Claire. But if not for Sean—"

"Sean? Is that who you picked up?" Tom tried to sit upright.

"Yes. He's a young man who needed a ride."

"A hitchhiker?"

"An antelope leaped out in front of his motorcycle. I couldn't just leave him there on the side of the road, so I gave him a ride."

Taylor leaned in the doorway. "Yeah. You'll love him. We don't think he's an axe murderer."

"I can bring him back to meet you," Willow offered.

"No ... not right now. But I'm glad to know he's not an axe murderer." Eyes still closed, he lifted his brows.

"Fine, then. Now drink some water before you get dehydrated." Willow held the glass out for him.

"Always the nurse."

"Some things just stay in our blood." Willow smiled.

Tom rose up on one elbow, opened his eyes, then quickly closed them. Sweat broke out on his forehead. He groaned. "The world's spinning again." He didn't move for a few moments, then he opened his eyes again and reached for the glass. He took a big gulp of water. "Thanks."

Daisy put her paws on the bed and licked Tom's face.

"Gross. Get that dog out of here."

"That's all right, Daisy. Off now." Willow gently pulled on her collar.

Tom swallowed another mouthful of water, then handed back the glass and gingerly lay down, scrunching his eyes closed as he did so. "Every time I move the spins start again."

"Tom, I'm Sean."

Claire looked up and saw Sean behind Taylor.

"I appreciate the ride. Hope you feel better soon."

Her heart revved up. Weakness slipped over her, and blackness edged out the light. She was going to faint. She couldn't, not in front of a stranger, especially not someone like Sean. She fought to hang onto consciousness.

A hand grabbed her arm, then Willow's smile came into focus. "You all right, dear?"

"I'm fine."

The darkness receded.

Sean moved to the living room.

Willow kept a steadying hand on Claire as they walked down the short hallway. "Tom, I'll be back with something for you to eat," said Willow. "Just as soon as we get the camp set up."

His expression troubled, Sean sat at the dining table, elbows braced against the tabletop and his chin in his hands. "He's got MS, huh?"

"Yes." Willow kept a hand on Claire until she was seated on the sofa.

"Why is he out here ... traveling?"

"Where do you think he should be?" Willow's blue eyes gleamed defiance.

"Well ... at home, or maybe in a care facility. I mean, something terrible could happen."

"Yes, it could, but terrible things happen at home too."

A shadow fell over Sean's eyes. "Yeah. That's true all right."

Willow leaned down and rested her hands on the table. "I didn't mean to be sharp. We're all just doing the best we can to live, and to do it in a way that has meaning and purpose. For some it's harder than for others."

Sean met her eyes and nodded. He didn't say anything more.

Admiration for Willow swelled in Claire's chest. She wished she could be like her—wise and strong and brave. Instead Claire was weak and afraid.

And she hated who she'd become.

CHAPTER FIVE

Sean's knee throbbed, and as he lowered himself to the sofa, pain shot straight through it.

Willow sat beside him. "I'd better have a look at your leg."

"It'll be all right." He didn't want to be any trouble … or owe these people anything.

"You don't know that, and I might be able to help." Willow met his gaze. "I'm a nurse. You can trust me."

A nurse? She didn't look like any nurse he'd ever seen, and he'd seen a lot of them. "No. I'm fine. Really."

Sean pushed off the couch and took a few steps, making certain not to limp. "See. Fine."

"Okay. But let me know if it starts giving you trouble."

"Sure." He didn't want to look like a wimp in front of the cute blonde, Claire.

Willow looked at the other women. "I'm hungry. Anyone else?" Her gaze settled on Claire.

"Maybe a little. I had a big breakfast."

"This looks like a nice campground." Willow moved through the RV, hanging onto handholds as she went.

"Nice?" Taylor draped one leg over the other and leaned against the back of the sofa. "No club house. No swimming pool. You call that nice?"

Willow gazed out a side window. "It's too cold to swim. And who needs fancy amenities? Look at these trees. I love the cinnamon-colored bark of ponderosa pine. They stand so tall and strong. We're in the midst of God's creation, and I'm going to gather some of those huge pine cones scattered everywhere. They'll make gorgeous Christmas decorations."

"Where are we going to store pine cones?" Taylor asked, rocking back and forth.

"Oh, I'm sure we can find room." Willow smiled, acting as if Taylor's derisive tone didn't disturb her in the least.

"Like we really need them. We can't collect everything you think is pretty."

What kind of friends were these people? Sean moved to the door. "I'll get the hookups taken care of."

Claire pushed off the sofa. "I'll help."

"Are you sure you're feeling up to it?" asked Willow.

"I'm better. Thanks."

Willow picked up Claire's cane. "You better take this, honey."

"Oh, all right. I guess I should." She accepted the cane and glanced at Sean before moving toward the door.

Her help would be nice, but what was wrong with her? Was she sick too? Sean stepped out of the RV, headed for the hookups on the side of the vehicle, and quickly connected them to the camp's facilities.

Claire watched him. She wasn't helping. Finally, she asked, "You've done this before."

"Yeah. My parents used to do a lot of traveling."

Claire chewed her lip.

Why had she offered to help if she had no intention of doing so?

"Oh. That's right. You did say that." She picked up a pine cone. "These are pretty."

He felt like he was back in school, all nervousness. Maybe her uneasiness was contagious.

Or maybe it was because she was so beautiful, only not in the ordinary sense. She had a kind of ethereal presence about her he couldn't quite grasp.

He hooked the last clamp, then pushed his hands into the pockets of his jeans and looked up through the trees. "Pretty impressive." He turned his gaze to the campground. "I guess I'd better find myself a place to sleep for the night."

"You could stay with us." Claire's face reddened and she glanced at the carpet of needles at her feet. "I mean, you can at least have dinner with us. You must be hungry."

"I am, kind of." He turned to their camping spot. "There's a barbeque pit and picnic table."

"We have hot dogs and marshmallows," Taylor said as she

27

stepped out of the RV.

Willow appeared at the door. "Baked beans too. I made up a batch two days ago." Guiding Daisy on the leash, she made her way down the steps.

"Let me help." Sean took the leash as the dog reached the bottom step.

"Thank you. One of these days she's going to trip me up." Willow pulled her jacket closed. "It's freezing out here."

"High desert. What did you expect in April?" Taylor turned to the grill. "I'll cook."

Claire and Willow glanced at one another, exchanging looks of surprise.

"Is something wrong with that?" Sean asked quietly.

Willow took him aside. "Taylor is almost never helpful."

"What are you whispering about? I can cook … a little." She flipped dark hair off one shoulder. "Anyone can make hotdogs." Eying the stationary grill, she said, "This thing is filthy. It needs a good scrub."

Claire didn't quite suppress a groan.

"Now what?" Sean whispered.

"If she's in manic mode we'll never eat—she'll be cleaning the grill all night."

"Taylor, let us help." Willow went to her side. "I know how to build a fire."

How did he land in the middle of this bunch? He'd spent too much of his life dealing with sickness. He wasn't about to do it again. The sooner he put distance between himself and this band of travelers the better.

কৈ∕ভ ভ⁄িৌ

"I'm no good at cooking," Sean said. "I'll get the slide-out taken care of and bring my appetite to the table." He grinned.

His smile chased away the sadness in his eyes and made Claire feel like life was full of possibilities. She forced herself not to stare at him and went in search of firewood. She felt stronger than she had earlier and managed to gather an armload of small pieces. Before she realized it, Sean was working beside her collecting larger chunks of wood. She couldn't think of anything to say, but that didn't seem to bother Sean. He kept working.

"I figure this will give us a good start." He headed back to camp, a pile of wood in his arms, still limping, though less than before.

Claire did her best to keep up, but her legs felt like rubber. She'd overestimated her energy level.

By the time they returned with the wood, Taylor and Willow had the kindling burning. Taylor took a couple of chunks of wood from Claire. "About time."

Claire held back a retort. Fighting with Taylor was never helpful.

Sean set his armload of wood at the edge of the campsite. "This should be enough for now. I'll get more later."

"You need to rest that knee of yours," Willow said. "Get off your feet." She sat at the picnic table and peered up into the trees. "It's glorious here. I don't know that I want to go a step farther."

"If we stay, there might be some disappointed dolphins," Claire said.

"I seriously doubt that," Taylor scoffed.

"Oh, I don't doubt it." Willow chuckled. "I think those dolphins will have just as much fun meeting us as we will have meeting them."

Claire sat beside Willow and stretched out her aching feet.

The fire popped and crackled and the smell of cedar and pine sweetened the air.

"Dolphins?" Sean sat on a nearby stump.

Willow pressed the palms of her hands together. "We're on our way to Florida to swim with wild dolphins."

"That sounds like fun, but just you four?" Sean raised one eyebrow, doubt showing on his face.

"Yes. Just us." Unreasonable anger flared in Claire. She couldn't keep quiet. "Do you think we *can't* do it?"

"No. I was just wondering …" He glanced at the RV. "Well, your driver is sick and the rest of you are women."

"Young man, tell me what being a woman has to do with it," Willow said.

Sean shook his head, his smile reemerging. "Okay. You got me. I'm sorry. I'm just not used to seeing a group of women traveling so far alone." He leaned forward. "How did you four end up out here and on your way to Florida?"

Willow looked at the sky. "I guess it's my fault."

"We all wanted to come." Claire brushed her hair off her shoulder. "We're part of a support group." Now what did she say? Sean didn't need to know about their problems, especially hers.

"We meet once a week," Willow said. "We talk about our troubles and help each other through life's challenges." Her eyes moved from Claire to Taylor. "We decided it was time to do something special, just us."

"Tom owns the RV." Claire pointed at the motor home.

"What about work?"

Taylor seemed unaware of the conversation. She was meticulously placing hot dogs on the grill and making certain they were in a perfectly straight line.

Like I'm going to tell you I'm on disability and that most the money I've got my mother gave me. "Well, Tom and Willow are retired. And Taylor is trying to become a professional country singer."

"It's none of my business anyway. I shouldn't have asked." He looked at the RV. "What about Tom? Is he going to be okay?"

Willow glanced at the coach. "I've been praying. The Father will take care of him."

"I used to believe that." Sean's tone had a bite to it. "But … well, I don't know what I think anymore."

"Your Father won't give up on you." Willow gave him a gentle smile to match the gentleness in her voice.

Why did Willow have to talk so much about God? She'd end up chasing Sean away. Willow didn't mean any harm, but sometimes it did get to be a bit much. "What about you? How long have you been traveling?"

"Nearly three years."

Why would a young guy spend so much time wandering? Did it have something to do with the sadness in his eyes?

Taylor looked up. "That's a long time to travel. How do you make a living?"

"I have savings, and I work here and there. 'Course now I have no bike."

"What are you going to do?" Claire asked.

Sean shrugged. "I don't know, but I'm definitely *not* going back to Monterey."

CHAPTER SIX

What was in Monterey that Sean detested so much? Claire glanced at him.

He was a puzzle.

She kept a hold of Tom's hand as he made his way down the steps of the motor home.

He took each with caution, legs quaking.

They shouldn't have let him drive. Now they were stuck and they hadn't even gotten out of Oregon. What would they do? She felt bad for Tom, but she was angry too. He should have been honest with them.

Tom let go of her hand. "I'm fine now," he grumped as his feet met the ground. Looking wobbly, he moved toward the fire, which crackled and snapped in the midst of camp. He held his hands, palms out, to the flames. "Feels good."

"Smells good." Claire sat on a wooden bench close to the fire. The aroma of burning cedar and pine reminded her of family campouts. If only she could go back to those carefree days. The times before she and Melissa had gotten sick.

It'd be nice to stay put. Each mile that carried her farther from home made her feel less secure, as if she were lost. She'd thought she was all grown up—at twenty-two she should be. Obviously she wasn't.

Willow smiled up at Tom. "I'm glad to see you out and about. Have a seat." She patted the bench beside her.

"I'm fine right here." He kept watching the fire, but his face reddened and he swayed slightly. "Maybe I will sit." He moved to the table and sank down on the bench seat, keeping as much distance between him and Willow as possible.

Daisy leaned against his leg and sniffed at his hands.

"Oh, look at that. She really does like you." Willow rubbed the dog's side.

"The feeling's *not* mutual." He folded his arms across his chest and out of the dog's reach. "Git."

"Come on, Daisy." Willow rested a hand on the dog's head. "I love you, even if that mean old man doesn't." Her eyes sparked mischief.

Daisy moved to Willow and rested her head on her lap.

Willow caught the dog's head between her hands and rubbed her forehead.

Tom didn't even glance her way. "By tomorrow I ought to be good to go."

Willow eyed him skeptically. "It might be better if we waited a few days, just to make certain you've recovered."

"I'll be ready."

She looked around the camp. "Where did Sean get off to?"

"He said he was going for a walk." Claire turned her gaze to the camp entrance. "He headed toward the road." Maybe he'd decided to keep on going. The idea deflated Claire's pleasure at being around the campfire with friends.

"I wonder if he'd drive for us. Only for a while. Until Tom's better." Willow cast a sweet smile toward Tom. "He's headed the same way we are."

A crow cawed from overhead. A different crow picked up the cry. The two hopped from one tree limb to the next, squawking at one another.

"We don't need him. I can drive." Tom lifted his right leg over the bench seat and straddled it, then lifted the other leg and turned around to face the table. He grasped his hands in front of him and scowled at a chirping chipmunk on a nearby stump.

"Maybe Sean *should* drive, hypothetically speaking." Claire glanced toward the road.

"There's only one way to find out." Willow stood.

But if Sean did the driving, he'd stay with them, and that would make her life more uncomfortable. She always felt awkward around men. "Maybe Tom's right. All he needs is a couple of days to rest and he'll be his old self."

"His old self? Is that really what we want?" Willow chuckled. "Tom, you're lovable and well-intentioned, but you never should

33

have been driving. You knew that before we left home."

"If that's what you believe, why did you let me drive?"

"Sometimes it's best to let God work things out. And I think he did by placing Sean in our lives."

Tom huffed. "How would you know what God wants?"

"I feel his presence and hear his voice." Her tone was reverent. "And I believe, if we allow, he will work out *his* will."

"You hear his voice." Tom smirked. "Okey-dokey, then. Glad we don't have to worry. As long as you know what God wants for us, we'll be just fine. We can trust you to get us to Florida."

Claire cringed inside. Any conflict was uncomfortable to be around, but especially spiritual conflict. Willow was right. God did speak to his people. Claire just wished she was better at hearing him.

Willow pursed her lips. "I don't claim to have special powers, just a special relationship. The Holy Spirit lives in me, and he guides me. I trust him." She turned a determined look on Tom. "You mean well, but we can't know how your MS is going to behave. You may not be healthy enough to drive … at least some of the time. And I'd hate to have the responsibility. If we're forced to take too many long stops, we'll never make it to Florida and back before winter."

"You sound as if we're part of a wagon train crossing the prairies." He turned away and took in a big breath, then with a shrug said, "Let me do a background check on him first. And if that comes out clean, then I guess it would be all right. He could bunk with me."

"I thought we were supposed to do this on our own," Claire said.

Taylor wandered into camp, arms full of wood. "We aren't now?"

Willow smoothed her skirt. "Oh, we were just thinking it would be nice if Sean joined us and drove the RV."

"He is kind of cute." Taylor dropped the wood beside the fire. "But too young for me."

He's not too young for me. Claire tried to smother the thought. His age didn't matter. He wouldn't be interested, at least not after he got to know her. And just taking this trip was complicated enough without adding the confusion of dealing with Sean. "Willow, you did a good job of driving."

Tom grunted. "Oh no. You're not driving my RV all the way to Florida. No."

"And why not?" Willow planted her hands on her hips.

Tom grimaced. "You just said you didn't want to."

"Well, that was before—"

"Before what? Before I said you couldn't?" Tom smirked.

Silence simmered.

"There's no one here who can drive my RV, not that far." He took off his glasses, studied them, then wiped the lenses with his shirt tail. Replacing them, he looked at Willow. "None of you ladies has enough experience."

Willow relaxed her stance. "I have to agree with you on that. Which must mean you're okay with asking Sean."

"Asking me what?"

Everyone turned and looked at the young man.

Tom cleared his throat. "Didn't know you were there."

"Just got back. What do you want to ask me?"

"Well, we've been talking about a driver. Everyone else thinks that I need some help." Tom looked at Sean from beneath shaggy eyebrows. "Wondered if you might be interested. 'Course I'd have to run a background check." He shrugged. "These days you can't be too careful."

Willow took a step toward Sean. "We'd feel more secure if you were driving the RV. Tom's just not healthy enough."

He stared at the band of travelers. "You're really nice people, but I've got things to do, places to go. I can't get distracted—"

"I'd pay you to do it," Tom said. "Just consider it another job to see you by. You'd get room and board, and I'll pay you more than minimum wage, which is better than you'd get at a lot of places."

"You'd be like a chauffeur." Willow doffed an imaginary cap.

Sean combed his fingers through his hair. "I thought you wanted to do this on your own."

Tom looked at Willow and Claire.

"We did. But maybe that's unrealistic. Everyone needs help from time to time." Willow closed the gap between her and Sean, and took his hands in hers. "It would mean so much to us."

"I don't need the money. I called my insurance and they're mailing me a check for the bike. Plus, I've got a friend to see in Colorado." He met her gaze. "I can't do it."

CHAPTER SEVEN

How did I get myself into this?

Tom's clean background check, that's how.

Sean clenched his teeth and stared at the road. After waiting three days Tom had improved, but Willow and Taylor didn't feel comfortable with him as driver and begged Sean to help them out. He should have told them no and stuck to it. He couldn't take living with people who were sick and looking for their place in a world that didn't want them. He'd grown up in that kind of meat grinder, and all he wanted was peace.

The radio shouted the Mamas & the Papas' "California Dreamin'." He'd had enough of the 1960s' bebop. He reached for the dial, but the Righteous Brothers replaced the Mamas & the Papas. That kind of oldie wasn't so bad.

"Oh, Sean, dear. I almost forgot. Here's the address in Salina, Kansas, where we'll be making a stop for mail." Willow handed him a note card. "You might want to let your family know."

"Make sure to send them something," Claire said. "Email just isn't the same for parents."

Sean stuck the card in his pocket. He doubted his parents wanted to hear from him.

"I just don't know how to thank you," Willow said for the hundredth time. "It's so kind of you." She tugged a straw hat down on her head and tied the strap under her chin. "I love to travel with the windows down, but that wind is creating a puzzle out of my hair. Is it bothering you?"

"No. I'm fine." He didn't say it, but he liked the smell of desert air. It somehow reminded him of his childhood and freshly washed laundry.

Willow peered out the window. "I know those brown bushes aren't Scotch broom, but they look like a desert version of it."

Couldn't she sit in the back with everyone else? She talked too much.

"Scotch broom is supposed to be a weed, but it's so beautiful I don't see them as weeds. There's nothing like their brilliant yellow blossoms, and when the pollen is heavy, the fragrance is absolutely aromatic."

Taylor leaned over the seat. "We burned Scotch broom. It's a nuisance weed whether you want to think so or not, and it will overrun a place."

"I love their blooms anyway." Willow peered down the road in front of them. "How far do you think we should drive today?"

"I don't know." The road wound up and down hills and valleys, the Eastern Oregon desert stretching out to the north and south and east as far as he could see. It looked lonely, kind of the way he felt, although how he could feel alone while surrounded by four eager travelers didn't make a lot of sense.

He'd been lonely most of his life. Now he preferred solitude, which he wouldn't be getting any of today.

Broken, his faith shattered, he'd left home three years before, searching for peace and time to himself. He didn't want anyone depending on him or requiring anything. He glanced at his companions in the rearview mirror.

They were probably going to need a lot from him.

He needed to find a way out. "We'll be coming into John Day pretty soon. Anyone want to stop?"

"Let's keep moving. We need to get some miles behind us," Tom said.

"Are we still heading east to Yellowstone?" Claire stood in the back, bracing her hands on the hallway walls.

Sean couldn't keep from glancing at her in the mirror. He liked her looks—tall and slender, long dishwater-blonde hair, and misty blue eyes.

There was something wrong with her, but no one had said just what yet. It couldn't be anything too bad. She seemed healthy enough. Other than that cane.

"My sister lives in Grand Junction. She's been … sick. Mom's hoping I'll check on her. I hate to wait too long."

"Oh, honey, why didn't you tell us?" Willow moved to the back.

"Of course we'll go straight to Grand Junction."

Tom blew out a hard breath. "Sure. No problem. We can do that." He didn't sound happy about the change.

After a stop in John Day, where they had a quick meal, they made good time moving across Oregon, then into Idaho the following day.

At least Willow had moved to the back, where she and Claire were both involved in novels. Taylor was in her usual spot—in front of her computer. Tom had taken the front seat.

The terrain changed as they descended from the high desert. There were no more trees. Grass and sagebrush squatted among rocks, splashing the arid landscape with subtle color. Broad ravines with flat tops on the rock buttresses framed the occasional pond offering refreshment to animals that lived in the thirsty country.

Sean caught Claire looking at him in the mirror and smiled at her.

She returned the smile as a blush crept up her cheeks.

Her appearance—was it the flawless skin? The wide-eyed innocence? Something reminded him of some of the women captured in the sixteenth century art books his mother always had on the bookshelf.

"You like that mirror?" Tom asked. "Had it made special so when my wife, Joan, was doing something in the back I could see her."

"Good idea. Makes it easier to see what's going on back there."

"I noticed." Tom smirked.

Changing the subject, Sean asked, "I'm hungry. How about you?"

"Starved. Time to look for a place to stop."

Tom was always hungry. He could really put it away, but one would never know to look at him.

Telephone poles stretched out in front of them, looking like tall, skinny scarecrows planted to protect the vulnerable terrain. By the lay of the land, it would probably be a long while before they ate. The last three days they'd gone through most of their supplies and had planned on buying fast food today, then restocking that night. Sean's stomach grumbled. He needed to be fed as well. "We should have stopped in Boise for groceries."

"Something will come along," said Willow. "And I've got mixed nuts left and a little guava juice. Anyone want some?"

Mixed nuts is right. Sean nearly laughed.

When no one responded to Willow's invitation, she said, "Well, I guess you're not that hungry."

Claire moved up behind Sean's seat and leaned toward the front window. He could smell her shampoo. *It* even smelled pure.

"There's a sign," she said. "Glenns Ferry."

"Hey. I saw that on Google," said Taylor. "They have a museum or something there, and a park."

"That's perfect," said Willow. "We can pick up groceries from a market and eat at the park."

"Glenns Ferry, then?" Sean needed to get out and stretch his legs.

"Let's do it." Tom said, and no one disagreed.

Sean watched for the next sign—two miles.

Once off the main highway, Sean steered the RV through the small farming community. "There's a sign for the Three Island Crossing and Oregon Trail History Center."

"That's it." Taylor closed her computer.

After a quick stop at a market, the group headed for the history center and pulled into a park alongside the river.

Willow stepped off the coach first. "Come on, Daisy."

The dog leaped out and hurried to explore the area.

Willow was moving more slowly than usual. "Lunch first, then a look at the Oregon Trail."

∽◌ ◌∼

Claire pointed toward the Snake River. "There—on the other side. Do you see where the ridge is cut into the hillside? That's where the wagons came down and then they took a ferry across the river."

"That's steep." Sean squinted. "Those people must have had a lot of courage."

40

Taylor sat on a wooden bench. "How did they do it?"

"Do what?" Tom asked.

Taylor rolled her eyes. "Cross the country in covered wagons. No roads, not even trails. No maps. And trusting a wagon and a pair of horses or oxen to get them up and over mountains and down steep trails like that. So many people died along the way."

"We're not in a covered wagon, but we're kind of like the early settlers, aren't we?" Claire tried to imagine driving a wagon down the narrow trail. She would have been terrified.

"You're kidding me, right?" Taylor challenged. "We're cruising in an RV, on a paved highway, and all we have to do is stop at a store or restaurant if we want to eat."

"True." What a stupid thing to say. Still, Claire tried to defend it. "I know we're not facing the kind of things the early settlers did, but we are taking a risk and traveling to places we've never seen."

"Oh yeah … with our laptops and cell phones." Taylor smirked.

"I could shoot a wild turkey or antelope." Sean shouldered an imaginary rifle and acted as if he were sighting game.

Taylor continued as if he hadn't said anything. "We're not fighting disease or Indians either." She looked at Claire. "You read too many novels. How many times have you read *Redeeming Love*? Or *Pride and Prejudice*?"

Claire didn't respond. It was no one's business how many times she read her favorite books.

"You're a total romantic."

"I am not."

"Well, you do go to sleep at night with a flashlight and a book." Willow sported a mischievous smile.

"Really?" Taylor nearly chortled. She glanced at Sean then back at Claire. "Been dreaming about a man? Anyone specific?"

Claire's face heated. What could she say to something like that? And what did Sean think? He must be mortified. She couldn't look at him. "You don't know anything about me, Taylor."

Tom stood. "Ready for the museum?"

Willow lowered herself to the bench. "I need to sit. My back's feeling grumpy. You all go ahead. I'll catch up."

"Why didn't you say something?" Tom moved to her side.

"I didn't want to whine."

"I'll stay." Claire didn't want to be with them, not after what Taylor said. "I'm kind of tired." She made sure not to look at Sean, but was he staring at her?

Willow removed her straw hat and fanned her face. "It sure is hot. Daisy and I will just stay here in the shade." She patted the dog on the head and gazed at the deep blue sky. After the others had moved on, she said, "Don't let Taylor get under your skin. She enjoys annoying people." She put her hat back on and looked at Claire from beneath the brim. "Did it bother you so much because you *do* have feelings for that young man?"

Claire shrugged. "I don't know him well enough to like him, do I? And he'd never be interested in me anyway."

"And why not?"

"My illness, for one. He's strong and healthy. Why would he want to hang out with someone like me?"

"Why wouldn't he? Have you told him about your condition?"

"No. And I don't intend to."

Willow placed a hand on Claire's knee. "He knows something's wrong."

"All he knows is that I use a cane some of the time. Is the rest obvious?" Claire couldn't keep a desperate tone from creeping into the words.

"He knows we're all part of the same support group, and that Tom has MS. He's probably figured out that you have something you're wrangling with. And you aren't as active as most young ladies your age."

"So I seem like—"

"There's nothing wrong with being sick, Claire."

"Everything's wrong with being sick. Not to you, but to someone like him ... I'm sure he has his choice of beautiful, *healthy* women. He doesn't have to settle for someone like me."

"Settle for you? Oh, Claire. You don't know how special you are." Willow leaned against her shoulder. "You're a beautiful woman with a gentle heart. You've been patient with Taylor most of the time, helped take care of Tom, even when he's being cantankerous. And you're always watching out for me. Why wouldn't Sean be interested? Especially if God's in the middle of all this. Maybe it was meant that Sean join us."

"Maybe, but that doesn't mean he's meant for me." An ache welled up inside. "Besides, I don't even think I can have children. Most men want families. And if I did have children, what kind of mother would I be?"

"A wonderful one."

Tears pressed against the back of Claire's eyes, and she shook her head slightly. "I'm not strong enough or healthy enough." She stood and looked at their surroundings—scrub grasses and sagebrush. Would she end up empty and dried up like this desert? She breathed in the scent of sage. "What am I even doing out here? Why did I come on this trip? For what purpose?"

Willow reached out and took Claire's hand. "Only God knows that, sweetie. You've got to trust him. He'll reveal all at just the right time."

CHAPTER EIGHT

Sean's eyelids were getting heavier with each mile.

Caffeine. After hours at the wheel, he needed some.

Farm lands sprawled west of Interstate 84. Rugged mountains, still topped with snow, lay to the east. The way the feet of the mountains rolled right down to the highway was startling.

He took a drink of water, screwed the lid back on, and set the bottle in the cup holder. Changing positions, he rubbed his eyes. He needed to be alert with traffic picking up as they approached Ogden.

Tom shifted in the passenger seat. "You need to rest?"

"I'm tired, but I'm okay to drive. Nice to have someone to talk to."

"I'm feeling pretty good. I can spell you."

That was the last thing Sean wanted. "Nah. I'm fine." He glanced at Tom. "You have family?"

"Just a brother in San Diego and a sister in Seattle. My wife's gone, and we never had kids."

"Oh. Sorry."

"We were happy. I guess I can be thankful for the years I had with her."

Taylor leaned over the seat. "Traffic is getting heavy." Her voice was tight. "And you're driving too fast. Slow down."

"I'm driving the speed limit." If she'd just shut her mouth and sit down, he'd be fine. Sean clamped his mouth before he blurted out the thought.

"Well, as they say, better late than never. We're not on a schedule. What would it hurt if you took it a little slower?" Her long dark hair fell into his face.

He swept her hair aside. "Everything's fine. And if you sit down, I'll be able to concentrate on the road better." All day long, Taylor's voice had badgered him. Too fast or too slow, too close to the car in front of them … too something. He gritted his teeth.

Taylor sat on the edge of the sofa, but she was probably

44

watching his every move.

He studied her in the mirror. Maybe she'd forgotten to take her medication. That's what the others said when she got in a mood. And his brother had been bad about taking medication. He said the meds made him feel lousy.

It would kind of stink to have to take something that made oneself feel awful. Maybe Taylor felt that way.

Willow put an arm around Taylor's shoulders. "No need to worry. He's a good driver."

Taylor brushed Willow's arm away. "How do we know that? We just met him a few days ago."

"He's done admirably," Tom cast over his shoulder. "I trust him."

At least someone trusted him. It was more than his father ever did.

Taylor slumped back onto the sofa and folded her arms across her chest.

Sean turned his attention back to driving. He didn't have time to worry about Taylor. "Thanks for the backup, Tom."

"Anytime." Tom grinned.

"Have any of you been to Midway?" Willow asked.

Sean braked as traffic slowed. "Sounds familiar."

"Oh, it's the loveliest little town up in the mountains, just east of here. It reminds me of some of the villages in the Swiss Alps."

"You've actually been to the Swiss Alps?" Claire asked.

"Oh yes. I used to travel a lot."

"What was your favorite place of them all?" Tom turned and looked at Willow, as if he really cared what she said.

"Oh, I don't know. There are so many spectacular locations." She chewed her lip. "I guess I'd have to say Scotland. It is so verdant and … and untainted. I could hear the Lord speaking to me through the very earth beneath my feet."

Claire leaned on the table and rested her chin in her hand. "I always wanted to go there." She sounded bereft.

"You should, then." Sean swung his head around and looked at her. As he did, he accidentally turned the steering wheel.

The RV lurched to the right.

"Watch where you're going!" Taylor shouted.

Sean corrected the steering. "Sorry." He stared at the road. What was the look in Claire's eyes? Despair? Why?

"Can we stop by Midway?" Willow moved to the front, behind Sean's seat.

"No," Tom said. "Need to keep moving. We don't want to get caught in the middle of hurricane season in Florida."

"The season starts in a month." Taylor glanced between him and the road. "There's no way we're going to beat it if we take a bunch of side trips."

"If we keep up this pace, we'll get through before it hits," said Willow. "But I, for one, do not want to hurry through this trip. And I have plans to spend time with my daughter and grandson."

"Willow's right. Who made you king, anyway, Tom?" Taylor pushed away from the table and walked toward the front. "When we first started this trip, you said no itinerary ... and here you are, pushing us every day."

Tom threw up his hands. "Okay, okay. I'm sorry. But hurricane season gets worse later in the summer. If we take too long we'll end up smack dab in the middle of it."

Sean pulled into the next lane and passed a slow-moving travel trailer. "I've been to Florida a few times. The weather's always been great, even in August."

"Isn't it awfully hot there in August?" Claire asked.

Sean shrugged. "Yeah. A little. But it didn't bother me. I don't see any reason to worry." Although hanging out with a bunch of travelers wasn't the greatest, he did like driving the coach. It was luxurious and, with a diesel pusher, it had enough power to respond. Even mountain passes hadn't been a problem.

Of course, the Rockies were coming up. That would be the true test.

Everyone turned quiet as they continued south and moved through Salt Lake City. Even Taylor was silent for a change.

Once free of city traffic, Sean picked up speed. Would Taylor notice?

"Hey, there's the cutoff," she nearly shouted.

"We're not going that way. We'll stick to the main highway."

"But Highway 6 is shorter. It cuts across to Grand Junction, plus we can save time that way."

Sean tightened his hold on the wheel. "This is a little longer, but it's an easier drive. I'd rather stick to the main highway. The other route cuts through the mountains, and it's just one lane each way. It'll be slower. And I don't know if there are cliff-side roads or not." He looked at Taylor in the mirror. That should convince her. He didn't want to be further out in the boondocks than they already were. What if there was a medical emergency? The idea instantly produced sweat above his upper lip. He was no good at emergencies. "And this time of year you never know when a spring snowstorm will hit."

"Oh." She sat back down at the table. "Whatever you want. You're the driver."

Sean loosened his grip on the steering wheel.

"Looks pretty tame to me," Tom said.

Mountains pressed in on either side, but the road ran between them with bordering pastures.

"I think I'll climb in the back and take a nap."

"Let me pull off and stop first."

"No need," Tom said gruffly. He pushed out of the seat and wobbled.

Sean ought to pull over and stop, but there was no holding the man back now.

Tom grabbed the sides of the seats and stepped through just as the RV hit rough roadway. He tottered.

Sean tried to grab him with his right hand, but missed.

Tom fell headlong into the living area of the RV.

"Tom!" Willow was at his side immediately.

Claire kneeled beside him. "Let me help you."

He raised up on one elbow. "Don't worry. I'm fine." He pushed himself up so he was sitting. "Willow, you move pretty fast for someone who's old and decrepit." He laughed.

Willow sat beside him. "I surprised myself." She giggled. "Come on, let Claire and me give you a hand."

47

They stood up together.

"You've got to be kidding me." Suspicion laced Taylor's voice. "Is there something going on between you two? You're both way too old for that kind of stuff."

"There's nothing going on." Tom's voice was brittle and sharp. "But if there was, we're not too old for any of it."

"You mean me and Tom?" Willow sounded shocked and stepped away from him. "We have nothing in common."

Willow sat on the sofa and pulled Daisy up beside her and held the dog against her chest.

The boxer licked her face.

"Willow, you shouldn't pick her up like that. She's too heavy." Claire sat on the sofa with the dog between them and patted Daisy.

"I'm all right."

When they reached the junction, the highway narrowed into a two-lane road, and they drove into a small town call Scipio.

Taylor opened her computer and studied the screen. "According to the map, we're going the wrong way."

"No, we're not." Sean glanced at her over his shoulder.

"You need to turn around."

Sean suppressed a groan. Why had he promised to help, again? Oh yeah, the money was good.

"Taylor, I checked the map on my phone. I'm pretty sure we're going the right way," Claire said softly.

"How can that be? We're not even on a highway. We're in a dinky, ugly town. It almost looks like a ghost town." Her voice quaked. "I'm not sure anyone even lives here. And why would they?" Her gaze went to the barren, sterile hillsides surrounding the community.

"Taylor, settle down," Tom snapped.

Sean did his best not to add his two cents. He'd had more than enough of her. "We need gas anyway. I'll take another look at the map. Will that make you happy?" He pulled into a gas station convenience store and stopped alongside the gas pumps. He turned off the ignition, then moved to the computer and looked at the map. It took a moment to point out her error. "See, we're fine. The junction to Highway 70 runs through the town." He straightened. "Now I've got to fill up so we can get back on the road. It's a good time for everyone to stretch their legs." He climbed out and moved to one of the gas pumps, swiped Tom's credit card through, and started filling the tank, the smell of gasoline drifting up from the nozzle.

With his cane draped over one arm, and looking only slightly unsteady, Tom stepped out of the coach and offered a hand to Claire and then Willow, who had Daisy on a leash.

Taylor was the last out. She refused his offer of help. "Why do people live here?" She pointed at the small, boxy houses nearby. "This place looks dead. Doesn't anyone believe in paint? Or in watering their lawns?" She blew out a short breath. "It looks the way I feel most of the time."

Willow draped an arm around her shoulders. "I think it's quaint. And you're too hard on yourself."

Tom joined Sean.

"What's with her anyway?" Sean asked.

"Who, Taylor?" Tom said in a whisper.

"Yeah."

"It's her condition mostly, I think. But I guess it could just be her personality. Kind of like me—grumpy." He grinned. "She'd do better if she'd take her meds regularly."

"Why doesn't she?"

"She's full of excuses, but a lot of people who have bipolar disorder don't take their meds. They like the highs too much, and the medication makes them feel like they're not actually feeling anything—kind of flat. Trouble is they can get so manic that they hallucinate and the depression can get real bad. Some even commit suicide."

Sean's mouth went dry. He didn't handle death well. "Has she ever done anything really crazy?"

"Her life's a full-blown roller-coaster ride, but this week's not so bad. Willow helps, I think."

So far Taylor had mostly just been irritating. As long as she didn't get worse …

Claire walked across the parking lot and stepped into the store.

He was tempted to ask about her, but what if Tom got the wrong idea?

She didn't seem to belong with the others. She was healthier, and young.

Tom stretched to the side. "I think I'll get myself a root beer. Can I get you anything?"

"Sure. I'll take a Mountain Dew. I can use the caffeine. And how about some Cheetos?"

"Maybe we should start looking for a place to spend the night. You look beat."

"I'll check with Taylor. She'll find us a place."

Using a cane, Tom moved toward the store.

Sean sighed. Hanging out with a bunch of old or sick tourists wasn't what he needed or wanted. But he couldn't leave them stranded in the middle of nowhere either.

CHAPTER NINE

Claire hadn't slept well. They'd stopped in a rest area outside of Richfield, Utah, where traffic came in and out all night. She propped her elbow on the windowsill and kept her eyes on the road. How had she ended up in front with Sean … again?

He glanced at her. "Tired?"

"Yeah. Didn't sleep much." She let out a long breath. "It seems like we've been driving forever. And I've never seen so much gray dirt in all my life."

"Yeah, there's a lot of it. Probably some kind of sandstone."

"There's a lot of salt in the ground around here," Tom said from the back, where he sat in the recliner. "Read about it in one of my travel magazines."

Sean leaned forward and peered at a sign. "We better stop and top off the tanks."

Claire eyed the signpost.

Next Services 106 Miles.

She didn't even try to hold back a groan. "A hundred and six miles?" Panic stirred up inside. Maybe her parents had been right when they said the trip was risky. They *were* in the middle of nowhere. She studied the inhospitable terrain, then checked her phone for a signal. No cell service. What would they do if something went wrong?

Sean pulled off at a tiny settlement. He gassed up while the rest of the group got drinks and snacks. Taylor took Daisy to a small grassy area alongside the station. Maybe she was having a better day.

Tom stepped out of the store with Willow at his side. He moved more slowly than usual and leaned heavily on his cane.

"You should lie down," Willow said.

"Not a bad idea. Claire, do you mind if I use the bed?"

"Of course she doesn't." Willow walked with him. "Claire can keep poor Sean company."

Sean scrubbed at a day's growth of beard. "She's been doing a

51

good job so far."

"Sure, Tom, you can use the bed," Claire said. Who cared if she wanted a nap? "But I don't know if I'll be any good at keeping Sean awake. I'm pretty sleepy myself."

"Maybe we can help each other. 'Course, if you really need a nap, then …"

"No. I'm fine," Claire said, but she wasn't, not really.

Taylor returned to the RV with Daisy. "She wants to run."

Willow stroked the dog's head. "Thank you so much for taking her out for me. I hope we can find a good place tonight where she can work out some of her vitality."

Claire climbed up the RV steps and made her way to the front, where she eased into the passenger seat. How was she going to keep up a conversation? She'd run out of things to talk about.

Sean pulled back onto the highway. "So, what do you think about traveling?"

"I like it—"

"Turn on some country music," Taylor called from the back.

Claire couldn't help but roll her eyes. "Mostly."

Sean laughed and turned the radio to a country station.

A man's gravelly voice crooned on about a woman being his honeysuckle and him being her honeybee.

"Taylor, what would you do if there wasn't Sirius Radio?" Sean asked.

"Why target me? We listen to Willow's inspirational music more than anything else."

"This is good music too," Willow said.

Claire shrugged. "Maybe I'll learn to like country." Anything was possible.

Desert grasses whipped sideways, and sand blew onto the road.

While Taylor and Willow joined voices with the radio, Claire continued her vigil of trying to think of something interesting to say to Sean. "The wind's picking up."

"Yeah, it's getting fierce out there."

"You said you grew up in California?"

"Monterey."

"I heard it's nice there."

"If you like wind and fog." Sean stared straight ahead and tightened his hold on the steering wheel.

"A friend of mine went to a writer's retreat there. She loved it."

"Yeah, well, I guess it's a good place for writers."

"Were you a surfer?"

"Not really. Just played at it a little."

"I love the ocean and always wanted to visit a California beach."

"You should." His tone was clipped.

What had she said to upset him? "Do you have family there?"

"My parents."

"No brothers or sisters?"

"No. I had a brother. He died."

"Oh. I'm so sorry." Why had she asked him so many questions?

"Yeah. Me too."

Something jarred the RV, and it swayed, careening toward the next lane.

"What was that?" Taylor hollered.

"Just the wind. We're fine." Sean tightened his grip on the steering wheel and jutted out his jaw.

He was troubled, but about what? Monterey? His family? His brother? Claire slumped down in the seat and decided not to say anything more.

The highway climbed through mountain passes and charged down the other side. Wind lashed the valleys, tossing dirt and dry grasses across the road.

"Slow down," Taylor said.

"We're good. Stop worrying."

"The wind could knock us right off the road."

"That's not going to happen." Sean's tone was sharp.

"Maybe we should pull off."

"For how long? Out here there's a lot of wind. It could last all day, all night, or all week."

"You don't need to get snippy about it."

Daisy whined.

"It's all right, sweetie." Willow reached out to Taylor, who sat on the other end of the sofa, and rested a hand on her arm. "We'll be just fine, dear. The Lord is watching over us."

"Stop with the God talk. You think he's watching over us? Why? Who is he taking care of?" Her cadence was more anxious than challenging. "He didn't keep Claire from getting sick—or Tom or you. And I'm half demented."

Claire didn't need to be dragged into Taylor's spiritual doubts. She had enough of her own. What had she done to deserve a life of pain and loneliness? *Why, God?*

"He has a purpose for our lives, dear. For all of us, just as we are." Willow took her hand.

Taylor snatched her hand out from under Willow's. "And he'll have a purpose when we fly off the side of this mountain?"

"Nothing of the kind is going to happen." Willow smiled gently. "His glory is all around. He wants us to see him in the midst of his creation, not the danger. And no matter what happens we can be thankful."

"So you admit there is danger."

Willow closed her eyes briefly. "No. That's not what I meant. I just thought it would be better if you tried to focus on the beauty, the glory of God, his workmanship. There are mountains that look like castles and stacks of stones that could be statues. And see those flat-topped bluffs? They're magnificent."

"Sometimes I think you're crazier than me." Taylor dropped back against the sofa, crossed her arms over her chest, and closed her eyes.

Claire glanced at Sean.

He'd dropped his speed all the way down to forty-five miles per hour, and his hands gripped the steering wheel so tightly that his knuckles were white.

Alarm thumped in her chest. "Should we pull off?" she asked under her breath.

"There's not a good spot along here. We'll be all right." He offered her a comforting smile.

Claire almost felt as if she'd been kissed. She turned her gaze to the stark beauty of the Rockies. What was wrong with her? She knew better than to let herself get caught up with a guy. It never worked out. But what did she know, really? She'd only dated a couple of boys in high school, and one had been a neighbor she'd known all her life. It had been like dating her brother.

As they continued climbing up and down mountain passes, Taylor didn't speak, not even when wind gusts buffeted them. She had moved to the table and was riveted on her laptop. Probably playing a game to help shut out her surroundings.

A blast of wind hit the RV, and Claire gasped. Her heart rate picked up uncomfortably, and she grasped the arm rest. How had Taylor's anxiety pounced on her? She'd be glad to get out of the mountains. She took Willow's advice and focused on the beauty of the landscape but couldn't shake the sensation of desolation. She took out her tablet and, using the unique rock formations as inspiration, jotted down ideas for a children's story. Maybe she could have it ready for the kids in church when she got home.

She got caught up in the story and lost track of where she was until Sean announced a vista point.

"How about we take a break?" he asked.

"That's a wonderful idea." Willow grabbed Daisy's leash.

Sean followed the exit ramp into a small parking area, where he stopped and turned off the engine.

There was only one other vehicle—an older model pickup with the tailgate down. It looked like someone had set up a display of some sort in the back.

A panoramic view opened up in front of them, revealing an expansive, deep canyon.

"Oh, how amazing," Willow gushed.

Tom shuffled out from the bedroom. "Where are we?"

"I don't know," Willow said. "But it's gorgeous." She hooked the leash on Daisy, moved to the door, and gingerly climbed out.

Claire followed.

"I don't know that I've ever seen anything so awesome." Willow shaded her eyes with her hand. "It looks like the Grand Canyon."

The wind billowed her dress away from her legs.

Daisy stood beside her, quivering with excitement and obviously wishing she were free to run.

"Not really," Sean said. "The Grand Canyon is a lot *grander*. Undeniably God's work. This is more like a mini Grand Canyon." He stepped over a barrier and moved across smooth stones toward the cliff edge.

Claire wanted to call out to him to be careful—

Willow did it for her. "Sean don't act foolish now. Be careful."

"I'm fine. This is interesting, and not a big drop-off. It kind of steps down." He lifted one leg and threw his arms out for balance. "I'm falling, I'm falling."

"I'm not watching." Willow turned her back to the cliffs. "Men. Come on, Daisy." She headed for a wooden bench and sat, stroking Daisy's head and neck. "You're more reasonable than any man." She hugged her around the neck.

Shaking her head, Claire joined Willow and sat on the end of the bench. A man that daring would surely find her boring.

Tom let out a low whistle. "Impressive view."

The wind tossed Claire's hair about her face so she caught the tendrils in her hands and held it back in a loose ponytail. She didn't really mind the wind. It always seemed to lighten her spirits, but today it was full of grit. "I've never seen anything like this. Those rock walls look like they were created by a huge mud flow—the way all the different earthen colors swirl across the cliff face."

"Well, they probably were, dear—during the great flood." Willow pointed to another section of the canyon. "That looks like a huge castle, and those stone formations remind me of plump mushrooms." She leaned back. "I think God had a good time when he created this place."

"Where are we anyway?" Claire asked.

"There's a signpost. Let's see what it says." Dust kicked up around Willow's sandaled feet as she moved toward the placard. She placed her hands on it and read silently, then said, "Early Castle Valley. Mormons settled here in the eighteen seventies. It was the last place Brigham Young called his followers." She shook her head slightly. "Those poor souls. I can't imagine how harsh life must have been for them here." Her gaze moved back to the sweeping valley.

Sean joined Claire and sat beside her. "This is tiny compared to the Grand Canyon. Wait till you see it, then you'll know real greatness. I never get tired of looking at it."

Who was Sean? Some of the time he seemed detached, and other times he could be thoughtful and sensitive. He made the Grand Canyon sound like something he treasured. "You've been there?" Claire tried to sound casual, but she couldn't forget how close he was to her.

"A few times, with my family. There are trips down into the canyon bottom. We should do that." He looked back at Willow and Tom. "Well, maybe not."

They all headed back to the RV, Daisy pulling at her leash. The dog acted as if she wanted to check out the display by the pickup.

Willow wandered over to the display. "Are these for sale?"

The woman nodded. "I'll give you a good price."

Willow looked at several pieces. "Did you make these yourself?"

"Yes."

"You're an artist." She glanced at Claire. "Come and look. They're beautiful."

Claire pushed off the bench, and darkness closed in around her. She'd forgotten her illness for a moment. Now reality forced her to remember. She grabbed hold of the back of the bench and waited for the blackness to pass.

"Steady there." Sean stood and grasped her arm.

His touch startled her. "I'm all right." The faintness receded. Claire smiled at him and wished she could stay right where she was, with his hand steadying her. Instead, she joined Willow where a Native American woman had bead work laid out on a colorful blanket.

She picked up a set of turquoise earrings. "These are striking."

"You should get them. I was thinking about these for my daughter." She held up a pair of dangling turquoise and opal earrings. "Do you think she'd like them?"

"I would, but I don't know your daughter."

"I barely do either." Willow turned to the woman selling the jewelry. "How much for these?"

"Twenty-five dollars."

"I'll take them." Willow fished the money out of her woven purse and handed it to the woman.

She dropped the earrings into a small velvet bag, tied it closed, and gave it to Willow.

Tom looked over the jewelry. "Where's Taylor? She'd probably like these."

"She stayed on the coach." Claire glanced back at the RV.

"Too bad."

Daisy sniffed at the display while Willow picked up a feathered headdress that looked like it was made for a chief. "If only she wasn't so fearful. I think her brusque exterior is just a cover for anxiety. Poor dear." She studied the headdress. "This is just right for my grandson. That is, if my daughter will allow me to give him something."

What would be wrong with a gift from his grandma? "Why wouldn't she?" Claire asked.

"It's a long story for another time." Willow's eyes glistened with unshed tears as she glanced up at the sky. "I'm trusting God to work it out by the time we get to Atlanta."

CHAPTER TEN

Claire sat at the kitchen table, sketching some of the interesting rock formations she'd seen at Castle Valley. Some would make charming animated creatures for a children's story.

"What are you doing?" Taylor asked.

"Just trying to capture a little of what I saw back there. I'd like to see if I can work some of the formations into a story."

"Oh yeah. You write children's stories."

"I try."

"Hey, the Arches," Tom said. "According to that sign, the turnoff is just ahead. We ought to go."

"Oh, we have to," Willow said. "Do you mind, Sean? I was there once when I was young. I've always wanted to go back."

"The Arches?" Taylor asked.

Claire rested her hand on her abdomen. She wasn't feeling so great. "How far is it?"

Willow moved to the front of the RV. "Who cares? We're on an adventure. Right?"

Claire held back a groan. Her stomach had been churning for the last couple of hours and the extra driving might thoroughly curdle it. She'd rather Sean pull off the highway and stop.

"From what I read, there are all kinds of natural stone archways. The pictures are pretty spectacular." Tom leaned on the sofa's armrest and gave Taylor a quizzical look. "How'd you miss it? You've been laying out plans for this trip on that computer of yours for weeks."

"Didn't interest me. Besides you keep us updated … all the travel magazines you have stashed."

Claire set her writing tablet aside and lifted her hair off her shoulders, holding it away from her neck. "What do you remember, Willow? Was it as special as Tom says?"

"You better make up your minds." Sean decreased his speed. "We're almost to the turnoff."

Willow closed her eyes for a moment while a smile played on

her lips. She opened her eyes, one at a time, and looked at her companions. "Actually, I don't remember much. It was back in my hippy days. I was stoned most of the time."

Tom rolled his eyes. "Is that all you did?"

"Of course not. And don't be so critical. You are part of that generation too. And you can't tell me you didn't smoke a little weed now and then."

"I didn't. Really." He held up two fingers, pressed together. "Scout's honor."

Willow's cheerfulness faded, and she said in a serious tone, "I'd like another chance to see it."

"Okay. So we're going." Tom looked at Taylor. "You up for it?"

She didn't respond.

His eyes latched onto Claire's. "You're kind of pale. You all right?"

"I'm fine," Claire said, her stomach lurching as they rounded a curve. What good would complaining do?

"I don't know what the highway is like," Sean said. "It might be a bear to drive. But we'll find out."

"I'm not going." Taylor slammed her arms across one another over her chest.

"Fine. We'll drop you off, then," Tom said. "Look there—a rest area—two miles."

Sean glanced at him in the rearview mirror. "I'm not leaving anyone out here on their own, especially not at a rest stop."

"She's a big girl. We can see the Arches, then come back and get her. She'll be fine."

"Taylor, please come with us," Willow pleaded. "It's a chance to see something special. And you'll be glad you did it."

"I said no." Taylor stuck out her chin, looking defiant, but there was fear in her eyes.

No one said a word for a long moment, then Tom spoke up. "I'm not about to miss out just because Miss Scaredy Pants is too afraid to go. It's not fair to the rest of us."

All the bickering was making Claire's stomach feel worse.

Taylor's eyes shimmered as if she was about to cry. "Drop me off. I'll be fine." She snapped her laptop closed and stowed it under her seat.

"Honey, please," Willow said.

Tom cleared his throat. "Sean, you heard her. Pull into the rest stop. It's coming up."

Sean glanced back at the travelers, uncertainty on his face, but he followed the exit off the highway.

A look of surprise touched Taylor's eyes.

Claire wilted inside. How could they leave Taylor behind?

Sean pulled into a parking area and stopped. "You really ought to come with us. I'm sure the road is fine—"

"Just don't take too long." Taylor pushed up from the table and headed for the fridge. She grabbed a bottle of water, then walked to the door and climbed out of the RV.

"We can't leave her," Willow said.

"Sure we can." Tom motioned for Sean to get moving.

"I'll stay with her." Claire took a deep breath and willed her lunch to stay put. "My stomach's not feeling good. I need a break from the motion of the RV." She moved to the door. "You go ahead. Have fun."

Sean's hazel eyes locked with hers. He slid pursed lips sideways. "I don't think it's a good idea—two women out here, alone."

"There are lots of people driving this highway. We won't be alone." Claire forced a brave smile. Was she being foolish? "We'll see you in a little while."

"Wait." Willow pushed up from the sofa, grabbed a paper bag and placed several other water bottles, two apples, and two granola bars in it, then handed the bag to Claire. "You might need this."

"Thank you." Her voice wavered a little, but Claire threw back her shoulders and stepped out of the motor home and moved toward Taylor, who sat on a stout stone wall built into a hillside. Claire leaned against the wall.

"What are you doing here?" Taylor twirled a flower between her fingers, then started stripping off the petals.

"I decided to stay. My stomach's upset. I need a break from the RV."

"Don't stay because of me."

"I'm not." Claire looked out over the desert. It was empty and bleak. She pushed herself up onto the top of the wall beside Taylor. So much of the country looked like this—like her life. Maybe most lives were desolate. Maybe people didn't talk about what they felt inside. Maybe they were afraid and lonely too.

Even if it were true, there was always hope. Even in the midst of the desert, there were occasional places of beauty.

The RV pulled away, taking with it the last of Claire's confidence. She glanced at the parking area and the restroom buildings.

No one was here, except her and Taylor.

A quiver prickled up her spine. A chill breeze blew down the neckline of her coat. "April in Utah is a lot cooler than in Oregon."

"Yeah." Taylor stared at the sidewalk in front of her.

A sturdy, little plant with clusters of yellow flowers had pushed up in the inhospitable soil.

Claire plucked a blossom and held it to her nose. It had a pungent aroma.

A blue Chevy van rolled into the rest area and pulled into a parking spot. Three young children, a man, and a woman tumbled out of the vehicle and headed for the restrooms.

The larger boy tugged on one of his sister's ponytails.

She swung around. "Cut that out. Mom, he won't leave me alone."

"Jacob, stop that. You two get along." The woman kept walking.

"Not alone now," Taylor said. "Too bad." She reached into her pocket and pulled out an iPod.

Claire didn't know why she didn't use it more on the RV, instead of making them all listen to country. She probably hoped to convert them all.

Thoughts of her sister Melissa pushed themselves on Claire. The two hadn't been close for years, though they once had been. Melissa reminded her of Taylor—reserved and hostile. She suffered from bipolar disorder too, but she was brave, never fearful like Taylor. She'd always been a daredevil. On family outings to the desert, it was always Melissa who opened the throttle on her motorcycle and scooted across the dusty ground, leaving everyone behind. When they were horseback riding, she'd call out, "Race you," then urge her horse into a sprint across open fields.

Claire glanced at Taylor. She'd never told her about her sister's condition. Maybe now was a good time. It might help them connect. She was pretty certain that in spite of Taylor's bristly exterior, she wanted a friend. Claire studied the sturdy yellow blossom, then plunged forward. "My sister is bipolar."

Taylor cast an I-can't-believe-you-just-said-that look at Claire. "Yeah. So?"

"I just thought you'd like to know. It kind of gives us something in common."

"Why? I don't have a sister who's bipolar."

Claire let out a frustrated breath. "No. But, well … I remember how hard it was for her."

"Oh, so now you feel sorry for me? You?" She stared at Claire through defiant eyes. "I wouldn't change places with you in a million years."

Claire looked away. She should have gone with the others. "Okay, I guess I don't understand."

"You guess?"

She forced herself to meet the fire in Taylor's brown eyes. "I want to. To understand."

Taylor's expression softened. "You don't, not really. But I appreciate the sentiment." She looked at the high mountain desert, her jaw set, turned up the music on the iPod, and put in ear buds.

It was so loud Claire could hear Loretta Lynn's burly voice from where she sat.

Taylor jumped off the stone wall and walked toward the restroom.

The energy drained out of Claire. She'd messed up … again. Taylor hated her more than ever.

A new vehicle chugged into the rest area behind her. Claire turned to see who the new arrival was.

The RV pulled into the parking area.

Why were they back?

Sean climbed out, followed by Tom, Willow, and Daisy. They headed toward Claire.

Claire edged off the rock wall and stood. "What are you doing here?" Dizziness swept over her, so she kept her hand on the wall until it passed.

"We just couldn't leave you two behind." Willow pulled Claire into a casual hug. "What kind of people would we be?" She cast a disapproving glance at Tom.

He looked as if he was trying to shake off irritation. "I can see the Arches another time."

"Where's Taylor?" Sean asked.

"Using the restroom."

"That's something we should all do before we hit the road." Tom headed toward the restrooms, looking weary and weak.

Claire suddenly wished he'd been able to see the Arches after all.

CHAPTER ELEVEN

"Only ten miles to Grand Junction, Colorado," Sean announced.

Civilization. Claire could hardly wait to see a decent-sized town.

The scenery had changed. A small, quiet river meandered alongside the highway with slender alder and birch growing amid waist-high grasses along the banks. Claire gazed at the mountains in the distance. Piles of white clouds rested on the peaks, looking as if they'd settled into a comfy easy chair. She could use one of those kinds of chairs. She adjusted the seat back slightly and stretched out her legs, but she didn't find relief from her stiffness and pain.

"What river is that?" Taylor asked.

"The Colorado," Tom said, holding up a magazine with a mid-page spread that looked like the area they were driving through.

"It's so small."

"Yeah—takes a while to pick up steam."

"It's quiet and peaceful here." Willow leaned over the sofa and looked out the window. She flinched and pressed her hand to the small of her back.

"Are you all right?" Claire asked.

Willow rubbed her back. "Just a little kink. That bed's not the most comfortable I've ever slept on."

Claire had to agree. She moved up close to the window and, with her cell phone camera, took a picture of the river. "My family will never believe this is the Colorado River."

A breeze tickled the treetops.

"I love the aspen and birch. They look like they're worshiping the Lord."

"Right." Tom lifted his brow. "Willow, I understand that your faith is strong, but not everything is about God. Couldn't you just say the trees look happy or something?"

Willow gave him a half smile. "They're God's creation, so why shouldn't they worship him?"

Daisy leaned against her owner's leg.

Willow ran a hand over the dog's head. "Isn't that right, girl?" She turned and sat back on the sofa. "Either way they are amazing, after so many miles of rock and scrub. I'd like to just stop right here and spend a little time sitting along the river." She closed her eyes and leaned her head back against the sofa.

"There's a KOA park up ahead," Tom said. "My membership is still good. My wife and I used to do a lot of camping. Miss those days."

"I'm supposed to stop at my sister's in Grand Junction," Claire said.

No one responded.

"I'm sorry. It's just that—I wanted to spend time with her. My mother's worried about her. And if we camp all the way out here that means long, expensive taxi drives."

Tom rested his arms on his thighs and leaned forward. "To tell you the truth, I'm ready to spend some time in the city. We've been driving through empty wastelands for days. If we stay in town a few days we can have a sit-down dinner somewhere. Spend time in a crowd. With people we *don't* know."

Taylor looked over the top of her computer. "There's a campground right off Highway 50, near town. It has a pool and showers."

"How about washers and dryers? I really need to do some laundry." Willow rubbed her shoulder.

Taylor looked over the information. "It says laundry facilities."

"I vote we stay in town," Willow said.

"That's it, then." Sean passed a slow-moving truck.

"I hope they have a hot tub," Tom said.

"Ah, that would be heaven." Willow smiled.

Tom patted Daisy when she wiggled in between him and Willow. "What do you say, Daisy? Ready to get off this coach? Maybe take a swim?" He rubbed underneath her chin.

Willow watched, a knowing smile on her lips.

When they pulled into the RV park, Sean paid an attendant with Tom's card and followed a map to their campsite. He nodded at the swimming pool as they drove past. "That's where I'll be in fifteen minutes." After reaching their assigned space, Sean finessed the RV into place.

"You're getting pretty good at this," Tom said. "Thank God we came across you when we did."

Sean raised his eyebrows and slid his mouth slightly sideways. He didn't look exactly happy.

"I'll get something cooking for dinner." Willow let out a soft groan when she got up from the sofa.

Claire's skin felt sticky from her earlier nausea. "Mind if I leave dinner to you? A shower would feel good right now."

"This kitchen is too small for group cooking. Go on ahead." Willow opened the refrigerator.

"I'll take Daisy out," Taylor offered. "Come on, girl." She clipped on the leash and headed outdoors.

Deciding she didn't want Sean to watch her hobble off with a cane, Claire left it behind and fought against the wobble in her legs. How she missed the feeling of power in her muscles that she'd once possessed.

In the shower room, she lost more of her strength as heat and humidity stripped it away. Though standing in the warm cascade of water felt good, she made the shower short, in case she wouldn't be able to make it back to the RV without asking for help and then being forced to use her walker. The idea of struggling along with Sean watching cut into her heart.

Wearing light cotton shorts and a shirt, Claire made her way back to camp, wishing she'd been less vain and brought her cane. Everyone, except Willow, sat outside. She eased into a patio chair between Tom and Sean. "Whatever Willow's cooking smells good."

"Spaghetti." Tom glanced at the RV door. "She's a good cook. But she's taking too long. I'm starving."

Willow stuck her head out the door and the wind caught hold of her shoulder-length hair and swept it off her face. It made her look almost young. "Would you like to eat alfresco?"

"Perfect." Sean stood. "I'll clean off the picnic table."

Tom started to get up, but one leg gave out, and he fell back into his chair.

Claire fought an impulse to help him.

He tried again and this time got both legs under him and walked stiffly up the steps and into the RV.

Taylor was typing like mad.

"What are you writing?"

"A song." She plucked a few notes on her guitar, then turned back to her computer and typed something. "Need to get it down while it's in my mind."

Claire gave a little nod. She'd heard that a lot lately. She laid her head back against the chair and closed her eyes. A breeze cooled her warm skin. Would her sister be glad to see her? It had been a long time since they'd been together.

Conversation during dinner was light. Claire and Taylor did the dishes afterward while Sean, Willow, and Tom snoozed in their chairs. If only Taylor would give her pointers on what to say to her sister, how to better communicate. She didn't dare ask. Taylor would just get miffed over Claire's ignorance, and rightly so. Claire had never taken the time to reach out to Melissa or to understand her illness. For too long, Melissa had only been an annoyance. Claire had been working through her own issues and didn't have the energy to take on Melissa's troubles too.

Guilt jabbed.

After the last dish was washed and put away, Claire called for a taxi and returned to her chair beneath the awning to wait. "I hope the driver knows where to find us."

"He'll know." Sean drank the last of his iced tea. "I have a friend I'd like to see. Do you mind if I hitch a ride with you? While you visit your sister I can catch a little time with him."

"Sure," Claire said, but she wasn't certain she wanted anyone with her. She might need to make a fast exit. Melissa's moods were unpredictable.

"I'll cover the cost."

"We can share."

By the time the taxi arrived, Claire's stomach ached and sweat trickled down her temples. What was it about seeing Melissa that had her so edgy? And on top of that, she felt weak. She'd have to take her

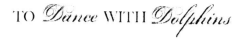

cane.

Sean held the door for her while she slid onto the backseat, then climbed in beside her. "Hey, this is kind of nice—I'm not driving."

"I'll bet you're tired of it."

"Yeah. I am." Sean's eyes went to half mast, as if he were hiding something.

He didn't want to be their chauffeur any longer—he never had. What would they do if he left?

She gave the driver Melissa's address, then sat back and stared at passing businesses. She and Sean should be chatting, but neither of them seemed to have anything to say. Frankly, all Claire could think about was her sister. What kind of reception would Claire get after all this time?

They moved into a neighborhood with wide streets and lots of trees. Children played basketball in a driveway court, others jumped rope on the sidewalk, and some rode bicycles.

How long had it been since she'd seen Melissa? Nearly three years? They'd exchanged only two letters and one Christmas card in all that time. They hadn't even stayed in touch over the Internet. Claire wasn't sure Melissa even owned a computer.

Gradually, the neighborhood changed. Homes looked old and unkempt—peeling paint, weeds in the flowerbeds, cars parked in the street. A knot tightened in Claire's stomach.

The driver pulled to the curb in front of a house that looked like it hadn't seen a paintbrush in half a century. "Here we are." He leaned down and gazed out the window. "Two thirty-one."

"Should we wait?" Sean asked.

"No. I'll be fine."

"What if she's not home? Did you call?"

"No. I guess maybe you should wait."

Claire stepped out of the car. Her heart hammered, and she prayed that it wouldn't kick up so much that it wouldn't quiet back down. Feeling faint and unsteady, she gripped her cane. Two steps up to a small porch. She stared at the door, then knocked.

The sounds of a radio or television carried from inside.

The door opened a crack. "Yeah. What do you want?"

"I'm Claire Murray. Is Melissa Murray here?"

"I don't know any Melissa. And I'm the only one who lives here." The door slammed shut.

Claire gazed at blistered blue paint. Now what? She knocked again.

This time the door swung open, revealing a heavy-set woman wearing a tightly cinched red-and-purple house coat. She pinched a cigarette between pudgy fingers. She glared at Claire from beneath thinly tweezed brows. "I told you I don't know no Melissa."

"Yes. But." Sweat trickled down Claire's back. Her hands trembled. She looked into the woman's weary eyes. "Do you know a Lisa?"

The woman's eyes widened. "Lisa? Oh, sure. She used to live here."

"Used to? The last time she talked to our mom, she gave this as her address."

"Yeah. But she moved a few weeks ago. I think she went out to California somewhere."

"You don't know where?"

The woman took a drag off the cigarette, held it in her lungs a moment, then blew smoke toward the ceiling. "No. She was in a hurry. You know her moods. She didn't even take any furniture with her."

"Oh. Well, thank you." Claire turned and gazed at the taxi, its deep blue blurred.

The door clicked behind her.

She needed to see Melissa, to reconnect. Why would she move and not tell anyone? Claire's legs felt like sticks, forcing her to lean hard on her cane as she shuffled back to the car.

Sean stepped out. "Claire?"

"She's not here. She moved to California." A tear trailed down her face. She swiped it away and tried to focus on Sean. "I guess I'll see her another time."

CHAPTER TWELVE

While Sean walked across a gravel parking lot, Claire sat in the backseat of the taxi, her cheek resting against the cool window, heart heavy. She'd really thought that she might be able to spend time with Melissa and begin to rebuild their relationship. Now all Claire could do was call their mother and tell her that Melissa was somewhere in California … maybe.

Sean headed straight for a construction site next to the lot. What was he doing? He'd said he wanted to see a friend, but the timing didn't make sense. Did his friend work construction?

No, it was way past working hours.

A man dressed in coveralls stepped out from behind a partially finished wall.

Sean moved toward him, hand outstretched. Yet the two's greeting looked reserved, not like friends who hadn't seen each other in a while.

The cab driver glanced at his watch. "Do you know how long he's gonna be?"

"No. Are you in a hurry?"

"Nearly time to clock out."

"I'm sorry. I'm sure he won't be long."

Sean and the other man talked for at least five minutes.

Claire rolled down her window, welcoming a cool breeze and the fragrance of a huge lilac blooming on a corner landscape. *Sean, hurry up.* She needed time alone—to think, then to sleep and close out the thoughts and questions.

If only she and Melissa could have the old days back, before their illnesses. They'd shared the fun in life, whispered secrets long into the night. But the year Melissa turned fifteen she changed, became unreliable and unruly, distancing herself from family and friends.

Claire swallowed hard. Or had it been the other way around? Had they moved away from her?

Just like Taylor, Melissa wasn't easy to be around. She had wide mood swings—deep depressions and unexplained agitation. Some days Melissa seemed like her old self, riding horses at the ranch or swimming in the river. And then there were the dark times, when she didn't come out of her room for days or did strange things like remodel her apartment, painting and decorating without ceasing, or making endless phone calls in the middle of the night. Claire could never predict how her sister would behave.

Staying a safe distance away was what people did when confronted with changes in friends or family. They didn't know what to do with the altered loved one that no longer behaved as they always had. Illness and disease transformed its victims. Claire knew it firsthand. As her illness took hold and she couldn't do what she'd always done, friends drifted away. She'd taken refuge at home. Her world grew smaller, life became quiet and lonely.

After Autumn married, nothing was the same—she had her own life. And with Melissa's emotional ups and downs, Claire made no real effort to breach the distance between them. Today had been her chance to try again.

If only there was some way to contact her, to make sure she was safe. Anxiety clawed at Claire's nerves.

The man and Sean shook hands again, and Sean sauntered back to the taxi. When he climbed in, he didn't look Claire full in the face.

"Where to now?" the driver asked.

"Back to the RV park." Sean glanced at Claire. "That is, if you don't have any more stops to make."

"No. None."

"Okay, then. Back to the campground." Sean relaxed into the seat, clasped his hands in his lap, and stared at the back of the seat in front of him.

Something wasn't right.

By the time they got back to the park, the sun was nearly down and the lights inside the RV glowed, soft and quiet. If only her heart could feel the way the interior of the coach looked.

Sean dropped onto one of the patio chairs. "I'll stay out here for a while."

"Sure." Claire grabbed hold of the railing and lifted heavy feet up the steps. Hand on the door knob, she stopped and studied Sean. There was definitely something wrong. What had happened between him and that man?

When she walked inside, Willow and Taylor were playing cards. Tom, a travel magazine resting on his chest, roused from a nap on the sofa. He was the first to speak. "You two weren't gone as long as I expected."

"How's your sister?" Willow asked.

"I don't know. She moved to California." Claire tried to sound casual but couldn't quite pull it off.

"Oh dear." Willow grasped her gently by the arms. "I'm sure she's fine. You'll see her soon. Maybe on our trip back we can swing by wherever she is."

A flicker of hope made Claire's mood lighter, but the weight quickly returned. "I don't know where in California, and I'm not sure how I can find out."

"Well, maybe by then we *will* know." Willow gave her a quick hug.

Tom closed the magazine and set it on the sofa. "It's fine by me, as long as it doesn't get in the way of my NASCAR drive."

"NASCAR?" Willow tossed Tom a troubled look. "You're planning to drive in a NASCAR race?"

"You bet. I've got it all worked out. They have something called the Richard Petty Driving Experience in Las Vegas. They give you a class and the right gear, and then you get to drive a NASCAR. It's safe. Even you could do it."

"But your—"

"Nothing's getting in the way of my driving. I've always wanted to do it, and I'm going to." He leveled a gaze at her as if daring her to object.

Willow shook her head but didn't say anything more.

Taylor didn't even look up. She played a few bars, then typed on her computer.

"You still working on that song?" Tom asked.

Smooth, Tom. Divert the conversation.

"I need to get it down while I'm hearing it. I think it's the best I've ever done." Her voice sounded slightly shrill. "Soon as I have it perfect, I'll play it for you." All the while she talked, she typed away.

"You've been refining it for hours. Ought to be perfect by now." He cast Claire and Willow a sideways glance and raised his eyebrows. "You been taking your medication?"

Taylor's fingers stopped, and she glared at Tom. "Whether I take my meds or not is none of your business." She returned to her keyboard.

"Tom, let her work on the song," Claire said. "She loves music and has a good voice, why shouldn't she go for her dream?" She turned to Taylor. "I'm proud of you for trying."

The door opened and Sean stepped in. "Hey." His brow was furrowed and his jaw looked tight. "Can I talk to you guys?" He sat at the table across from Taylor, cleared his throat, and looked at Claire.

Whatever was in his eyes made her stomach twist. Was it guilt?

"Well … I've got a job. I need the money."

"A job? You already have a job—driving for us." Tom leaned forward, arms on his thighs.

"Yeah, but this one pays more."

Sean was taking another job?

"Where is it?" Tom asked.

"Here in Grand Junction."

Tom narrowed his eyes. "What kind of job? For how long?"

"Construction—clean up and some carpentering. That friend of mine needs the help."

A drum thumped in Claire's chest. He wasn't going to travel with them anymore.

Tom stood. "How long will the work last?"

"He's got enough to keep me busy all summer and into fall."

"We can't cool our heels here until then." Tom clenched his hands into fists.

Taylor stopped typing. "You expect us to wait here for the next five months?"

"No. Of course not. I'm sure you can find someone else to drive you. I can't pass up a chance like this."

"But you promised," Taylor said.

"I never promised to drive the whole way. I just agreed to help you for a while." Sean held out his arms, palms up. "I have to do what I have to do."

Claire shrank back. How could they ever have thought they could do this?

"No problem. I'll drive." Tom's voice rumbled.

"Not a good idea." Willow tapped the cards on the table. "You don't know how you'll be feeling from one day to the next."

Taylor stared at Sean. "You lied to us—you *and* Tom. Tom said he could drive, and he couldn't. No matter what you say, you did promise to stick with us, and now you're dumping us for a second-rate job in this stupid town. What are we supposed to do now?"

"I've been feeling pretty good," Tom said. "No reason I can't take over the driving."

"Who are you kidding?" Taylor shook her head. "You're *not* doing good."

"Good enough to drive."

"We'll have to go back." Tears built up behind Claire's eyes. She'd go home, a failure with nothing to show for having tried. Nothing. Everything would be the same. She'd liked Sean, maybe too much, but now … He didn't care about them. He only cared about himself. And any hope of finding whatever it was that God had for her on this trip was gone.

"We don't have to decide anything tonight." Willow stood beside Tom and rested a hand on his arm. "We'll sleep on this and make a decision in the morning."

Tom scowled, the lines of his face so deep they reminded Claire of the wrinkles of the Shar-Pei her friend had once owned.

"I don't need to think about it." Tom cast an angry look at Sean.

CHAPTER THIRTEEN

Claire rested her book on her chest as Tom and Sean approached, chatting. They came from the direction of the pool and both had wet hair and dripping swim trunks, towels draped over their shoulders. Sean, tall and lean, was a contrast to Tom, whose age and illness had stripped away the strength of his youth.

That morning the group had met and gone over Sean's decision once more. The tension in the RV had been so heavy Claire could have sworn a Midwest thunderstorm had descended upon them. In the end, Tom agreed to post an ad for a driver in the local paper. The two men seemed fine with the new arrangement, but the idea of going ahead without Sean heaped another burden on Claire's heavy heart. She'd never see him again.

Sean caught her staring and gave her a little wave.

She sat up in the lounger. "Did you have a nice swim?"

"Hot tub," Tom said. "No way am I swimming. Not these days."

Sean pushed back wet hair. "Felt good. You ought to try it."

"No, thanks." Claire felt faint, but fought back the weakness, still not wanting her limitations displayed in front of Sean. It was silly, especially now that he was leaving them.

Tom toweled his hair. "Since we're going to be here at least another night, we ought to try out one of the better restaurants in town. My treat. What do you say?

Sean's head was already nodding.

She shrugged. "I can pay my own way."

"No. I insist. I know just the place. Saw it in a travel magazine." Tom headed for the RV. "I'll tell Willow and Taylor."

Claire rose from the chair, but her legs barely held her.

Sean extended a hand.

There was no rational reason not to let him help. Still, she hesitated before grasping his hand. "Thanks. I'm a little unsteady today."

A look of pity mixed with curiosity shadowed his eyes.

Now was not the time to tell him more about her illness.

"Glad to help."

As they stepped inside, Willow hurried toward the back of the RV. "Do we have to dress for dinner?"

"My guess is it might be frowned upon if you showed up in your birthday suit." Tom chuckled.

"Well, I don't know about that." Willow flipped her hair over her shoulder and wiggled her hips.

The light from Taylor's computer screen made her face glow. "From what I see online, I'd say dressy casual."

"I have just the perfect dress." Willow stepped into the bedroom.

It was a bit thorny, everyone getting ready at once, but the five of them managed. Claire was putting in her earrings just as the taxi pulled up.

Taylor was the first one out the door. Tom helped Willow, and Sean gave Claire a hand down the steps.

Despite the questioning looks she would certainly get from people, Claire brought her cane along. At least it was less obvious than her walker or wheelchair.

Taylor climbed into the front seat, and Willow slid in beside her. Tom, Claire, and Sean crowded into the back.

"Are you sure this is all right? There's not too many of us?" Willow asked the cab driver.

"No problem. I do it all the time."

"We're heading for the Winery Restaurant," Tom said. "Do you know where that is?"

"Yes, sir. Good choice. And it's not far—downtown on Main Street." He stepped on the gas and maneuvered through the RV park.

Traffic was light and they clipped along.

Claire's spirits lifted. Maybe this would be fun.

The taxi pulled off the street and into an alley alongside a brick building.

"It's awesome." Willow stepped out of the taxi.

Gas lamps sat on brick ledges nestled among ivy that enveloped a brick wall. A grapevine canopy over the alley framed the entrance, an overly large wooden door.

Tom paid the cabbie, then offered Willow his arm. "Looks like a nice place."

"Sure does," Taylor said and turned to Sean. "But I don't understand why he's with us."

Sean stopped. "You're right. I can find another place to eat."

"Not on your life. Never been one to hold a grudge and not about to start now." Tom clapped a hand on Sean's shoulder. "A man's got to find his own way in the world."

"Thanks, Tom. I appreciate that."

The five of them moved to the entrance.

"Never judge a book by its cover." Taylor yanked open the door.

The interior greeted them with vintage charm. The walls were rustic wood, and soft light filtered in through stained-glass windows.

If Claire's mood were lighter she could fully enjoy the distinctive character of the restaurant. But she couldn't shake the cloud of her sister's move and Sean's desertion.

Tom led the bunch to a reception desk. "We have reservations."

"Your name?"

"Tom Cantrell."

The maître d' glanced down at a register. "Yes. Reservation for five?"

"That's us."

He picked up five menus. "Right this way."

The band of travelers followed him through a maze of people, wooden tables, and chairs. Each table was arranged with elegant place settings and candles. They moved past a quaint bar, well stocked with wine. The smell of grilling meat, herbs, and seafood drifted through the room.

"Will this do?" the maître d' asked, standing beside a table that sat alongside a brick wall.

"It's perfect," said Willow.

Before the maître d' could pull out a chair for her, Tom stepped in and did it. Sean helped Claire and Taylor, then took the seat between the two. He gazed around the room. "So, Tom, extra benefits to keep me on?" He lifted a brow. "Might work."

Tom grinned. "Order anything you like."

Willow leaned toward Tom and quietly said, "It must be good or there wouldn't be so many people here."

Taylor unfolded her napkin, tipped her face toward the ceiling, and placed the napkin over her face. She blew on the fabric, making it ruffle slightly.

Claire's stomach clenched. Why would Taylor do that?

"What are you doing?" Tom asked.

She dragged the napkin off her face. "Nothing."

Clearing his throat, Sean picked up his menu. "Well, let's see what there is to eat. I'm starved."

Everyone opened their menus, and Tom let out a low whistle. "A bit pricey."

"Oh dear, Tom. We don't have to eat here," Willow said. "It's way too expensive."

"Price doesn't matter. Sorry I said anything."

"But you've been paying for everything," Willow said. "We can't continue to put this kind of burden on you."

"Look. Let's get this straight. I have plenty of money. I owned my own business most of my life, made wise investments, and when I sold the business I made a big profit. Why don't you let me enjoy spending a little of it?" He smiled broadly, then held the menu up to better light. "Sometimes it's good to treat ourselves."

Claire wilted inside. Money, a nice restaurant, and good food wasn't going to change anything. Her life would go on just as it had before they'd set off on this trip. Muffling a sigh, she scanned the menu. Veal medallions, New Zealand Rack of lamb—no. She wasn't about to let Tom pay those kinds of prices. Seafood bisque—more reasonably priced and more palatable for her touchy stomach. "I think I'll try the seafood bisque."

"That sounds amazing." Willow fanned herself with the menu. "Oh, the best I ever had was in a little café in Paris." She set down the menu. "I'll try it."

Tom leaned back, clasped his hands over his chest, and intertwined his fingers. "I'm having the Alaskan king crab legs."

Sean peered at his menu. "They're eighty dollars!"

"A man's got to splurge once in a while." Tom smiled broadly.

Sean closed his menu. "I'll have the lamb chops."

Taylor patted her face with the menu.

"Taylor, dear, do you know what you want?" Willow took the menu from her.

"Do they have filet mignon?"

"They do."

"I'll have that." Taylor grinned, looking almost as if she'd had too much to drink.

A waiter approached, took their orders in a reserved manner, and walked away.

"I've got to pee." Taylor pushed her chair away from the table and stood.

"I need to go to the restroom too." Willow stood as quickly as possible and followed Taylor.

Melissa had done things that made no sense also. Like moving without letting anyone know where or why. Where was she?

"What's up with Taylor today?" Sean smoothed the tablecloth in front of him.

Tom leaned forward and lowered his voice. "She's been off for a few days. I don't think she's taking her medication."

"Is there any way to make her take it?"

Tom shrugged. "I don't know. Maybe Willow can talk to her. She won't listen to me."

When Taylor and Willow returned, Taylor didn't look like she was any more in control of herself than when she'd left. She held her dress away from her legs and sashayed toward the table. "Too bad they don't have music. I'm in the mood to let go." She dropped onto her chair.

Claire gripped the seat, doing her best to stay put. She wanted to leave. She'd seen this kind of thing before, with Melissa.

ॐ ॐ

Sean walked Daisy back to the RV while she pranced on the end of the leash.

"Thank you, Sean," Willow said. "It looks like you two had a nice walk."

"She's got energy to burn. Loves to chase rocks." Avoiding eye contact with Claire, Sean gave Daisy a good rub down. "I'm going to miss you, girl." He unhooked the leash, and Daisy trotted over to Willow.

Willow scratched her behind the ears, hugged her around the neck, and looked up at Sean. "And she's going to miss you."

Sean glanced away.

Claire sat in the patio chair right next to Willow, ignoring Sean. He didn't like her being mad at him, even though she did have a right.

"I have an appointment to look at an apartment tomorrow. I appreciate your letting me stay until I can get into one."

"You're welcome to stay as long as you need," said Willow.

Despite Taylor's strange behavior at last night's dinner, Sean had had a good time. His charges had seemed more like friends than an obligation. Especially Claire. But, when they'd accepted his defection with grace, that only piled on more guilt. He needed to get away, clear his mind. "I'm going into town. Actually I have some business to take care of."

Claire sighed, the small sound full of disappointment.

"I've got a cab coming. It should be here any minute." He leaned against a small tree, pretending nonchalance. When the cab rounded the corner a minute later, he felt like he'd been saved from a coming inquisition.

But from whom? Claire and Willow wouldn't have confronted him. Was it his own heart that questioned his decision?

"See you later." He flagged down the taxi.

"'Bye," Willow and Claire said in unison.

Sean climbed into the backseat, pulled the door closed, and gave them a wave. He needed to think, and he couldn't do it with those blue eyes staring at him.

"Where to?" the cab driver asked.

Sean hadn't thought that far ahead. "Uh, is there a movie theater in town?"

"Yep."

"Take me there."

"Sure thing."

When the taxi pulled up in front of the theater, a billboard advertising the latest Spielberg movie caught Sean's eye. That would be a good enough distraction. After paying the driver, Sean walked up to the ticket window. "One, please." He slid ten bucks to the clerk, took the ticket and his change, and stepped into the lobby.

It smelled of popcorn, which would usually tempt him into buying a bag, but today he wasn't hungry. He got a Coke, found a seat in the theater, and sank down, waiting for the movie to start.

There was nothing wrong with his setting out on his own. He had a life to live.

Advertisements flashed across the screen, but all Sean could think about was Claire. Her sweet face drifted through his mind— blue eyes, a soft smile framed by silky blonde hair. She was beautiful, but his attraction was about more than that. She wasn't like anyone he'd ever known. Although unsure of herself, she possessed a quiet strength hidden within her gentleness. Something was wrong with her health, but what?

He dropped his head back against the seat. He couldn't fall in love with her. He wouldn't.

Music swelled and the movie appeared on the screen.

If he didn't drive the RV, Tom would. That would put Claire and the others in danger. Tom meant well, but he wasn't capable. If something bad happened, it would be his fault. *I'm not responsible for their choices. Just forget about them and watch the movie.*

But his mind remained with his friends. He'd never meant for them to become friends. If he left, he'd be deserting them, going back on his word. But if he stayed, what help was he really? They all faced a bad end, and he didn't want to be part of it. *Or do I?*

Sean couldn't sit there anymore. He pushed to his feet and headed for the exit. By the time he reached the lobby, he had the taxi company on the phone. He paced the sidewalk while he waited for his ride.

Finally a taxi pulled up, and Sean climbed in and gave the driver the name of the RV park. They'd been pretty accepting of his decision. Maybe they didn't care who drove.

No one was around when Sean stepped out of the cab.

The RV was closed up. Where were they?

Probably meeting with a new driver. He'd be off the hook.

An Explorer pulled up and Tom climbed out of the front seat. "Surprised to see you back so soon, Sean."

Willow and Claire stepped out, followed by Taylor.

Everyone stared at him.

"Did you find a driver?"

"I didn't think that was any of your concern." Tom frowned at him.

"I guess it isn't. If you found one, that's good. I won't have to worry about you."

"Who asked you to worry about us?" Taylor planted her hands on her hips and glared at him. "We can take care of ourselves."

"I know that." Sean should just have left well enough alone. "So ... *did* you find a replacement?"

Tom blinked once, slowly. A smile lifted his lips. "Nope. You looking for something to do?"

"Maybe. I heard you might have a job."

Claire's face brightened with a smile. "We've been praying for just the right man."

Tom studied Sean. "We *have* been praying. And I'm not so sure it's you." He stared hard at Sean. "You walked away from your responsibility pretty easily. How do we know you won't do it again?"

They seemed so forgiving. Sean hadn't expected rejection. What did he do now? "I understand your lack of trust. But I figured out something tonight. You're not just a job to me anymore. You're my friends. And I never betray friends."

Tom held his gaze. A smile emerged and he held out a hand. "Okay. You've got a job ... and friends."

That night they all went to bed early since they were leaving the next morning.

A stink drifted through the RV.

"For crying out loud, Daisy," Tom groused. "Willow, she's your dog."

"Fine," Willow said.

A window slid open a moment later.

Sean lay on his back, arms folded under his head. "'Night, everyone."

"Good night," Claire said.

"'Night," said Taylor.

"God bless you all," said Willow.

"Good night, John-Boy." Tom chuckled.

Sean closed his eyes, feeling more relaxed than he could remember feeling in a long time. He didn't know why he was here, but this was certainly where he belonged.

CHAPTER FOURTEEN

The travelers headed east, continuing their journey into the Rocky Mountains. And Sean was still driving.

Claire smiled and snuggled into the recliner.

The highway was like an ocean wave, rolling through the mountains, reaching for greater heights, then breaking over each new rise. Blue skies and mountain peaks gradually disappeared behind a building wall of clouds.

Taylor glanced out the side window. "It looks like bad weather is on its way."

"Could be," Tom said. "Never know this time of year. And at these elevations anything can happen."

"How high are we?" Claire studied a mountain top in the distance.

"The last sign said ten thousand feet." Sean looked at her in the rearview mirror.

"My goodness." Willow looked up from the Bible in her lap. "That's awfully high."

"Well, I guess you'd know about that," Tom said. "Getting high, I mean."

Willow shot him a snarky look. "That was a long time ago."

Voice laced with anxiety, Taylor asked, "Do you think it will snow?"

Sean looked over his shoulder at Taylor. "I doubt it."

Actually, Claire's aching body said otherwise. A climate change was definitely coming. Willow had been moving slower than usual too.

Taylor hadn't been backseat-driving since they'd left Grand Junction, which had to be a relief to Sean, but she did seem agitated. Her fingers flew over the computer keys while the heels of her feet bounced. She'd been to the fridge at least three times and downed that many bottles of pop.

They needed a break.

"Can we stop at the next rest area so we can get out and stretch a little?" Claire asked.

"That would be heaven." Willow rubbed her right shoulder.

The miles to the next rest stop seemed endless. By the time they pulled off and parked, Claire's legs and feet were on fire.

Walking might not be an option anymore.

She eased herself up and moved toward the door. *Take my walker or not?* She grabbed her cane.

"We better put on our coats." Willow slung a parka over her shoulders. Instead of her usual cotton shift and sandals, she wore sweat pants, walking shoes, and a parka. "It looks pretty frosty."

Claire shrugged into her jacket, pulled on a hat and gloves, opened the door, and gingerly descended the steps. Every movement sent spikes of pain into her feet and legs.

A snowflake drifted from the sky, then another and another.

"It's snowing!" She stared up into the gray, blinking as flakes dropped onto her eyelashes.

Tom scowled at the sky. "Great. That's all we need. I was hoping we'd get out of these mountains before bad weather hit."

"There's nothing to worry about," Sean said. "Spring storms don't last long."

Willow slowly made her way to a concrete table and eased herself onto the bench seat. "It's freezing out here."

"You forgot something," Tom said as he exited the RV, holding a leashed Daisy and a folded blanket, which he placed on the bench beside Willow.

"How nice of you to take care of Daisy … and me." Willow moved onto the blanket and pulled her coat more tightly around her.

The pain in Claire's feet eased slightly. "I think I'll take a little walk."

"Have you lost your mind? It's snowing." Taylor propped her hands on her hips, as if she were a disgruntled mother.

"I wish I could go, but I'm just not up to it." Willow shivered. "My body doesn't like this kind of weather."

"I'll keep you company." Tom stood beside her.

"Let's share the blanket." Willow got up, partially unfolded it, and smoothed it out.

Tom sat. "Thanks."

Was something brewing between the two of them? The idea made Claire smile. They'd be good together.

Tom puffed air into the sky. "Besides, at this altitude I don't think I could walk and breathe at the same time."

"I'm going inside. It's freezing out here." Taylor headed for the motor home.

Sean moved toward Claire. "I'll go with you. Need to stretch my legs after all those hours behind the wheel."

Claire stared at a couple of different pathways, thankful she wouldn't be alone, but wishing that she didn't need a cane for walking.

"Which way looks good to you?"

The least challenging, the one with the slight slope and a not-so-scary drop-off. "That one should be fine." She moved forward, doing her best to ignore the pain in her legs.

"You up to this?" Sean came beside her, matching her pace.

"Sure. Why not?" She smiled up at him. "Too many hours sitting, plus the cold weather, brings out the worst in my muscles. A walk should help."

Neither of them spoke for several minutes. The trail curved and dipped, branching off a few times. At each fork, she randomly chose between the options.

Clearing his throat, Sean finally broke the silence. "Do you ever get mad?"

"Everyone gets mad. Are you referring to something specific?"

"You know, being sick. You're young and ... beautiful."

Claire cheeks heated up. "And using a cane?" She lifted it off the ground.

He glanced at it. "This is supposed to be the best time of your life. You ought to be having fun. Instead—"

"I am having fun." Claire turned a full-beam smile on him. She hated living the way she did, but at the moment there was honestly nowhere else she'd rather be than at Sean's side, winding their way along this trail in the Rocky Mountains.

"You know what I mean. Your life is so … limited. I don't know exactly what's wrong with you, but it's clear you have a lot of pain and weakness." He paused.

Should she tell him? No. At least not yet.

"Don't you ever wonder why? Why you?"

Couldn't she just focus on his thinking she was beautiful and ignore how limited her life was for a moment?

No. He deserved an answer. A real one.

She stopped and faced him. "Yes. I do get mad sometimes. And I don't understand why me, but asking why doesn't help. I don't know if there is an answer. Or maybe there is one but I'm not supposed to know what it is. When I've prayed about it in the past, I've come to the conclusion that I'm supposed to trust God and keep living my life."

"That's what I don't get. You're a person of faith. Don't you feel betrayed?"

Way to go right to the biggest doubt in my soul, Sean Sullivan. Claire shrugged and walked along the path again. "Maybe a little. I don't really know how I feel. You should talk to Willow. She's a lot wiser than me."

Sean tugged her to a stop again, then peered at her with his warm hazel eyes. "I want to know about you, not Willow."

What was he saying? That he cared for her in a special way? If so, she might melt beneath his gaze. "I … I try to live one day at a time, and I pray for a cure."

"And if one doesn't come?"

"Then I'll pray for strength and courage." She tried to sound strong, but she wasn't. She wanted to be strong and healthy more than anything, and if it never happened, she wasn't sure she could ever really count on God the way she knew she should.

A strong gust of wind swept the fresh powder into the air.

She pulled her hood tighter around her face and led the way farther down the trail.

As the snow fell and the world grew quiet, they kept walking, snow dancing about them. It felt almost magical.

"I want to know why, Claire. None of it makes sense. Why does

God allow good people to suffer? People like you and my brother?"

"I don't know, but I don't blame God." A blast of wind sent shivers through Claire. They ought to go back to the coach, but that would mean ending this one-on-one time with Sean.

"He could do something about it if he wanted to." Sean sounded defiant.

She didn't understand why God didn't heal everyone. Why he allowed suffering. "This is what I know. God created a beautiful, perfect world. People messed it up, not him. He gave us choices, and we made the wrong ones."

Sean snorted. "I believe, but I never have gotten that. It's messed up. How can we be held accountable for what a man and woman did thousands of years ago?"

"I'm not a Bible scholar, Sean, but I put myself in Adam and Eve's place and I know that, if I'd been there, it would have been me who sinned."

"You really think that?"

Claire nodded. "And if you'd been there, it would have been you."

With a bit of shock in his eyes, Sean pursed his lips.

The wind intensified, howling and pelting them with snow. The path before them was covered in white. Claire's stiffness returned and her pace slowed. Her legs ached, and her feet felt frozen.

"Looks like this might be more than just a normal spring snowfall," Sean said, glancing back at the trail.

Their footprints were hidden beneath snow.

"I wish I'd worn my boots," Claire said.

She carefully found her footing to head back up the trail. "You said your brother died, but you never told me what happened."

"It's not something I like to talk about."

"Sometimes it helps to talk. I can't imagine what it must feel like to lose a brother."

Sean hunched deeper inside his hoodie. "It was bad. He was sick his whole life. All we ever did was run him back and forth to the hospital and to doctors, searching for better treatments, some way to save his life. He suffered a lot." He swiped at his eyes. "Nothing helped."

"I'm so sorry, Sean. It must have been awful."

"It was … for everyone." He shoved his hands in his pockets. "We watched him die one day at a time, and each day my parents died too. Everything was about Benjamin. I felt like an orphan most of the time." His voice caught. "And then I felt guilty about being mad at him, at them. It was like being stuck in a nightmare, and I couldn't wake up." Sean stared into the white storm. "I was the only one home when he died."

Claire fought to hold back tears. "How terrible for you. I'm so sorry." No wonder he didn't want to spend time with her. She was sick and maybe even dying, like his brother.

"It was a long time ago." His eyes were no longer warm or kind, but brittle and angry.

A few moments later, the path became two, and Claire had no idea which one to take. "Do you know the way?"

Sean grabbed her hand. "Yeah. I think so. We'll figure it out."

A tiny bit of warmth came through her glove, but the temperature had dropped more and fear crept inside.

They kept moving, but visibility shrank to only a few feet in front of them. Another fork in the trail emerged from behind the white veil.

Sean pulled the ties of his hoodie closed. "I'm not sure which one to take here."

Panic flashed through Claire. Where was the rest area? How far had they walked, caught up in their conversation?

Sean checked his phone. "And we don't have a signal."

Could they find their way back to the motor home, or would they be moving farther away, into the wilderness?

As dramatic as it sounded, they could die if they wandered too far.

She leaned on her cane to keep upright on her shaky legs. "What should we do?"

"Stay put. If we keep moving we might become even more lost. The storm will likely break up soon. Someone will find us. The gang will call for help."

"But it's so cold." Would someone find them in time?

Sean looked around. "If we get out of the wind, it'll help."

He steered Claire toward a stubby evergreen with a broad trunk and a hollow center with one side partially rotted away, creating a natural barrier.

"This should help." He took a large pocket knife and cut several evergreen boughs and spread them out on the floor of the hollow tree.

"Get inside."

"But it's not big enough for both of us. What will you do?"

"I'll be all right." Sean set her cane against the outside of the tree, then helped ease Claire down.

She huddled inside, pressing against the rotted wood.

Sean sat in front with his back to her, his hoodie pulled down over his head.

What if he froze to death? They both could. Claire opened her coat and stretched out her arms. "Lean back against me."

Sean didn't argue with her. He rested against her chest, and she put her arms around him.

They stayed like that, huddled against the storm, freshly cut boughs enveloping them in a sharp, tangy fragrance.

"I should never have decided on a walk, especially not this far," Claire said. "I didn't think it would get so bad. I'm sorry."

"It's not your fault."

Claire had been careless, wanting time with Sean, wanting to be close to him, rather than paying attention to staying safe.

Now they were close—so close they might die together.

Claire's shivers grew and her hope faded.

"Someone will find us. We'll be fine." Sean drew his legs up close to his chest.

Claire should ask for God's help, but she couldn't hold the truth back. *God, how can I believe in your mercy? You haven't protected me from this disease. My sister is sick ... and missing. Sean's brother died a horrible death. Why shouldn't I think that it might be your plan for us to die under this tree today?*

Wouldn't it be ironic if her illness had nothing to do with the way she died? What if she could have been living differently, not letting her sickness restrain her?

"Are you all right?" Sean asked.

Other than regrets and life questions pummeling her? "Just cold. How long does it take for hypothermia to set in?"

"Someone will find us before that. Or the storm will blow through."

Claire rested her cheek against his back.

"Just don't sleep. Okay?"

The minutes passed and the world was only wind and snow. Claire's eyelids began to fall.

What if no one came?

It seemed unfair to die like this—arms around the first man she thought she might be able to love.

And he didn't even know how she felt.

CHAPTER FIFTEEN

The wind quieted and the snowfall slowed until there were only occasional flakes.

Had Claire ever been so cold?

Sean stood. "How are you feeling?"

"Warm and toasty." She pulled her coat closed and struggled to her feet. "Do you think we should try to find our way back now that the weather's gotten better?"

"No. I don't think we're far from the rest area. If we stay put someone will find us." He pulled out his cell phone and checked the time. "It hasn't even been two hours since we left." He held up the phone and swung around slowly. "Still no signal."

"It feels like we've been here forever. I hope they come soon."

Sean put his arm around her. "Just trying to keep us warm."

"I know." He wasn't interested in her in any way other than friendship and warmth. If only he were, though.

"Sean! Claire!" A strong voice rang out across the trail.

"Here! We're over here," Sean yelled back.

Two men dressed in Forest Service uniforms appeared, both sporting huge smiles.

The taller of the two extended a hand to Sean. "Glad we found you. I'm Mike."

The other man shook their hands. "Kelly."

"Sure good to see you." Sean shivered.

Mike took off a pack, pulled out what looked like a space blanket, and wrapped it around Claire. "You have some friends who are worried about you. That was a pretty wild squall, but they're not that uncommon this time of year." He draped another blanket over Sean. "How you holding up? Any frostbite?" He looked at Claire's face and ears, then Sean's.

Sean pulled the blanket tighter. "I think we're okay, just cold."

Kelly took out a thermos and poured hot coffee into a cup. "This should help warm you." He handed the mug to Claire.

"Thank you." She took a few sips. The heat felt good as it went down her throat. She passed the cup to Sean.

Mike took Claire's pulse. "On the slow side, but within normal limits." He checked Sean's. "You're in good shape."

Sean took another drink of coffee, handed the cup to Claire, and she finished it off.

"Let's get back to the RV." Sean put a protective arm around Claire. "Can you walk?"

"I think so."

Mike led the way, with Claire and Sean following. Kelly brought up the rear. It didn't take long before Claire's weakness took over and her heart battered erratically inside her chest. She didn't remember coming so far. Her knees threatened to give out, and she relied more and more on her cane. "Can we rest? I don't think I can go any farther."

"We're almost there," Mike said. "How about we give you a ride?" He and Kelly locked hands, creating a swing between them. "Have a seat."

It would be less embarrassing to accept their help than to fall on her face. Claire handed Sean her cane and sat.

They hadn't gone far before the rest area came into sight. And never had a rest stop looked so good. Claire stepped out of her seat. "Thank you for the lift."

When they walked into the parking area, the door of the RV flew open. "Oh, thank you, Lord!" Willow shouted and started down the steps.

Tom followed. "Boy, are you a sight for sore eyes!" He grinned, and lines cut deeply into his face.

Taylor hurried past Tom and Willow. "I thought you were dead." She threw her arms around Claire and hung on.

Claire hugged her back. Taylor cared about her this much? "We're fine. Really."

Mike got a clipboard of paperwork out of his SUV. "Let's get you indoors where it's warmer," he said and moved toward the RV.

Once inside, Willow wrapped blankets around Claire and Sean while Mike jotted down some notes.

He handed the clipboard to Sean. "I need you to sign this report."

Sean signed and handed it back. "It was just a stupid mistake. We didn't expect the weather to get so bad."

"You and a lot of other people every year." The forester gave the pen and clipboard to Claire. "Folks from outside the area don't realize how fast the weather can change up here."

Willow put an arm around Claire. "I prayed and prayed. The Father is so good to us."

Claire wanted to agree with Willow, but guilt over her doubts swamped her. "Sean found a place to shelter us from the wind."

"And she was smart enough to share body heat," Sean said.

"Oh really?" Tom grinned. "Good thing."

"It was about survival," Sean said.

Claire wished it had been about more than survival.

"Yeah. Sure. I get it."

"There's hot soup on the stove," Willow said.

Claire signed and handed the report to the rescuers. "Thank you for your help."

"No problem." Mike tipped his hat. "It's part of the job. Glad everything turned out okay."

⁖⁘⁙ ⁙⁘⁖

Intermittent snow continued throughout the day and night and much of the following day, keeping the travelers shut inside. Claire didn't mind and took advantage of much needed rest and extra time to work on a story.

After three days of stormy weather, the clouds parted.

With a gust of chilled air, Tom came inside the RV, Daisy on the leash. "Been here long enough. Time to hit the road."

Taylor looked up from her computer. "Is the snow cleared?"

"Looks pretty good out there." Tom unhooked the leash, then pulled off his gloves. "The Loveland Pass is between us and Denver. We can go through on Highway 70 or take the old route on Highway 6, up top. I was talking to a fella yesterday who said it's spectacular." He took off his coat.

95

Why would Tom want to take the old highway? It was probably snowed in.

"How safe is the road? How big are the lanes?" Taylor asked.

"Well, it's not a freeway," Tom said.

Taylor shook her head. "No. I'm not taking an icy, cliff-side road."

"Aw, come on, where's your sense of adventure?" Tom laughed.

"Claire and Sean's close call wasn't enough adventure for you?" She gripped the edge of the table. "I'm not doing it. I'll get a different ride ... with ... someone. And I'll meet you on the other side."

Tom cast Sean a disappointed look. "Highway 70 it is, then. At least there's an amazing tunnel."

Taylor turned pale. "Tunnel?"

Claire rested a hand on Taylor's arm. "I'm sure it's not bad. It's a freeway, after all."

That seemed to satisfy Taylor, because she didn't argue anymore. Once they were on the highway, Claire settled on the sofa with Daisy beside her.

The dog rested her head on Claire's lap.

The weight of it was somehow comforting.

"That dog knows good people." Willow glanced at Tom, who had reclined in the lounger. "Except she seems to like Tom, and he can barely tolerate her."

"I never said I didn't like her."

"You did."

"No, I said she'd be a nuisance."

"And is she?"

"I admit she's been pretty good ... all except for the stink she's always making in here."

"Just a little fluffing. She can't help it."

Sean slid into the driver's seat. "Everyone ready?"

"You bet." Tom moved to the front passenger seat.

They hadn't traveled far before white-barked aspens crowded the hillsides, their lime-green leaves shimmering in the sunlight.

"I came through here once in the fall," Willow said. "It looked like the Lord had taken out his paintbrush and splashed the hillsides with yellow. Truly glorious."

Taylor let out a huff. "God and trees. God and mountains. God and rocks. Is there anything that doesn't make you think of God?"

Willow scrunched her face as if she were thinking. "No. It wouldn't be right to leave him out of anything. This earth is his. He created it—for our pleasure."

"Can't you keep it to yourself at least?"

Willow protested mildly as Sean flew past Vale and all its lovely shops and continued their climb over the Rockies.

"I've had enough of mountains." Taylor went to the fridge and got another pop.

"You keep downing those sodas like that and pretty soon you'll float away," said Willow.

"Using the toilet more means we have to dump more often," Tom added.

Taylor jabbed the bottle toward him and twisted off the top before sitting down.

Taylor's moods had been as up and down as the mountain passes. If she still wasn't taking her medication, it could mean all kinds of trouble. Claire's sister had cycled often, leaving painful memories in the wake of her undisciplined decision.

Taylor needed to stay in control, as the results of an episode could be drastic.

"Here it is—Loveland Pass and the Eisenhower Tunnel." Tom looked at the women in the back of the RV. "Did you know it's the highest vehicular tunnel in the world? Over eleven thousand feet in altitude."

Claire pressed her back into the seat, the rhythm of her heart irregular. They were about to drive through a mountain?

Taylor closed her computer and stared at the approaching tunnel. "It's so steep."

"A seven percent grade and nearly two miles long." Tom's voice was animated, like a kid on Christmas morning.

As the concrete tunnel closed in around them and shut out the world, a moment of claustrophobia enveloped Claire, but the feeling passed, replaced by delight as they rolled down the long, steep descent into the valley at the foot of the mountains.

Taylor closed her eyes. "I just want this to be over."

"Sean, you know not to ride the brakes," Willow cautioned. "You'd hate to heat them up."

"I know," Sean called back. "I'm being careful."

Taylor looked up. "Can the brakes go out?"

In a calming tone Willow said, "No. Sean knows what he's doing, and the brakes are in good shape."

The grade got steeper, and the tunnel seemed to have no end. The passage was both thrilling and terrifying at once. At the sight of daylight ahead, Claire's excitement faded. She'd probably never travel that part of the road again.

"I never want a repeat of that," Taylor said as they drove into sunlight.

Of course she hadn't liked it. Taylor was afraid of everything. What had happened in her life that made her so fearful?

"It was exhilarating." Willow clapped her hands.

Of course Willow loved it. Claire smiled.

"Won't be long before we're out of the mountains." Tom slipped in a CD and the friendly voice of John Denver echoed through the coach.

Taylor put her hands over her ears. "Can't we listen to something else?"

"It's perfect," said Willow, with a smile for Tom.

They rolled eastward. A broad valley came into view between mountain peaks.

"Denver, straight ahead," Tom said. "This is a milestone. We've put the Rocky Mountains behind us."

As they got closer the city seemed to glisten in the sunlight. It was bigger than Claire had expected, sprawling across an endless, flat prairie.

The highway became congested with cars, which set Taylor off again.

"Slow down!" she said. "Watch out for that truck. I swear that driver is sleeping."

Eventually they left the city and Taylor's shrill commands

behind. As they moved into the expansive prairie, Claire had the odd sensation of heading out to sea.

With Denver several miles behind them, Sean asked, "Vote for a break?"

Everyone agreed.

He pulled off at a rest area that sat in the middle of a plain of short grasses and brush, brightened by colorful wildflowers. He stopped beneath a tree and everyone climbed out. After using the restroom, they settled at a table.

Warm, dry air blew through the picnic area, catching hold of tree leaves and making them twirl.

"I love the wind." Willow breathed in deeply through her nose, then turned her gaze on the distant Rocky Mountains. "They're magnificent, aren't they?"

"Yep," Tom said. "But I'd rather think about food. I'm starving. You gonna make us something to eat?"

Willow turned sharp blue eyes on him. "Since when did I become your servant?"

Tom started to answer, but he swayed and nearly fell off the bench. Tom grabbed hold of the table and righted himself. "Just a little wobbly."

Claire moved toward the RV. Tom wasn't fine. He just wanted everyone to think he was. "I'll get you a patio chair."

"I'll get it." Sean hurried ahead, opened an outside compartment, and grabbed a chair. "Here you go, Tom." He set the chair beside the table.

"Thanks." Tom cautiously moved to the chair.

"Maybe we ought to stay here tonight," Willow said. "Rest a while before we move on. Enjoy the beauty and majesty of the mountains we've just conquered."

Tom used his shirt sleeve to wipe moisture from his forehead, then pointed at a nearby field. "What's Taylor up to?"

Everyone turned to stare at Taylor, who had wandered into the field.

"Picking wildflowers, looks like." Willow stood. "That sounds like fun. Plus they'll add a bit of color to our table." She eyed Claire.

"You up for that?"

"Sure. Just want to take a picture first." She snapped a photo of the mountains and sent them to her Facebook page. "The last time I frolicked through a field I was probably eight."

"You guys stay put. We'll make lunch when we get back." Willow offered Claire a hand up. "Or you can do it and have it ready for us when we get back." She tossed Tom a saucy look.

When Willow and Claire approached Taylor, she seemed unaware of them. Arms filled with a variety of wildflowers, she skipped through the meadow, tossing petals around her.

"Taylor?" Willow called. "Can we help?"

Taylor didn't answer. She kept on skipping and started singing "You Are My Sunshine."

What was wrong with her? It wasn't like her to sing something other than country, or to frolic in the field. Alarm spilled through Claire, but she picked some flowers while watching Taylor, who kept on singing and dancing through the field.

When Willow had a bouquet, she approached Taylor. "Come on, honey. It's time for lunch." Willow's tone was that of a mother. "Come on, dear."

Taylor hugged the flowers to her chest. "I'm not hungry."

"You don't have to eat, but why don't you come back with us anyway?"

Taylor allowed them to escort her to the picnic area. While everyone else ate, she sat on the ground, continuing to sing the same children's song while she made a chain out of the flowers.

"What's up with her?" Sean asked quietly.

"My guess is a manic episode," Willow said. "I didn't see her take her medication today, and maybe not yesterday."

Melissa had been like this at times, joyfully caught up in her own world—lost to the real one.

It always left Claire with a bittersweet feeling. While it was nice to see her sister acting happy, the happiness wasn't real, and the crash after the mania was always painful to watch.

Sorrow swelled in her chest.

I'm so sorry, Melissa. I didn't understand.

CHAPTER SIXTEEN

Sean had traveled much of the country, but never Kansas. Now, as they cruised through the state, quiet, rolling hills threatened to lull him to sleep. There were few trees, but a big sky watched over spring grasses that carpeted the countryside.

Willow braced one hand on the back of his seat and leaned over his shoulder.

The scent of musk settled over Sean.

"We have a mail pickup in Salina. How much farther do you think it is?"

"Less than an hour."

"Maybe I'll hear from my daughter." Willow's voice sounded wistful.

Sean glanced in the rearview mirror.

Willow retreated to the recliner and looked ready for a nap. Tom snoozed in the seat beside Sean, but Taylor kept her eyes on the skies, as if watching for tornadoes.

A quick shift of his gaze showed Claire on the sofa, head resting against the back cushion, eyes closed. She'd said she hadn't been feeling well.

Sean didn't want to care about her health, but couldn't help himself. If only she could find a doctor who could help her.

"Do you think there will be any tornadoes out here?" Taylor asked.

"Skies are clear," said Willow. "I'm sure we have nothing to worry about."

If they ran into a severe thunderstorm or a tornado, Taylor would be a mess. Sean looked at the open prairie outside the front window. Where would they go if there was severe weather? There was no shelter anywhere.

Willow's back, Tom's MS … Sean was used to their health issues, yet he'd be glad not to have to worry about them when the trip came to an end.

But Taylor—she got under his skin. Her disagreeable moods and chronic fear was almost more than he could take.

Everyone, including Taylor, was asleep when he passed a sign announcing their exit. He relaxed his hold on the steering wheel. His tired mind and body needed a break. "Next exit, Salina," he called out.

Tom opened his eyes, seeming slightly disoriented. "Already?"

Sean smiled. "Yeah—already. You've been asleep for the last seventy or so miles."

"Nah. I wasn't asleep that long."

"Whatever you say."

"Can we stop at the post office first thing?" Willow dropped the footrest of the recliner.

"Sure."

Sean checked on Claire in the rearview mirror.

She looked pale and had a hand pressed against her chest.

A thump of alarm went through him. "Claire, you all right?"

"I'm … okay. Just a little startled. I can't believe I slept so long."

"You needed it, dear." Willow patted her leg. "We all did. And poor Sean has been driving the whole time."

"That's what I get paid for." He chuckled and watched the road once more. "I don't mind. Really."

"I'll find the post office with the GPS on my phone." Tom fiddled with his phone.

Moments later a woman's voice said, "Take the next exit on the right, then turn right onto Ninth Street."

Tom peered at the phone screen. "I hate using this thing. I'll get the RV GPS fixed while we're stopped over in Salina."

Sean followed the exit off the highway and turned onto Ninth. Salina looked like a peaceful town with older homes, shaded by aged elm trees, reclining behind large front porches. Large trees also lined the streets.

"Everything looks so friendly here, so homey," said Claire.

"Yeah. Kind of makes you feel welcome." Following the directions given by the sweet voice on Tom's phone, Sean took a left on Elm Street. A few minutes later he passed the post office and pulled onto a side road. "Here we are." He swiveled his seat to the right. "What did we do before GPS?"

"We used a thing called a map." Willow hitched herself to her feet.

Tom eased out of his seat and moved to the back door.

Sean followed.

Willow bent to give Daisy a pat. "I'll be right back for you. Now stay." She retrieved some mail from the kitchen shelf, opened the rear door, and stepped down cautiously, then hobbled toward the post office door.

"Slow down before you face-plant in the middle of the street." Tom did his best to catch up to her.

Sean waited for Taylor and Claire. Although he didn't expect any mail, he'd dropped off a postcard to his parents a few states ago—a quick note letting them know where he was and where they could send mail. His mother might have gotten something off to him.

There was a short line waiting for one clerk.

He took his place beside Claire, trying to ignore the tantalizing, sweet fragrance emanating from her. "So, you'll probably have a lot of mail today."

"Maybe. I have some to post too. Good old-fashioned snail mail." She held up a few envelopes. "What about you?"

"I'm not expecting anything."

Willow stepped up to the counter. "Willow Lambert, general delivery, please."

The clerk walked down a row of shelves and returned a few moments later with a large manila envelope. "I need to see some ID."

"Here you go." Willow presented her identification, and the clerk handed over the envelope. "Thank you." Willow pressed it against her chest and spun toward the rest of the crew. "It's from my daughter."

Tom picked up a small stack of mail—bills, mostly. Taylor seemed surprised to receive a couple of letters. There was a small stack of mail for Claire.

Sean stepped up to the counter, acting nonchalant, but his nerves skittered inside. "Sean Sullivan. General delivery."

The clerk checked his ID, left, and returned with an envelope.

"Thanks." He palmed the letter.

His mother's handwriting.

He didn't want to open the envelope. Why would he want to when every word from home carried memories and guilt?

"Now aren't you glad I told you to send your mother something?" Claire asked, wearing an endearing smile that tugged at his heart.

"I guess so."

He knew what his mother would say. She'd ask how he was, tell him how much she missed him, and ask when he was coming home.

Maybe never. How could he tell her that?

There might be something he needed to know, so Sean walked across the street, sat beneath an oak tree, and opened the envelope. He scanned the letter. Nothing new. And then his eyes stopped. His father had suffered a small heart attack and a stent was put in. He was doing fine. But for how long?

Sean climbed back in the RV. Why didn't his father ever listen? He'd been warned about carrying too much stress.

Willow had gone through the contents of her envelope, which contained a flier of some sort. "Oh dear. I don't understand."

"What's wrong?" Claire asked.

"My daughter sent me a flier about a 5K run. She wants me to do it with her and Carson." She shook her head. "I can't run. What am I going to do? I know how she is. If I say no, she'll think I don't care about them and that I'm only thinking about myself."

"How can she expect you to do something like that?" Claire asked. "She knows about your back and your fibromyalgia."

"Yes, but she believes everyone can do whatever they put their minds to. She won't understand."

Sean slid the letter back into the envelope. That was his father. Always expecting too much out of people.

Tears traced paths down Willow's cheeks, and she covered her face with her hands. "I messed up ... bad, in the past. If I don't do what she wants now, she'll never forgive me."

If constantly cheerful Willow lost hope, what did that mean for the rest of them? Sean tossed the envelope into the glove compartment.

"It's been a decade since she left home. She said I'd ruined her life and that she'd never speak to me again."

"Obviously she didn't mean it." Tom gestured at the mail. "She's speaking to you."

"I've heard from her a handful of times since she left. But I've never met my grandson, who turns ten this summer."

"The one you bought the feathered headdress for?" Taylor asked.

"Yes. I've been praying she'll let me see him. And that she'll forgive me." She folded the flier in half. "My wild ways did ruin her life." She sucked in a quaking breath. "Once upon a time, drugs, alcohol, and men were all I cared about. I moved us from place to place. She never got to settle anywhere." Another tear traced its way down her cheek. "She had a lonely and frightening childhood."

Her eyes settled on Claire. "When I found the Lord, my life was restored, but not Melody's. She rejected me and everything I stood for. And I can't blame her. All I can do is pray that one day she'll know the Father and that she'll forgive me."

Claire reached out and grasped Willow's hand. "I know it will happen. One day. How could she not love you?"

Willow patted Claire's hand. "Thank you, honey."

"All that's behind you. You're not that person anymore," Tom said. "And if she can't see it, then you shouldn't bother with her."

Willow looked hard at Tom. "She's my daughter. I love her. And my grandson."

Sean didn't have the energy to deal with Willow's crisis. She needed a solution. "What about a bicycle?"

Willow turned to Sean. "What do you mean?"

"I've seen lots of community races. Some people run, some walk, and some ride."

"I don't know if my back or my muscles will let me ride a bike."

"What about a recumbent bike?" Claire asked. "My dad has a friend who uses one."

"I don't know. Maybe." Willow tilted her mouth in a half smile. "The Lord will have to provide it. They're expensive."

Tom rested a hand on Willow's back. "Do you think he'd use someone like me? I can get it for you." He stared at her. "That is, if you really want to try."

Willow laughed. "Of course I want to try. Thank you." She smiled. "I think you've got a good heart inside that tough exterior of yours, Tom Cantrell. God is using you to bless me."

He stepped back. "I want to help, but it doesn't mean I have to start being nice to everyone." Mischief sparkled in his eyes.

"Of course not." Willow grabbed a tissue and dabbed at her eyes before gently blowing her nose.

"You've got a lot of work ahead of you, if you want to ride and actually finish," Tom said. "You're not in the best shape."

"I know that." Willow straightened her spine. "God does too."

Sean got behind the wheel and drove through town looking for a place to park for the night as the others admired the old homes, government buildings, and churches.

When Willow exclaimed over a particularly stunning church, Sean pulled to the edge of the road. It was an Episcopal church with steeples and stained-glass windows. A verdant yard lay behind an ornate iron gate.

"I wonder what it's like to have services in a place like that," Tom said.

"The place doesn't matter," Willow said. "God will meet with his children anywhere."

Tom didn't look convinced. "I think all that finery would be distracting."

"Maybe, but if a person has a real relationship with God every distraction will fade." Willow's tone was testy. "Are you one of those who don't like worship services?"

"No. But I don't believe in all the frills, not for me anyway."

Willow said no more, but her expression softened.

Sean pulled back on the road. It was time to find a place to stay for the night.

A Walmart sign peeked out down the road.

A few moments later, he pulled into the parking lot. "We can stay for the night, maybe even longer. Everything we need is close by.

We'll see if we can find a bike for Willow and do a little shopping, stock up on supplies."

"Are you sure it's all right?" Claire asked.

"I'll check it out." Tom searched for information on his phone. "Yep. Here in Salina, RVs are welcome in Walmart parking lots."

Sean pulled into a spot in the periphery of the parking lot and shut off the engine. He turned and looked at the group. "Let's eat out. There's a restaurant just down the street."

"Sounds good to me. I'm hungry." Tom was already reaching for the door handle.

"You're always hungry," Taylor said.

Tom patted his stomach. "A steak and garlic mashed potatoes should hit the spot."

"Okay, so dinner it is. Let's go." Sean stood and moved into the living area.

"I'm not hungry." Taylor pushed her wallet into her pants pocket. "Kenny Chesney has a new CD I want to get."

"You can do that after dinner," Tom said.

"No. I'm doing it now." Taylor stepped past Claire and Willow, walked down the steps, and headed for the store.

Tom shrugged. "Guess she doesn't have to eat if she doesn't want to." He gazed down the street toward the restaurant. "That's quite a hike."

"We can drive," Sean said. "I'm getting pretty good at parking this thing."

"I'm fine," Willow said. "And I've got to get into shape for that bike ride."

"I can walk," Claire said. "But if Tom—"

"I can do it." Tom pulled himself up to his full height.

"Do you think Daisy will be okay here by herself?"

"She can guard the home front," Tom said. "No one's going to bother her."

"I'll take her out for you when we get back." Sean pocketed the key.

"Okay. Thank you." Willow pressed a kiss between Daisy's eyes. "We'll be back soon, girl."

After exiting the RV, Tom and Willow walked side by side, and Claire and Sean fell into step behind them.

⁓⊙ ☉⁓

Sean finished off the last of his burger. "That was good."

Claire folded her napkin and set it on the table beside her plate.

"You finished?" Tom asked. "You left more than half your meal."

"I can't eat another bite."

Willow sipped sweet tea. "I'm afraid I ate too much of mine."

"If we stay in town, I'd like to come back. That was good, wholesome food. Reminded me of home cooking." Tom scooted his chair back and rested a hand on his stomach.

Claire leaned forward. "Can we find a laundromat tomorrow? I figure we all need to get caught up on our dirty laundry."

"Sure," Sean said. "I've got a bunch to do."

A waitress walked by, and Claire waved her down. "Can I have a to-go box?"

"Sure thing. I'll be right back." The waitress trotted off.

"Maybe Taylor will want to finish this for me," Claire said.

Not long after, the band of travelers walked toward the Walmart, accompanied by cool evening air and the rustle of leaves in the trees. Sean had a book waiting in the RV, but held himself back to the snail's pace of his companions and quashed his frustration.

A sheriff's car whistled past, then an ambulance with its siren wailing.

Willow glanced at the sky. "Heavenly Father, please take care of whoever's in trouble."

Both the police car and ambulance pulled up at the Walmart entrance.

"Wonder what's up?" Tom hurried his steps slightly.

By the time they reached the RV, a second police car had joined the first.

Sean stepped into the coach. "Taylor?"

A thud of apprehension went off. He took a quick look around

108

and then poked his head out the door. "She's not here."

"Oh dear." Willow headed toward the store. "I hope she's not in trouble. She hasn't been doing well lately."

When the four of them stepped inside the entrance, an uproar of some kind was going on in the back.

A clerk approached them. "Please. Go back to your vehicles. You can return as soon as the police leave."

"What's happening?" Claire asked.

"Some lady's off her rocker. And she won't let anyone help her. They'll have to use a stun gun on her."

"No!" Claire hurried toward the back of the store.

Sean had never seen her move so fast. Taking long strides, he caught up to her.

Taylor's shrieks echoed down the aisle.

"She's in trouble." Claire turned the corner and skidded to a stop.

Taylor stood in the middle of the electronics department.

The place was a mess—CDs strewn about, racks overturned.

Claire approached one of the officers. "I know her. She's my friend."

The policeman sized her up. "Do you think she'll listen to you?"

"Maybe." Claire moved closer.

Taylor backed into the corner made by two racks, her arms filled with CDs.

"Taylor, it's me … Claire."

Taylor glared at her. "You want to lock me up too?"

"No. Of course not."

"I just want to buy some CDs. I have a credit card, but they won't take it."

"We'll get you some. But first, let's go home."

Tears spilled from Taylor's eyes. "I don't have a home," she wailed.

Claire stepped closer.

"Stay back!" Taylor lifted an arm as if readying to hurl a CD at Claire.

Claire spread her hands and moved a step closer. "I won't hurt you. I'm your friend—Claire, remember?"

Taylor had a lot more muscle than Claire. If she couldn't trust Claire and tried to push her way past ... Sean tugged Claire's sleeve. "Maybe you should leave this to the police. She's not in her right mind."

Claire pulled free. "Taylor, let's go to the RV, and you can show me what you've done with your new song."

Taylor stared at her for a moment, then lowered her arm. "It's pretty good."

Claire reached out her hand. "We'll work on it together."

"Grab her!" someone shouted from behind Claire. Officers rushed past, pushing Claire aside and bounding toward Taylor.

"No!" Claire cried out. She lost her balance and fell sideways, her head and shoulder hitting the floor as Taylor screamed.

CHAPTER SEVENTEEN

Claire opened her eyes but couldn't see very well.

"That woman's bipolar, not a criminal." Willow told a police officer. "Please. Don't do that."

Sean kneeled beside Claire. "Are you all right?"

The scene came into focus.

A cop put handcuffs on Taylor, who was hurling profanities at him.

"Don't do that!" Willow stood in front of the officer. "She needs to be in the hospital, not jail."

Claire cautiously sat up and rubbed her shoulder. The world was spinning. "My head hurts."

Sean put one hand under her elbow, and with his other, pulled her up.

She held on to his arm and moved toward a police officer. "Willow's a nurse, and she's right. Taylor's not dangerous. She's sick. She needs a doctor."

Taylor stared at Claire with suspicion in her eyes.

"Can't you take off the cuffs?"

The other officer pushed up his cap. "We understand your concern, ma'am, but for now they have to stay—for her own safety. Maybe the EMTs can give her something to calm her down."

The one who cuffed Taylor steered her toward the store entrance.

Claire, Sean, Willow, and Tom followed the officer, Willow continuing to explain Taylor's condition.

When Claire stepped outside, the cool evening air startled her. It was pleasant—no harsh lights or department store smell, no CD clutter.

But there was the ambulance—a reminder that nothing was normal or pleasant. Two EMTs stood beside the vehicle.

"No!" Taylor blurted. "No hospital!"

The older EMT took hold of her arm. "Everything's going to be fine. We'll take good care of you. The hospital here in Salina is one of the best." He smiled, but Taylor fought him.

"Taylor," Sean said, "they aren't going to hurt you. They're just trying to help."

Though Sean likely had never been around someone in a manic crisis, he still cared enough to make things easier on Taylor. Claire's heart warmed. "We're here for you, Taylor." She turned to the EMT. "Can I ride along?"

"Sorry. It's against policy, ma'am."

Taylor clamped a frightened gaze on Claire.

"Taylor, we'll follow right behind you. I promise. And everything is going to be fine. The doctors will know what to do."

Taylor seemed to relax a little as she sat on the gurney.

"Can you lie down for me?" one of the EMTs asked. "We'll get an IV going."

"I'm not lying down."

"Come on, Taylor," Tom said. "They won't hurt you."

"We can do the IV sitting up if you like."

Taylor stared at him but didn't respond. She looked frightened and utterly miserable. At least they were trying to give her as much dignity as possible.

The driver closed the doors, cutting off the view of Taylor.

Claire stepped back. "Poor Taylor. What's going to happen to her?"

"She'll come out of this episode." Willow rested a hand on Claire's back. "You'll see."

They walked back to the RV, with Tom and Sean following them.

"I'll take Daisy out," Sean offered as he hooked the leash on the dog.

By the time Claire negotiated the steps of the motor home, her head felt as if it were about to explode. She lowered herself to the sofa, her legs and feet burning and her shoulder throbbing.

Willow sat beside her. "You took a terrible fall. A doctor should have a look at you."

"I'll be fine. But I could use some pain medicine."

Willow got the pills and water, and took them to Claire. "How is the pain?"

"Not too bad."

"Those policemen didn't have to be so careless."

"They were just doing their job." Tom sat at the table. "They couldn't let Taylor destroy the store." He planted his elbows on the table and leaned on them. "She never let on that she could get so crazy."

"She's not crazy." Claire felt like a mama bear protecting a cub. "She's ill. All she needs is medicine, just like you and me and Willow. But she's not crazy."

"If people with bipolar disorder don't take their meds, they can become manic to the point of losing their hold on reality," Willow said. "With proper care, she'll be fine."

Sean climbed into the driver's seat. "What's the name of the hospital?"

"The ambulance driver said they're taking her to Salina Regional Health Center." Tom took out his phone. "I'll look it up." He scrolled through the phone directory. "Four hundred South Santa Fe Avenue."

"Let's go see how she's doing." He drove through the parking lot and pulled onto the street.

"Poor Taylor needs our prayers." Willow took Claire's hand and reached out for Tom's. The three bowed their heads. "Father God, Taylor is lost right now. She's afraid and confused. She needs you. *We* know how much you love her, but I don't think she does. Draw her close. Let her know that you are with her and are protecting her. Give the doctors wisdom and discernment. Make sure they give her just the right treatment. And, Lord, show us what we can do to help dear Taylor."

Claire's heart ached. *Lord, please hear our prayers. And help me to be the kind of friend Taylor needs. I don't want to let her down, not like I did Melissa.*

"Thank you for watching over us all and for listening to our prayers. Amen."

Salina Regional Health Center was a brick building, larger and nicer than the usual small-town hospital.

Sean somehow maneuvered the RV into the emergency-room parking area.

Claire moved to the door with difficulty. Her legs were heavy and weak—the uproar and her fall had taken a toll. Using extra care she gripped the handrail and took the first step down. She managed the next before her legs went out from under her.

Sean grabbed her around the waist and steadied her. "You need to see a doctor."

"I lost my balance is all." She took a deep breath and pushed away from him.

Sean watched her. "Your head bounced off a concrete floor."

"It was nothing. Just a little dizziness," Claire said, though her head throbbed. "Right now we need to think about Taylor." She moved toward the emergency entrance. With each step her feet felt as if she were walking on hot coals, and the pain moved up into her legs. She tried to walk normally but couldn't. She'd forgotten her cane in the RV.

"You're not fine." Sean hurried through the door and grabbed a wheelchair that was parked just inside and wheeled it up to her. "Sit. I'll push you."

"I can walk on my own." Wheelchairs drew attention—people stared.

"Claire, use the wheelchair," Willow said gently. "We all need help sometimes … even when we want to be independent."

"All right." Claire eased into the chair.

Sean approached a woman at Admitting. "We had a friend just come in on the ambulance. Taylor Reaves."

"Oh yes." She looked at the group. "Are any of you family?"

"No. Just friends," said Claire. "She doesn't have any family in the area. Can we see her? I promised her we'd come."

The nurse's tone softened. "She's being seen by a doctor right now. You can wait over there, and he'll be with you shortly."

They retreated to a waiting area. Tom got himself a pop from a machine while Willow poured herself some coffee. Claire considered getting a cup for herself, but she didn't want to hobble over to the machine or roll the wheelchair there. Though, the aroma might disguise the antiseptic odor, the worst part about hospitals. And the smell clung on clothes for hours. She'd change when they got back to the RV.

"You want anything?" Sean asked her.

"Thank you. Yes. Coffee?" Sean to the rescue.

He moved to the coffee pot and filled a Styrofoam cup. "Cream and sugar?"

"That sounds good."

He handed the cup to Claire. "Careful it's hot."

Tom sat at the end of a cushioned bench. "I knew something like this would happen. Never should have brought her along."

"Taylor deserved a chance," Claire said through clenched teeth. "Just like the rest of us did." She set her coffee on an end table and snatched up a magazine and leafed through it, the pictures flashing by unseen.

Doors that led to the Emergency Care opened, and a young man in hospital scrubs walked into the waiting room. He headed toward them. "I'm Doctor Whitson. Are you with Taylor Reaves?"

Sean stood. "Yes."

"How is she?" Claire leaned forward in the chair.

The doctor glanced at a chart. "I'll need your names. Taylor gave us permission to speak only to the friends that she listed."

"I'm Claire Murray."

"Willow Lambert."

"Tom Cantrell."

"Sean Sullivan."

"Good. You're all on the list." He lowered the chart. "We gave her something to calm her, and she's stable. The report that came in with her on the ambulance says she's been diagnosed with bipolar disorder."

"That's correct," said Willow.

"I've sent for her records. But what I know at present is she's experiencing an episode of psychotic mania. Do any of you know what medication she's been taking?"

"Oh yes. I brought it with me." Willow dug into her purse, took out Taylor's pills, and handed them to the doctor.

He looked at them and jotted down information on the chart. "Has she been taking these regularly?"

"No. She's terrible about being consistent." Willow snapped her purse closed. "And she doesn't like us interfering."

The doctor added more notes.

"Is she going to be all right?" Claire asked.

"Yes … in time. I'll speak with her physician in Oregon, and we can begin the process of bringing her back. It will take time to get her medication up to appropriate levels and for Taylor to stabilize. Until then she'll have to remain in the hospital."

"How long will that be?" Tom asked.

"Hard to say—could be days or weeks."

Tom knit his brows but didn't say anything more.

"Can we see her?" Willow asked.

"Not tonight. And not tomorrow. Check back in a couple of days. She'll need a little time before she's up for visitors."

"Okay. Thank you, doctor." Willow offered a grateful smile and a slip of paper. "Here's a list of numbers where we can all be reached if anything changes."

"Glad to be of help." He turned and walked back to the treatment rooms.

Sean turned to the group. "We might as well go back to the Walmart, if that's all right with you."

"Fine by me," Tom said.

Willow nodded. "But, Claire, while we're here, you should see a doctor."

"I'm feeling better. My headache is almost gone."

"What about the dizziness?"

"Gone. I'm fine. Really. Let's just go." She'd spent too many days in hospitals being probed by doctors. They always meant well, but were rarely helpful and often made her feel worse. Just the smell and sounds of the hospital made her feel sick. Why spend one extra minute in that atmosphere? And though she dreaded the walk to the RV, she wasn't about to use the chair. She stood, and her legs were still a bit wobbly.

"Here, lean on me," Willow said and grasped her elbow. Together they headed for the bus.

Once back at the Walmart parking lot, everyone prepared for bed, but no one seemed tired enough to sleep, so Willow made hot chocolate.

Tom sat at the table, his cup cradled between his hands. "What do we do? We can't just hang out here indefinitely waiting for Taylor to get well."

"You want to just leave her?" Claire asked. *Would you be as quick to leave me?*

"She's in good hands. And once she's ready to leave the hospital, someone will come for her."

Claire gave him a hard look. "What if it were you? What if your MS put you in that hospital? Would you expect us to leave?"

Tom thought a moment. "Yeah. I wouldn't want your plans ruined because of me, not if I was going to be down and out for a long time."

"He has a point," said Sean.

Tears pricked Claire's eyes. "I thought we were more important to each other than that. I wouldn't leave you alone in that hospital, Tom. But obviously you'd leave me … or any one of us."

"Hey, you're not Taylor." He looked from Claire to Willow to Sean. "She's been a pain in the backside from day one—whining, depressed, giving us a hard time, and keeping us from doing some of the things we wanted to do." He made a fist with one hand and pressed it into the palm of the other. "If we don't keep moving, we'll never get to Florida. We'll never even see a dolphin, let alone swim with one."

Willow ran her hands along Daisy's side. "I can't imagine leaving Taylor, though. It doesn't feel right." She cast a compelling look at Tom. "And no matter what you say, I wouldn't leave you."

Tom stood. "Maybe we ought to just forget this whole thing. We're just kidding ourselves anyway. We're never going to swim with any dolphins." He stared at Willow. "And you're not riding a bike in a race. Taylor's never going to have a hit song. I'm not driving on a NASCAR track."

Willow stood and faced him. "I thought you were a better man than this. I thought you had more courage than this." Tears filled her eyes. "I'm disappointed in you, Tom Cantrell." She stared at him for a long moment, then turned and walked to the back of the motor home where she disappeared into the bedroom and shut the door.

Tom sat on the sofa, his bluster gone.

"I'm not going to desert Taylor. I'm staying," Claire said.

Sean shook his head. "Be reasonable, Claire. What are you going to do here?"

Claire let out a breath. "I'm going to be a friend."

CHAPTER EIGHTEEN

The next morning Tom had made coffee before Claire even crawled out of bed, and he was sitting at the table enjoying a cup.

"Smells good." She poured herself a mug of it and glanced around. "Where's Sean?"

"Don't know. He was gone when I got up. The dog's gone too, so I figure he took her for a walk."

Claire sat on the sofa, mind wrangling itself around the how-tos of staying in Salina. Hotels were expensive, and so were taxis. She had most of the money her mother had given her, but she hated to use it all. She'd have to learn the bus system.

Willow emerged from the bedroom and shuffled down the short hallway. She barely glanced at Tom when she stepped into the kitchen. "Good morning, Claire." She filled the kettle with water, set it on a burner, and turned on the stove. "It would have been nice if someone had remembered to heat up some tea water when he made the coffee." She placed a tea bag in a cup, then sat on the sofa next to Claire.

Tom grunted. "Good morning to you too."

"I've decided to stay with you, Claire." Willow combed her fingers through her hair. "After Taylor recovers we can travel home together."

Anxiety about being alone slipped away. "I'd love that, Willow, but I don't want you to give up your trip. You were the one who thought of swimming with dolphins. And what about seeing your daughter and grandson?"

"I've considered all that, but I'm staying. Maybe my daughter will come and see me in Oregon later this summer." She eyed Tom. "I really do want to swim with the dolphins, though, but that's not on a specific time schedule."

Tom looked back at her and slurped his coffee.

Of course Willow was jabbing at him, but why did she have to give up so much? However, that woman had a strong will. If she wanted to stay, she would.

The kettle whistled, and Willow gingerly pushed up and shuffled to the counter. She poured water into the cup she had prepared and dipped the tea bag several times. "It would have been so nice to float in the warm ocean, see dolphins coming to greet us ... up close and in the wild." She removed the tea bag, then returned to her place on the sofa.

Tom set his cup on the table. "Look. I'm sorry."

Willow blew on her drink. "Sorry means you want to change, Tom. Is that what you're saying?"

"I was wrong." He kept his eyes on the table. "I barely slept. I kept thinking about what you said, and ... well, it's hard to admit to yourself that you've been acting like a horse's behind."

Wearing a slight smile, Willow gave him a look that said, *I told you so*. "Yes. It is."

"I want to stay until she's better, if Sean agrees." His tone was sincere and contrite.

They might all stay? That would mean the adventure could continue.

"Agrees with what?" Sean stepped through the door and unhooked Daisy's leash. "There you go, girl."

The dog licked his hand, then trotted to Willow. Daisy rested her head in her owner's lap and wagged her stub of a tail.

"Good morning, sweetie." Willow stroked the top of her head and looked up at Sean. "We've decided to wait here for Taylor to get better. And we hope that includes you."

Claire held her breath.

"I don't have anywhere else to be, so ..."

"You'll wait too?" Claire could barely stay in her seat. All that worrying for nothing. Kind of reminded her of the Bible verse that said today had enough worries of its own and not to borrow from tomorrow.

He smiled. "Why not?"

"My agreeing doesn't mean I don't have reservations," Tom said. "There are no guarantees that Taylor won't go off the deep end again. And what will we do if she does?"

"We'll cross that bridge when we get to it." Willow took a sip of tea. "I don't expect anything like what happened this week. We know what to watch for—strange behavior, disconnecting from the rest of us—and we'll make sure she doesn't miss any of her medication."

Apprehension fused with the bubble of hope rising in Claire's chest. Taylor *was* unpredictable. And what happened at Walmart could have been worse. Or what if Taylor went into a deep depression and did something awful, like kill herself? The depression experienced by those with bipolar disorder could be that very deep.

"I'm hungry." Tom rubbed his stomach.

"As always," Willow said under her breath.

"Let's eat, get the GPS fixed, and find Willow a bike." He grinned. "She has a race to prepare for, and we have the time to help her."

Three days later, Taylor was allowed visitors, and Claire was the first to see her. She knocked on the door. When there was no response, she opened it a little. "Taylor?"

"Come in." Taylor's tone was flat. She sat in a chair near the window and stared outside.

The room looked like many others Claire had visited through the years—pale green paint on the walls, a narrow, metal bed with a light and medical devices on the wall behind it, a single sink and mirror, and one chair for visitors. Claire crossed the room and stood beside her. "It's a beautiful day. Maybe we can take a walk this afternoon. Are you feeling up to it?"

Taylor turned slowly and looked at her. "What are you doing here?"

"The doctor said you could have visitors. I wanted—"

"No. *Why* are you here?"

Taylor wanted more than a pat answer, but Claire's heart for Taylor would probably sound insincere. "I care about you. We all do."

"You *all* care about *me?* Right."

"We do care." Claire gave her a sideways grin. "It is true you haven't made it easy." She tried to keep her tone light. "But in spite of your moods and your sour attitude, you've grown on me ... us.

And we'll be staying in Salina until you're released, and we can finish our trip together."

"You're going to wait? Aren't you afraid of what I might do?"

If she lied Taylor would be able to tell. Plus, after what she'd gone through, Taylor deserved the truth. "Yes, a little. But we think that, with help, you'll be just fine. And that you're worth the risk."

Taylor's eyes brimmed with tears. "I don't trust myself. I might do anything."

"When we decided to take this trip, we agreed to stick together. We had plans. We all needed to get out of the ruts we'd fallen into and learn to live again. I didn't expect it to be easy. Did you?"

"No."

"We're friends ... and friends stick together."

Tears cascaded down Taylor's cheeks. "I haven't had a *real* friend in a long time."

Claire handed her a tissue from the box on the windowsill. "There's one condition."

Taylor sniffed. "What?"

"You have to take your medication every day. And you have to give us permission to be the med police." She smiled.

Taylor laughed and wiped at a tear. "Okay. You have a deal. And I'll do my best not to get mad about being policed."

It was June by the time they got back on the road. Claire thought about sitting up front with Sean when they left Salina, but Tom grabbed the spot first. She settled on the sofa beside Willow instead.

Finally, they were on their way again. But everything was different now.

She glanced at Taylor, who sat in her customary spot at the table. Her crisis had bound the travelers together, into real friends who were facing an uncertain future together.

Willow threaded a needle and knotted it. She placed a button against the front seam of her blouse.

"Is that the button?" Tom asked. "The infamous button?"

Willow gave him a hard stare. "It's just a button."

"It's the button that flew into someone else's food." Tom laughed.

Willow's cheeks flushed. She pushed the thread through one of the holes in the button.

"Guys." Claire shook her head. "That happened over a week ago. Do you really need to bring it up now?"

"The way it came off and landed in that guy's soup ..." Tom snickered.

Sean joined in the fun. "I have to admit when you walked over to his table to ask for your button back ..." Sean broke into laughter.

"All right. Enough." Willow pushed the needle into the fabric and pulled it up through another hole in the button.

There were a few more twitters of hilarity.

"I've always wanted to visit Branson."

Claire didn't blame Willow for changing the subject.

"I can't wait to hit the casinos," Tom said.

"There's no gambling in Branson." Willow pushed the needle through the button hole.

"What? I thought ... I'm sure I read—"

"No. No gambling. But there are lots of great shows to see, and a showboat called the Branson Belle that offers entertainment and meals while passengers enjoy a trip around Table Rock Lake." Willow's eyes lit up. "I can't wait."

"That sounds *very* exciting." Tom's sarcasm couldn't be missed.

"Sean, how far is it to Branson?" Claire asked.

"We've got about four hundred miles," Sean said. "We should be there before dark." He glanced back at Taylor. "Could you do a little research on your computer and find a good place to stay while we're there?"

Claire added a note on her Facebook page. *On our way to Branson, Missouri. Pictures soon.*

Taylor opened her computer. "I'll do a search and see if I find a good spot, then send the info to your phone, Tom. That way you can get directions off your GPS." She frowned. "Isn't Branson for old people?"

"It's for anyone who likes to have fun. And we're going to have a great time." Willow pulled the needle up and tugged the thread taut. "Maybe we can do a little fishing. That is, if I'm able to sit in a boat." She rubbed the small of her back. "All the bicycle riding I've been doing has my back in a fit."

"You're getting stronger."

"That I am."

The RV passed through farm country with plants sprouting in tilled soil and big, open fields lined with wind turbines. Across some of the flat lands, oil rigs looked like giant grasshoppers as they pumped oil out of the ground.

When the wind swept through thick, deep grasses, they reminded Claire of the hay fields back home. The wildflowers looked like the ones growing throughout the woodlands there.

Country music drifted from the radio. Claire got caught up in the tune and lyrics and soon she was singing along.

"I thought you hated country." Taylor acted as if a miracle was happening right in front of her.

"I thought I did too." Claire laughed, then grew more serious. "You're good. I think you could make it as a country star. Keep working on your music and see where it takes you."

Claire and Taylor sang along together, and by the time the song came to a close, they were both laughing.

"Who was that singing?" Claire opened her writing tablet, flipped to a new page, and wrote *Country Artists I Like* across the top.

"Blake Shelton. He's one of my favorites."

"I like him too," Willow said.

"Aw, come on." Tom changed the station. "We need some real music—seventies rock."

Grinning, Claire leaned her head back on the cushions and closed her eyes.

The tires hummed over the highway, occasionally thumping through a rough patch.

Claire dozed off to the sounds of Jefferson Airplane, and when she woke up, the station was on local news. The landscape had changed. The road wound through hills covered with forests of oak, maple, and ash. Some areas were so dense it didn't seem there was room for even one more tree. When they rolled over the crest of a hill, she peered down on the treetops. They looked like a mass of green umbrellas.

The weather had changed too. Dark clouds hid the sun. Some piled up high into the sky, looking like giant anvils.

Taylor strummed her guitar, occasionally stopping to write out notes in a tablet. Periodically her gaze went to the skies. "Looks like a storm's brewing." She set the guitar in its case and snapped the lid shut.

"Nothing on the radio about weather warnings," Sean said. "Probably just a run-of-the-mill kind of storm."

"Weathermen don't know everything." Taylor scooted close to the window and looked out.

"No need to be afraid," said Willow. "The Lord has us in his hands."

Taylor turned a startled look on Willow. "So you think there's something to fear?"

"No. We don't *need* to fear."

"But you wouldn't have said there was nothing to be afraid of if you didn't think the storm that's coming is going to be bad."

Apprehension prickled through Claire. Was Taylor going off the deep end again so soon? Had she taken her pills? Willow wouldn't have allowed her to miss, and she counted the pills each day.

"We might get a storm, but everything's going to be fine." Willow stroked Daisy's back. "See how calm Daisy is. She always knows when something's not right."

"She's not used to this kind of weather any more than we are." Taylor's voice had taken on a high pitch.

"Calm down." Tom's tone held a warning, but was still friendly. "We're almost to Branson."

Taylor closed her eyes, took a few deep breaths, and opened her computer. "I did find a place to stay. It's near a lake. Looks pretty nice."

Tom smiled and flashed Taylor a thumbs-up. "Sounds good. Can't wait to get my line in the water."

125

Claire pictured Tom wearing waders and casting a fishing line. All she'd have to do is pudge him up a little and he'd make a great character in one of her stories.

Willow moved to the bench seat across from Taylor and gazed out the window. "This is a beautiful place. It reminds me of home."

Taylor only nodded and watched the sky. "How much warning do you think you get if a tornado touches down?"

Willow glanced outside. "Taylor, dear, the weatherman's not predicting tornadoes."

"Here's the turnoff," Tom almost shouted, then rolled down the window and leaned out.

Sean took the exit and followed a winding road that led into a wooded area.

Flashes of blue showed between the trees, which weren't as crowded here, where trails meandered through the forest and along the lake shore. It offered peace to visitors, and Claire was ready to soak it in.

"I see the lake," she said. At least they'd made it off the highway before the storm hit.

"I think that's the office." Sean pointed at a wood cabin and pulled into a graveled area. "I'll see about getting us a campsite." He turned off the engine, climbed out, and strode toward the small building.

"I hope they have spaces available." Tom rubbed his hands together. "I'll bet they have some good bass fishing."

About five minutes later, Sean jogged back to the RV. "We're all set. I got us a spot that's not far from the lake."

Everyone cheered.

He followed a narrow roadway through the campground, stopping in front of a space with thick grass carpeting the spot where heavily leafed trees sheltered the area from the sun. "Here we are."

He and Tom got the RV set up just before the storm hit. Dark clouds swirled above, and rain splattered the thirsty ground as they scurried inside.

"This is going to be a humdinger." Tom stared out the window.

Trees bent before the winds. Limbs slapped together as if they were clapping.

"It looks bad." Taylor moved to the sofa and pulled a blanket up to her neck, even though it was warm in the RV.

"We'll be okay," Claire said, reassuring herself as much as Taylor. "Storms come through all the time."

"What about tornadoes? Look at that wind. I've heard what can happen to RVs when they get hit."

"Taylor, don't worry. Most of the storms that come through here don't produce tornadoes."

Maybe an anti-anxiety pill would help. "I'll get you something to calm you." Claire moved to where they kept the meds.

"No. I want to be able to think clearly … just in case."

"All right. But try taking some deep breaths."

Claire and Willow sat on either side of Taylor and breathed in and out in unison, leading her.

Claire began to get lightheaded. "Taylor, I planned to cook dinner tonight, but can you help me?"

A branch slammed against the window, and Taylor let out a squeal.

"Remember, Taylor, the Lord is with us." Willow gently brushed a strand of dark, thick hair off the younger woman's face.

Taylor nodded but kept watch outside, chewing on her lower lip.

Claire stood. "Why don't you shred some cheese? I'll cook the hamburger. Willow, can you take care of the lettuce and tomatoes?"

"Sure."

Nerves fraying, Claire took the ground beef out of the fridge. *Lord, keep Taylor calm.*

Another branch skittered across the top of the RV.

And keep us safe.

They were, after all, in tornado country.

CHAPTER NINETEEN

A tornado never came. And Claire was thankful the bad weather moved through rapidly, though it did leave behind a confusion of leaves, limbs, and other rubble.

Even though she was clearly frazzled by the storm, Taylor did better than expected. After it was over she took out her guitar and strummed part of a song. "I've never seen a storm like that."

"Us West Coasters are storm wimps." Sean grinned. "*Real* thunderstorms only happen this side of the Rockies, you know."

"Back home, storms are fun," Claire said. "Except during fire season. One year we actually lost several acres of timber on our ranch after lightning sparked a blaze."

Taylor pressed her palm over the guitar strings. "I don't like them and never will."

"I know you don't want to hear this, but you can count on more." Tom headed for the door. "I'll check for damage."

"I'll give you a hand." Sean followed him out.

Willow gazed out the window. "What a sight." She grabbed a couple of dish towels and a large trash bag out of a kitchen drawer, then shuffled toward the door. "We better get it cleaned up."

Claire pushed to her feet. She was exhausted and hurting. Physical labor sounded like torture. "Taylor, we could use your help."

She glanced out the window. "You guys can handle it. I really need to get another song polished up. I'm out of practice, and we're not that far from Nashville."

"Okay." Claire forced herself not to say more and went out to help the others. Taylor wasn't fighting physical pain. She should be helping.

The warmth of the sun caressed Claire's cheeks, but the humidity was worse than before the storm. The air smelled like moist earth. Storms in Oregon usually cooled things down and freshened the air. A pang of homesickness nudged her.

"Look at this mess." Willow picked up a small orange and blue life jacket. "I hope the child this belongs to is okay."

Claire cleared a couple of small branches off the picnic table and dropped them into the fire pit. "These will help with an evening fire." She wiped leaves and debris off the table while Sean and Tom inspected the RV. "Is everything okay?" Claire asked them.

"Yeah. Just a few scratches and a couple of small dents. I can have it repaired when we get home." Tom sat at the picnic table, face flushed. "Good thing your bike was still on the rack. That wind would have tossed it around like a kid's toy."

"It's all right, then?"

"Yeah. Fine."

Sean stared at the motor home. "What's Taylor doing?"

"Working on a song," Claire said. "When we get to Nashville, she's hoping for a chance to perform."

"Could use her help," he grumbled.

"Yeah, it's frustrating. But maybe we need to be more understanding. She is talented, and I think we need to encourage her."

Willow picked up what looked like the remains of napkins and dropped them in the trash bag. "I don't think being a professional musician is a good life for her. It's almost impossible to break in, and if you do, it's a rough life—constant travel, pressure to produce more songs, criticism, and fighting to stay on top."

"You seem to know a lot about it," Sean said.

"In my youthful travels I came across all sorts of people." Willow added more brush to the fire pit.

"It might be hard, but what isn't in life?" Claire tossed soggy paper plates in the trash. "Yesterday Taylor told me she wants to visit Loretta Lynn's childhood home in Butcher Holler. She's crazy about Loretta Lynn."

"You mean the place that was in the movie? *Coal Miner's Daughter*?" Tom asked.

"Yes. But the real home. I guess tourists can visit."

"Where is it?"

"I already said in Butcher Holler. Kentucky. Outside a town called Van Lear."

"Oh great." Tom scowled. "Another side trip? I wish she'd told me."

"What's the harm?" Sean eyed Tom. "Aren't we on vacation? Maybe you should lighten up a little. Do some exploring."

"Oh, it'll be fun." Willow's eyes sparkled with mischief. "And maybe you'll find out what a holler is, Tom." She shot him a smile.

"I know what a holler is. It's what you do when you call the pigs in for dinner." Tom laughed.

"You don't know, do you?" Willow picked up a large branch heavy with leaves and laid it beside the fire pit. "A holler is a low spot between two hillsides." Using her best southern drawl, she said, "It's all right. Doesn't mean you ain't smart."

Claire giggled.

"Fine. I got it," Tom said. "And you shouldn't be lifting any heavy branches. You could hurt yourself."

"Since when are you worried about me hurting myself?" Willow plunked a hand on her hip.

Tom didn't seem to know how to respond.

After wiping the bench seat off, Willow sat down. "Thank you for caring." She glanced around the campsite. "It looks like we got the worst of it."

"Anyone hungry?" Tom asked. "I seem to recall some cheesecake in the fridge."

"Is that all you think about?" Sean gave him a fake punch in the side. "You're getting a little pudgy around the middle there, old man."

"I think about other things … like … well, I'll think of something later." He laughed.

"A cup of tea and a bed sounds just right to me," Willow said. "I'm worn out."

The following morning, the pain in Claire's legs and feet drove her out of bed before anyone else was up. She took an extra pain pill and an anti-inflammatory, then quietly slipped outside and sat in a chair beneath the broad limbs of an oak. Would the suffering never end? On mornings like this her mind went to all the years past and the endless days ahead, days of sickness and suffering. She didn't think she could do one more day, let alone a lifetime. Why couldn't she have a disease with a cure?

She closed her eyes and tried to pray, but couldn't get past her misery.

A friend had once told her that when she couldn't pray she should whisper the name of Jesus.

"Jesus. Jesus. Jesus."

Comfort came to her, sweeping away some of the gloom.

She opened her eyes and took a sip of coffee. Its warmth felt good in her empty stomach.

A young couple, hands linked, walked along a trail that meandered past the campsite.

"Good morning," the cheery blonde woman said.

"Good morning." *Please don't stop. Keep walking.*

"That was a powerful storm yesterday," the man said in a southern accent.

They stopped.

"It was."

"We get them all the time back home in Okmulgee." The woman glanced up at the man. "Right, honey?"

"Sure do. And worse."

"Today looks better," Claire said. She didn't have the strength to carry on a conversation with strangers, especially ones who were blissfully happy.

"It does." The woman looked at the clear sky. "Well, have a nice day." The couple wandered on.

Claire sighed. Why couldn't she have a normal life like that? Did they know how lucky they were? They had each other and their health. They weren't worrying about making it through one more day.

A conversation she'd had with her mother pricked her conscience. *"Everyone has troubles. We might not see them, but they're there."*

It was true. But some troubles were worse than others. And most people's difficulties had a beginning and an end. Hers just went on and on—no end in sight.

The RV door opened and Tom stepped out, a mug in hand. "Howdy."

"Hi."

He looked up at the sky, just like the woman had. "Beautiful day. Perfect for fishing."

"Fishing? Today?"

"Sure. I already called down and reserved a boat for us." He sat on the bench at the picnic table. "You like to fish?"

"It's okay. I haven't gone for a long time."

He took a drink from his mug. "Good coffee."

"Thank you."

"I plan to catch our dinner. With everyone's help, of course." He glanced at the door. "If they'd just get up. Need to be on the water early." His voice crackled with frustration.

By the time everyone was up and had eaten, early morning had faded. But Tom didn't give up. He'd rented a golf cart. Pulling up in front of the RV, he beeped the horn. "Everyone ready?"

Did she have a choice? Claire stood. She hated being a spoilsport. "I'm coming."

The cart was crowded with gear and fishing poles, but Claire and Willow managed to find a place to sit. Sean and Taylor walked behind.

When they arrived at the marina, Tom paid for the boat rental and life vests. Taylor strapped hers on immediately. "Why aren't you wearing your life vests?"

"It's just a lake." Tom didn't try to conceal a smirk. He headed for the boat, his limp less obvious than usual.

A short time later, and her mood slightly improved, Claire settled in the kicker boat.

When everyone was seated, Sean started the engine, then untied the boat from the dock and shoved off. He returned to his place in the back and grabbed hold of the tiller. "Where to?"

"Head straight across. We'll fish along that shore over there. It's still in the shade."

"Okay. Here we go." He revved the small engine and they puttered across the lake.

The boat sat low in the water, too low. Were there too many of them for the size of the boat?

Taylor hugged her life vest. "How did I let you talk me into this? The boat could sink."

"It's not going to sink." Tom didn't disguise his irritation.

"I hope you're right. 'Course, I won't be the one in trouble if it does. I'm wearing my life vest."

"We're fine. We can all swim," Tom sniped back. "And what are you worrying about anyway? There's not a cloud in the sky and no breeze."

Please stop. Claire hated bickering. After Melissa's and her illnesses set in, the two of them had a lot of bad days, which often erupted into verbal wars. Since then, petty quarreling made her squirm.

Willow leaned against the side of the boat and trailed a hand in the water. "It's lovely out here, Taylor. Try to enjoy yourself." She smiled at Tom. "We all need to relax."

"I am relaxed."

"Will you teach me how to fish? It's been a long time."

If Claire wasn't mistaken, Willow's request almost sounded flirtatious.

"Sure." His tone was lighter. "I figured I'd help you ladies out."

As they moved across the water Claire realized just how big the lake was. It was a long way to shore. Even a good swimmer would be challenged. She eyed her life jacket. Maybe Taylor was smart to wear hers. Sean wasn't wearing one. Would he think she was being ridiculous if she put one on? Nothing seemed to bother him. Yet she knew his heart was scarred. She'd seen it in his eyes, heard it in his voice, especially when he talked about his brother.

It only took about fifteen minutes to reach the opposite side of the lake. Sean turned off the engine and threw out the anchor.

Immediately Tom went to work preparing a pole for Willow. It was ready to go in a matter of minutes. He cast the line, then handed the pole to her. "Hang on for just a minute while I get Taylor set up. Then I'll show you what to do."

"Don't bother." Taylor looked out over the water. "I hate to fish."

"Fine." Tom shook his head. "Why did you even come along?"

"Nothing better to do."

"There's good bass fishing here. A guy at the marina told me if we wanted bass, we should use this bait called a Wiggle Wart lure."

Willow laughed. "What a silly name."

Tom showed her how to handle the pole and how to cast.

"Oh, I do remember," she said. "And I love to fish."

Sean got a jig set up and handed the pole to Claire. "Have you fished before?"

"Not since I was little."

"Okay, well you want to cast your line out like this." Sean sat beside her, took the pole, and showed her how to do it, then reeled in and handed it back to her.

"I don't know what to do with it." She wanted to be good at something. Her illness had stolen most of her abilities. Before getting sick she'd been athletic, taking part in a variety of sports, and she'd worked alongside her family on the ranch. One of the most painful losses had been school. She'd had to withdraw and finish at home.

"Here, like this." Sean reached around her and helped hold the pole.

Claire's heart tripped over itself, but she didn't mind. He smelled good, like fresh linens and soap.

"Okay, so hold the reel this way." With his hand just behind hers, he put his thumb on the top of the reel, kept his index finger on the line, and wrapped his other three fingers around the handle, touching her hand. "Then you open the bail to release the line. Keep your finger on the line so it doesn't get too loose."

His closeness had Claire discombobulated, but she managed to follow his instructions. "Now what?"

"You want to bring your pole back and then throw out the line, like you're throwing a ball. When you do, take your finger off the string. After that, move the bail back, to keep the line from unwinding, and then you can reel in slowly."

Claire gave it a try but kept her finger on too long, and the line didn't go anywhere. Her bait dangled in front of her. "That was awful."

"No, it's all right. Give it another try." Sean smiled at her in that charming way of his, and she almost let go of the pole.

She could ask Sean to help, which meant his arms would be around her again, but what was the use anyway? He didn't like her in that way.

She looked behind her to make sure no one was there and then cast again.

The line sailed out over the water and the jig plopped in.

She moved the bail back into place and reeled in just a little.

"Good! That's just right. You're a natural." His eyes connected with hers a moment longer than necessary.

Her heart rate picked up. Maybe he *did* have feelings for her.

Sean cleared his throat. "Now, what you want to do is let that bait settle on the bottom, then give it a little tug, pop it up a couple of times to entice a fish. If you get a bite, pull up real quick to set the hook."

Claire tugged on the line and then waited for a bite, her mind on Sean. Even if he did care for her, nothing would come of it. He'd made it clear he couldn't get involved with someone like her. She needed to stop thinking about him. It was hopeless.

All of a sudden the boat rocked.

A pulse of alarm thumped through Claire, and she looked over her shoulder.

Willow stood, struggling to keep her balance.

Claire's stomach dropped. Willow shouldn't be standing in the boat.

"Hey, take it easy," Tom teased. "You don't want to tip us. Sit down."

"It's easier to cast when I'm standing." Her arms outstretched for balance, she tipped forward, then straightened but threw herself too far back.

The boat rocked violently.

Then, as if she was waving down a plane, Willow threw her arms up and back, wobbled wildly, and with a squeal, pitched forward out of the boat.

CHAPTER TWENTY

"Willow!" Claire screamed. She stood and the boat rocked harder.

Spitting out water and gulping in air, Willow slapped at the surface. Her skirt floated and swirled around her, tangling with her arms while she tried to tread water. She barely managed to stay afloat. "Someone help me!"

Tom leaped in after her, simultaneously shoving the boat farther away from him and Willow. He swam to her and grabbed her hand. "I've got you."

Tom had a hold of her, but seemed unable to swim toward the boat with Willow in tow. She went under, and he dragged her to the surface, but they both fought to stay afloat.

"Claire, throw the rope!" Sean yelled as he started the engine.

Claire wobbled toward the rope and cast it out, but it only made it half the distance. She pulled it back in.

Tom tried to swim toward them while hanging onto Willow, but couldn't make it. His head went below for a second, then popped up.

"They're drowning!" Taylor shrieked.

Claire threw the line again. "Lord, help them."

And missed once more.

If she didn't get it right, they could drown. She dragged the rope back in. Praying, she tossed it toward her friends.

This time it landed within reach, but as Sean steered toward them, the rope got pulled away.

Sean maneuvered the boat beside Tom, who grabbed the side while still hanging onto Willow. Sean reached for her. "Give me your hand."

Willow let go of Tom and took Sean's hand.

He towed her to the boat and lifted her in.

Claire took hold of Willow's legs and helped haul her aboard.

She was shivering hard.

Claire put her arms around her in an offering of warmth and comfort. "You're safe now."

Sean helped Tom crawl in next.

Tom sat on the seat in the front. "You all right, Willow?"

"Yes. Just cold." Her teeth chattered and her lips had lost their color.

Sean turned the boat toward the opposite shore. "We need to get you two dried off and warmed up."

Taylor looked like she was about to cry. "I thought you knew how to swim."

"I do," said Tom. "But I guess the shock of the cold water, and with my MS, I'm no good at swimming anymore. Or at saving anyone."

"I can swim a little," Willow said. "But the water knocked the wind out of me, and my back felt like it was going into a spasm. All I could do was try to breathe."

"We'll go back to the motor home, and you can get into some warm, dry clothes." Claire continued to hold Willow. "Thank goodness you're all right. You scared me half to death. I don't know what I'd do without you." She tightened her hold on Willow.

"Oh, you're such a sweetie. But I'm just fine. You never had to worry. The Lord was with me."

Still, doubts assailed Claire. Willow could have drowned. She didn't, but how much of that had to do with God and how much was the help of friends? Life could change in a moment. The thought sent a tremor through Claire.

When they reached the dock, Sean tied off the line while Tom, Willow, and Claire climbed out of the boat and into the golf cart.

"You go ahead," Sean said. "I'll be there after I check in the boat and gear."

"I'll help," Taylor said.

Claire scooted into the driver's seat and drove home.

By the time Sean and Taylor reached the RV, Tom and Willow were dressed in dry clothes, wrapped in blankets, sitting in the sun, and no longer shaking.

Claire stepped out of the coach with mugs of hot chocolate. "This should help warm up your insides." She handed the drinks to Tom and Willow.

"Thanks, hon." She gave her a hug, then turned a smile on Sean. "You saved our lives. Thank you." She pulled the blanket closer. "I never thought that falling into a lake would be so dramatic."

"I'm just glad you're both okay," Sean said.

They'd all planned on going to a Larry Gatlin and the Gatlin Brothers show that night, but Willow opted to stay at the motor home, saying she was in pain from her fall and the climb back inside the boat. Claire wasn't feeling well and remained behind with Willow.

Claire wanted to cheer when Taylor climbed into the cab with the guys. It was like watching a miracle. Before Salina, Taylor never would have been able to go out on the town, not after going through something like what had happened today. She would have gone into a tailspin of anxiety.

Willow and Claire sat in the chairs outside and watched the taxi drive off.

"Isn't it amazing that Taylor is going out?"

Willow nodded but seemed distracted.

"Willow, are you not feeling well? Are you sick?"

She didn't answer for a long moment.

"I'm not sick, but I'm not all right either." She sighed. "I should be filled with thanksgiving. Instead, I'm down in the dumps. Days like today remind me how much I dislike my body. I want to be strong and healthy. The old me would have been fine in the water today. I'd have made it to the boat on my own and climbed back in, easy as pie." Tears washed into her eyes. "Yet here I am ... all gimped up. Sometimes it just makes me so mad." She wiped her eyes with the edge of the blanket. "I really wanted to ride in that race, but who am I kidding? I'll never be able to do it."

Claire swallowed hard. What could she say? Willow was the one she relied on—the one who was strong, wise, full of faith. She'd never seen her like this. If Willow couldn't stand up to her weaknesses, then who could?

"You'll do it. I know you. You're strong."

"Oh yes, that's me—strong. Even my name, Willow. A willow bends in the wind. Its limbs are weak. That's who I really am."

"But a willow also dances in a breeze. It's flexible—that's how I see you." Claire reached over and rested a hand on her arm. "Today was just a bad day."

Willow shook her head. "You all think I'm so tough, but I'm just like everyone else. I get mad and depressed. And sometimes I don't understand why God allowed me to end up like this. I used to be fun-loving, the one involved in everything. I enjoyed working hard and playing hard. But now …" She wiped her eyes. "Oh, I hate feeling like this. What must the Lord think of me?"

"He loves you. No one is strong and full of faith all the time. You're allowed to have real feelings." Claire grasped Willow's hand. "But you *are* strong. And you have great faith. You help everyone around you. And I'm thankful for you.

"This morning I was feeling really low. I hated how I have to live and I had, once again, convinced myself I had no future. But today was amazing. I went fishing. And then I helped my friend when she fell in the lake. We all helped each other—Sean, Tom, you, me, and even Taylor. We didn't have to think about it. We just did it."

Willow sniffed and wiped away tears. "You're right, but sometimes it seems impossible to make it through even one more day."

"I know exactly how you feel. But I'm learning to take care of the body I'm in, and not think about tomorrow." Claire hugged Willow. "I love you so much. I'm so glad you have more days to live."

Willow smiled. "You're right. It was a good day."

CHAPTER TWENTY-ONE

After they all gave the RV a thorough cleaning, Claire settled into the corner of the sofa, resting against a stack of pillows. She picked up the book *Redeeming Love*, her reward after helping her companions, and got lost in the tale of romance and redemption.

The door opened and Willow stepped into the RV. "Who wants to do something special today?"

"I do," Tom said. "In fact—"

"Good. I met a gal who needs help serving at a local mission." She smiled brightly.

Everyone stared at her.

"That's nice, but I plan on going to the World War II museum." Tom folded his arms over his chest.

And I want to read.

Willow settled a hard gaze on Tom. "It's not difficult work. We'll just help serve food and hand out clothing items." She planted her hands on her hips. "I told her we'd do it."

"What?" Tom's face reddened.

"You volunteered us without getting our okay?" Taylor asked.

"Willow, you really should have checked with us first." Sean combed his fingers through his hair. "I know you have a good heart, and you love spontaneity, but you should have asked."

"You're right. I'm sorry. But it was a spur-of-the-moment thing and she really needed someone." She shrugged. "I didn't think any of you would mind."

"I mind," said Tom.

"That's fine. You don't have to help. But I'm going to." Willow closed her eyes and took a breath. "If any of you want to come along, Dolly is picking me up in fifteen minutes." She grabbed her cane and disappeared out the door.

Claire closed her book and set it aside. "Willow's always here for us when we need her. I don't want to let her down."

"Yeah." Sean didn't sound entirely certain he agreed.

140

Tom scowled. "What about the museum?"

Sean released a sigh. "I suppose we can help Willow and this friend of hers, then go." He clapped Tom on the back. "Or we can go to the museum tomorrow."

Taylor closed her computer. "I'll help."

Claire opened the door of the RV and made her way down the steps.

The others followed to Willow sat at the picnic table.

Willow looked at them. "Did you change your minds?"

"Yeah. We're with you." Tom scratched his chin. "But after we're done I'm going to the museum."

"That would be great." Willow stood, a smile on her face. "I knew you'd come."

"You guilted me into it."

"I did not. You listened to the Holy Spirit, that's all."

A maroon minivan stopped at the campsite, smelling of burning oil and trailing white smoke behind it. A middle-aged woman with blonde hair pulled back in a ponytail leaned out the van window. "Willow, I do declare, you're a marvel." She looked at the group. "Are you all helping?"

"All of them," Willow said. "Everyone, this is Dolly. Dolly, these are my friends, Tom, Sean, Taylor, and Claire." She nodded at each person as she said their name.

"Thank you so much for helping out. You all are lifesavers. Climb on in."

Tom and Sean took the cramped backseat, Claire sat in the middle with Taylor, and Willow sat up front.

It took three tries to get the side door to shut, and the van had a shudder that went along with the smoke. *Please keep this thing running.* If it was still in one piece when they headed home, Claire decided to sit in back so Sean and Tom didn't have to.

Dolly turned in her seat and looked at her passengers. "I love how God answers prayer. This morning when I found out I was on my own, I had no idea he'd provide so many workers. This is wonderful." She turned back around. "We'll be helping folks in town. The weather is supposed to get hot, so I doubt we'll have many stay after lunch to visit."

Claire had never worked with the homeless. All she knew about them was what she saw on the news. While driving through cities, she'd seen people sitting on the street with a sign or huddled beneath a blanket. They always looked dirty, sometimes sick. They scared her. How would she know what to say to them?

Dolly pulled into a parking lot in front of a one-story, white brick building. Belying her age, she bounded from the van while tossing out instructions. "Willow, can you help me prepare the meal? And you too?" She nodded at Taylor.

"Sure."

"I need you fellas to set up tables." She unlocked a door and stepped into what looked like a storeroom. "It's a shame it's going to be so hot. I like it best when we can set up the clothing and other items outside. But this time of day the sun is unbearably hot out front." She looked at Claire. "After the tables are up, can you help the men size the clothing and set out the sheets and blankets?"

Claire had no time to respond before Dolly traipsed off toward a large kitchen.

"Okay, let's get busy. People will be here any time."

"Tables?" Tom called out.

She stopped and pointed toward the back of the room. "Over there. We have to set up and take down every time we use the building. There are other groups who meet here." She walked toward the kitchen.

"Willow, we'll make sandwiches." Dolly turned to Taylor. "Can you open cans of fruit? Someone donated a bunch of fruit cocktail, bless their hearts. Fruit cocktail is always a favorite." Her ponytail bounced as she walked. "Oh, and we've got some fresh carrots someone dropped off."

Joy bubbled up in Claire. This was going to be fun. "Where are the clothes?"

"Oh, over there along the wall in those boxes and bags. I haven't had a chance to go through them yet."

Tom and Sean carried a table to an area in front of the kitchen and set it up. "Is this where you want these?" Sean asked.

"Yes. That's just right. Thank you. Can you set up six of them in that spot and then another four over there, just out of the sun, for the clothing?"

When the tables were up, Claire, Tom, and Sean went to work sorting the clothes.

"Has this stuff been washed?" Tom put a shirt to his nose.

"I'm sure it has been." Claire glanced at Dolly. She couldn't imagine that someone who cared enough to do this kind of work would be careless about cleanliness. She pressed a garment to her nose.

It had a faint floral fragrance, probably from a fabric sheet.

Claire held up a pale yellow little girl's dress. White ruffles edged the bottom and it looked brand new. She'd had one like it when she was young—a good twirling dress.

Oh, to be so carefree again, when life seemed like a delightful adventure. Sometimes she'd try to remember what it was like not to worry if her heart was going to race, or if she might faint, or wonder if she had enough strength to join friends on a shopping trip. What was it like to live without pain and do the things she loved, like riding horses or dirt bikes? No. She couldn't remember what it was like to be pain free.

They hadn't been working long when people started trickling in. At first people were quiet and didn't visit much. Dolly and Willow handed out meals along with encouragement, both acting like gracious hostesses at a dinner party. Soon their enthusiasm had some visitors smiling, even chatting.

Once the clothes were sorted, Claire refilled drinking cups and mugs of coffee and even joined in a few conversations. Some people shared their latest news or sorrow. She wasn't scared anymore, but she still wasn't sure what to say. Dolly seemed to know exactly what was needed to put a smile on each face.

Taylor hung back with the guys and mostly watched.

Lots of people left after they'd eaten, but some wandered over to the tables of clothing. By that time, Claire's feet and legs hurt badly, and her heart was beating too fast. Her body went weak. What if she fainted? Or ended up needing to be rushed to the ER to stop a spell of tachycardia?

Lord, help me. I want to stay.

A little girl with big brown eyes and dark brown hair caught back in braids picked up the yellow dress. Her eyes alight, she held it in front of her and smoothed the fabric. "Mama?"

A tiny woman, whose eyes held the sorrows of the world, joined the girl. "That's beautiful, Jasmine. And it should fit."

"Can I have it?" She looked from her mother to Claire.

"Of course you can." Claire glanced at the mother. "As long as your mom thinks it's all right."

The woman gave her daughter a nod.

Claire kneeled in front of the child. "Yellow is the perfect color for you."

Jasmine clutched the dress against her chest as if she held a treasure. "I'm going to be beautiful." She whirled about.

Claire's throat ached, the memory of her own days of twirling so close. She'd had a magical childhood. What had this little one experienced? She couldn't imagine.

Jasmine's mother looked through the women's clothes.

"I think I've got something you might like." Claire searched through the clothing until she found a pair of jeans and a nearly new blouse that looked about the right size. She handed them to the woman. "What do you think?"

She held the blouse out in front of her. "This is nice." She looked at Claire, but only briefly. "Thank you."

"You're welcome." Helping the needy gave her a feeling of worth.

The guys were drawn in too. Tom assisted a boy who needed a blanket, and Sean worked to match up a pair of shoes and socks for an elderly man. When they found the right pair, Sean seemed just as excited as the man he was helping. He assisted him with putting on the socks and shoes, even tying the laces.

Tears pooled in Claire's eyes. What would it be like to be so poor that you couldn't afford a pair of shoes or even socks? Sometimes she forgot how blessed she was.

The afternoon went by in a flash. After the dishes were washed and everything was stored away, Dolly asked, "Is there anywhere you'd like to go before we head back to camp? I owe you big time. You were an immense help today."

"I was kind of hoping to see the World War II museum," Tom said. "Is it far from here?"

"No. I can have you there in two shakes. You're going to love it."

They visited the museum, where Tom marveled over the historical photos and displays of war uniforms and weapons, then they had a meal in a local diner. After that they stopped at an antique mall where Tom purchased a piece of glassware for Willow after she mentioned how much she liked it.

Claire spent a lot of time sitting while everyone else shopped, but she had fun people-watching, especially Tom and Willow. Clearly something was going on between them. The way they teased one another and showed kindness to each other made Claire happy inside. She liked the idea—grouchy old Tom and free-spirited Willow. They'd be perfect together.

By the time Dolly finally headed back to the campground, Claire was exhausted. She and Sean were squished into the backseat. His proximity made her uncomfortable, but even so, her weariness got the best of her, and she nodded off.

Sean nudged her. "Time to wake up, sleepyhead."

Claire opened her eyes. She was leaning against him, probably drooling on his shoulder. "Oh!" She sat upright. "I'm sorry. I didn't mean to use you for a pillow."

"My pleasure." He flashed a smile at her before stepping out of the van and offering her a hand.

"Thank you." She was stiff and had trouble getting her legs to do what she wanted. Her head spun and her stomach tumbled. For a moment she thought she might lose her lunch. That couldn't happen. Not in front of Sean. "I think I'd better lie down. I'm not feeling well."

"Are you sick?" Willow asked, placing a hand on Claire's forehead.

"No. I just did too much."

"No fever." She took Claire's pulse. "Oh my—you're tachycardic. You need to get to bed."

"She's got tachycardia?" Sean asked. "Maybe we should go to the ER."

"I'll be fine," Claire said, but she didn't feel fine now. "I just need to rest."

"You're sure?"

"Positive."

Willow put an arm around her and walked to the bedroom. "You get yourself a nap."

Her eyes were sad, but Claire didn't see pity in them, only concern. "Thank you, Willow."

"I'll get you some water." She disappeared.

A moment later, Sean looked in. "You sure you're all right?"

"Yes."

A shadow seemed to fall over his face. He compressed his lips. "Okay, good. Sleep." He moved away.

Claire cringed.

He hated that she was sick. He could barely even look at her.

She turned her back to the door, unable to hold in her tears. When Willow returned with the water, she pretended to be asleep.

CHAPTER TWENTY-TWO

Sean climbed into the driver's seat, put the keys in the ignition, then swiveled the seat around so he could see into the back of the RV. "I've seen all I want of Branson." It hadn't been as much fun as he had hoped, with Claire being under the weather a lot of the time. He'd kept his distance.

Willow patted the sofa next to her, inviting Daisy up. "I loved the shows, and Tom even managed to catch a few fish. Without me being in the boat it was a lot easier."

Tom looked back at her from the front seat. "You did a good job of cooking them."

"Okay. We had a good time, but now, Nashville or Van Lear?"

"I did some checking," Tom said. "It's over seven hundred miles to Van Lear and *way* out of our way. I don't see any reason to make that kind of side trip."

"I told you." Taylor closed her mouth and looked like she was trying to get control of her temper. "I … told … you … Loretta Lynn grew up in Butcher Holler, which is just outside of Van Lear. Her childhood home is there. And they give tours. I can't be this close and not go. I know that just being there will inspire my songwriting." Taylor's tone had turned pleading.

"She did say that." Claire leaned back in the recliner.

"You taking your meds?" Tom asked.

"Yes. Tell him, Willow."

In an overly sweet voice, Willow said, "Yes, Tom, she's been taking her medication. I oversee. Remember?" She rested her forearms on her thighs and leaned forward. "Is there a reason you don't want to go to Van Lear? Are you not up to it?"

"I'm doing okay. But I … well, I don't want to miss my chance to drive on a NASCAR track. I'm scheduled—"

"You're still planning to do that?" Willow straightened. "I have to be frank—it's a ridiculous idea."

"Well, whether you think it's ridiculous or not makes no

difference. You're not my mother." Tom pushed back in his seat and stared out the front window.

"I wish you two would quit fighting," Claire said. "If we go to Van Lear, how much extra time will it take?"

"Probably two or three days." Sean didn't really care where they went, but he was getting sick of Tom always insisting on his way. "Is that going to interfere with your plans?"

Tom continued to stare out the window. "No." He blew out a resigned breath. "We can go to Van Lear."

Taylor pressed her palms together and leaned back in her seat. "Thank you, Tom. We'll get you to the racetrack on time."

He glared at the console for a long moment, then leaned on the seat's armrest and fixed Taylor with a challenging gaze. "You want to give it a try?"

"What, drive a race car?"

"Yep."

"No. But I'll cheer you on."

"If you can do it, maybe I can." Willow gave him a mischievous look.

"Oh, I'd like to see that."

"Well, glad we got that settled." Sean turned his seat toward the front, started the engine, and put the RV into gear. "Van Lear, here we come."

They headed out across Missouri and on to Illinois. It wasn't long before hillsides gave way to open flat lands. Farms and ranches sprawled across the countryside.

"It's amazing! I'm going to be in Illinois," Claire said.

"What's so special about Illinois?" Tom asked.

"So much history happened there. It feels like the place where west meets east, and I've never been so far east before."

Taylor looked up from her computer. "What kind of history?"

"It's where Abraham Lincoln grew up. And Lewis and Clark started their cross-country journey at Wood River, Illinois. There was the Great Chicago Fire, and the Chicago World's Fair was a huge deal in its time."

"And don't forget it's the home of the Chicago Bears." Tom

grinned.

Sean looked at Claire in the rearview mirror. Her sweet face brightened his disposition. "Hate to disappoint you, but we're just barely going into Illinois. The highway passes through the southern end of the state only." He offered her a smile.

∼∘℮ ℮∘∼

Claire was glad to see Sean smile. He'd seemed aloof since she'd been sick, almost unfriendly, leaving her feeling like a cloud was hanging over them. Maybe there was hope for a friendship, if nothing else. "It's all right. I'm just grateful to be a part of this adventure."

"We can stay overnight at the town of Mt. Vernon," Taylor said. "It's in Illinois. And about halfway to Van Lear."

"Perfect." Willow crossed her legs at the ankle and winced. "Ouch. Ouch. Ouch." She stood and stretched her leg. "Sciatica."

Willow must be in real pain. "Do you need to get out and walk? Or maybe an ice pack will help."

"The cramp is easing up." She stood for a couple of minutes longer, then sat back down on the sofa.

"I'll see if I can find a place in Mt. Vernon where we can park tonight. And maybe I can dig up more history for you, Claire." Taylor offered a smile Claire's way.

∼∘℮ ℮∘∼

Mt. Vernon was a small town, made up mostly of older homes with tidy front lawns and orderly flower gardens.

Claire rocked the recliner upright and gazed out the window. "Where are we staying?"

"I thought Taylor was going to find a place for us," Tom said.

"I'm looking."

Tom swiveled the captain's chair and turned a playful look on Taylor. "They have a Walmart." He grinned. "Well, maybe that's not such a good idea."

"I'm not going to freak out, if that's what you think."

"I don't think that." Tom sounded defensive. "Can't you take a joke?"

"It was a mean joke." Taylor studied the computer.

"I don't see anything wrong with staying in a Walmart parking lot again," Sean said. "It's free and close to shopping."

ॐ ॐ

The next morning, breakfast was ready when Claire limbed out of bed. Taylor had made coffee, toast, and scrambled eggs. She was apparently in a hurry to get moving.

After eating, Taylor and Claire did the dishes while Willow tidied up the RV. Sean and Tom studied a map, trying to figure out the best route.

Taylor set a mug in the dish drainer. "Sean, how long will it take us to get there?"

"At least five hours."

"I can hardly wait." She scraped a little leftover egg into Daisy's dish. "Here you go, girl."

"You're full of energy this morning," Willow said from the comfort of the sofa.

"I'm just feeling good." Taylor dipped a plate into sudsy water. "Do you think we'll have time to go out to Butcher Holler today?"

"Doubt it," Sean said.

"There will be time tomorrow." Willow smiled at Taylor.

She rinsed the plate and set it in a tiny dish drainer.

Claire toweled the plate dry. "If we wait until tomorrow, we won't have to hurry through the tour. We can take all the time we want."

"That's true." Taylor rinsed another plate and handed it to Claire, then drained the sink and quickly wiped it out. "I just hate to wait. It's a place I've dreamed about seeing for so long."

CHAPTER TWENTY-THREE

The Kentucky countryside was a delight to the eye. Claire had never seen such intense shades of green, nor the variety of hues. Fields looked like emerald carpets. Trees were leafed out in such stunning garb it was as if they were preparing for a party. And the hillsides were blanketed by lush pastures and forests crowded with oak, maple, and pine. Horses grazed farmlands bordered by white wooden fences.

The scene's perfection reminded Claire of a postcard. "I think this is one of the most beautiful places I've ever seen." She snapped pictures with her phone. "My parents will love this."

"It is stunning." Willow watched the passing landscape. "I don't think I've ever seen so much green in all my life. It almost hurts to look at it." She turned and beamed at Claire. "God used a special paintbrush when he created this part of the world."

Taylor looked up from the book she was reading. "Do you really believe that?"

"Yes, I do."

Taylor's mouth turned down, and she shrugged and went back to her book.

If only Taylor could fully appreciate God's workmanship. Claire felt a prodding in her spirit. She needed to worry about her own gratitude, which was lacking.

As the miles flew by, her eagerness intensified. Kentucky and Butcher Holler had never been points of interest on her horizon, but the idea of taking a peek at the past of someone as famous as Loretta Lynn had grown more appealing.

The fact that Claire was so far from home and feeling mostly unafraid was a happy surprise. She'd felt trapped at home, the nucleus of her life all about being sick. But now, she was beginning to believe it could be about something else, and she could barely wait to see what it was.

The road wound up and down through the mountains, and finally Sean drove into the cozy little town of Paintsville. It had a lot of homes made of brick with big porches and pillars in the front—a perfect place to welcome neighbors on warm summer afternoons.

There was some sort of town celebration going on. It looked like most everyone in the county was out on the streets or in the city park.

"I wish we could stop," said Willow. "This looks like fun."

"Well, we can't." Sean had a tight grip on the steering wheel as he maneuvered the RV through the crowded roadways. "There's no place to park this coach, and we need to find Paintsville Lake. They have RV campsites there."

A sign inviting people to the U.S. 23 Country Music Highway Museum caught Claire's attention. "Oh, look. It says there's going to be entertainment, and anyone is invited to sing." She turned to Taylor. "That would be a good experience to help get you ready for Nashville."

Taylor's eyes widened and she shook her head. "No. My songs still need work."

"Oh, come on," Claire said. "This is the perfect place. It's small and friendly."

"No." Taylor slumped down in her seat and went back to reading her book.

"Well, you lucked out," Tom said. "The entertainment is on Thursday nights—that was yesterday."

Taylor scowled at him.

He turned his attention back to a map on his cell phone. "Sean, you gotta go back the way we came and take Highway 40 out of town. You missed the turn off."

"Why didn't the GPS catch that?"

"Maybe you should've been watching closer. There must have been a sign. Paintsville Lake is a state park."

Sean circled the block and made his way through the crowded streets and then up to a narrow roadway that wound through the forest.

"There's a sign," Claire said. "Paintsville Lake."

Tom chuckled. "It's about time."

"There sure are a lot of skinny curving roads in this area," said Willow. "Good thing about it is that it forces you to slow down and get a better look at what's here."

Sean pulled up to a hut, where a friendly-looking woman leaned on a counter at the window.

"How many nights?"

"Well … probably two."

"Do you want a full-service site?"

"Yes."

"Okay, that'll be twenty-nine dollars a night."

Sean handed her Tom's credit card, then glanced at Tom. "That's reasonable. This is a nice place."

"Here you are." She handed Sean a pamphlet and a receipt, along with the credit card. "Nice spot with a view of the lake. Just follow the road. The sites are clearly marked."

"Thank you." Sean drove into the campground.

Paintsville Lake was picturesque and peaceful. The water was so still, trees and plants reflected in it like a mirror. This would be a good place to unwind.

"Maybe we can stay a few days," Claire said.

"I've got a date with a racetrack, remember?" Tom glared over his shoulder at her.

Of course. How could I forget?

"Oh my, this is lovely," Willow said.

"Here's our spot." Sean backed the RV into the site, then climbed out.

Claire was the next one out. She breathed in the fragrance of wildflowers and pine.

Willow moved to the door and made her way down the steps, while gazing at the lake. "I think I want to stay here forever." As she took the last step, she closed her eyes, as if soaking in nature. She missed the step and tumbled to the ground.

Alarm spiked through Claire. "Willow!"

Sean was beside Willow immediately. "Hey, there."

She opened her eyes and smiled through clenched teeth. "Oh dear. I can't believe I did that."

"Well, you're supposed to be looking at where you're going," Tom teased, but it didn't disguise his concern. "You all right?"

"I'm fine. Just a little shaken up." She tilted her head back and brushed her hair from her face and grimaced. "Ooh. I think I twisted my neck. Those legs and feet of mine. They can't be trusted."

"Can you stand?" Sean offered her a hand.

Willow pushed to her feet. "See? Just fine."

He helped her to the picnic table. "Are you hurting anywhere else?"

Willow inspected her body. "I think I'm still in one piece." She rubbed her neck. "I'll likely be sore for a few days."

"Maybe you should see a doctor," Tom said.

"No. I'll be all right. Besides, that would mean driving all the way back into town. I'd rather be here."

He sat next to her. "You can't scare me like that. I'm not a well man." He winked.

How fond of Willow was Tom? Claire hoped it was a lot. Everyone needed someone to care about, and to be cherished in return.

The next morning they set off with directions to Loretta Lynn's house. Narrow roads wound through a dark forest.

"Kind of reminds me of *Deliverance*." Wearing a devilish grin, Tom hummed a bit of the movie's theme song.

"Cut that out, Tom." Willow wagged a hand at him.

"It is spooky," Taylor said. "Maybe this wasn't such a good idea."

"Of course it was a good idea," Willow said. "We're going to have an awesome time."

"Here's Millers Creek Road. Van Lear should be right ahead." Sean leaned over the steering wheel, peering out the window. "Oh yeah—Possum Hollow Road. We have to be close."

As the RV moved through Van Lear, Claire's stomach churned. It was the epitome of a coal-mining town—run down, buildings in disrepair and badly in need of paint. Loretta Lynn grew up here, yet she managed to rise from poverty to fame. Seeing it firsthand made it real, more than just a story. It was a testament to one's determination.

Loretta Lynn's ability to overcome adversity gave Claire hope. She had a steep mountain to climb, but maybe it was possible to reach the summit. *Lord, I'll climb, but you have to help me.*

Somehow or other, Sean found the way to a boulder with Butcher Holler written on it in white paint. He stopped.

The pavement ended and the gravel road was narrow.

"I don't know if I ought to take this vehicle through here. We might not be able to get back out."

"If you can get in, you can get out," Tom said.

"Okay." Sean kept going.

He hadn't gone far when a large two-story house appeared in the midst of the forest. It had old barn siding that looked as if it had never seen a lick of paint and was now dark from years of weather. It sat on a shelf between two hillsides.

"Tom, that's a holler, the little valley there." Taylor grinned.

Sean pulled as far to the side of the road as possible. "I'll have to back out. There's no place to turn around."

There was a small, rustic barn, along with what looked like an outhouse. A cute wooden-framed well stood in front of the home.

Taylor hurried out of the coach. "I can't believe I'm here! Look at this place. It's incredible."

Tom slowly stepped off the motor home. "It's just an old, run-down house."

A white-haired man wearing a flannel shirt and blue jeans hobbled onto the front porch from the house. He braced his hands in his back pockets. "You here to see Loretta Lynn's home?"

Taylor pushed to the front of the group. "Yes. Is it all right? I mean, are you letting people in today?"

"Well, sure. Just cost you five dollars, is all." He smiled from behind pale blue eyes. "Per person."

Sean paid the fee and the travelers climbed the wooden steps to the porch. "I'm Herman Webb, Loretta's brother."

"It's good to meet you." Taylor reached out and shook his hand. "I can't believe I'm here with Loretta Lynn's brother."

Herman offered a tolerant smile. "Well, come on in, and I'll show you around. I just ask you not to touch nothin'."

They filed through the front doorway and into a small entry. Wallpaper that looked as old as the house covered every vertical surface. Photographs of Loretta Lynn and her family were displayed in all the rooms. The pictures gave a glimpse into her life of poverty and her career. A small coal-burning hearth sat against the center wall in the front room. It couldn't possibly have provided enough heat for the entire house.

Claire shivered at the idea of the cold winter nights spent here.

Herman shared a few family stories as he moved through the house.

The group followed him into a tiny kitchen. There was an antique stove with a big boiler on it and a white-washed table holding old-fashioned kitchen gadgets and pots and pans. How did Loretta's mother cook for her huge family in such a small space?

Loretta's bedroom had a rickety chest of drawers and a bed covered with a hand-sewn quilt. A guitar sat on the bed.

Was it the one she'd had as a child?

No. Probably just a prop.

Claire moved past Taylor, who looked at every photograph, read each note posted on the walls, and studied the details of the rooms as if she was trying to imprint them on her mind. Several times her eyes filled with tears, but she swiftly wiped them off.

The starkness of life here took Claire's breath away. How had Loretta Lynn escaped this kind of poverty? Where did she get the courage to even try? *I couldn't do it.* Fear ground through her. If she couldn't find that kind of courage, she'd never overcome the privation that accompanied chronic illness.

After they'd seen everything, including the horse in the barn, they boarded the coach with waves and *thank you*s to Herman.

"Oh, those poor dears," Willow said. "I can't imagine living like they did."

Taylor took out her guitar. "Loretta Lynn is my hero. She's even more incredible than I knew." She strummed the guitar. "I have a new song. I feel it inside. This place is an inspiration." She played a few notes. "Seeing what she accomplished makes me want to work harder for my dream."

"That's exciting," Claire said.

"It touched me too," Willow said. "I had no idea that being there would affect me so deeply. What a precious lady. And God … He lifted her out of that life." She smiled. "I'm going to work harder on my bike so I can ride with my daughter and grandson. I'm not giving up."

Before they left the next morning, Willow went for a bike ride, in spite of sore muscles from her fall. Tom watched from a park bench, and Taylor sat beside him. She had a new song written that she practiced nonstop. She seemed almost manic about it, but Claire didn't detect any mania, only joy in the art of creating.

"I've got to be ready by the time we get to Nashville. It's my chance. Maybe I can sing in one of the honky-tonks there. Tootsie's is the most popular. I could get discovered."

"You'll do it. And you'll be great."

Taylor smiled at her. "Thanks for believing in me, Claire."

Claire returned the gesture, but inside she agonized. It was easy to believe in someone else's dream. But what was her dream? Would she ever figure out what she wanted from life? And if she did, would she have the courage to go after it?

CHAPTER TWENTY-FOUR

Sean maneuvered the motor home through heavy traffic. He never liked busy freeways, and right now Nashville's rush hour made him wish they'd skipped the city altogether. He liked solitude, probably because he'd spent hours on empty Northern California beaches when he was young. When the anguish at home became too much, he sought solace there.

"Okay, Tom, which way now?"

Tom used a magnifying glass to read a map on his phone.

"Why don't you just make the map bigger?" Sean chuckled.

"Then I've got to jockey it around. This is easier. Can't believe the RV's GPS went out again." He adjusted his glasses. "Okay, Two Rivers Campground is the next exit. Says here it's only two miles from Opryland. So we'll be right in the thick of things."

"Super." Sean made no attempt to disguise his sarcasm. Nashville wasn't his dream. He took the exit to Music Valley Drive. A shade tree and a lounger—that's what he needed. And no matter what anyone wanted to do, he was reclining and napping for the rest of the day.

"We're here." Taylor said. "Nashville." Her tone was reverent.

After checking in, finding their site, and parking, Sean stepped into the living area of the RV. He stretched from side to side. It felt good to be out of the driver's seat. "I'm ready for a break. Let's take a few days off the road."

Taylor studied her computer. "I agree. They have everything here—swimming pool, game room, and bathhouses. A long, hot shower would be fantastic."

She smiled at Sean, and he noticed her captivating brown eyes. Her good looks hadn't escaped him the first time they'd met, but since then he'd been so preoccupied with her disposition he hadn't paid much attention to her appearance. She was pretty—tall and slender with long, chocolate-brown hair.

She didn't seem to notice his appraisal. "We're really close to the Grand Ole Opry, and the Country Music Hall of Fame is just across town. There are a bunch of honky-tonks down the street from there, on Broadway. The one place I really want to see is Tootsies. All the greats sang there."

"Not today. Not me, anyway. I'm going to kick back in a lawn chair and take a nap." He strolled outside, and the heat hit him like a wall. It was muggy, but with the breeze kicking up it would be comfortable enough in the shade.

After taking care of the hookups, Sean and Tom put up the awning. Then Sean hauled lawn chairs out of the storage compartment, and Tom set them up beneath the awning.

"I'll take this one." Sean carried a lounger to a grassy spot beneath a small tree and opened it up. He stretched out on it and closed his eyes. The breeze cooled his skin and carried the sweet aroma of freshly watered grass. This was just what he needed—a little quiet and relaxation.

Willow's voice called to him. "We're going swimming. You want to come along?"

Sean opened one eye. "Nah. I'm good right here. You go ahead." He closed his eye and willed his companions to leave. They'd been in close quarters too many days. He needed some time to himself.

"Okay. We'll see you later."

Sean raised one hand in a halfhearted wave, then slipped into sleep.

The group's chatter woke him. He watched them approach. What a bunch of characters. Tom and Willow both used a cane. Willow and Claire had their towels wrapped around them, but Tom had his draped over one shoulder, at ease with his paunch. Taylor, confident of her good looks, had no towel at all.

His gaze gravitated to Claire. She walked gingerly, but managed to pull off a fairly fluid stride and keep up a gentle demeanor. Why did she have to be so beautiful … and so sick?

"I'll put together a nice fruit salad," Willow said as they came into camp. "I'm sure we've got everything we need."

"I'll help." Taylor hurried to the steps of the RV.

"I'm going to get changed." Tom tromped up the steps behind

Taylor, his legs seeming to move in slow motion.

Claire's towel drooped below her chest, and she quickly rearranged it so she was completely covered. She sat in one of the chairs. "Did you get a nap?"

"I did." Sean pushed the back of his chair up so he was sitting more upright. "I feel better."

"Good. I think we're going downtown tonight. Taylor wants to check out the honky-tonks and see if she can get a spot onstage."

What happened in Salina, Kansas, didn't feel far enough away. "Not a good idea. Too much stress."

"She's going for her dream. And she should."

He shook his head. "She's not ready. It hasn't been that long since the episode in Kansas. She was stressing herself out then, and she's still doing it."

"That was brought on because she wasn't taking her medicine."

"This whole trip's been nothing *but* stress for her." Sean shrugged. "It's not up to me. You guys do whatever you want. But I'm not going to encourage her."

"We all need encouragement at one time or another." Claire stood. "I'm going to change." When she walked away, she limped slightly.

Claire needed to lighten up on herself too. She was doing way too much. Why did these people push so hard?

ঙ৹ළ ৩৹ৎ

Claire woke with a heaviness in her spirit. Morning gray waited for sunrise outside her window.

Willow still slept, so Claire quietly rolled to her side and dropped her feet to the floor. She'd start the coffee.

Daisy looked at her but didn't bother to lift her head.

Claire pulled on a bathrobe and picked up her phone. A message blinked at her.

Odd. Someone had called during the night.

She stepped into slippers, scuffed to the kitchen, and put on the coffee, then moved to the door and walked outside. The cool morning air smelled of rain. The phone in her hand summoned her, but she stopped for a moment to gaze at the sky where the rising sun cast pink across a smattering of clouds.

She looked at the return number. Her mother. Lowering herself into a chair, she puzzled over the call. Why would she have called in the middle of the night?

Claire dialed and waited.

Several rings. No answer.

It was too early. She should have waited for a more reasonable hour to call.

Someone picked up.

"Hello. Is that you, Claire?" Her mother's voice reminded Claire of an old sweater—threadbare and limp.

"Yes. It's me. What's wrong?"

A long pause. Then a trembling breath.

"Mom? Is everything all right?"

"No. I have … some news."

"Is it Daddy?" Her stomach clenched. "Did something happen?"

"No, it's not your father. It's Melissa."

"You heard from her?"

"Yes. No. I'm so sorry, Claire … your sister went to heaven."

At first Claire thought she'd misheard. "She what?"

"Melissa died. She … killed herself … yesterday afternoon."

"No!" Everything whirled around her. "She wouldn't."

A sob came over the phone. "She's gone, Claire."

A deep ache rose in her chest. "But why? Why would she do that?"

"She left a note. That's how the authorities found our number. She said she couldn't do it anymore. That life was too hard." Her mother sobbed. "If only I'd done something. There must have been something I could have done."

"No, Mom. It's not your fault. You always loved her. You were a good mother." Her breath caught.

Melissa had been waiting for someone to care. When it'd been so long since they'd reached out, all she could think of was ending the suffering.

Why didn't I stay in touch? I should have cared more. "I'm coming home. I'll get on a plane today."

"Wait, Claire, honey. Melissa specified ... there is to be no service. She asked a friend to be responsible for her ashes." Sobs tumbled from the other end of the phone. "I won't even have her ashes."

"Oh, Mom. I'm so sorry." If only she was there with her mother so she could hold her and let her cry as much as she needed. "I'll be there as soon as I can."

"No. There's no reason for you to do that. You need to finish what you started. You're so close to your goal. And I ... I don't want you to end up like Melissa—brokenhearted and without hope. Please."

Stay here? So far from home? No. It wasn't right. Her sister had died.

Sobbing, a shuffling noise, then her father's voice. "Hi, sweetie. Your mom and I will be fine. Autumn is on her way here. We'll call you later today or tomorrow, okay?"

"Sure, Daddy. I'm so sorry. It doesn't seem possible that she's gone."

"We love you."

The phone went dark.

Claire stared at it for a long time, the silent void filled with grief. Tears came—first a trickle, then a flood. She cried for the days when they had loved each other, for the days of distance that had separated them like a gaping chasm, and for the life that had ended, leaving no second chances.

The creak of the RV door penetrated her consciousness.

"What is it, Claire?" Sean made it to her in two long steps.

"It's my sister—Melissa. She's dead. She killed herself."

Sean hugged her and held her tightly against his chest.

She pressed in close, but even the strong beat of his heart and the strength of his arms offered no comfort.

"What's happened? What's wrong?" Willow asked.

"Her sister died." Almost in a whisper Sean added, "She killed herself."

"Oh dear, Claire. I'm so sorry."

Willow's hand caressed Claire's back, warm and soothing. Then the refuge of her arms was added to Sean's.

"The Lord has her. He has you too."

Claire broke away. "Does he? How? By letting my sister suffer the way she did?" She pushed the heels of her hands against her eyes. "Leaving her in misery until she couldn't do it anymore? Does he love me like that? My whole life is about suffering. How is that love?" She didn't give Willow a chance to answer but, instead, turned and stormed away.

How could God be all about love if he let people suffer? She'd never treat someone she loved that way.

CHAPTER TWENTY-FIVE

Grief-stricken, Claire wandered through the RV park. She longed for relief from the ache in her heart, but there was none to be had. Even her prayers for peace went unanswered.

She sat at the pool but barely noticed the children playing in the water. Like a mist, she felt only partially present. At the picnic area she fed the birds potato chips someone had left. The sun heated up the afternoon, and she walked back to the coach.

Tom and Sean were off somewhere. Willow was making tea, and Taylor sat at the kitchen table, typing. Claire sat across from her. Did Taylor have answers for what had happened to Melissa?

Claire didn't ask.

There were no answers.

Taylor stopped typing and unexpectedly reached out and rested a hand on Claire's arm. "I'm sorry. I don't know why people do things like that." She looked out the window. "No, actually, that's not true. Sometimes, when I'm tired of the fight, I've thought about it."

"Please. Never do that." Claire grasped her hand, squeezed. "Please."

Taylor looked at her. "I won't. I promise." She went back to typing, then stopped. "It's not your fault, you know. Sometimes life is just too hard, and no one can help."

Claire could barely breathe. Sometimes life *was* too hard. There had been times when she herself had wondered if death was her only answer.

Willow wrapped an arm around Claire's shoulder and leaned down close. "Can I get you something to eat?"

"I'm not hungry."

"It's nearly two o'clock. I know how weak you feel when you skip meals."

She ought to do it for Willow. It would make her feel helpful. "Okay. I'll try."

"A tuna sandwich?"

164

"Sure, but just half." She pushed up from the table. "I'll help." Standing in the kitchen preparing food made life feel closer to normal. When lunch was ready, Willow picked up her Bible, and she and Claire took glasses of tea, the sandwich, and sliced apples outside and sat in the shade.

"It's really getting warm." Willow lifted her hair off the back of her neck.

Claire bit into the tasteless sandwich. "Summer's here."

Daisy trotted down the steps of the RV. After a good scratch behind the ears from Willow, she moved to Claire and rested her head on her lap.

"Aww, what a sweetie. She knows you're sad. She always knows when I need her."

Claire ran a hand over Daisy's head. "I do need you today." She gave her a piece of her sandwich, and Daisy swallowed it down without chewing. Claire chuckled. "More than likely she was just hoping for a handout."

"Well, that too." Willow smiled. "She can be a mooch."

The chargrilled aroma of a barbecue at one of the other campsites in the park carried memories of family picnics. Forcing down a lump in her throat, Claire leaned back in her chair and gazed at the underside of the tree's canopy. Those days when the whole family would get together were gone now.

Her phone chimed. She looked at the caller's number.

"Hi, Mom."

"Hello, Claire. I just need to know you're all right."

"I'm not, but I will be. What about you?"

"The same."

"I'm coming home. I need to be there."

"I understand … and I want you here. But I'm afraid that if you come, you won't go back. You'll never finish what you started. And I can't bear to lose two daughters."

"You said that before. What do you mean?" Claire twisted a button on her shirt.

"When you left, I was afraid for you. I didn't want you to be so far away and vulnerable. But from your text messages and Facebook posts, it's clear this trip has been good for you. And it's important that you stay with your friends and see what your journey is all about. I've been praying, and I know God is up to something. I don't know what it is, but I'm certain it's important. He has so much more for you than a life tucked safely away in the Oregon countryside with me and your father."

"I wouldn't stay there with you forever, Mom. Just for a while. Until things are better."

"I can't tell you what to do. But please pray about your decision first."

"I will. I promise." She heard the laughter of a little one in the background—Travis, Autumn's son.

"Gamma!"

"Oh, your sister just got here. We'll call you later. I love you."

"I love you too." Claire clicked off. Her chest ached. If only she were there. She'd gather that little boy up in her arms and pull her sister into a hug. Tears spilled over.

"How's your family?" Willow asked.

"Okay, I guess. Mom sounded better."

Willow straightened her legs and crossed them at the ankles. Her familiar, well-worn sandals looked like she'd shined them. As she wiggled her toes, the nails glistened with soft pink polish. "Each day has its own sorrow, but that isn't the totality of our life. It's so much more than that. I'm sorry you're going through this kind of grief." She pressed her hand over Claire's.

"I'm not exactly shocked. Melissa's been sick a long time, swinging between highs and lows. She talked about … doing something like this, more than once."

"I never had a sister or a brother. When my parents passed on, I grieved, but they'd lived their lives. It's not the same as losing one so young." Willow's eyes glistened. "I guess the closest thing I know to what you're feeling was the loss of my daughter."

A pulse of surprise zipped through Claire. "I thought you just had the one daughter. I didn't know one had died. I'm so sorry."

"No. She didn't die. I'm talking about Melody. The day she walked away from me, it felt like a death. I thought it would have been easier if she had died. At least that way she wouldn't have rejected me." She closed her eyes and took a deep breath. "I'm so thankful she's giving me another chance. I'm so blessed."

"I don't understand how you can be at peace with your life. You're in pain every day. And there is so much you can't do."

Willow smiled at her. "I don't always feel blessed, but it's not about what I feel. It's what I know. And I know there is so much that I *can* do. Claire, our bodies may be broken vessels, but we are whole in Jesus."

Willow's words were like a balm. If only Claire could hang on to them, make them part of who she was.

"Your dear sister forgot how much the Father loved her."

"How can you know that?"

"If she had remembered, she would never have taken her life."

"Sometimes it's hard to feel loved when all you hear is the clamor in your brain, and sadness claims most of your days." Claire's heart was shredded. "Do you think she's in heaven?"

Willow nodded. "You told me she knew the Lord and loved him." She smiled softly. "She's certainly in his presence."

"But you just said she didn't know his love."

"She simply forgot for a time. We live in a dangerous, fallen world where God doesn't orchestrate our every step. We have free will."

Claire let out a long sigh. "I wish he had stopped Melissa." Tears burned her eyes. "Sometimes her days were so dark. If only I'd been there for her." She took a sip of tea. "I need to go home. I need my family."

"I understand. But I'll miss you."

"Mom and Dad want me to keep traveling. They're afraid if I don't, I won't come back and finish."

Willow's eyes widened, and she didn't respond for a moment. Then she asked, "What do you think?"

Claire knew the answer. It terrified her. "I think they're right. I won't finish. My life will go back to the way it was before I left. But how can I not go home?"

"What do you think the Father wants you to do?"

Claire closed her eyes briefly. "I don't know what he wants."

"My dad died when I was almost fifteen, Mom when I was seventeen. I was too young to be out on my own, but I couldn't bear the thought of staying in my parents' house with Aunt Marge and her brat of a daughter, Summer. That was her name, but she was anything but sunny." Willow crossed one leg over the other. "One night I packed my stuff and got as far away from home as I could. I thought it would help. It didn't. I was miserable and scared … for a very long time. I did everything wrong—drugs, booze, counterfeit friends. None of it helped me. And then I found the Lord and he gave me a new life."

"To know you now, all that seems impossible."

Willow leaned toward Claire and grasped her hand. "Pray, honey, and see what he says to you. He loves you more than any of us do, and he's the only one who knows what's best."

A gust of wind swept through the camp. "Thank you. I will pray. Take some time to decide."

"Maybe you can spend some time with him now. Here, use my Bible." Willow picked up her Bible off a side table. "I've got work to do inside." She stood and slowly made her way toward the RV. She didn't complain about her obvious pain.

Claire stared at the Bible. Where should she begin? She opened to Psalm 28.

Her eyes went to the sixth and seventh verses.

"Praise the Lord! For he has heard my cry for mercy. The Lord is my strength and shield. I trust him with all my heart. He helps me, and my heart is filled with joy. I burst out in songs of thanksgiving."

Claire pressed the Bible against her chest and closed her eyes.

Had he heard her cry? Would he give her strength? Would she ever know joy?

Yes. His Word was true. He had never lied to her.

CHAPTER TWENTY-SIX

Claire added a flat iron to her bag and zipped it closed. It was time. A car horn beeped, and she glanced out the window—the taxi.

"I'll get that for you." Sean stepped into the room and lifted the bag off the bed.

"Thank you." She took in a quaking breath. Her heart felt like it might fly out of her chest. It was as if she were leaving home again.

In a way she was.

Sean followed her out the door.

Taylor was leaning against the RV, but she straightened and unsuccessfully attempted a smile.

As Claire made her way down the steps, Willow and Tom pushed out of their chairs. Claire gripped the handrail, her legs weak and wobbly.

Willow smiled in her motherly way. "You've got everything you need?"

"I think so." Claire glanced at the taxi. "If I don't come back, I'll send for the rest of my stuff."

"I'm counting on seeing your beautiful smile again soon." Willow cradled Claire's face in her hands. She kissed her cheek, then hugged her. "Oh, I'm going to miss you."

"I'll miss you too."

Sean gave the taxi driver Claire's bag.

Taylor looked like she might cry. "I can't believe you have to miss the Country Music Hall of Fame. It's going to be amazing. I'll take pictures for you." She gave Claire a quick hug. "Good luck."

The driver put Claire's bag in the trunk, then opened the back door and stood beside it, waiting.

Claire moved to Tom. "One word of advice—smile more. You look almost handsome when you do." She cast a playful glance at Willow. "I'll see you soon."

Tom didn't smile, but he hugged and hung on like he didn't want to let go. "You come back to us. Things won't be the same without you."

Claire blinked away tears. She wouldn't be back.

She turned to Sean. How should she say goodbye? She couldn't hug him.

Before she had a chance to decide, he reached out, pulled her into his arms, and gave her a tight squeeze, then stepped back. "Good luck to you and your family."

"Thanks." Claire swallowed hard and held back tears. There was a lot to cry about, but not now. She dredged up a smile. With a last glance at her friends, she climbed into the taxi and settled into the backseat.

The driver closed the door and climbed in behind the wheel. The smell of cigarette smoke emanated from him. "The airport?"

"Yes, please." She stared at the back of his head. She couldn't look at any of the dear people watching her leave.

"What time is your flight?" He put the car into drive and moved away from the RV … and her new family.

"Noon."

"We've got plenty of time."

The airport was huge, with masses of travelers flowing in and out of the front entrance, up long escalators and longer corridors, looking like ants on a mission.

Claire picked up her ticket at the kiosk, then, with her bag in tow, she wandered into the concourse, leaning on her cane as she went. She wandered through a store, but soon her legs ached and felt like they were made of rubber.

Wishing the airport were smaller, she returned to the concourse.

A coffee shop.

That's just what she needed—a Frappuccino drink and a chair. There was no line at the counter, so she ordered and took her drink to a small table in the corner of the shop, tucking her cane out of sight.

She stared at her phone for the longest time, envisioning her family and what they were doing. There would be visiting relatives and neighbors flowing in and out of the house, as well as more food than could be eaten, along with lots of hugs and tears. The idea of it set the muscle above her right eye to twitching. Her stomach churned.

She'd be glad when the ordeal was all over.

Her phone chimed.

Sean? Why was he calling? "Hello?"

"Hey there. I wanted to come in and sit with you, but I don't have a ticket so security won't let me. I'm in the lobby."

"Oh, well …" He had come to the airport to see her? "I haven't gone through security yet. I'm getting coffee. But you don't have to wait with me."

"You missed the *I want to* part of what I said. I'd like to sit with you."

"Oh. Okay."

"I'll be right there."

A few moments later, Sean strode into the espresso bar. He waved and walked to the table where she was sitting. "Coffee—good idea." He sat across from her.

"Did you want to get something to drink?"

"Not right now."

Claire looked at the clock. She couldn't think of a thing to say. What did he want?

He clasped his hands in front of him on the table. "I hope you don't mind my being here. I figured you could use some company … since your flight has been delayed."

"It has? I didn't even notice."

"Two hours."

"Why?"

"My guess is heavy storms on the East Coast. I heard they were getting hit pretty hard today."

Claire held in a groan. Her muscles were already growling at her, and a migraine was coming on.

"It'll be good to see your family."

"Yeah."

His hazel eyes radiated kindness, and maybe something more.

Did she dare tell him the truth?

He probably didn't want to hear it. But she needed to tell someone.

She let out a long breath. "Actually, it won't be good. At first I longed for home, but now that I'm faced with being there, all I can think about is the agony of putting on a smile and talking to people I barely know. Repeating platitudes about Melissa being in a better place and how she's finally happy. Mom and Dad will be trying not to cry, and Autumn will be bossing everyone around."

"I know how you feel. I've been there."

"Autumn isn't exactly bossy. She's sweet, actually, but someone has to be in charge, and she's always been the one. She always knows what to do." Claire stared at the tiled floor.

Its high sheen glinted at her.

"It will be harder on Mom now."

"What do you mean? Why now?"

"Before this happened, both Melissa and I were sick. Now there's just one sick daughter who needs her. There's going to be a big hole where Melissa used to be."

Sean leaned on the table. "So, it seems like your family was close. When did things start to go wrong?"

"There was a time when life was about having fun—climbing trees, horseback riding, and riding dirt bikes. Melissa was always full of mischief and fun ... until she started acting peculiar. She'd either be storming through a project while she rambled on about it at a hundred miles an hour, or she'd sleep all day and refuse to leave her room.

"Then the diagnosis came—bipolar disorder. Mom and Dad were devastated, but they hoped for better days. Melissa went off the deep end. She called herself crazy but refused to take her meds. It was an awful time. Finally, she ran away to Las Vegas, where she stayed with a friend. I don't know how she ended up in Grand Junction."

Sean studied the palms of his callused hands. He lifted his eyes to her. "You said you were both sick?"

The question hung in the air.

Claire had dreaded this moment. She knew it would come. Now that she was leaving, it really didn't matter. She met Sean's penetrating gaze. "I have a disease called dysautonomia."

"Never heard of it."

"Most people haven't."

"How bad is it?"

Claire shrugged. "Depends."

"Can you die from it?"

"Not usually. A lot of people like me live a full life." Claire wanted to be truthful, but she heard the lie. Dysautonomia might kill her.

"What does it do to you?"

"On an average day or a *really* bad day?" She gave him a crooked smile.

"How about an average day."

"I have a lot of heart issues, like tachycardia and sometimes bradycardia—my heart is either going too fast or too slow. My blood pressure drops, and when it drops fast, I faint. I'm tired a lot. Sometimes dizzy. Pain in my legs and feet make it hard for me to walk. My stomach is unhappy a lot of the time, and on days like today I get migraines."

Sean's eyes warmed with compassion. "That's a lot for an average day. You do a good job of covering up."

"I've had a lot of practice. No one wants to hang out with a sick person all the time."

"So, what happens on a really bad day?"

"Let's just say it's a big accomplishment to get out of bed. And sometimes I end up in the ER."

"There isn't a cure?"

"I keep hoping they'll find something. Right now I'm supposed to eat a lot of salt. Kind of funny—most people have to stay away from it. And believe it or not, I take a medication to increase my blood pressure."

"That's a new one." He chuckled, then turned serious. "What about a specialist?"

"I've seen so many doctors I've lost count. Lots of specialists. In the beginning they thought I had lupus, then Lyme disease. One time I had to swallow a small camera, and it took pictures of my insides."

Sean made a face. "Sounds like fun."

"Let's just say it was interesting." She picked up her drink and swirled the straw, then took a sip. "This trip was a chance for me to be someone other than the sick one. I hate being sick all the time."

"Yeah. I know all about that." Sean turned his attention to something in the concourse.

"How do you know? Are you sick?"

"No." Sean stood and pushed his hands into his pockets. "I told you about my brother, but I didn't tell you that he had cystic fibrosis."

"I'm sorry." Silence wedged itself between them.

Sean let out a deep sigh. "He fought hard, but it killed him anyway." He looked up and down the concourse. "It's over now." Sean looked tense, like a runner waiting for the starting gun. "I guess I ought to go. I need to do a little shopping."

"Oh. Sure. It was nice of you to come by." And now he was in a big hurry to get away … after he'd heard about her illness.

"Stay in touch."

"I will."

"'Bye." He turned and walked away, heading back into the concourse.

It would be the last time she saw him. One more thing to grieve over.

Claire took a book out of her purse. It was the kind of day that required a good read. *Pride and Prejudice* seemed appropriate.

CHAPTER TWENTY-SEVEN

After a while the chair in the coffee shop became too hard, and Claire moved into a waiting area where there was a smattering of chairs.

Still more than an hour before her plane boarded.

She opened her book and tried to read, but her mind was with Sean and the others. Finally, she rested the book in her lap.

A woman cradled an infant against her shoulder, swaying gently from side to side.

Why couldn't Claire have that? She would have been a good mother. Instead, she was grieving, sick, and would never know what it felt like to hold her own child. She'd never know the pleasures of a complete life.

The thought was absurd. No life was ever fully complete.

A gravelly cough rumbled from across the room. An elderly man pulled a handkerchief out of his pocket and covered his mouth until his cough quieted.

A young woman sitting next to him patted his back, and a little boy climbed into his lap and rested his head against the man's chest.

"I'm fine," he reassured the woman beside him while he stroked the boy's blond curls. His gnarled hand quaked slightly, but a quiet smile rested on his lips.

Obviously he wasn't fine. But he seemed at peace.

If only Claire could experience that kind of peace. If she asked him where it came from, what would he say?

Her phone chimed.

She fished it out of her purse.

Autumn's number flashed on the screen.

"Hi, Autumn. Is everything all right? I'm about to head out."

"Yes. Well, as all right as it can be under the circumstances. How about you?"

"I'm … managing. I'm still at the airport waiting for my flight."

"When do you leave?"

"I was supposed to take off at noon, but the flight is delayed until two o'clock—bad weather on the East Coast, I guess."

"Is the weather all right there? Maybe you should wait."

"All we have here are a few clouds."

"Oh." Autumn sounded disappointed. "I've been thinking."

It was never good when Autumn started a conversation with *I've been thinking*. Claire took a quick breath. "You think too much."

"You're right, but someone's got to do it."

Neither of them spoke for a long moment, then Autumn said, "I don't think you should come home. Not now anyway."

"I've already been over this with Mom."

"I understand that you want to come, but there's nothing any of us, including you, can do to help Mom and Dad. They'd love to see you, but this is a path they have to walk on their own. We can't do it for them. And you have something important you need to do."

"What do you mean?"

"You set out on a journey, Claire—an important journey. I haven't said anything, because I didn't think it would help, but the last couple of years you've been kind of fading away. You're not you anymore. I feel like I'm losing you. And after Melissa ... well, I really want my sister back."

Weariness, like a heavy blanket, fell over Claire. She had changed. How could she not? "I'm still me ... mostly. I can't be who I used to be."

"I know. And I don't expect that. But I really think you're kind of lost. I'm afraid for you."

What did Autumn see happening? *Am I about to throw away my life?*

The question terrified her.

"I understand what you're saying, but I need you and Mom and Dad. I lost Melissa too. And I want to be there so Mom and Dad know I care."

"They know. Mom's not just being nice when she says not to come home. She really thinks you need to stay with your friends."

Claire leaned back in her chair and crossed her ankles. "It doesn't feel right to be here having a good time when I know what's going on there."

"You can't depend on feelings. The only way you'll find what you're looking for is to stay on track."

What was she looking for? What if she didn't find it? "I can't cancel on such short notice, not without losing the money I paid for my ticket. Disability doesn't go far. I can't afford to throw money away."

"If you come home now, you'll lose a lot more than money."

Autumn was right. Money wasn't the issue.

"Okay. I'll think about it and call you." Claire turned off the phone and put it back in her purse. She closed her book, held it against her chest, stood with the help of her cane, and walked along a row of windows.

The city stood, colorful and daunting, daring her to stay. Should she?

She turned her back to the view and leaned against the windowsill.

Taylor stepped into the lobby. Willow followed with Tom, who rode in a wheelchair pushed by Sean.

What were they doing here? And why was Tom in a wheelchair? Her wheelchair.

Willow waved and hurried toward her. "Claire!"

"Hi."

"Thank the Lord you're still here." Willow gave Claire a hug, the smell of White Musk perfume enveloping them.

"Tom, you're in my wheelchair."

"Yeah. Bad day. But that's not what I want to talk about. We're here to stop you." He looked at the others. "We don't think you should go."

"I just talked to my sister—"

"I've prayed about this." Willow rested her hands on Claire's arms. "And I'm certain the Lord wants you to stay."

Claire dropped her arms to her sides. What was going on? Her parents, Autumn, Willow—were they right?

"Honey, we know if you leave, you're not coming back. And God is doing something in our lives. We feel it, all of us."

"I agree with Willow," Taylor said. "It's not the right time for you to leave. If you do,"—her eyes shimmered with tears—"you could end up like your sister."

"This is a chance to find your life," Tom said. "I don't know exactly what's going on, but I've changed. I have hope, and I've got plans for my future. Most impressively, I don't feel like I want to tear someone's head off anymore." He glanced at the others. "I see changes in all of us, even you, Claire. We're like a family. And I'm convinced if we stay together, we'll figure out God's plans for us."

⁊⁊ᎶᎶᎶ

An announcement that Claire's flight was boarding came over the PA. Sean fidgeted. *Please stay.*

She turned and looked at the security gate. "I haven't even gone through security. What happened to the time?"

"It's now or never," Sean said, his nerves taut.

Claire closed her eyes for a moment. "Okay. I'll stay."

A wave of relief rolled through Sean. Why? He had feelings for her, that was it, but they would only lead to trouble, more misery. He'd have to keep his distance, which wasn't going to be easy. He wanted to spend time with her.

"Oh, honey, I'm so happy." Willow pulled Claire back into her arms.

Sean wanted to hug her too. Instead he smiled and said, "Good choice."

What was wrong with him? She'd been so close to leaving. That would have fixed everything. He could never commit to anyone who was disabled. Guilt filled him. He knew her illness shouldn't make a difference, but he'd had enough sickness in his life, more than anyone should have to bear.

Claire's soft blue eyes held hope, in spite of all she'd lived with. She'd had enough too. But there was nothing she could do to escape it.

Shame at his cowardice flooded Sean. "Good thing you only have a carry on." He lifted it off the floor. "Let's get back to the park. Taylor, can you push Tom?" He looked at Claire. "Do you need help?"

Hope and maybe even happiness flashed across her face. "No, I'm fine. Thank you."

But she wasn't fine. And he knew she never would be.

CHAPTER TWENTY-EIGHT

The next morning, Taylor was in a hurry to get going, but even with all her complaints about everyone moving too slowly, the travelers didn't make it to breakfast at a nearby café until eleven o'clock. Taylor had her guitar and wouldn't relinquish it, so they had to wait for a table with extra space. They didn't set out for the Country Music Hall of Fame until well past noon.

Claire was in no mood to visit the museum or a honky-tonk, but she didn't want to disappoint Taylor, so she reluctantly agreed to join the others.

A cab dropped them off in front of an impressive, huge, angular building.

Claire suppressed a groan. She wouldn't have the stamina to see many of the exhibits. *Why didn't I bring my wheelchair?*

Tom and Willow seemed to be in good spirits, but their moods weren't going to be enough to carry them all the way through the massive museum. Walking all that way would have consequences.

Taylor checked her guitar at the front desk. "This is incredible," she said and set out, acting like a tour guide.

The exhibits of country music greats and memorabilia were enough to distract Claire for the first forty minutes or so, but eventually the pain crept in. Pushing past it, she focused on the exhibits of gold records, photos of musicians, their stage clothes, guitars, and posters. There were even cars that had belonged to country stars.

Taylor rattled on about the performers like Roy Clark, Dolly Parton, Johnny Cash, Hank Williams and, of course, Loretta Lynn.

Sean was pleasant but seemed only mildly interested. Tom made fun of anything he could. How did Willow tolerate him? For reasons Claire didn't understand, they were happy with each other. They'd clearly paired off.

After strolling through the museum for more than an hour, Claire began to panic. She needed to sit down. Her legs felt like they might give out at any moment, and it seemed as if the pain in her feet had spread to the rest of her body. She found a water fountain and took a pain pill along with a couple of ibuprofen.

Half an hour and she should feel better.

Sean sat on a cushioned bench and watched a video about Trisha Yearwood.

She moved toward him, hobbling but trying not to. She lowered herself to the bench.

"You gotta watch some of this. She's a fantastic performer."

Claire was just grateful for a place to sit, but pretended to be interested in the video. "Do you know where Tom and Willow are?"

"Last time I saw them, Taylor was giving them the life history of Waylon Jennings, and Tom looked like he'd been cornered by a bear." Sean laughed. "A light and friendly one."

"You should laugh more."

He looked aghast and ducked one shoulder so it bumped into hers. "What, I don't laugh enough?"

"No. It's just that when you do ... well, you look and sound happy."

"And the rest of the time?"

"You don't."

He returned to watching the video with a perceptive dip in his mood.

Claire placed her hands on her hips and pressed, trying to take some of the pressure off her back. She shouldn't have said anything. Why did she have to turn even a casual comment into something more? "I never knew sitting could feel so good. I don't know if I can walk any farther."

"Probably should have brought your wheelchair."

"I know, but I can usually get by without it. And I hate using it."

"I can tell. It's hasn't left the storage compartment since we left Oregon, except for Tom using it yesterday." He straightened his legs. "Claire, it's a tool, that's all. It's not a flag of surrender."

Is that how she saw it? As a sign of surrender?

"Do you need a wheelchair?"

"No. I'll be fine. I took a pain pill. I just need to rest and wait for

181

it to kick in."

Taylor sauntered up to them. "Come on. There's a film about to start."

"You go ahead," Claire said.

"Okay." Taylor glanced at her watch. "It's getting kind of late. The film is about thirty minutes long. When it's over I'll get my guitar and meet you at the exit."

"Sounds good," Sean said.

Tom and Willow joined Sean and Claire. Willow sat beside Claire. "It feels so good to get off my feet. I probably won't be able to walk for a week after this." She slipped off a sandal and rubbed her foot.

Claire's mood dipped. If only rubbing her feet helped. How was she going to see the rest of the museum plus go to the honky-tonks?

"Who's coming to the show?" Taylor asked.

Willow and Tom looked at one another. "We are." Willow rose with help from Tom. "Claire?"

"No. I'm staying put for now."

"I'll stay with her," Sean said.

"I'm fine. I'll just watch this video."

Sean ignored Claire's comment. "We'll meet you at the exit." After the others had gone, he stood. "I'm getting you a wheelchair. You're in pain, and I'm not about to have you faint and hurt yourself. You look terrible."

"Thanks a lot."

"I mean you look like you feel awful." He grinned. "I'll be right back."

She didn't have time to object again before he strode away. He was right, but the idea of being pushed in a wheelchair again, especially by Sean, made her stomach ache.

Claire kept her eyes on the Trisha Yearwood documentary and tried not to think about her pain or the coming humiliation. Why did doing something fun always come at a price?

Sean returned with a wheelchair. It was black with big chrome wheels. "How about that? Just ask and you will receive." He grinned and parked the chair beside Claire. "Shall we see the rest of the museum, madam?"

She eyed the contraption.

He laughed. "I swear you're looking at that chair like it's a snake."

"Would you want to ride in it?"

The humor left Sean's eyes. "No. I guess not."

Claire sat in the chair and let Sean push her. She attempted to engage in conversation and make comments about the displays, but she didn't really see them. All she could think about was the chair. Would she be tethered to one someday? What would she do then? Take Melissa's way out?

Sorrow squeezed her chest.

No. She couldn't do that to her family.

Tom, Willow, and Taylor were waiting when Sean and Claire reached the exit.

An employee of the museum approached Sean. "Sorry, sir, but you can't take the wheelchair out of the building."

"Oh. I'm so sorry." Claire stood and nearly toppled over.

Sean steadied her. "Look. I just need it for a few minutes. We're heading up the street to Tootsies." Sean slipped him a twenty-dollar bill. "I promise to bring it right back."

The man stuck the money in his pocket. "Okay. Go ahead."

Sean saluted him, motioned Claire to sit back down, and pushed her into the afternoon heat.

She plastered on a smile, though she was embarrassed. She could walk. Sean had just wasted money.

"Now, where are the honky-tonks?" Sean asked.

"The phone shows they're just a couple of blocks up." Willow nodded in the direction of Broadway. "I'm not sure I can walk that far, especially in this heat."

"I've been resting all the time Sean's been pushing me. Why don't you use the chair? I'll walk." Claire stepped out of the chair, thankful to be on her feet again, despite the pain.

"Can you make it, sweetie?" Willow asked.

"I'm sure I can. It's your turn to have someone push you." She smiled as brightly as she could.

"Okay. Thank you." Willow sat and rested her arms on the arm supports.

Tom moved behind the chair. "I'll take care of you."

"Can you do that?" She rested a hand on his.

"No problem. I'm getting a second wind." He started up the sidewalk.

Taylor followed.

Claire walked beside her, spikes of pain jabbing her feet, in spite of the pain medication. "Are you going to sing tonight?"

She hefted her guitar slightly. "I'm ready, if I can find a spot." She stopped and looked back at the museum. "All of the greats in country music fought for their place. So can I."

Claire gave her hand a squeeze. "I know you can."

"You are courageous, dear," Willow said. "But God will make a way at the perfect time. Only perform tonight if you really think you're ready."

"Tonight is the night." Taylor stepped around the wheelchair and strode up the street, not bothering to wait for anyone else.

"I hope she's right," said Willow.

"She is. I'm sure of it." Claire watched Taylor. She was going after her dream.

"What makes you think she even has a chance?" Sean asked. "Tootsie's is pretty famous. New singers have to come back again and again before they can get a spot on stage. And who knows what will happen if Taylor gets to perform, once she's up in front of an audience."

"I just think this is Taylor's time."

"Yeah. Her time to be humiliated," Sean said.

By the time everyone made it to Broadway and the little purple building called Tootsie's Orchid Lounge, Claire could barely keep up. The humidity and high temperature were oppressive, and each step drained her endurance.

Taylor stood at the corner of the building. "Thought you'd never get here."

"Well, let's go in," Tom said. "Might as well get this over with."

Taylor shot him a defiant look before stepping inside.

Claire followed. Tootsie's wasn't what she'd expected. It was dark and not very big, definitely not glamorous. It smelled of beer and cigarettes. On one side of the room was a bar in front of a wall crowded with photographs of singers who had performed there—people like Kris Kristofferson, Willie Nelson, Waylon Jennings, and Patsy Cline. Tables clustered on the other side of the room, and a small stage stood in the front just inside the entrance. A short stairway in the back led to a second level. Both levels were already crowded, and it was barely five o'clock.

Waitresses moved through the sea of people, carrying trays of drinks and food and taking orders.

"Did you know the Grand Ole Opry used to be right behind here? When Loretta Lynn sang, her husband would come here and hang out. She'd stop by after performing." Taylor turned and looked at the pictures on the wall. "See, that's her right there." Her eyes darted to the empty stage.

Sure Taylor was nervous, but who wouldn't be?

Willow got out of the wheelchair and sat at one of the few free tables. "Thank you for the ride, Tom."

"You're welcome."

"I'll be right back." Sean pushed the chair out the door.

Taylor and Claire joined Willow and Tom. "Should you see what you have to do to sign up?" Claire asked.

"Yeah." Taylor stared at the stage, then got up and went to the bar. She talked to a woman, who pointed at a man standing in the back of the tavern. She moved across the room, looking apprehensive as she approached him. They chatted a few minutes, then she returned to the table. "They don't have a slot for me." She shrugged. "I guess I'll have to wait for another night."

"That's all right, dear. I'm hungry. We can have some dinner and enjoy the show." Willow patted the chair next to her. "Sit by me."

A waitress took their drink orders, and they settled back to enjoy the entertainment.

After an introduction from the stage manager, a tiny woman with long blonde hair, dressed in blue jeans and wearing cowboy boots, stepped onto the stage. She sat on a wooden stool and played a guitar while she sang. She was good, but Taylor was better.

"That should be you," Claire said.

The blonde finished her love song, received exuberant applause, and strummed her guitar as she led into a new tune.

Taylor slumped in her chair, sipped a Coke, and listened.

The man Taylor had talked to earlier made a beeline toward her. "Taylor, you got a few songs ready to go?"

Taylor shot up straight in her chair. "Yeah, I sure do."

"Well, you're going on. My next act didn't show. It's your lucky night." He grinned.

"Thanks." Taylor tossed her long hair off her shoulder as the man walked away. "That's the entertainment manager." She stood, tugged on the bottom of her shirt, and smoothed her hands over the front of it, then took out her guitar and tuned it.

Sean rejoined them. "The chair is happily home again."

"Taylor's up next," Claire said.

"Really? I thought it was hard to get a spot." Sean sounded more apprehensive than excited. He leaned close to Claire and whispered. "Do you really think she should do this?"

"Of course. She's worked hard." Frustration sifted through Claire, but she forced a smile. "And we've got perfect seats."

Taylor slung her guitar over her shoulder and tightened the strap. She tapped out the beat of the music with the heels of her boots. "It's really getting crowded in here."

"That's good, right?" Claire's heart thrummed. She was probably as nervous for Taylor as Taylor was for herself.

No. Taylor was scared. She was visibly shaking and looked pale.

"Taylor, would you like me to pray for you?" Willow asked.

Taylor glanced around. "Sure, but do it silently." She tapped the body of the guitar with her nails.

The manager stepped up to them. "Okay. Five minutes. Be ready when I call your name."

Taylor nodded and watched him walk away. She pressed a hand to her chest. "I don't know if I can do this."

"You're going to be great," Claire said. "You'll see."

Sean leaned close to Taylor. "If you're not ready, you don't have to do it."

"Of course she's ready." Claire smiled at Taylor. "She's been working a long time for this chance."

"Claire's right. I am ready." Taylor smoothed the front of her shirt.

The woman who was singing finished her set, gave a little bow, and walked off the stage while people clapped.

The manager ran up the steps and stood in the center of the small platform. "A big round of applause for the little lady!" He clapped, then took hold of the microphone. "Tonight we have something special for you. A brand-new face here at Tootsie's. I hear she has the voice of an angel and a special song for you. Welcome Taylor Reaves!"

Taylor moved out of her chair and, looking as stiff as a mannequin, made her way up the steps. She stood behind the microphone and stared at the crowd.

Taylor didn't look good—maybe she wasn't ready. Claire's stomach ached.

"Thank you." Taylor adjusted the microphone, cleared her throat, and let her fingers rest on the strings.

Then—nothing.

She stood there looking petrified.

"Lord, help her," Willow said in a quiet plea.

Taylor strummed a few notes. Stopped. Stared at the floor in front of her, then out at the lights. Plucked a few more notes. Didn't sing. And then she mumbled, "I'm sorry," ran off the stage, and disappeared out the front door.

"Oh no. Taylor." Claire stood and hurried after her.

When Claire stepped outside, Taylor was running down the street.

"Taylor! Wait!"

Sean joined Claire.

"I should go after her."

"Leave her alone. She needs time to herself." He stared at the fleeing woman. "I tried to warn you, but you kept on her. Why?"

All of a sudden, Claire could see how much she had contributed to tonight's disaster. "I wanted to help."

"I know you didn't mean for this to happen, but it did. Are you trying to live out your dream through Taylor?"

"Of course not. Why would you think that?"

Sean rubbed the back of his neck. "Sometimes you push too hard. Not just Taylor, but yourself."

"We have to—that's the only way we can do anything. And you didn't even believe in her. She could have done it. She's talented enough."

"Maybe she is, but sometimes we've got to put away our talent and our dreams, and move on to something else."

"Like you? Is that what you think you did? Moved on?" He looked at them as if they were the only ones with problems, but he had serious issues himself. The aggravation burst from her lips. "You're not moving on, you're running. What are you running from, Sean?"

He stared at her, his eyes like flint. "You want to know?" He walked to the corner of the honky-tonk, planted his hands on the wall, and leaned into the building, looking at the paved sidewalk.

Claire followed. Had she gone too far? "Yes. I do."

Sean swung around and faced her. "My brother's dead because of me. I let him die. I wanted him to die."

"No. Your brother died from cystic fibrosis."

Sean gazed at a street light. "Sometimes I prayed he would die." He looked at her. "Yeah. I did that." Sean shook his head slightly. "He was crushing our family. My parents didn't have a life. I didn't have a life." He shoved his fingers through his hair. "The day he died I was the only one home with him. I ... I didn't try hard enough. I could have done more." Tears washed into his eyes. And then there was something more than tears—regret, self-loathing. He sucked in a deep breath. "My brother's dead because of me."

Her anger melted away. She reached out and rested a hand on Sean's arm. "I understand. I do. You're not a monster. You wouldn't be here helping us if you were." She squeezed his arm gently. "Your brother died because it was time for him to go. It wasn't your fault."

And Melissa's death wasn't Claire's fault either. Her sister made the choice.

Tears trailed down Sean's face. "Why did he have to die?"

Claire didn't know what to say. She sent Willow and Tom a look of panic.

Willow stepped up and rested a hand on Sean's back. "The Lord knows about these things. We don't understand. We can't. It's just too painful." She put her arms around Sean.

He leaned against her and cried.

Claire's heart ached for him, but Taylor needed someone too. Claire had to go after her. "I've got to find Taylor."

Sean straightened. "Go. I'm okay."

With a nod, Claire headed down the street.

"You can't go by yourself," Tom called after her.

"I'll be fine." She kept moving.

About a block down the street, Taylor sat on a bench in front of another honky-tonk.

Claire took a seat beside her. "Glad I found you. Don't think I could have walked any farther."

They watched the traffic and people moving past.

Claire finally said, "I'm sorry."

Taylor rested her hand on the neck of her guitar. "For what?"

"I messed up. I shouldn't have pushed you."

"You didn't do anything wrong. I wanted this." She glowered at the sidewalk. "But I couldn't do it. I just couldn't. I'm never going to now that I've wasted my chance. My life is going to be a big, fat nothing. I'll just keep on being me—a weirdo. A loner." She leaned her back against the building and stared at the street lights.

"That's not true. You're not weird. You're beautiful and talented. And one day—"

"No. There's never going to be a 'one day.'"

"What if we work on it together? I don't even have a dream … or a real friend, except maybe you."

Taylor looked at Claire. And then a hint of a smile lifted her lips. "Friends? Now, that would be something." She slung an arm around Claire's shoulders and pulled her into a hug. "And hey, what about your stories? I'd like to say I know an author."

"I've thought about it, but who am I? I just write for fun and the kids at church."

"It might become more."

Claire shrugged. "Who knows? Maybe." Was it possible? Could she actually write for a living?

The idea terrified her.

It was too big of a goal.

Claire hugged Taylor back and held on. Willow was right, God had a plan for them. They just needed to wait for his perfect time. He'd show them.

CHAPTER TWENTY-NINE

Taylor's guitar felt awkward in Claire's hands as Taylor showed her where to place her fingers for different notes and chords and how to strum to create various sounds. Claire threw her head back and laughed. "Loretta Lynn I am not. This is hard. I don't know how you do it."

The RV swayed and nearly unseated Claire.

"Sean! What are you doing?" Taylor gripped the edge of the table.

"The road's winding. Do you want me to drive straight when the highway curves?" He glanced back at her. "We're driving through the Smoky Mountains. They may not seem like much when you compare them to the Rockies, but they're not a prairie either."

"Sorry."

"I'm done for now." Claire handed the guitar back to Taylor. "It'll probably be easier when we're not driving." She turned to Willow. "Do you think Tom's going to be all right?"

"Yes." Willow glanced toward the back, where Tom had headed a while ago. "He just needs some rest. Setbacks are part of his life."

Claire nodded. She picked up a deck of cards sitting on the table. "Anyone feel like playing rummy?"

"Not right now." Taylor worked through several chords, stopping occasionally to write down words to a song she was working on.

"Willow, do you want to play?"

"No. I just can't put this book down. I've got to see what happens."

Claire sat there for a few minutes. What to do to pass the time? She could work on a story, or … She glanced at Sean. Maybe she could mend some of what had happened between them. She climbed into the front passenger seat and snapped the seat belt into place. "Do you mind having company?"

Sean didn't look at her. "I can always use a distraction. It's going to be a long day."

She adjusted the seat backward a notch. "It's a lot more comfortable up here."

The highway flew by.

"The Smoky Mountains always sounded so romantic when I read about them in a book. But they're nothing much really, more like hills."

"Well, I don't suppose they felt like hills when families traveled through here back in the eighteenth century."

"No. Guess not." She studied the heavily timbered mountains. "I can't imagine doing something like that."

"Brutal. And deadly. It took courage."

"Why do you think people did it?"

Sean tossed her a sideways look. "When you want something bad enough, you'll do anything."

"That's not what you were saying the other night."

"I wasn't talking about me. I'm talking about people like you, people who take risks." He glanced at her. "And I've been thinking about what you said last night. And I think I understand a little better now. You push because you have to. I want to keep things safe and under control."

"Yeah. But I took a risk with someone else's life." She plucked a piece of lint off her shirt. "I'm sorry about what I said. I shouldn't have blown up at you like I did. And it's none of my business anyway."

"No. You were right. I am running." He shook his head. "I don't know what I think about all of it. I wish I'd been different, better to my brother. Now it's too late. And every day I walk around feeling like I have a big hole in my middle. And I know I can't run far enough to forget or to fill the hole."

"I'm sorry. I wish I knew how to make it better. I know how it feels to lose someone you love."

"Thanks, but I don't want you to care. I don't want you to help." He sounded sullen, but not angry.

Still, Sean might as well have punched her in the gut. Weren't they friends? Why didn't he want her to care?

"You don't need to be worrying about me," he said more kindly. "You have enough troubles of your own. And besides, I've got to work this out myself." Sorrow lay behind his eyes. "Let's just forget about what happened."

She didn't want to care. But how could she turn something like that off? A person's heart didn't have a spigot. She stared out the window until sleep claimed her.

Claire startled awake as Sean braked hard. "Where are we?"

"Atlanta."

She gazed out the window. They were in the midst of a monstrous city and a freeway that was nearly as big.

There were at least eight lanes of traffic each way, and they were all crammed with buses, trucks, and cars.

"Wow. I'd hate to drive in this every day."

In spite of the riotous surroundings, the architecture of the city was fascinating and cultured. If only there was time to stop and explore.

But she didn't even bring up the possibility. Tom would raise a stink.

"Hey, Claire, you ready for that game of cards now?" Taylor asked.

"Sure, I'll play." She unclipped the seat belt and pushed out of her seat. "Not sure what good it will do me. You always win."

Taylor laughed. "Guess you need some practice."

"I need something to think about besides this traffic. It's terrifying."

"Yeah." Taylor gazed out the window. "I'm trying to ignore it."

"The Lord's looking out for us," Willow said.

As Claire settled across from Taylor, Tom emerged from the bedroom. "Looks like we're in the middle of an ocean of cars."

"Are you feeling better?" Willow asked.

"Yeah. At least I can move around. Think I'll keep Sean company." He made his way to the front, a bit unsteady on his feet.

A game of rummy did its job of distracting Claire. The miles ticked by as she lost one hand after another. Gradually traffic became lighter, and Claire was able to enjoy the scenery.

Pink and purple flowers bloomed in the freeway median and pine trees fused with a jungle of heavy foliage beyond the highway.

"Look at those roads. I've never seen such red dirt. Strange." Taylor smiled and laid down her cards. "Rummy."

"Again?"

"Want another try?"

"No. I'm done." Claire moved to the recliner. She was overly warm. Even with air conditioning, the air felt hot and muggy. Midsummer in Georgia apparently meant high temperatures, high humidity, and a high chance for thunderstorms. All highly miserable.

Taylor put away the cards and pulled out her computer. She seemed to be completely at ease for the first time on the trip.

Friends. She and Taylor were friends. Who would have thought it possible? When they'd first set out, Taylor had a knack for getting under Claire's skin. Claire had been disappointed when Taylor hadn't chickened out and stayed behind. Everyone had been on edge in those early days. Now they were close.

All except Sean.

He and Tom got along well, but other than that, Sean had kept mostly to himself, especially after Nashville.

Claire hurt for him. He carried a terrible burden. And even though he was a believer, he hadn't been able to give his burden to God.

Who was she to judge? She wasn't doing a very good job of that either.

Fatigue enveloped Claire. Feeling older than her years, she closed her eyes. Would she always feel this way? Willow had said Claire needed to make peace with who she was, including her illness.

But how?

"I'm tired. I'm going to take a nap."

Willow set her book in her lap. "Are you okay?"

"Yeah." Claire made her way to the back and lay down on the bed. She was only twenty-two, with most of her life ahead of her.

What if she felt like this forever? What if she got worse? Her future rushed at her—a dark, bleak tunnel. How could she face it?

Sleep. She needed sleep.

CHAPTER THIRTY

"Only twenty miles to Savannah," Sean called.

Claire opened her eyes and stared at the ceiling. How long had she been asleep?

"Anyone know a good place to stay?"

"I'm checking things online," Taylor said.

Claire sat up, her skin feeling sticky and damp. She looked out the window. Everything outside appeared soggy. Moss draped the trees alongside the highway. She climbed off the bed and walked into the living area.

The windshield wipers swept rain off the front window.

"Are we in a storm?"

"Just a little rain." Willow looked up at Claire from her spot beside Tom on the sofa. "Did you have a nice nap?"

"Yes." She lifted her arms over her head and stretched. "I'm still half asleep." Dizziness swept over her and she caught hold of the table edge.

Claire wobbled past Taylor at the table on her way to the front and dropped into the passenger seat.

Sean glanced at her. "Hey."

"Hey." Her mouth felt pasty and she was sure she had dragon breath. She opened the glove compartment and fished out a peppermint candy. "Twenty miles to Savannah?" She unwrapped the mint and popped it in her mouth.

"Yep."

She looked over her shoulder at Willow. "Are you excited that we're so close to your daughter?"

Willow pursed her lips and nodded. "I pray she still wants to meet."

"Hey, you want to stay at the beach?" Taylor asked. "There's a camp called River's End."

"You think we can get a spot?" Sean changed lanes.

"Unlikely, but it *is* the middle of the week, so maybe. Doesn't hurt to try." Tom pulled out his phone.

"It's the perfect spot," Taylor said. "Close to the beach. We can walk there."

"That would be fabulous," Willow said.

"I'll call." Tom dialed the number after Taylor read it off to him. "Hi, this is Tom Cantrell. I'm traveling and need a spot for my RV." He waited while the person on the other end talked. "I'm in Savannah now. I need something today." He broke into a big smile. "No kidding? That's perfect. We'll take it." After giving his information to hold the space, Tom shut down the phone. "We got one. It's a miracle, really. Someone just called in and cancelled. We can stay up to two weeks."

Willow pressed her palms together. "Thank you, Lord." She leveled a serious look on Tom. "It would be wonderful if we could stay several days. That way I can have more time with my daughter and grandson. Is it possible for you to change the date of your NASCAR drive?"

"It wasn't easy to get the reservation." Tom's jaw tightened. "I don't know if they have any others."

She gave him a pleading look.

"I'll check it out."

Oh, he was smitten all right. He'd never change his NASCAR plans for anyone else.

Sean maneuvered the RV through Savannah. It wasn't a big city like Nashville or Atlanta, but more like a town. Large southern-style homes like the ones in movies and described in books, lined the streets. Wisteria and honeysuckle, intermingled with lush greenery, hung from trellises and draped across spacious front porches. Claire imagined the sweet fragrance that wafted over the verandas. Spanish moss enveloped trees, drooping from heavy limbs of giant oaks.

"There is so much Spanish moss here. Don't you love it?" Willow asked. "It's so mysterious looking."

"More like messy and spooky-looking," said Taylor.

"This is outstanding," Willow said. "I've never seen anything like it, except in photographs. And I thought this kind of moss only grew in the bayous."

"I don't think we're far from bayou country," Tom said.

"I'm not going near those swamps—bugs, alligators, snakes." Taylor shivered.

"I doubt we have to worry about any of those," Sean said. "But turtles might be a problem." He chuckled.

"Turtles?" Willow kneeled behind the front console. "Oh, look at that—a turtle-crossing sign. How sweet. I wonder if we'll see any."

Claire barely caught a glance of the sign as they drove past. Funny, like the deer-crossing signs posted in Oregon.

Sean continued on until they came to a sign that said River's End Campground. He slowed and turned into the camp. It was packed with RVs and tents. "Don't see any open spots. We must have gotten the last one." Sean checked in, then returned to the RV. "Got the directions to the site." He handed a pamphlet to Claire. "Here you go."

She glanced through it. "There's tons to do here. Lots of history. They even have Civil War reenactments."

Sean backed into their spot. They had close neighbors on either side, but there was also a nice shade tree. "We're only three blocks from the beach and a lighthouse. They've got a swimming pool and a couple of bathhouses, which will help keep the sand out of the RV."

"I saw a cute little convenience store." Willow reached for her purse.

Sean climbed out of the driver's seat and stepped into the living area. "Sorry, Willow, forgot to tell you, Daisy is welcome here in the park, but she's not allowed on the beach."

"Ah, poor girl." Willow stroked the dog. "She loves the beach."

Daisy leaned against her, tail beating the air.

"Beachcombers don't like the little gifts dogs leave behind." Sean snorted.

"Yeah, and sharks probably think dogs make nice snacks." Tom laughed.

"Tom. Really?" Willow straightened and made a show of being mad.

Claire stepped into the back. "When is the race you're entering with your daughter?"

"In a few days." A pained expression crossed Willow's face. "I don't know if I'm ready."

"Have you talked to your daughter?"

"Not since we made the arrangement. It was an uncomfortable conversation. I'll call, just not now." She ran her fingers across her forehead and massaged her temples. "I have to let her know where we're staying and double-check to make sure she still wants to do it." She turned to Tom. "Would you like to take a walk on the beach with me, gallant sir?"

"Are you up for it? It's been a long day."

"I can't wait."

"Okay then, after I give Sean a hand with setting up."

"That's all right. You go ahead," Sean said.

"You sure?"

"Absolutely." Sean stepped out of the motor home and went to work, taking care of the awning first.

Claire took her cane and descended the steps, Taylor following.

Tom gave Willow a hand down.

She stopped and took a deep breath. "Do you smell that?"

"What?" Tom asked.

"The ocean." She drew another breath. "I love it. I'm so happy to be here." She smiled at Tom, and the two headed toward the beach, walking slowly.

"Come on, Claire. Let's go." Taylor headed out of camp.

Claire hesitated. Should Sean be left with all the work? "Do you need help?" She'd rather spend time with Sean than walk the shoreline.

"No. I'm good. Besides, I'm on the payroll. You're not." He smiled. "I'll be down in a while. After I take Daisy for a walk."

"Oh yes. Poor Daisy."

He set the bracing for the awning. "Go on. Have fun."

Claire turned and caught up to Taylor. Obviously Sean didn't want to spend time with her. More and more, he sought out his own company. He was probably sorry he'd ever joined them. She could understand, after what he went through with his brother. She turned her attention to the beach. It didn't do any good to think about Sean.

Tom and Willow were already several yards down the beach, their hands linked as they walked. Every once in a while Willow would laugh and look up at Tom like he was someone special. Was she in love?

"Look at those two," Taylor said. "Do you think old people have feelings like ... well, you know. Do they want to have sex?"

"I don't know. I guess ... maybe." Claire giggled. "I can't imagine Tom being romantic. He can be such an old grouch."

"Yeah, a grouch who's crazy about Willow."

The beach was nothing like the ones in Oregon. These waves were quiet, almost gentle. And there were no big rocks standing in the water, nor any cliffs bordering the shore. The sand mounded in low dunes sprinkled with blowing beach grasses. The smell was the same, though.

She breathed deeply of the pungent scent of salt and sand, then stuck a toe in the water. "It's almost warm."

Taylor stepped into the water, and a small wave cascaded around her ankles. She waded out a long way, but the water didn't get deep. Using her foot, she splashed water toward Claire and laughed.

Staying close to the shore, the two walked along the beach.

"Claire, why did you come on this trip?"

"I wanted to get away from home, and I hoped to find a purpose for my life." She bent and picked up a smooth white stone. "I hoped I'd find out more about myself. Maybe even discover happiness."

"You're not happy? I thought you were." Taylor frowned.

"I'm not unhappy, exactly. It's just that I never thought my life would be ... like this."

"Like what?"

"Slow and careful. Painful." She tossed the rock into the surf. "Everything's hard. Even this walk. I'm not taking a stroll on a sandy shore. I'm gritting my teeth and walking on this sand. It's not supposed to hurt, not when you're only twenty-two. I'm tired of pain—tired of being tired. Tired of worrying about whether or not I'm going to faint or end up in the hospital because my heart accelerates so much it can't pump blood."

"I'm sorry."

Tears burned. "There's no freedom in living the way I do. When I think of doing something fun, I always have to measure whether or not I can do it—is it worth the consequences? I want to run and leap and dance." She watched a seagull dip over the waves. "I know I need to make peace with it, but I haven't been able to. I pray and feel better, then something happens and I'm mad all over again." She bent and picked up a colorful shell. "If I could find peace, then I'd consider this trip a success."

"I didn't get it. But I think I understand better now."

Claire couldn't hold back the tears any longer. Trickles became rivers.

Taylor put an arm around her. "I can't imagine being so young and so sick." She gave Claire a squeeze.

Claire wiped at her cheeks and choked down sobs. "I'm just feeling emotional today and having a pity party."

Sean ambled down the beach toward them.

She couldn't let him see her like this. She brushed away the remnants of tears, took a deep breath, and did her best to look composed.

"He's pretty cute." Taylor gave Claire a devilish smile. "I think he likes you."

"Me? He barely even speaks to me."

"That's because he likes you. And he doesn't want to."

"You think so?"

Sean looked lonely, walking on that great big shore all by himself.

CHAPTER THIRTY-ONE

The morning of the race, Willow flitted around the RV like a hummingbird darting from flower to flower. She went from heating water in the kettle to packing a beach bag with essential items to peering out windows to check on the weather, then moving to the front of the RV to see if her daughter had arrived. "She said she'd be here by eight thirty."

Claire had never seen her so on edge. "I'm sure she'll be here. Why don't you go outside and enjoy some morning air? I'll get you a cup of tea."

"That sounds nice." Willow started for the door, then turned and looked at Claire and Tom. "What if she doesn't come?"

Tom offered her a smile. "Oh, she'll show up."

"I'm sure you're right. I'm worrying over nothing." Willow opened the door and stepped out.

Claire made a cup of herbal tea and took it outdoors.

Willow had wandered toward the nearby road. She looked one way, then the other. "She's late."

"Come sit down. She's only a few minutes late."

When Willow was seated, Claire handed her the cup. "She'll be here. I'm certain of it."

"True. I'm just excited." Willow sipped some tea, then set her mug on the patio table. With her hands pressed between her knees, she bounced her legs. "I just can't seem to quiet down. Even when I was reading my Bible, I couldn't concentrate."

"It's understandable. You haven't seen your daughter in a long time." Claire gave Willow a reassuring smile. "Enjoy your tea, and save some of that energy for the race."

Obediently Willow sipped. "That tastes lovely." She closed her eyes and took a deep breath. But instead of settling down, she said, "We should be on our way. The race is scheduled to begin at ten." She looked at her watch … again. "Eight forty-five."

Tom made his way down the RV steps. "There's plenty of time."

Sean returned from a morning walk with Daisy. He bent, patted her, and unclipped the leash.

The dog went straight to Willow and tried to jump into her lap.

"No. You're too big for that." She pressed a kiss to the dog's face. "Did Uncle Sean take you for a walk?"

"Sean, you running in the race?" Tom asked.

"Yeah. Figured I'd give it a try." Sean grinned. "It's been a while, but it should be fun."

Tom turned to Claire, then looked at Taylor as she stepped out of the RV. "I guess that means the three of us will be cheering. That is, unless you intend to run, Taylor."

"You've got to be kidding. I'm way too old for that kind of thing."

"Thirty-one is *not* old." Willow gave her a playful look.

"Maybe not, but I'm out of shape." She looked down at her thin, shapely legs. "This body hasn't done any running since high school, but I'm pretty good at cheering." A crooked grin lifted her lips. "When I want to be."

A sky-blue minivan pulled up in front of the campsite.

"Oh! It's her." Willow stood, eyes pooling with tears. "It's been so long." She took a step toward the van.

The woman driving climbed out. She was tiny, with short blonde hair, and she looked like a younger version of Willow. "Mom. Hi." She stood her ground and didn't make a move toward her mother.

Willow closed the distance between them. "Melody, I'm so glad to see you." She didn't embrace her but reached out and touched her hands briefly.

A small, skinny, towheaded boy ran around from the other side of the van. "Grandma?" Wearing a big smile, he walked up to Willow and threw his arms around her waist. "I've been wanting to meet you."

Willow hugged him. "Carson, I'm so happy you're here."

He stood back and gazed up at her, as if he were meeting someone of great importance.

"You are so grown up." Willow bent and kissed his cheek, then ruffled his hair.

"I'm more than four feet tall now." When he smiled, the freckles scattered across the top of his nose seemed to spread out onto his cheeks. "And I'm real strong for ten."

"I can see that." Willow straightened and looked at her daughter. "Thank you for coming … and for bringing Carson."

"This reunion is long overdue." Melody looked at her mother with affection. Her gaze turned to Willow's bicycle. "I guess we better get your bike loaded. We don't want to be late."

"First, let me introduce you to my friends." Willow turned to her comrades. "Everyone, this is my daughter, Melody, and my grandson, Carson."

Tom stepped forward. "I'm Tom Cantrell. Nice to meet you, Melody." He patted Carson's back. "And you too, young man."

After the others had greeted Melody, Taylor closed Daisy inside the RV, and Sean helped Melody load Willow's bike onto the rack on the back of the van.

Melody moved to the driver's door. "Looks like we're all set. I brought some chairs and a cooler with food and drinks, and there's still room for everyone."

Carson grabbed hold of Willow's hand. "Mom, can I sit in back with Grandma?"

"Sure." She glanced at her mother and offered a fleeting smile. "You are all he's talked about for weeks now."

"Good," said Willow. "Then we're even." She rested a hand on his head. If people could hug with their eyes, she was certainly doing that.

"Shotgun," Sean called as he took the front seat.

Everyone else piled in the back.

He leaned toward Melody. "Hope you don't mind."

She laughed. "No problem, if that's where you want to sit."

Jealousy knotted in Claire's stomach. Melody was one of those extra pretty girls who jumped out of bed in the morning looking breathtaking. Some things just weren't fair.

After arriving at the park, it took Melody a few minutes to find a parking spot. "We better get to it. We still have to sign up." She, Carson, Willow, and Sean disappeared into the crowd.

After they returned with numbered vests worn over their shirts, Sean unloaded Willow's bike while Tom, Taylor, and Melody took out the chairs and cooler and set them up along the course.

Longing rushed through Claire. If only *she* had a vest and was taking part in the race. And if she was *normal*, she might have a chance with Sean. A dark mood threatened to overrun her, but she chased it off. Her disability was not going to ruin this special day.

"Okay, here's some water for you." Tom put a water bottle in a holder on the front of Willow's bike. "Make sure to stay hydrated. It's already getting hot, and the humidity is high."

"I'll be fine, but thank you. You're such a help."

Tom's smile deepened the lines in his face, but the look in his eyes was youthful. "Let's pray."

Pray? Tom wanted to pray?

He took Willow's hand. "Don't look at me like that. I believe in prayer." He winked at her. "At appropriate times."

Everyone gathered around, except for Melody, who hung back.

"Melody?" Willow released Tom's hand and extended it toward her daughter. "Will you join us?"

Melody hesitated, then took a step forward. "Sure." She grasped her mother's hand and Taylor's.

Tom bowed his head.

Claire closed her eyes. It would be difficult to concentrate on the prayer with Sean's hand in hers.

"Lord, I know how much you love Willow. And I'm asking that you help her today. Give her the strength she needs and let this be a spectacular day for her. I also pray for Carson, Melody, and Sean. Give them strong legs and the endurance they need to finish. And I ask that you make this a treasured memory they can take with them after the race is over. Amen."

Sean gave Claire's hand a gentle squeeze, and her stomach did a little flip.

"Oh, Tom, thank you." Willow gave him a big smile. "Well, I guess it's time to line up."

Willow went to get her bike, and Tom turned to Melody. "Are you going to be running next to your mother?"

"Why? Are you worried about her?"

"Yeah, a little. A 5K is quite a ways for her, even if she's riding a bike."

"Don't worry. We'll be running laps, so if she gets overly tired she can always sit out the remainder. And Carson and I will stay close to Mom."

"Thanks."

"Tom, she'll be fine," Taylor said. "She's been preparing for weeks."

Tom, Taylor, and Claire stood on the sidelines as the others made their way to the line. When the gun was fired and the racers took off, everyone cheered. Sean went to the front, his stride long and effortless.

He was good. Maybe he'd win.

Willow had a wobbly start, but, after a near fall, she pedaled away on the paved pathway, Melody on one side of her and Carson on the other.

A lump of emotion fixed itself in Claire's throat at the sight of the three of them together.

"Well, they're off," Tom said, fishing a bottle of water out of the cooler, and then siting in a patio chair. He swigged a gulp of water. "I wonder how high the temperature is already."

Claire sat in the chair beside him, and Taylor dropped into the one next to Claire.

A welcomed breeze carried the heady fragrance of jasmine and gardenia. The air was heating up, but joy pushed aside Claire's discomfort.

It didn't seem long before the first runner appeared. It was a tall, lanky man wearing a red baseball cap. Sean was next.

"Go, Sean!" Claire shouted. She glanced at Taylor. "He might win. Who knew he could run?"

Tom stood. "Yeah." He barely glanced at Sean. Instead, he watched the trail.

Several racers ran past.

He kept watching.

Willow appeared with Carson and Melody running alongside

her. She was still pedaling. And although she was flushed, she looked happy and gave them a triumphant smile as she rolled past.

Carson waved.

"Well, how about that," Tom said. "She's still riding." The pride in his voice couldn't be missed. This time he remained standing until the runners came around again. Willow was still going strong. He grabbed a hand towel out of a beach bag sat, and wiped sweat from his forehead. He downed several mouthfuls of water, then pushed back to his feet to watch.

Several runners and bikers passed. But not Willow.

"Where is she? She should have come past us by now."

Claire smiled. "We'll see her soon, I'm sure."

Finally, Willow came up the pathway, Carson and Melody on either side. She pedaled slowly, but kept moving. A few yards from the starting line, she slowed and stopped. "You two go on. I'll cheer for you."

Carson and Melody stopped. "Are you okay, Mom?" Melody asked.

"I'm fine, just old." She laughed. "I'll be waiting for you."

"All right."

Carson gave his grandmother a hug. "You did good, Grandma." He took off, running ahead of his mother.

Willow pushed her bike off the trail and parked it. "Whew, that was hard. But fun." She wiped her forehead.

Tom hugged her. "I'm so proud of your effort."

"I really wanted to finish, but we can't always have everything. I rode about half of the way. That's pretty good for an old lady." She blew out a big breath. "An old lady who needs to sit down." She lowered herself into the chair Tom had vacated.

"Here, how about some cold water." Tom took a bottle of water out of the cooler Melody had brought along. He opened it and handed the drink to Willow.

"Thank you." Willow took several swallows.

Together, Tom, Willow, Taylor, and Claire waited for the racers.

The first runner to appear wasn't Sean, and it wasn't the one who'd been in the lead most of the race. Instead it was a teenage boy

207

who sprinted across the finish line, looking as if he was barely winded.

Sean came in fourth and high-fived Tom. "I did it." He sucked in oxygen. "Not bad for being out of shape."

"I had no idea you could run." Willow handed him a bottle of water.

"I was in track in high school and college. But it's been a few years." He chugged down some water.

When Carson and Melody ran across the finish, they lifted their arms over their heads in triumph. Both wore big smiles.

"That was fun," said Carson. "Can we do it again?"

"Well, not right away." Melody was breathing hard as they joined the group. "But one day."

"I'm so proud of you." Willow hugged Carson.

"I'm proud of you too." He smiled up at his grandmother.

Melody joined them. "He did a good job." She turned to her mother. "And so did you. I know that wasn't easy for you."

"I wanted to do it. I love you, and I've enjoyed spending time with you."

Melody's eyes filled with tears. "I love you too, Mom." She wrapped her arms around Willow. "I've missed you."

Willow held on to her for a long moment. "I've missed you so much, sweetie." She took a step back and cradled Melody's face in her hands. "I'm so sorry for the way I raised you. If I could take it back I would."

"You know, I've thought about those days a lot. That life—it's part of who I am now. And I like me." She smiled. "It wasn't typical, definitely not perfect, but it's our history ... together. I'm sorry for staying angry for so long. Will you forgive me?"

"Of course. You have a right to be angry. I was young and irresponsible, and you suffered because of me." She hugged her daughter. "Are you sure your good will isn't all those endorphins running through your body? You know, a runner's high?"

"No. I've been aware of my anger for a long time, and I've been waiting for the right time to ask your forgiveness. Today is it." Melody wiped away tears and looked at the group. "So, is anyone hungry? I made a picnic."

"I'm starved," said Tom. He reached for Willow's hand, and a smile passed between the two of them, the kind shared only between couples in love.

Over the next few days, Willow devoted a lot of time to her daughter and grandson. Their last night there was the Fourth of July, and they spent the night on the beach, roasting hotdogs, eating s'mores, and watching fireworks just like other families. It was magical.

Willow's answered prayer gave Claire hope for her own.

CHAPTER THIRTY-TWO

Sean struggled to stay awake. He'd spent a lot of the previous night thinking about home instead of sleeping, and he'd be glad to have the day's drive behind him.

Willow leaned on the back of his seat. "How far to Panama City Beach?"

He glanced at her over his shoulder. "Less than four hundred miles. We'll be there today."

"The beaches there are mind-blowing," Tom said. "You're going to love it." He beamed a smile at Willow. "Ocean's warm as bath water."

"I don't know if I like that," Willow said. "The weather is so hot and steamy, cool water sounds better. Oh, it doesn't really matter. We're so close. Soon we'll be swimming with dolphins."

"Can't count on seeing them. They've got a mind of their own," Tom said. "Remember, they're wild."

"Oh, I know we'll see dolphins. We didn't come all this way for nothing. God will see to it that we get to swim with them."

Sean furrowed his brow. "I'm not so sure God's in the business of herding dolphins just so people can get a thrill."

"No. But he loves us, and he understands how far we've come and how important this is to us. He can make anything happen. Look what he did for me and my daughter." She wiped at her eyes. "I hated to say goodbye. Being with Carson and Melody was the most precious time in my life."

Tom put his weight on the arm rest and leaned closer to Willow. "Maybe we can go back."

Willow gave him a questioning look. "When and how are *we* going to do that? And why would *we* be traveling all the way to Georgia together?"

Tom sank back into his seat. "I don't know. Just sounds nice." A satisfied smile rested on his lips.

"I guess you'd better hire Sean on permanently, then, if you want to keep traveling."

Sean shook his head. "Hate to disappoint you, but I've got other plans. I like you guys, but it's time I got my feet back in the waters of the Pacific, the ones around Monterey specifically." What would it be like to be home, with all its unpleasant memories?

"I've never been there," Claire said. "Is it like the Oregon beaches?"

"No, better." He tossed her a smile in the mirror. "You'll have to visit Monterey one of these days. There's no place like it."

"You're going to see your parents?" Willow asked.

"Yeah. It's been a long time since I've even talked to them. Too long."

"Shame on you." Willow softened the remark with a smile.

"Sorry to say, but that's right. When I saw you with your daughter and grandson, I knew I had to see my folks." His mother always said she missed him, but his father was a different story.

"I'm glad."

"You know, if you and Tom want to keep traveling you'll need a driver. Maybe you ought to learn."

"I already know how, kind of. Remember? I got us to the campground back in Oregon."

"Barely got us there," Tom said.

"Tom and I will have to talk about it. If we decide I can drive, I'll need a teacher."

"And that would be …?" Sean narrowed his eyes and half grinned.

"Well, you, of course. We have a lot of road left for you to teach me."

He let out a sigh. Willow was an intelligent woman, but what kind of driving pupil would she be?

Willow squeezed his shoulder. "I think it's wonderful that you're going to see your parents, but I'll miss you." She looked back at Claire and Taylor. "We all will."

"Hey. I'm not gone yet." In truth, he wasn't ready to say goodbye to his new friends. But he wasn't about to let them know that. "I have to finish my end of this bargain."

Willow pushed herself up and moved to the sofa, sitting with care. "I don't know if my back will ever be the same after that bike ride."

"You'll feel better, just need to do a little floating around in the warm waters of the Gulf." Tom grinned. "Maybe I ought to get a bike too."

"That's a great idea," Claire said.

"I agree. We could ride together—when I can ride again." Willow cast Tom a smile.

Tom on a bicycle? He probably couldn't maintain his balance long enough to stay upright. Sean didn't say anything. Life was hard enough for Tom. And the least of Tom's worries was bike riding. He still planned to drive on a NASCAR track. In his condition, anything could happen during that event.

"I'm going to lie down," Willow said. "I didn't get much sleep last night, and I think we must be in for some changeable weather. My muscles are screaming at me."

Tom gazed at the sky. "The clouds *are* building up."

Willow moved to the back of the RV, stepped into the bedroom, and closed the door behind her.

"I don't like the looks of those," Taylor said. "And when I checked the weather report, it was calling for thunderstorms."

"That's what keeps this place so green. Guess we should be thankful," Tom said.

Taylor didn't need to know, but if they got hit by a bad storm, there was no shelter. And tornadoes were part of Alabama life. There was nothing they could do about it but trust God.

Wait.

Was Willow rubbing off on him?

There was a time when Sean's faith had been solid, but since his brother's illness and death, he wasn't sure about God. Where had he been when Benjamin needed him?

"No reason to worry about the weather. We'll be in Florida before you know it," Tom said.

"They have tornadoes there too." Taylor peered at the computer screen.

"But that's rare," Claire said.

When Sean drove through the next town, signs posted directions to the nearest shelters. It was little comfort. The signs were likely there because tornadoes were a real threat.

He scanned the darkening sky. The smell of rain was in the air. They were going to get it, but not knowing exactly what *it* might be made his palms sweat. He wiped them on his pants. Monterey was sounding better and better.

A snort came from Sean's right. Tom had nodded off and his chin rested on his chest. He'd likely have a sore neck when he woke up.

Sean checked the mirror.

Claire had fallen asleep too. Taylor worked on her computer and kept watch on the skies.

Sean was as alone as he could be on the coach. He watched green flatlands roll by, but his mind carried him back to his childhood.

It had seemed as if everyone was always on watch since his brother was sick most of the time. There were countless trips to the local hospital, and others to the clinics and hospitals in San Francisco to see specialists. Days were filled with treatments, the sound of his brother's struggle to breathe, and his mother's weary face and haunted eyes.

There had been good times too. He and Benjamin visited the pier to fish as often as they could, under the bay's misty-blue skies and gentle, rolling waves. But even when they were having a good time, Sean never forgot how sick his brother was. Would he have a bad spell? Would Sean know how to help? If things got bad would the EMTs get there in time?

The day Benjamin died, Sean had been out in the yard, tossing a Frisbee for their dog, Chuck. When he came inside he could hear Benjamin wheezing. In the end, there'd been nothing he could do except call the paramedics. They had taken Benjamin, but it had been too late.

Even now, as Sean drove down a highway in Alabama, the details of that day bombarded him—Benjamin quiet and still on the gurney, morose expressions on the EMTs' faces, no siren as the ambulance pulled away.

His stomach knotted. If he let Claire into his heart, would their days be all about life and death the way it had been with Benjamin? He couldn't go through that again. He couldn't be responsible.

A wall of rain charged toward the RV, drenching the road and tearing Sean from his thoughts. He slowed down.

It wasn't only rain. Oversized balls of ice bounced off the road and drummed against the roof of the RV.

"Is it a tornado?" Taylor's screech almost turned into a yell.

Tom snorted and sat up.

Claire roused. "What is it?"

Sean turned the wipers on high, but they did little to disperse the ice and rivers of water coursing down the windshield. "Hail."

Tom put on his glasses and peered into the deluge. "Maybe you should pull over. Those hailstones are big enough to pound holes in my coach."

Willow emerged from the bedroom and sat at the table across from Taylor. "The storm woke me." She gazed out at the downpour. "I've never seen it come down like that."

"In the movie *Twister*, there was always hail before a tornado," Taylor said.

"Hail doesn't mean we're going to have a tornado." Willow rested a hand on Taylor's. "Deep breaths, dear."

"There were tornado watches in the weather report."

"Yes, and we can thank God it wasn't a warning." Willow glanced out the window.

"What's the difference?"

"A watch means conditions can produce a tornado, but a warning means a tornado has been spotted."

"The last time I looked, there were just watches. I've lost the Internet connection."

Sean turned onto a side road. "I'll see if I can find a place to wait this out."

There wasn't any place to pull off.

He continued, moving slowly, trying to see through the deluge.

"Are we in Alabama?" Willow asked.

"Yeah. For a while now." Sean kept driving, but the hail didn't let up.

Taylor clasped her hands tightly on the top of the table. "This is awful. Are we lost?"

"We're fine," Sean said. "I know how to get back to the highway."

"If we don't get carried away by a tornado first." Taylor's voice sounded shrill.

Wind whipped the RV. If Taylor was right, they were in big trouble.

Gradually the hail stopped and the rain lightened up until sunlight peeked through the clouds. Fields the color of jade seemed to vibrate with life beneath the glimmer of the sun.

Willow stared out the window. "If I was an artist, I'd want to paint this. I think it's greener here than in Kentucky." Her gaze moved to an old country store. "Can we stop? I'm dying for an orange pop. I woke up thinking about it. That's Carson's favorite." Willow caught Sean's eye in the mirror. "And good job of driving through that storm, by the way. Thank you."

"Yeah. Thank you," Tom said and clapped.

Everyone joined in.

Sean gave them a small bow from his seat. The RV splashed through puddles as Sean pulled into a dirt parking area alongside the store. Mist drifted above the earth.

The store's shiplap siding had once been painted white, but time and weather had chipped away some of the color. Two aged gas pumps stood out front.

"This place is a wonder," Willow said. "I feel as if we've stepped back in time."

"Yeah, you can get bait, fishing gear, and while you're at it, you can get married too," Taylor quipped.

What? Sean scanned the store windows. A notice promoting weddings was posted on the front of the building, alongside a big red sign advertising Coke, a poster promoting a sale on sugar, fishing bait, and tackle. He chuckled.

He climbed out of the RV and headed for the store, avoiding sloppy mud. He opened the door and a bell's ring blended with the squeak of ancient hinges.

A scrawny-looking man wearing overalls stared at him from behind a pile of cabbages.

The bins of cabbage, beets, and potatoes weren't something Sean had ever seen in a Fast Stop station.

The man stepped into the aisle between vegetable bins, hands in his pockets. "How do. Anything I can help you with?"

"I'm just looking for something to drink."

The store smelled of pipe tobacco and plums.

"Right over there in the cooler." He nodded toward the back of the store.

The jingling bell and creaking hinges announced Willow, Tom, Claire, and Taylor.

"That was quite a storm come through," the man said.

"Sure was." Sean headed for the icebox. There wasn't a lot of choice. He grabbed a single coke for himself, a Pepsi six-pack, and one of orange soda.

Taylor joined him. "Had to see this for myself." She glanced at the man in overalls and spoke in low tones. "Reminds me of *Green Acres* reruns. And weddings? Can you imagine a wedding in this place?" She surveyed the room. "Where?"

"I think it's charming." Willow opened the refrigerator door and grabbed an orange soda. "Can never have too many," she said to Sean with a wink.

Claire stood in front of a basket piled with plums. After picking up one, she held it under her nose and breathed in.

Sean sidled up to her. "You planning on buying some of those or just smelling them?"

"The smell reminds me of home. We had plum trees on the ranch. My sisters and I used to wait until they were ripe, then we'd climb up the tree, sit on a branch, and eat ourselves sick. There's nothing better than warm plums right off the tree." She placed a few in a small paper bag.

"This isn't anything like where I grew up, but it feels homey somehow." Sean grabbed a bag of corn chips, then walked up to the register and waited while Willow paid for her drink. "Nice store," he told the man in overalls. "And I couldn't help but notice your advertisement for weddings."

"Yes, sir." He pulled a handkerchief out of his pocket and wiped sweat from his face. "You thinking on getting married? We can set you up. We've got a nice little chapel out back. My wife would be proud to help you and your young lady." He glanced at Claire.

If only she could belong to him. "She's not my young lady. I was just curious."

And even if Claire was his young lady, he'd never get married in a place like this. She deserved to have a spectacular wedding.

An image of her in a long white wedding gown flashed through his mind. Devotion for the woman in his imagination crashed over him before he could dispel the image.

"Well, you let me know if you two change your minds. Easy as pie to get your wedding license—no waiting period." He smiled, blue eyes shimmering with mischief.

"We're going to take Daisy for a walk," Tom said and escorted Willow out of the store.

Sean opened his Coke and took a swig as Claire walked up to the register. "Well, I guess we need to get back on the road if we want to make it to Panama City Beach today."

"That's where you're heading?" the man asked.

"Yeah. Got sidetracked by the storm."

"I love the beaches down that way. Me and the wife go whenever we can. You have a good time."

"Thanks. We will." Sean headed outside. Where did Tom and Willow go? He took another drink of his soda and spotted them and Daisy walking out of a building just beyond the store.

Willow wore a peculiar expression as she and Tom approached the RV, their hands clasped.

Taylor and Claire sauntered out of the store and joined Sean.

As Tom and Willow approached, Willow burst into a smile. "We have news." She looked at Tom then back at the others. "We're getting married." She linked her arm with his.

"What?" That couldn't be right. Tom and Willow?

"We had a look at the chapel. It's adorable." Willow gazed up at Tom. "We love each other."

"We do." Tom circled an arm around Willow. "So we figured why not? We're not getting any younger."

"You can't be serious," Taylor said. "Married? Here?"

"Yes. It's perfect. This is a charming place, and the chapel is quaint." Willow leaned against Tom.

Sean looked at the building with its peeling white paint and dirty windows. He didn't see quaint. Rustic, maybe. "Well, it's none of my business what you do."

"I think it's wonderful. I'm so happy for you." Claire hugged them both.

"Don't you need a license?" Taylor asked.

"Yes," Tom said. "And now that Willow has said yes, I'm going to find out how to get one. I'll be right back." He headed for the store. Willow skipped a few steps to catch up and walked inside with him.

The two reappeared a few minutes later. "The owner said there's a courthouse in town. And there's no waiting period in Alabama." Tom patted his pocket. "I've got the directions right here."

What did Tom think he was doing? He and Willow weren't anything alike. She was a fanatical Christian, and Tom rarely even spoke about God. It would never work.

A few minutes later, Tom emerged from the store, a piece of paper in hand. "Got them. Let's go. His wife's going to set up while we're in town."

Willow approached Claire. "Do you think you could oversee while we're gone?"

"Absolutely. Don't worry about any of it."

Sean took off with Tom and Willow. What had gotten into them? It was crazy to get married, especially in a shanty. And they were both sick. Tom had MS, for crying out loud. His life would likely be short.

Town was only a few miles from the store, and the clerk in the small courthouse didn't blink an eye over Tom and Willow's request for a marriage certificate. In fact, she congratulated them.

Tom and Willow were acting like kids. They were being irrational. Someone needed to talk sense into them.

Once Sean parked the RV beside the store, he took Tom aside as Willow disappeared into the bedroom. "Are you sure this is what you want? You two don't even get along most of the time."

"Sure. We just bicker, but that's mostly for fun. She's an uncommon and loving woman, and I'm lucky to have won her heart. There's no reason we shouldn't get married." He clapped Sean on the back. "Don't worry about us. You should be thinking about yourself. If you don't get over being afraid to love, you'll live out your life alone and unhappy."

He wasn't afraid—he was being reasonable. But even as he silently argued with Tom, Sean knew the truth. But he didn't know what to do about it.

Tom glanced at the bedroom door. "I've been given a second chance. I loved my first wife and I miss her, but she'd like Willow, and she'd be happy for me." He nailed Sean with a searing gaze. "When you meet the right girl, you need to follow through, not hold back. You might not have another opportunity."

Tom didn't know anything about what Sean should do with his life. The last thing Sean wanted was to be saddled with someone who was sick and, in all likelihood, would continue to be sick until the day she died. He'd had all of sickness he could take.

Willow stepped out of the bedroom wearing a peach dress with a sheer layer over it. She held her arms away from her body. "How do I look?"

"You're beautiful." Tom kissed her cheek. "Time for me to clean up."

Willow went with Claire and Taylor to check out the chapel. When she stepped inside, her gaze roamed over the room and a smile brightened her face. "It's perfect. Thank you" She gave them each a quick hug. "I can't believe I'm doing this."

"Me either," Taylor said.

"I think it's wonderful." Claire looped her arm through Willow's, and they walked outside. "You need a bouquet. I noticed some wildflowers in the field."

219

"They'd be just right."

The ladies gathered wildflowers, and then walked back to the RV. Taylor made a wreath out of some of them. "This time I'm not out of my mind," she said when she placed it on Willow's head. "And you're a flower child again." She smiled. "You look so pretty."

"Thank you." Willow hugged her, then Claire. "I guess it's time." She looked at Sean. "Don't look so glum. Be happy for us."

Sean scrambled to his feet. His heart wasn't in this, but he had to at least act supportive. "I am happy for you." He gave Tom a friendly slap on the back.

"Thanks. I better get over to the chapel." Tom dropped a kiss on Willow's cheek. "See you at the church."

"See you."

Tom hurried out ahead of his friends.

"Come on, Daisy. We can't get married without you." Willow clasped the leash on the boxer and led her out of the RV.

Willow, Claire, Sean, and Taylor walked to the chapel together. Sean opened the door and the ladies stepped inside.

Tom was already up front, waiting.

The chapel wasn't what Sean expected. A wood floor gleamed in the afternoon sunlight streaming in through narrow windows. Mahogany benches had been polished, and each had a white bow attached to the end closest to the middle aisle. A lace-covered table stood at the front of the room, holding a burning candle and a large, black leather Bible. A short, stout woman sat at a piano, softly playing an old hymn.

The man from the store stood in front of the table. He'd changed into a suit. Was he a genuine chaplain?

Sean ushered Claire and Taylor to a bench, and they sat together while Willow waited in the back.

When the pianist looked at the pastor and he gave her a nod she changed to a new song, unfamiliar, but exquisite. The pastor motioned for them to rise and Claire and Taylor stood.

Sean followed their example.

The bench was short, forcing Sean to stand close to Claire, too close. Her arm brushed against his, but he forced himself not to look at her and watched Willow.

She started down the aisle, her eyes on Tom. A soft smile rested upon her lips. She was stunning and she didn't limp. Interesting what love could do for a person.

When Willow reached the front of the room, Tom caught her hand in his and they faced the chaplain.

He spoke about love, commitment, and the Lord. The shop owner was no longer that funny little man in the store, but a man of God. The chapel might be old and in need of paint, and sitting behind a run-down store that sold fishing gear and bait, but that didn't matter. At this moment, it was the Lord's house.

As Tom and Willow gave their lives to one another, Sean couldn't tamp down the joy rising up inside.

They'd found each other … just as they should.

Sean was also acutely aware of Claire sitting beside him. Was it possible God had brought them together?

He glanced at her.

She looked at him, their eyes held, and something sparked between them.

What did he *really* feel for her? Was it pity or love?

CHAPTER THIRTY-THREE

Sean pulled into the parking lot of the Comfort Inn hotel, where Tom and Willow had stayed the previous evening.

The newlyweds waved from the entrance.

"They look happy." Claire opened the door, trying to ignore the thorn in her heart.

Sean climbed out.

"This is going to take some getting used to," Taylor said. "Tom and Willow married. It's bizarre."

"I think it's wonderful and romantic," Claire said. Would there ever be a marriage for her? She quickly released the thought and greeted Tom and Willow. "Good morning, lovebirds."

Willow smiled as she walked up the steps. "Hello, everyone."

Claire pulled Willow into her arms and gave her a tight squeeze. "I'm so happy for you."

Willow hugged her back. "Thank you, sweetie." She glanced at Tom. "It's finally time we swam with dolphins." She laughed, the sound reminiscent of wind chimes in a gentle breeze.

"That, and do some fishing." Carrying one overnight bag, Tom struggled up the steps of the RV.

Sean brought in the other bag. "Are you all set for Panama City Beach?"

"Ready to go," Tom said, settling on the sofa beside Willow.

Taylor was in her usual spot at the table.

Claire moved to the front passenger seat. She looked at Sean, but he barely glanced at her. Was something bothering him?

The look that had passed between them at the wedding had felt like a spark of electricity. She knew he felt it too. Maybe that's what was wrong. Was he afraid of what might happen between them? If not, she was scared enough for both of them.

They left the surprising events and memories of the country store and its chapel behind and set off for Florida.

Miles passed and the hours dragged.

"We're close to the state line," Claire said, looking at a map on her cell phone. "It won't be long now."

Taylor closed her computer. "I'm not about to miss our first moment in Florida."

When they passed a sign welcoming them to the state, cheers erupted from everyone.

"I can hardly wait to get there," Willow said.

Claire's mind carried her back to their first day on the road. It felt like another life. The trip had seemed impossible. Yet, like a fairy tale come true, they'd crossed the country and were about to reach their goal—swimming with wild dolphins.

"Hey, Sean," Tom called. "Willow and I were talking, and we'd like to stay at the Holiday Inn hotel. It's right on the beach."

"Sure. We can drop you off."

"No. We want everyone to stay there."

"Count me out," Taylor said. "I can't afford it."

"My treat."

What had become of Tom, the grouch who'd started the trip with them? Mile by mile he'd changed. And when he fell in love he'd become even happier. "Tom, you've been so generous, but I'm starting to feel guilty," Claire said. "You've already paid for so much."

"It's my pleasure. I've got plenty of money. And I'd like us to do something special together." He moved up behind Sean. "I'm rescheduling my NASCAR drive. When I call later today, should I add your name to the list?"

"Sure. That sounds great. I've never driven a NASCAR anything before."

∞☯ ☯∞

Claire could hardly wait to get a glimpse of the ocean, as Sean drove the RV through the town of Panama City Beach.

"Look at all the palm trees." Taylor moved to the sofa and stared out the window. "They're so tall and regal-looking."

Sean followed the road around a big curve, and the view opened

223

up, revealing a white-sand beach that reached down to an aqua-blue sea.

"There's the ocean!" Claire said.

The coach bounced as they crossed a drawbridge that spanned an inlet, next to a marina.

Willow gaped. "I've never seen so many boats."

Sean maneuvered around a tight curve. "I'd sure like to give sailing a try."

Tom clapped a hand on his shoulder. "Maybe we can take a crack at it while we're here."

The two-lane highway followed a shoreline that could only be seen occasionally through gaps between hotels that stood along the beaches.

"It's so beautiful. I've never seen white sand, or water that is so many shades of blue and green." Delight spilled from Claire. They'd actually made it.

"Yeah. Amazing," Sean said. "I'll be coming back."

"Be watching for the hotel." Sean studied each entrance as they approached. Most of the hotels looked new.

"There it is!" Taylor cried.

Claire moved to the sofa and looked out the window.

A large sign welcomed visitors to the Holiday Inn, which stood at least twelve stories and was surrounded by palm trees and broad-leafed plants.

Sean turned into the parking area and drove under the covered parking to check in.

"You stay put. I'm going in." Tom was smiling, but he couldn't hide the weakness in his legs as he climbed out of the RV. Fifteen minutes later he reappeared and walked around to the driver's window. "We're on this end. There's an elevator that will take us up to the tenth floor and our rooms. I got three adjacent. And we'll have a great view."

Two cars parked behind them.

Sean started the engine. "I'd better get this monster out of the way. Everyone go ahead and get off, then I'll park and find a luggage cart."

"I'll give you a hand," Claire said. But just what could she do to actually help?

Willow put Daisy on the leash and headed for the door. "I can't wait to see our room. Daisy's not a problem, is she?"

"No. Just paid a pet fee."

Willow, Tom, and Taylor headed toward the outdoor elevator.

"Keep an eye out for a spot big enough to park this thing," Sean said.

They had traveled only a short way down the row when she pointed out a parking area designated for RVs.

Sean parked. "I'll be right back." He walked toward the hotel entrance.

Claire collected the overnight bags and set them by the door, then got Taylor's computer and guitar. The rooms would most likely have refrigerators, so she put a few food items in a bag. She'd just finished when Sean exited the hotel, pushing a cart.

"It was the last one," he said as he stepped inside the RV. "Hey, you've been busy. Thanks." Sean loaded the larger bags first, then added the smaller items Claire had gathered and Taylor's guitar. "All set?"

"Oh yes."

After they reached the elevator, which ran on the outside of the building, Claire stepped in and leaned against the wall while Sean jockeyed the cart into place.

He pushed the button and smiled at her, his hazel eyes almost balmy.

Claire grabbed hold of the handrail, willing her legs to remain sturdy enough to hold her. If only those amazing eyes would see her and not her illness. "You know, I'm more than dysautonomia. It's not who I am." Had she said that out loud?

"I know." The guitar started to slide off the cart, and Sean secured it, then looked at her. "I do know, Claire. Really."

CHAPTER THIRTY-FOUR

The elevator had big windows on two sides and the doors were mostly glass. As it first left the ground, dizziness swamped Claire. She pressed a hand against a window and closed her eyes for a moment to control the vertigo. When she opened them her gaze went to the breathtaking view of the Gulf Coast with its sugar-colored sand and vibrant gulf waters. "This is like a dream. I never expected such an exotic resort." She wanted to put her stuff away, run to the beach, and fling herself into the ocean.

The elevator stopped and they stepped out. A walkway followed the outside of the building, bordered by a waist-high wall. It was disconcerting at first, and Claire stayed close to the building and away from the wall.

"Taylor probably didn't like this much." Sean grinned and kept moving, counting off the room numbers until he reached 1031. "This is Tom and Willow's room." He knocked.

Tom answered the door with a big smile. "Howdy. How do you like it?"

"I haven't seen much," Sean said. "But so far … very nice."

Tom took his bag and set it on the floor. "Your room is ten thirty-two, and the girls are in ten thirty-three." He unloaded Willow's bags. "Make yourselves comfortable. We'll see you later." He winked and closed the door.

"Do you ever remember Tom winking?" Claire said.

"Can't say that I do." Sean grinned.

Claire led the way to her room and knocked when she got there.

Taylor flung the door open. "Come in. You won't believe this place. It's amazing." She crossed the room to a balcony. "Look at this."

Claire and Sean followed her, leaving the cart outside the door. When Claire first stepped out on the balcony, the height made her light-headed and she grabbed hold of the railing. "We're so high."

"Oh yeah. Takes a little getting used to. But we can see

everything from here."

The balcony looked down on a huge swimming pool bordered by palm trees, and huts with grass rooftops. Beyond that, the sand reached to the ocean waters.

Wind, carrying tantalizing sea air, caressed Claire's face. She brushed it aside and breathed deeply. "I could get used to this."

Sean peered at something offshore. "Hey, someone's parasailing. I can't wait to get down there. I'm going to try that." He watched the parasailer, then moved back inside. "Where do you want your bags?"

Taylor plopped down on the bed closest to the sliding glass door. "Put mine over there by the dresser."

"Can you set my bag on my bed?" Claire grabbed her overnight case and carried it into the bathroom, which was near the main door.

Taylor got her guitar. "Thanks for bringing up my stuff."

"No problem. Guess I'll check out my room."

"Tom wants to have dinner at the hotel restaurant at six o'clock," Taylor said.

"Okay. See you then." Sean pulled the door closed.

Claire put away her things, then grabbed a bottle of iced tea and sat at the patio table. She leaned her head back against the chair and closed her eyes, allowing the breeze and smell of the Gulf to wash over her. It would be perfect, if only she were stronger. Would the longing to be healthier and sturdier ever yield? *Lord, give me the strength and courage to do all that I can, and the peace that only you can give to accept my weaknesses.*

Claire took a few photos of the view and posted them on her Facebook page with the caption, *Can you believe this is the view from my room?* Then she posted a note to her mother, telling her a little about the last couple of days and asking how she was doing.

Melissa would have loved this—she'd have joined Sean parasailing. A spell of melancholy settled over Claire.

Taylor sat across the table from her. "So this is what it feels like to be rich. Always wondered."

Claire took a drink of her tea. "I could stay here the rest of my life." She let her gaze rest upon the grandeur that sprawled out in front of her.

After dinner everyone decided to check out the beach. Tom and Willow strolled leisurely along the water's edge, arms linked, caught up in a private conversation.

Taylor waded into the water. "It's so warm! You've got to try it." She moved deeper into the water, then walked parallel to the shoreline.

Claire took off her flip-flops and walked to the water's edge, where small breakers lapped at her toes. "I never imagined it would feel this warm, truly like bath water." She stepped deeper in, relishing the caress of water and soft sand.

Sean pulled off his T-shirt and threw it on the beach, then splashed past Taylor and dove beneath a wave. He came up, took a gulp of air, and brushed his hair off his face. He turned toward shore wearing a big smile.

Sean was beautiful to look at—tall, slender at the waist, with a broad chest and lean, muscular arms. His dark, wet hair curled onto his forehead.

"This is worth every mile driven." He held out a hand to Claire. "Come on in, deeper."

"I'm still in my clothes."

"So?"

"They'll get soaked."

"So?"

Maybe it didn't matter. Shorts weren't much more than a swimsuit bottom, and her dark-blue blouse was light cotton and sleeveless. But … take his hand? She wasn't about to let him manipulate her. He had no plans for them.

The sensation of waves catching at her ankles, sand slipping away beneath her feet, and Sean's outstretched arm overwhelmed Claire with emotion. Her breath caught in her chest, and the world spun.

No. Not now.

She willed herself to remain calm and upright, then took a step toward Sean. Instead of taking his hand, she lifted her arms and held them out from her sides and moved deeper into the water until it was up to her chest. When the next wave washed in, she leaned back and allowed it to carry her toward shore. She was weightless and agile, moving fast. She felt young and healthy.

It was like finding a treasure she'd forgotten existed.

When her feet found the bottom, she stood up. Laughing, she flipped back her hair. Even the sting in her eyes and the sharp, salty taste on her tongue was delicious.

Staring at her, Sean moved toward her, admiration in his eyes. And something more.

She glanced down at her clothing. Could he see through her blouse? She dropped her arms, turned around, and pulled her shirt away from her skin.

"What's wrong? Is something wrong?"

"No. Nothing. You … you were just looking … at me …"

Sean chuckled. "You caught me. But you can't blame a guy for looking at gorgeous."

He was so close he could touch her. Water beaded on his chest, and for a moment he acted as if he would embrace her. Suddenly he turned and dove into another wave.

Claire plopped down into the water, joy swelling inside. For a short time, she'd left behind the real Claire, and so had Sean.

What if she could always feel like this? Was it possible?

Maybe. Tom seemed so much better since he and Willow had fallen in love. Was love enough? Or was that just a girlish dream?

Taylor had left the water and now walked down the beach. Sean moved on, heading toward a parasailing boat a couple of hundred yards away. Tom and Willow had found beach chairs that sat right behind the hotel.

Claire headed to the hotel, trying to turn her thoughts to the goodness in her life and the beauty that surrounded her right now. Clearly, she couldn't change who she was and needed to make peace with that. She just didn't know how … not in any lasting way.

And was accepting the same as giving up?

When she got back to her room, she showered, changed into dry clothes, and lay on her bed, exhausted. Sleep was all she wanted.

She had just started to nod off when Taylor walked in.

"I thought we were going out tonight."

Claire pried open her eyes and looked at her friend. "I'm really tired. Think I'll stay in."

"I'm not going without you. And I want to go. So get up."

Claire groaned and rolled onto her side. "Really?"

"Yes. Really."

She pushed herself upright. "Okay. But I need to put myself together." She took extra care with her looks, combing her hair into a twist and pinning it with a tortoise shell barrette. She slipped on a casual summer dress, its powder-blue color especially flattering. Would Sean look at her the way he had on the beach?

By the time she and Taylor went downstairs to the outdoor nightclub at the pool, music was playing and people were milling about. Some were dancing. Real life, the ranch, and Cinnamon all seemed far away, a part of someone else's life.

Sean found her. "Do you want to dance?"

She wanted Sean to like her, not think about what a poor dancer she was. "No. I'm not any good at it."

"I didn't ask if you were good." He smiled.

"Okay. But don't say I didn't warn you." She let him pull her into his arms. She'd never been held by a man before, except her father. She felt stiff and clumsy, but in Sean's arms, she was barely aware of her pain.

He smelled of aftershave and looked more handsome than usual. His hand on her back felt warm, protective. Should she press in closer? She wanted to, but she couldn't even look at him.

As if reading her mind, he gently drew her nearer.

Before she knew it, she'd rested her cheek against his shoulder, feeling as if she belonged there.

If only it were true.

The music stopped, but she didn't want the dance to end. They stepped apart. What should she say?

A man with a microphone leaped onto a small stage and announced that karaoke was starting.

Willow walked up to her. "Let's do it—you, me, and Taylor."

"Sing?"

"Yes. It will help Taylor break the ice. And it'll be fun. I've done it before."

"I don't know how to do karaoke." Claire's stomach churned. Willow would persist until she gave in and ended up on the stage.

"It's easy. The music plays and the words are on the screen. You'll see." Willow took her hand and led her across the room to Taylor, who stood at the bar. "We're going to sing karaoke and we need you to help us."

"No way."

"Aw, come on. I want to do it. So does Claire."

Claire would have differed with Willow had she been given a chance.

"I need both of you." Willow gave Taylor a pleading look. "Please?"

"Okay." The word seemed to fall out of Taylor's mouth in slow motion. "But what song?"

"What about the latest Carrie Underwood tune? We all know it. It's been playing on the radio for the last few thousand miles."

Taylor nodded tentatively. "I guess."

Willow turned toward the stage. "We'll do it," she called out and waved at the man.

"I think we have some singers. Come on up."

Willow pulled Claire through the crowd and up the steps onto the stage.

Claire stared at the sea of faces. Her heart raced. How had she let Willow get her into this? What if she fainted?

"We've got three beautiful young women here," the announcer said. "And what song do you want to sing?"

"Do you have Carrie Underwood's new single?"

The man looked at the disc jockey, who nodded. "We sure do. Good luck." He stepped off the stage.

The music started, but it sounded too loud, too fast. What were the words? She couldn't remember. She was going to be sick.

Willow didn't look nervous at all. She held the microphone in front of the three of them.

Words flashed onto a small screen on the stage to their right.

Taylor and Willow sang out, but Claire missed the first line, then quickly caught up. They sounded terrible. Surely they'd get booed off the stage.

But the crowd cheered them on.

By the time they got to the second verse, they were doing much better. Taylor's voice grew stronger. Claire didn't sound too awfully bad, and her nerves had quieted down.

When she spotted Sean in the audience, she tried to read his expression. What was he thinking? He wore a satisfied smile and had a look in his eyes that she'd seen before—was it admiration or maybe longing?

Claire managed to make it through the song without fainting or getting sick. When she, Willow, and Taylor finished, the crowd clapped and roared their approval. Claire felt like cheering too, especially when it was Sean who cheered the loudest of all, his eyes on her.

Was there a real chance for them? Or was this just a game to him?

CHAPTER THIRTY-FIVE

What was that noise? Claire dredged herself from sleep.

The phone.

She fumbled to find it on the bedside table. "Hello."

"Time to get up." Willow sounded way too cheerful.

Eyes closed, Claire rolled onto her back. Why was Willow calling? She pried open one eye and looked at the clock—seven thirty.

"Did you forget to set your alarm? We're going to Shell Island."

"Oh no! Why didn't my alarm go off?" She looked more closely at her clock and groaned. She'd set it for p.m. instead of a.m.

"Tom scheduled a taxi to take us to the shuttle."

"How long do we have?" Claire asked through a yawn.

"About forty-five minutes."

Claire let out a heavy breath. "All right. I'll wake up Taylor."

"We'll see you in the lobby." The phone went dead.

Claire hung up the phone and pushed herself upright. Every inch of her hurt. And she could already feel the burning in her feet. "Taylor. We have to get up."

Grumbling came from the lump in Taylor's bed.

"That was Willow. We only have forty-five minutes until we leave for Shell Island."

Taylor pulled the blanket over her head.

Claire sat up and dropped her feet over the side of the bed. When they hit the floor it felt as if needles were poking into her soles. Last night had been too much. But it had been worth it. She smiled.

∾◦⊙ ⊙◦∾

After a breakfast of coffee and bagels, Taylor and Claire headed down to meet Tom and Willow.

Sean caught up to them just before they reached the elevator.

233

"Good morning, ladies." He looked like he was in a good mood.

"Good morning," Claire said.

Taylor gave him a nod.

How did he do it? How did anyone jump out of bed in the morning ready for the day? Had she been like that before she was sick?

No, she'd never been like that.

Taylor stepped into the elevator first. She gripped the handrail and stared at the floor. The doors closed and they started down. "I hate all the windows. I can see too much."

"Just look out at the view. It's spectacular." A look of what might be compassion touched Sean's face. "And did you notice that we can see the sunrise from the entrance of our rooms and the sunset from the balcony? Great layout."

Sean was so confident, yet Claire couldn't think of anything to talk about. What could she say after last night? Had something really happened between them, or was she making too much of a dance and a little flirting? People flirted all the time.

"Ready to swim with the dolphins?" Sean asked.

"Yes, but I'm a little nervous. They *are* wild."

"Could this thing be any slower?" Taylor griped. When it stopped at the ground floor, she stepped out the moment the doors opened. "I could barely breathe in there."

Sean threw Claire an amused glance, and the two followed Taylor.

Tom and Willow stood by the front entrance. Two small coolers sat on the sidewalk beside them. Tom looked like the typical Florida tourist—canvas hat, sunglasses, bright orange shorts, and flip-flops. He held up a hand of greeting. "Morning."

"You look like you're ready for the beach," Sean said.

"And how about me?" Willow did a small twirl, her gauzy peach dress swirling away from her body. A gust of wind nearly snatched her floppy hat from her head. She resettled it and adjusted her sunglasses.

"You look beautiful," Claire told her. "I think I need to be more creative." She looked down at her jean shorts and tennis shoes. She shifted her beach bag to the other shoulder.

"We're going to need some gear," Tom said. "There's a shop at the park where we catch the shuttle."

Once they got there, they all purchased snorkeling gear, and Tom and Sean bought swim fins. They also bought snacks and drinks, then the taxi took them through the large park to the shuttle.

The shuttle looked like a pontoon boat—open on all sides with a roof and bench seats. Tom and Willow moved to the back, and Sean, Taylor, and Claire sat on the bench across the aisle from them.

Nerves skittered through Claire. She'd never been on the ocean before and, as horrible as she felt, should not be venturing out at all today. But she might not feel any better tomorrow or the next day. They'd come so far, and this could be her only chance to do something thrilling like swim with dolphins. She had to tough it out.

A handful of other passengers stepped aboard and found places to sit.

"Not crowded," Willow said. "I expected more people."

"Could have something to do with the time," Taylor said, voice laced with sarcasm. She stuck her legs out in front of her and folded her arms around her waist. "As soon as we get there, I'm going to find a shady place and take a nap."

The captain started the engine and backed away from the pier. He turned the boat and headed out of the harbor.

Claire pressed a hand to her stomach. "How far is it to the island?" she called.

"We'll be there in less than twenty minutes. But I can't take you around to the west side this morning. The tide's not cooperating with our schedule. I'll drop you at the beach on the lagoon side, and you can walk to the west beaches."

Silence settled over the group.

"How far is the walk?" Tom finally asked.

"Not bad, less than a mile. It's easy walking, just follow the shoreline. Don't try cutting across. You might run into a rattlesnake. And there's a lake, so you never know about gators. There's nothing on the island, no businesses or houses, not even an outhouse. Once I leave, you're on your own."

A thud went off in Claire's gut. Snakes? Alligators? Completely on their own?

What had they gotten themselves into?

The boat cut smoothly through the calm waters of the bay. There was nothing to worry about. She was certain the shuttle wouldn't drop people off in a place that was dangerous. She focused on the beauty of the Gulf. She'd never seen seawater that was such a deep shade of blue. It looked even more intense when contrasted by the pale blue sky, dotted with wisps of white clouds.

A small fish leaped out of the water, a dolphin close behind. The fish leaped again, swimming for its life.

"Look! That dolphin's trying to catch a fish," a boy shouted.

Everyone moved to that side of the boat to watch the fish hurl itself through the water.

The chase went on a few seconds longer until the dolphin won out, succeeding at catching its breakfast.

The skyline of hotels lining the beach grew smaller as the shuttle cruised across open waters and headed for the island. As they approached, there was no sign of humankind, unusual in a world of sun and tourism.

The boat headed into a beach and slid out a catwalk that reached the shore. "I'll be back this way every hour. Last trip of the day is at five o'clock," the skipper said. "Don't miss the last run, or you'll be spending the night."

Passengers unloaded and the ramp was hauled back in. The boat moved into the lagoon and set off toward Panama City Beach. The other passengers headed down the shore and quickly disappeared as they rounded the island.

There was nothing—no shops, no bathrooms, no people. Just large dunes where grasses and small trees grew. Did the snakes and alligators ever come down to the beach?

Willow adjusted her hat and looked down the water's edge. "It's wonderful how Florida has preserved this place. Civilization is close, but it doesn't feel like it." She walked to the water and waded in. "And I've never seen water this clear. You can see the sandy bottom, just like you're looking through glass."

Taylor stepped into the water. "Weird. I can see my feet perfectly."

Willow turned and gazed down the beach in the direction the other passengers had gone. "I wonder how long it will take to get to the other side of the island."

"Only one way to find out." Tom picked up one of the small easy-carry coolers and held his arm out to Willow. She waded back to shore, hooked her arm through his, and the two of them started walking.

Sean grabbed the other cooler and strode up the beach.

Claire would have gladly stayed put. It was beautiful right where she was. Walking all the way to the other side of the island would take all of her strength. "Maybe if we wait, the dolphins will come around to this side of the island."

"Not likely. If we want to see dolphins, we're gonna have to hoof it." Tom adjusted his grip on the cooler and kept walking, his left foot dragging lightly across the sand.

If he could walk it, so could she. Her snorkeling gear in one hand and her beach bag in the other, she ambled along, trying to keep up. She should have brought her cane. Along the edge of the water, the sand was compact enough that it shouldn't sink.

Taylor ran ahead, and Sean walked beside Claire. Back in Oregon, when they'd talked about swimming with dolphins, this was not what Claire had imagined—walking on an empty beach with the sun beating down so intensely that she was sweating. There was no shade. The only place that had trees also had snakes and gators.

She kept moving. The island had the same white sand that swept into the beaches in front of their hotel. The dunes were so white they looked like a winter landscape.

The beach would have been an easy walk for most people, but Claire's heart pounded hard, fast, and erratically. Her body ached and she was lightheaded. She stopped walking. Maybe cooling off in the water would help. She stepped into the ocean. Even though it was warm, it was refreshing. She splashed water on her arms and chest.

Tom and Willow joined her. "Are you all right?" Willow asked.

"Not so great," Claire admitted. "I need to rest." She walked out of the water and sat down.

Willow sat beside her. "It's hot out here. We should have brought an umbrella."

Taylor ran back toward them and then waded in and gazed at the water's surface. "Oh!" She backed up in a hurry.

"What?" Tom stepped in and slowly moved toward Taylor.

"Tom, you be careful," Willow said. "There are bull sharks around here."

Sean splashed alongside Tom.

"It's a jellyfish," Taylor said. "I've never seen one like this. It's huge. In the center it has what looks like a clover traced in pink, and the outside edges are lined with the same pink color."

Tom and Sean strained through waist-deep water to get to Taylor.

"Don't touch it," Willow ordered. "We don't know one jellyfish from another. You don't want to get stung. I'm a nurse, but out here I wouldn't be much help."

The men joined Taylor and stood looking down at the water. "You should see this," Tom said.

"I'm fine right where I am," Willow said.

Claire would have liked to see the jellyfish, but she was too exhausted to move. If only she could take a picture of it.

Finally Taylor, Tom, and Sean walked back to shore. "I'll look that up on the computer when we get back." Taylor stopped and picked up a shell. "This is pretty—pink. Here's another one." She picked it up.

"Lots of shells here. Guess that's where the island gets its name." Tom gave Willow a hand up. "Ready, wife?"

"I'm ready." She turned to Claire. "Are you up to it?"

Claire pushed to her feet, but the earth tipped and the sea and sky spun. She sat back down. "I don't think I can keep going. It's the heat and walking."

"How about a ride?" Sean scooped her up in his arms, smiled at her, then started walking.

His arms felt hot, but strong. "You don't have to carry me."

"What are you going to do? Fly?"

"No." This was humiliating. "I can wait for you right here."

"We drove all the way across the country so you could swim with dolphins. I'm not about to leave you here on the beach, only steps away from them." He tightened his hold.

Claire quit arguing. She wanted to see the dolphins, and she didn't exactly dislike being in Sean's arms. "Okay. Thank you." She glanced behind them.

Taylor grabbed the cooler Sean had been carrying and followed the others.

By the time they reached the west beach, Tom and Willow shuffled through the sand, looking like they were on their last legs.

Taylor splashed into the water.

Sean was sweating and slightly breathless.

Claire could imagine how much his arms must ache. "You can put me down now."

He set her on her feet, but for a few extra moments continued to hold her.

Claire stepped back. "Thank you for the ride." She felt stronger now, but she wouldn't have minded remaining in Sean's arms a little longer.

The other passengers from the boat had congregated a few hundred feet farther down the shore. They had set out towels and were sunbathing.

Willow bent and picked up something. "What a beautiful shell. It looks like an exquisite fan." She held it up so everyone could see.

Claire looked out at the Gulf. Even though she'd been willing to stay behind, now that she was here, she was eager for a dolphin experience. They'd come all this way—it would be awful to leave without getting close to one.

"You feeling better?" Sean spread out a towel for her.

"Yes. I think I got overheated."

"I'd like to do some snorkeling," Tom said. "Does anyone know how?"

"Yeah," Sean said. "I've got some experience." He held up his snorkel. "It's pretty easy, really. And we got dry snorkels, which helps. They have a little valve here on top that will seal shut and keep water out when you dive under. But in case you do get some in the tubing, you can clear it with the purge valve. Just pinch this flexible hose here." He showed them how to pinch it closed. "Then blow out a short burst of air." He demonstrated. "You're likely going to get water in your mask. It's easy to clear. Just pull the bottom of the mask away from you face and blow out your nose."

Everyone put on their masks and practiced the techniques.

"Okay. I'm ready," Willow said. "How do I look?"

"Gorgeous." Tom chuckled.

"You've got that right." She laughed, then walked deeper into the water. "Do you think they come in close?"

"I saw photos of some right in front of people who were standing close to shore." Tom donned his gear, along with the fins, which made walking extra difficult. He waded in and took Willow's hand. The two of them moved further out into the water together until they were chest deep.

Taylor waded back in. "I don't see anything," she whined.

Sean put on his fins, then moved into the surf. "I wonder if we'll see any." He looked back at Claire. "Come on."

She moved into deeper water. Swimming used to frighten her. She never knew how her body would react. Would her muscles cramp or her heart get erratic? Since yesterday's experience, though, she felt no fear and couldn't wait to feel the buoyancy and freedom the ocean offered.

She kept moving forward. Her nerves zinged. Would it really happen? Would a dolphin come close? She studied the surface, searching for signs of one.

"They'll come," Willow said. "Just be patient."

For what seemed like a long time, the adventurers waited.

Then a dolphin swam right up to Willow and lifted its upper body out of the water.

With a squeal, Willow fell backward. Quickly pushing to her feet, she searched the water, but the dolphin was gone. She took off her mask. "Oh, he came so close. It was amazing!"

"You could have reached out and touched it," Claire said, putting her mask on in a hurry.

"I didn't see it," Taylor complained.

"You just have to wait," Claire said.

A flash of something beneath the surface.

Probably just a fish.

All of a sudden the smiling face of a dolphin rested on the surface of the water a few feet in front of her, making clicking sounds at her. The elegant creature edged closer, watching her.

Did she dare touch it? She reached out and rested her hand on the top of its head.

Immediately it retreated.

She turned to Sean. "Did you see it?"

"I did. Wow!" He moved closer to her. So did Taylor, Tom, and Willow.

The others who had ridden out on the boat with them moved down the beach and joined them in the water.

Everyone waited and watched, and then the dolphin returned. Another one joined the first. Before they knew it, there were four staring at them, acting as if they wanted to interact with the strangers who visited their beach.

And then all of a sudden the dolphins disappeared beneath the surface.

Claire dove after them.

They were there, spinning and darting after one another. They plunged to the bottom, then rocketed to the surface, all the while communicating in a series of clicking noises that reverberated through the water.

One swam past, and Claire reached out and touched it, running her hand along its rubbery, smooth skin.

Needing air, Claire reluctantly surfaced, removed the snorkel from her mouth, and sucked in oxygen.

Tom and Willow were floating on the surface. "You need to dive deeper," Claire said. "Get closer. They're extraordinary."

Where was Sean?

She plunged beneath the surface again.

He was there, surrounded by the fascinating creatures.

Claire swam toward them, feeling weightless, agile.

A dolphin came near, gazed at her, then nudged her with its nose.

She reached out and touched it, then swam alongside it with her hand resting on its back. It was as if she'd been set free, no longer bound by the constraints of her disease.

Then Sean was beside her. Together they surfaced, gulped in air, and returned to their ocean friends.

The dolphins circled them, swam away, then back.

Claire tried to mimic their moves, swimming with them, up and down. She didn't want to leave them, but her lungs screamed for oxygen and she had to surface.

This time when she surfaced, she felt weak. She needed to rest.

Unwilling to give up completely, Claire adjusted her mask, and using the snorkel, floated on the surface, and watched the activity below. The dolphins played with Sean as he swam among them, his sleek, athletic body looking almost dolphin-like itself.

Then one approached Tom and Willow. It was pure joy to watch their dream come true. Taylor swam toward one and it nuzzled her hand.

And then, the dolphins swam away, their clicking vibrating through the water. As quickly as it had begun, the dance was over.

Claire swam to shore and sat in the shallow water, watching the dolphins diving and skipping across the surface of the water in the distance, still chattering and chirping to one another. "Thank you," she whispered, more to God than to the dolphins.

Willow swam in and sat beside Claire. "It was better than I ever imagined. I'll remember this all my life." She laughed. "Who would have thought? We did it! We actually did it."

Tom moved onto the beach, leaving Taylor in the water. "Willow, you want something to drink?"

"Yes." She stood and waded to the shore, then tossed her snorkeling gear on the sand. Unfurling a towel, she spread it out on the beach, sat down, and accepted a sweet iced tea from Tom. "Thank you."

"Claire. Sean. Can I get you something?" Tom asked.

"No, thanks."

"Later," Sean said.

Taylor walked down the beach.

Claire left the water and sat on a rock outcropping that reached into the water. Hugging her knees to her chest, she gazed at the ocean, feeling as if she were brand-new. She'd done something she'd never imagined possible.

Sean sat beside her. "Incredible, huh?"

"I didn't want it to end."

He turned his eyes on her. "You looked like you were dancing with the dolphins."

"That's how it felt. At this moment, right now, I feel like I can do anything."

Sean leaned closer. Too close. "Maybe you can."

Was he going to kiss her? Claire had never been kissed before. Her skin hummed.

Sean moved away and turned his face back to the ocean. "Maybe God's going to heal you. Today you didn't look sick at all."

A weight intruded on her blissful mood. "God can heal, if he chooses. But just because I felt good swimming today doesn't mean I'm going to get well."

"Why wouldn't he?"

"I don't know why he heals one person and not another. I just know I've got to trust him."

"Maybe you have to want it. Do you?"

Sean's words struck a familiar, painful chord. "You think I don't want to get well?" Claire bit down on her lip, holding back tears. "I long to be whole and healthy more than anything." She narrowed her eyes and peered at him. "Why does it matter to you anyway?"

"I care about you."

"Enough to care even if healing me is not part of God's plan?"

He shifted his gaze to something in the distance. "I care about you no matter what."

His body language said otherwise.

Friends. That's all they could ever be. There was no future for them. Sean couldn't accept her as she was, and she couldn't accept him, because he needed her to be someone she wasn't.

CHAPTER THIRTY-SIX

The dolphin encounter changed everyone. Sean could see it.

Tom and Willow seemed to be even more in love, not just with each other, but with the world. They savored each new experience. And Tom was less afraid to show his more tender side. However, that likely had more to do with Willow than the dolphins.

Taylor found joy in the small pleasures of life. Though her negativity had already been decreasing, it diminished even more after the day on Shell Island. Some of the time, she actually seemed lighthearted.

And Claire? She had a peace about her that Sean had not seen before. Conversations with her parents were more upbeat, and she often sang or hummed while she went through the day.

A pang of regret jabbed at him. Since the day they swam with the dolphins, Claire had been standoffish. Not unfriendly, but the camaraderie between them was no longer there. He missed it.

Had their time with the dolphins changed him? Maybe. He thought he'd managed to control his feelings for her—being friends was enough. He could keep his distance and his unshackled lifestyle.

But he couldn't rid himself of the image of Claire dancing with the dolphins. Even now it made him smile. Her supple, slender body moving through the water alongside the wild animals tugged at his heart. She was beautiful. He wanted to love her, but when he thought about it all he felt was panic. The shame and fear he'd carried inside since his brother's death wouldn't let go, wouldn't allow him to love her or anyone else.

ംരോ ഇൈ

The travelers stayed in Panama City Beach for three additional days. The ladies spent time on the beach and made trips to local shops. Tom and Sean filled their days fishing at the pier, where they both did well.

Sleeping arrangements changed in the RV as they prepared to leave town. The newlyweds got the bedroom, and Claire and Taylor moved to the sofa bed. Surprisingly, Taylor didn't complain. Sean took the kitchen table fold-out, which was not very comfortable, but he figured it was for a good cause. Besides, there was no other option.

Leaving Panama City Beach behind, Sean pulled onto the highway, glad to be on the road again. Florida had been amazing, but now it was time to head west, toward home. He glanced at his friends in the rearview mirror. It wouldn't be long before he would say farewell to these unique people. That saddened him, but it had to be done.

Looking into the future, life seemed tedious. Still, he knew the sooner he put distance between himself and Claire, the better. He needed to find his own way, one that didn't include her and her troubles. Was he heartless? Maybe. The experience with his brother had created deep scars that no one could heal.

Willow said God healed wounded hearts, so why not his? Why couldn't he be free to love anyone he wanted?

Even Claire.

He pushed her from his thoughts.

Driving through southern Mississippi and Louisiana was like making one's way through a massive, endless swamp. A good deal of the road was a causeway that carried drivers above fuzzy, green marshes and tributaries that smelled like overripe vegetation.

To have been one of the first explorers through the area must have been harrowing. They would have navigated the waters in boats, swatting at mosquitoes and staying alert for alligators and snakes. The fact that any of the early explorers had survived was a marvel.

"Bad weather is in the forecast." Taylor's voice rose, tugging Sean's interest to the conversation behind him.

"How bad?" Tom said.

"I don't know. Looks intense to me."

Daisy nosed Sean's arm.

"Hey there, girl. Are you worried about the storm?" He gave her a quick pat.

She rested her head on arm of his seat.

"Come on, Daisy," Willow said. "Leave Sean alone. I'm done with my Bible reading for now, and I'll give you a good tummy rub."

Daisy's tail wagged and she trotted away.

"Daisy and I aren't afraid of a little blustery weather. We have the Great I Am with us."

Sean glanced back at Taylor and saw worry in her eyes. He understood the difficulty.

After a long day of driving that included a few rain showers and some impressive cumulonimbus clouds, Sean pulled into a rest area just outside Houston, Texas. They had a dinner of fresh fish and stir-fried vegetables over rice, then the ladies tidied up the RV while Sean and Tom went to work on the dishes.

Tom gathered plates and scraped the leftover rice into a container.

Sean filled the sink with sudsy water. "We should get an early start in the morning."

"How early?" Taylor asked. "I want to sleep in."

Sean turned and looked at her. "You can sleep while I drive, you know."

She frowned at him.

"The weather report calls for storms tomorrow. I'd like to get out of Dodge, er … Houston, before they roll in. They're supposed to get worse by the afternoon."

"Okay. I'll get up." She took a seat at the table, opened her computer, and typed something in. In a few seconds she spoke with a wobbly voice. "They're forecasting severe storms. Possible tornadoes."

"No need to worry," Willow said. "The Lord will take care of us."

Did God really care about things like storms? In some ways Sean felt closer to God since beginning this trip, but he'd also seen enough suffering that he questioned more. Why did God allow so much hardship to fall on his children?

The next morning, Sean put coffee on, then took Daisy for a walk.

The sky was gray, the air dense and damp.

"We better hit the road," he told the dog and headed back to the RV.

"Do you think you could be any louder?" Taylor asked when Sean pulled the door closed. She pushed up on one elbow. "People are sleeping here."

"Were sleeping," Claire mumbled.

Sean poured himself a cup of coffee and sat, elbows propped on the table. "Sorry. It's not like there's a lot of room to get up without waking people who are in the same room."

Taylor rolled onto her back and glared at him. "It's still dark."

"Sun's just coming up. And if we want to make it to Fort Stockton ahead of the storms, we need to get moving."

"Okay." Taylor pushed up, rolled off the bed, and prodded Claire. "Come on. If I'm up so are you."

"Already?" Claire brushed blonde hair off her face and combed it back with her fingers.

"Has the forecast changed?" Taylor asked.

Sean shook his head and took a drink of coffee.

"I thought we didn't have to worry about tornadoes in the summer."

Taylor's voice already grated on his nerves, and the day was very young. "Spring is the worst time, but storms come through any season of the year. It'll probably just rumble a little and drop some rain." Even though he downplayed the storm, his gut told him it might be a bad day for a lot of people.

As they made their way through Texas, a tornado advisory, followed by a blaring alarm, blasted from the radio.

"Didn't I see a sign a few miles back that we were entering Pecos County?" Taylor asked.

"Yeah."

"There's a tornado warning for Pecos County!"

"It's a big county, Taylor." Sean scanned the sky. The cloud movement looked peculiar.

"Is there a tornado coming?" Alarm shuddered through her voice.

"Not that I can see." Sean stepped harder on the gas pedal. They were only a few miles from a campground. He'd feel better if they got off the highway. This was desolate country—no place to shelter from a storm.

Tom studied the map on his phone. "Take the next exit."

When Sean reached it, he let out a relieved breath with a glance at a wicked-looking sky.

"Make a right turn off the exit, and it will be right down this road."

Sean turned into the campground. It was nothing special, but at least they weren't exposed on the open highway. There was no attendant at the entrance, so Sean drove through and searched for a space. They could pay later.

The road was rough and littered with potholes. Leaning over the wheel with his shoulders hunched up, Sean rolled forward slowly, trying to avoid the biggest holes.

Although most of the spots were taken, there were only a few campers out and about. Finally, he found a spot about midway through the camp. He let out a breath and tried to relax as he backed in the space. "I'll get us set up." He climbed out and, keeping an eye on the dark clouds, took care of the hookups.

While Daisy nosed around, Tom and Willow set out five chairs and sat down. "I doubt there's a tornado coming," Tom said. "I had a buddy who used to live east of here, and he said they'd get warnings all the time and then nothing would happen."

"You're probably right," Sean said.

Tom looked around. "It's nothing to write home about, but at least we've got water and power and a place to sleep for the night."

"Looks like a ghetto." Taylor stepped out of the RV. "Can't we find a nicer place?"

"It's just one night." No matter how run-down it was, no way was Sean going back out on the road, not today, not with a storm brewing.

Taylor dropped onto a chair.

The wind picked up and caught hold of the trees, whipping the limbs into a frenzied state. Fear prickled through Sean. The air tasted of dust and felt heavy, and the look of the clouds had him spooked.

"What's for dinner?" he asked, trying to sound nonchalant.

"I have no idea, but maybe I better take a look in the kitchen." Willow stood and her dress billowed away from her legs. With her face turned into the wind and eyes closed, she caught the fabric between her hands and pressed it down. "I love a good breeze, but this is getting wild."

Claire stood in the doorway, looking at the sky. "I don't trust these clouds. They're really stirring things up."

"If a tornado came through, what would we do?" Taylor said.

No one spoke for a long moment.

Finally Tom said, "We could stay in the shower house. It's a brick building, which is a lot better than a motor home. 'Course, I doubt we'll need to worry about a shelter. The warning was a long ways back down the road."

Sean wasn't sure he agreed with Tom. The clouds looked brutal.

"We're not in a town. What about sirens?" Taylor paced.

"You'll get a weather alert on your phone," Tom said.

Taylor looked at her phone. "There's a tornado warning still in effect. We might as well just stay in the showers until the warning is lifted." She headed for the bathhouse.

Come on Daisy," Willow said and hurried to catch up with Taylor. "I don't see that it'll hurt."

Tom followed Willow. "Whatever makes you feel safe, dear."

"I'm fine—trusting God with the weather, but caution is wise."

"We're coming," Sean called.

Claire joined him.

Taylor ran to the shower door. "It's padlocked," she yelled.

Portable bathrooms stood less than fifteen feet away. They would be no help.

Sean strode up to the building. A sign was plastered on the door—Closed for Repair. "Let's check the men's side." He walked around the building.

Same thing. Padlocked.

He walked back to the group. "They're locked too. I guess we'll just stay with the motor home and do like Willow said—trust God." Tension worked its way across his back. They could be in trouble.

"Why in the world would they both be closed?" Tom asked. "I'll see if there's a manager around who can unlock at least one of them. And I'll find out if there is a place to shelter … just in case."

"I'm coming with you." Willow took Tom's hand and they headed toward the camp entrance.

Sean, Claire, and Taylor returned to the RV. The few campers they'd seen earlier had moved indoors. By the time they reached the coach, the squall howled. A patio chair lifted and flew by, nearly hitting Sean in the head.

"We better get inside." He, Claire, and Taylor picked up the remaining chairs, stashed them in the loading compartment, and ran for the door. He helped Claire and Taylor up the steps, then stood in the doorway and kept an eye on the clouds. His stomach dropped.

Churning and black with debris, a tornado bore down on the campground.

Taylor screamed.

"Where are Tom and Willow?" Claire pushed past Sean. "We have to find them."

"We can't worry about them right now." He looked toward the front of the park.

There was a ditch alongside the road, but the tornado would be on them before they reached it.

"Get inside!"

The RV would provide no protection if it took a direct hit, but it might shelter them from flying debris.

He pulled the door shut. "In the bathroom!"

Taylor and Claire squeezed inside the tiny room.

"Get in the tub."

Claire and Taylor wedged themselves into the cramped space.

Sean grabbed the largest cushion from beneath the dining room storage and pressed it over the top of them. "Hold it down over you." He closed the door, then turned and looked for some kind of shelter. As he pulled another cushion out of storage, the RV rattled and pitched. He scrambled beneath the table and pulled the cushion over him, doing the best he could to protect his head.

The storm screamed. Branches and debris bombarded the coach.

It shuddered and Sean expected it to blow apart at any moment.

The sound of breaking glass mixed with Taylor's screams.

Sean envisioned Taylor and Claire being snatched away and tossed into a tree or a building. "Lord, we need you now. Please help us." He huddled against the bench, gripping the cushion. What would his parents think when they got the news of his death? He should have called them, should have answered his mother's letter, gone home to see them.

The tempest seemed to stall, unable to make up its mind whether to hit the RV straight on and decimate it or barrel past and spare it and its occupants.

Sean waited to die, and then the wind was slightly quieter, then grew more calm and hushed.

The tornado had gone by without destroying him and his friends.

He waited a few minutes before he lifted off the cushion and climbed out from beneath the table, quaking inside.

He'd never been so close to death.

"Claire? Taylor?" he opened the bathroom door. "Are you all right?"

At first, the only answer was weeping, then Claire said, "We're okay."

Sean removed the cushion and tossed it down the hallway.

Taylor and Claire emerged. Taylor shook violently and was crying. "Is it gone?"

"It's gone," Sean said. "And we're okay." He put an arm around her shoulder and gave her a squeeze. "Everything's going to be fine."

Taylor moved past him, looking around the front room as if she was trying to convince herself it was still intact.

Sean pulled Claire into his arms and held her against his chest.

She clung to him and wept quietly.

He smoothed her hair. "Thank God you're all right."

Claire looked up at him. "I thought we were going to die."

"Me too, but we didn't."

"What about Tom and Willow?" Claire moved out of his arms and to the front door.

Sean followed her.

Claire stared at the wreckage. "We've got to find them. And Daisy." A sob escaped her. She stepped out of the coach and nearly fell, but grabbed the railing and righted herself.

Sean reached for her. "Be careful."

The park was nearly unrecognizable. Trees had been stripped of foliage, and cars and trailers were strewn about like toys. There were cries for help and wails of pain coming from all over.

Sean was unable to move. What should he do? How could he help?

God, show me.

And then, clarity came to him. He looked at the girls. "We've come through this alive. I don't know why, but we did. And now we need to help these people. Maybe we'll find Tom and Willow."

"What if they're dead?" Taylor sobbed.

"They're not dead. They made it. I know them." Sean tried to sound convincing.

Claire shook her head. "I'm not a nurse. Willow's the nurse. Willow is the one who knows what to do."

"She's not here, but we are. First thing, we'll start moving through the debris, get people out from under the rubble."

Claire straightened, her tenacity unmistakable. "Okay. We're going to need bandages. I know Willow had an emergency kit. It's in the lower compartment of the RV."

Sean opened the section. "What's it look like?"

"I'm not sure … I think its brown leather."

Sean rummaged around. A few moments later, he held up a bag. "Is this it?"

"Yes."

He handed it to her.

Claire opened it. Taking out bandages, she gave some to Sean. "You'll need these." She grabbed more bandages and tape, then turned to Taylor who sat on a stump, crying. Claire kneeled in front of her. "I know you're scared and shaken up, but right now there are people who need us." She took Taylor's hand. "We need you."

Taylor nodded. "Okay."

Claire straightened. "You can come with me."

"There you are!" Willow shouted. "Oh, thank the Lord!"

Willow!

She and Tom, Daisy at their side, hung on to one another and staggered toward the motor home.

Blood trickled down Tom's forehead. "You made it!" He grabbed Sean in a bear hug. And then laughed. "We all did." Tears coursed down his muddied cheeks.

Claire and Taylor both grabbed hold of Willow. The women held one another for a long moment.

"I was so scared," Taylor said. "I was sure you were dead."

Willow stepped back. "It was a miracle. We were up by the road when it hit, so we jumped into the ditch, praying like we never have before. And it skirted us." She looked at the RV. "It's still standing and in one piece. Amazing. Thank you, Lord."

Tom moved along the RV, checking it for damage. "Not bad. A few dents and a couple of broken windows." He stopped and studied a back tire. "We'll need to get this replaced."

Someone cried out from a nearby trailer.

"We found your medical supplies," Sean said. "Are you and Tom able to help the injured?"

"I'm ready," said Willow. "Tom?"

"Ready. Just let me get a call made for help first." He pulled out his phone, called 911, and gave the operator their location and a few details.

Sean hauled water bottles, sheets, and blankets from the RV compartment. "We're going to need these," he said, handing them to the ladies.

When Tom hung up, his face showed no relief. "They're swamped with calls but said they'll get someone here as soon as possible."

"Come with me." Willow looked at Tom. "I'll need your help too."

"I'm with you, sweetie."

"First, let's see about your head wound." Willow took a quick look. "It doesn't seem very deep."

"It's not a big deal," Tom said. "You can doctor it later."

"There are people who need help," said Sean. "Minutes might mean the difference between living and dying."

"Right," Tom said. He took Willow's face in his hands. "My head is fine. Don't worry. We've got other people who need our help right now."

Sean took a quick look at the injury. "Not pretty, but it isn't life-threatening. You and Willow go with Taylor. Claire and I will work together. We'll meet back here."

Tom, Willow, and Taylor set off.

Sean and Claire went the other way, following cries for help.

The next hours became a blur as others chipped in to help. An ambulance eventually arrived, along with city emergency crews. Those healthy enough to help sifted through debris, hefted doors and furniture off of people.

Sean never knew what he'd find beneath. One woman had a hunk of glass wedged in her side. She hadn't survived. Beside her, a little girl, her body twisted, was also gone.

Most had wounds like broken bones, contusions, lacerations. But what about the wounds that weren't visible? How long would they take to heal? Would they ever?

When the last person was loaded into an ambulance, Sean, Claire, Tom, Willow, and Taylor returned to the RV. Willow lovingly cleaned Tom's head wound and bandaged it.

No one spoke. Depleted of energy and overwhelmed by what they'd seen, they settled into chairs outside the coach, still alert to the needs of others.

People milled about, some searching for possessions, others just walking. There was nothing else they could do.

Sean looked down at his clothes.

Blood had soaked into his shirt and pants. The blood of those he'd helped … and those beyond help.

Empty, he leaned forward on his thighs, hands over his face, his thoughts on the woman and little girl who had died. Had God been good to them? *It makes no sense. It seems like you take and give life without reason.*

"It could be a lot worse," Tom said.

Sean looked at Tom. "Yeah, for you maybe. But some people didn't make it today. What do you have to say to them?" Tears came unbidden, like a flood that couldn't be held back. Sean didn't understand.

Was he supposed to? Could anyone?

"We prayed and he didn't answer." He turned a defiant look on Willow. "You always say God hears us and answers prayer. What about today? Where was he today?"

Willow studied her hands, rubbing them together. Then she looked at Sean, eyes filled with sorrow. "I don't have an answer for these kind of tragedies. All I know is that the devil is the ruler of this world, and he spreads evil and all kinds of hardship. God loves us, and when we grieve he grieves with us. He cares for the wounded and binds up their wounds. He uses all things in life—the good and the bad—to strengthen and to teach those he loves and to draw them closer to himself."

Sean sighed. Could he trust God that what Willow said was true?

"God sees the beginning and the end. Unlike us, he sees the death of his children as a step into a better life."

A glimmer of hope flickered inside Sean. The little girl he found wasn't suffering. She was in heaven, living a new and better life.

And her mother?

Sean prayed the two were together. His eyes caught Claire's.

She reached out and took hold of his hand and held onto it.

There was no reason for words.

CHAPTER THIRTY-SEVEN

Like a soft breath, relief floated through Claire when Sean pulled onto the highway. They'd been in Fort Stockton too many days, but finally, with repairs on the RV completed, they were headed west once more. Putting Fort Stockton and the tornado behind her was a comfort, but would she ever truly be able to leave what happened on that terrible day in the past? Or would it stay with her for a lifetime?

Everyone was shaken up, but Taylor seemed the most damaged. She kept a watch on the skies and the weather report throughout the day.

A trauma like the tornado and its aftermath could set off a bad episode. They all looked out for her and made sure she took her medication. It seemed Taylor knew that and was guarding against it as well.

Claire had demons of her own. Nightmares tormented her, and she dreaded sleep. In the midst of a dark dream she'd find a body, turn it over, and look into the face of her sister.

Her mind turned to the days ahead. She'd come on this journey with an indistinguishable goal, feeling as if the rest of life would be empty and dreary if she didn't do something to change it. But the trip hadn't been the magic bullet she'd hope for. She still didn't know what she wanted, except to see beyond her disease, have a purpose in life, and find friends who would stick with her even though she was sick.

Everyone else on the trip was changing and fulfilling dreams, or at least trying to. Had she changed? Had she accomplished anything? Anything lasting?

Lord, why am I here?

You had the courage to come on this trip, a voice spoke to her heart. *You've been a friend to Taylor. You danced with dolphins. And you made a difference when the tornado hit.*

All of that was true, but *she* wasn't different. She was still just Claire, who sorrowed over the loss of her old life. And still had no clear purpose for what was left of it.

Willow leaned against Tom. "It was an adventure," she said, jarring Claire out of her reverie.

"Not the kind of adventure I was looking for." Taylor rested her elbows on the table and stared out the window.

Adventure? Is that what this was all about? Claire turned to Willow. "Is adventure enough? Is that why you came on this trip?"

Willow lifted her hands. "Oh well, I love an adventure and God knows I wasn't living one when I left Oregon. But no, that's not why I came. I believe in walking through doors that God opens. If I do that, I'll find his will for me. It doesn't have to be something big or life changing. In fact, I think the small things in life can have the biggest impact. With every person we meet, there's an opportunity to touch their lives. That's a gift to us and to them. I just want to make the world a better place."

"I like that." Claire leaned back against the sofa cushions. She'd been looking for something big, but maybe change had been right in front of her and she just hadn't seen it.

"Willow, you ready to learn how to drive this thing?" Sean said.

"Now?" Moving to the front, she leaned on the console and stared at the road.

"Sure. We just passed a sign for a rest stop. Good place to pull off."

"Well, I guess now is as good a time as any."

After a brief break, the gang was ready to head out.

Willow settled into the driver's seat, while Sean took the front passenger seat. Willow glanced over her shoulder and smiled at Tom.

"I can't believe I'm going to let you do this." Tom laughed. "I've got my fingers crossed." He leaned over her shoulder and dropped a kiss on her cheek. "You'll do fine."

Claire moved to the recliner so she could get a better look at Willow. This she had to see.

Willow tightened her seat belt, then looked at Sean. "Remind me. Why am I doing this?"

"It's time for me to head home—see my parents. Someone needs to drive."

"Oh. Right." Willow's expression was tender. "I'm glad you're going to see them."

It was good that Sean was going to see his parents, but a pang of grief jabbed Claire. She would miss him. "When are you leaving?"

"I figure when we get to central California."

Was that regret she heard in his voice?

"That will give you plenty of time to practice, which you're going to need," Sean said.

"Appreciate that." Taylor didn't attempt to disguise her sarcasm.

"I'm praying," Willow said, then turned on the ignition.

"This is just like driving a car, only you've got to remember you have a bus behind you." Sean chuckled.

"Got it." Willow pressed the gas and drove through the rest area and onto the entrance ramp without mishap. "It feels so big ... and wide."

"You'll get used to it." Sean edged onto the console and leaned close to Willow. "You need more speed. Give it some gas."

She did as he said, and with everyone silently watching her and the road, she eased onto the highway. "Thank the Lord there's almost no traffic." Tightly holding the wheel, Willow sat rigid in her seat and kept her eyes straight forward.

"Relax a little. You've got this." Sean said, but he looked like he might be ready to take the wheel at any moment.

Willow cruised along and gradually seemed to get the hang of driving the RV.

Claire moved to the table and sat across from Taylor. "That was scary at first," she whispered.

"I almost had to take an anti-anxiety pill." Taylor grinned.

They hadn't traveled far when the wind started. It tugged at white clouds, stretching them across the blue sky like strands of cotton candy. Prairie grasses sailed. Gusts buffeted the coach, but Willow coped well.

They passed a large sign publicizing the Petrified Forest National Park.

"Can we stop?" Willow asked.

"I read about this place," Tom said.

"Let me guess. In one of your magazines?" Taylor teased.

"Yeah. And it's real interesting."

"Okay, let's stop," Sean said.

While in the park, they had lunch, then decided to drive the loop through the geological formations, this time with Sean at the wheel.

Claire's heart wasn't into sightseeing. It was with Sean and his upcoming departure. After he left, she'd never see him again. The thought made her stomach ache. Why had she allowed herself to care?

They toured painted deserts, petrified forests, Indian ruins, and studied petroglyphs. Claire's mood improved by the time they returned to the highway. She'd taken a lot of pictures to post online. After her mother saw them, it would be fun to read comments.

They weren't far from the Grand Canyon and should reach it before the day was done. Was it as remarkable as people said? She'd heard it could be a life-changing experience. She hoped so.

Willow protested slightly when they drove past Flagstaff without stopping. She'd wanted to do some shopping at the town's specialty shops, but Sean followed the signs to the Grand Canyon instead.

The pine forests in and around Flagstaff had raised Claire's hopes of spending time among the pines, but they soon left the trees behind and once more trekked across desert country.

"This road doesn't drive along the rim of the canyon, does it?" Taylor moved to the console and gazed out the front window.

Sean glanced at her. "I don't know."

"I hope not."

"Either way, it'll be fine." Sean braked to miss a jack rabbit. "Did he make it?"

"Yep." Tom put his hands on the dashboard and leaned forward. "He's hightailing it."

"I've never been to the Grand Canyon." Taylor leaned her shoulder against the window. "In all the pictures, it didn't look like this. So desolate."

Tom rolled his eyes. "We're not there yet."

"You're going to love it," Willow said. Daisy climbed onto the sofa, and Willow scratched her behind the ears. "And you'll love it too, Daisy girl."

"Who wants to ride the mules to the canyon floor?" Tom asked, leaning on the arm rest and looking into the back. "You stay overnight at a lodge that sits along a creek."

"Are you kidding?" Taylor shook her head. "No way."

"You're safe. Mules are surefooted, and they've been going up and down that trail for years."

"Not another word." Taylor held up one hand, palm out. "You can't convince me."

Claire agreed. The last thing she wanted to do was ride a mule down a narrow cliff-side trail. What if she fainted or fell off?

"Tom's right," Sean said. "It is safe. I went a couple of times, with my family. But we can't go anyway. To get a spot on a trip to the bottom of the canyon you have to make a reservation a year in advance. And even if they had a spot for us, it's not an easy ride. Hours on the back of a mule, in the heat." He shrugged. "You guys couldn't do it."

"We've done a lot of things you didn't think we could." Willow moved up to the front, behind Sean. "We've done things *we* didn't think we could. I'd like to try something new and different while we're here."

"I'll check it out," Tom said, and started a search on his phone.

Claire wasn't up to any more challenges. She was tired, her body hurt, and Sean was going home.

She wanted to go home too.

CHAPTER THIRTY-EIGHT

As they approached Grand Canyon National Park, Claire's weariness subsided some and was replaced with anticipation. The cry for home became hushed.

When they reached the entrance, Sean stopped and everyone climbed out, including an overly excited Daisy, who wrapped her leash around Willow's legs in her frenzy to explore.

"Oh dear." Willow tried to untangle the leash. "Help."

Sean took Daisy by the collar. "Come on, girl." He carefully led the dog around Willow until the leash fell free. "I'll keep her."

"Thank you. Sometimes she forgets she's all grown up."

Everyone gathered in front of the park sign.

"Let me get a picture." Claire got out her phone. "Stand to the left of the emblem and the writing so I can get that in too." The friends clustered together and smiled at Claire, who clicked off a couple of photos.

"Okay. Now you." Sean moved out of the group and took Claire's phone.

Claire joined her friends and stood beside Taylor, with Willow and Tom on her other side.

As Sean struggled to control the dog and hold the phone still, Claire giggled.

"Can you send me a copy, so I can send it to Carson and Melody?" Willow asked. "Carson wanted to come. Maybe one day we'll visit together."

"I'd sure like that," Tom said. "Do you think he'll like having a grandpa?"

"Absolutely." Willow dropped a kiss on her husband's grizzled cheek.

"I'll text a copy of the pictures to all of you." Claire took a photo of a hyperactive chipmunk, then dropped her phone back into her purse.

After paying for a campsite and getting a map of the park, the travelers drove to the campground. Claire stepped out of the RV, behind Willow and Sean. The aroma of pine enveloped her, reminding her of home.

"No campfires," Sean said. "Too dry this time of year."

"Well, I didn't come here to roast marshmallows anyway." Willow said. "I want to see the canyon. How far is it from here?"

"Not far." Sean held up the map. "According to this, we're right here." He pointed at a spot on the map. "And this is where we want to be, only about a fifteen-minute walk to the rim and then about five more to the visitor center."

Tom took the map and studied it. "After we get set up, let's go down there." He took Willow's hand. "You up to it?"

"I am. But I want to see the canyon." She put on a sun hat along with a smile. "Maybe we can see the visitor center tomorrow."

"The canyon it is." Tom took her hand and they headed toward one of the viewing areas.

Taylor and Sean fell into step alongside Claire.

She barely kept up, feeling the pinch of her shoes with each step. She looked down at her swollen feet. *Please, no flare-up now. It will ruin everything.* "I can't wait to see it."

"You're gonna love it." Sean picked up a couple of pinecones and juggled them until they dropped. "I need practice." He grinned.

Thoughts of self faded when Claire caught sight of the north rim across the massive canyon. She moved to a fence that ran along the ridge. The most extraordinary sight stretched out before her—magnificent, majestic, frightening, humbling, breathtaking. A place layered with colors and textures, a place where God's presence dwelled.

A complex mix of emotions flowed through her. She felt small in this grand place, yet better understood her significance when she looked at what God had created. For she, too, was part of his creation and valued by him.

Willow gave her a side hug. "Unbelievable, isn't it?"

Claire couldn't take her eyes away from the deep and endless crater with its gold, red, and brown rock structures, crevices, and shadows so deep they seemed to have no bottom.

"They have a place with better views," Sean said. "Follow me."

They moved to a rock buttress with steps that led to a natural outcropping with a fence that protected visitors from falling. A small child could crawl under, or an adult over, if they wanted to.

Claire's stomach tumbled at the thought. She walked to the edge, keeping a hold on the fence, and gazed at the monstrous gorge.

It undulated through rocks and cliffs, reaching down to the Colorado River that cut its way between spires, chasms, and rock walls.

The cry of a hawk echoed across the thermals, and a breeze tousled her hair, carrying with it the smell of sage and dust. The idea of riding mules into the canyon was tantalizing. What an incredible experience it would be.

"Anyone hungry?" Sean leaned against the fence and looked at Claire and Taylor.

"Starved." Tom rested his hand on his stomach. "As usual."

Who could think about food? Claire remained where she was.

"Let's go back and make some dinner." Willow held Tom's hand. "We can talk about what we want to do while we're here." They moved slowly toward the campsite.

Claire stayed a few more minutes. No matter how long she remained, the wonder of it would not grow old. Finally, she started up the rock stairway and met Taylor almost at the top. "Didn't you go down?"

"No. Not this time." She turned and headed up the steps.

Dinner was simple—hamburgers and fruit salad. Claire ate in a hurry. She wanted another look at the canyon. "Anyone want to walk back to the viewing area with me?"

"I will." Sean dropped his paper plate in the trash.

"I'd love to, but I really need to lie down," Willow said.

"I'll keep her company." Tom threw a loving glance at his wife.

Taylor climbed up the steps of the RV. "I'm going to do some research."

"Okay." Claire looked at Sean. "I guess it's just us."

Just them? Again? It seemed they were always being thrown together, and it wasn't easy, not with the way she felt about him.

Spending time alone with Sean at the rim of the Grand Canyon was certain to stir up feelings she needed to keep restrained. She probably shouldn't go with him, but today wasn't a day to be sensible.

They wandered toward the viewing area.

"Glad you came?" Sean asked.

"Here? To the canyon?"

"Yeah, that, but the trip too."

"Of course. It's been wonderful. Better than I imagined."

"But …?"

Claire looked at him. "No 'but.' I'm glad I came. But …"

He chuckled.

"Okay, there is a *but*. I wish I could do more. It's been great to be with everyone and to see the country, but I want to experience more. I hate that my disease holds me back. I get mad."

"I'm sorry. It's a bad deal."

"I just try to be thankful, but I'm not always good at it."

They reached the rim.

"Careful, this section doesn't have a fence," Sean said. "So no fainting." His lips lifted in a crooked smile.

He'd made the statement in jest, but it wasn't funny. "I promise—no fainting."

Sean sat on a boulder and looked out over the canyon. "It's pretty amazing."

"I've seen photos, but they can't even begin to reveal what this is like."

The yip of a coyote echoed through the park.

"We have company." Claire sat on a smaller boulder beside Sean's.

"Probably a lot of them around here."

As the sun dropped below the rim, the canyon went from yellow to red and orange. Even though she knew there was no future for her with Sean, it was still wonderful to share the sunset with him. It was a time to cherish.

"I've been here a few times with my family. When Ben was still alive, we had a great time." His expression revealed a happy memory. "We took the mules down to the bottom of the canyon. You'd like it."

"I think I would." She let out a breath and straightened her legs on the flat rock. "How long has it been since you've seen your family?"

"A few years."

"Do you miss them?"

"Sometimes. But we were never close." He turned his gaze to the deepening purple sky. "Mom and Dad were always busy taking care of my brother. Not much time for anything else, like my basketball games or track meets."

Claire's heart ached for Sean. What would it be like to be an invisible child? "I'm sorry. I wish I could give you a do-over."

"Do-overs only happen in movies and books. They're not real, Claire."

"Why not? You could come back here with your parents, ride the mules to the canyon floor, and create a new memory."

Sean plucked a blade of grass. "It's no use, not now. We're not close. That's never going to change."

"I can't imagine what that would be like. My sisters and I all got along when we were younger. And my family went camping and horseback riding often. We liked to do things together. Until Melissa and I got sick … and then …" A stark truth glared at Claire.

She was her family's sick kid. She felt like she'd been punched in the stomach. "I'm like Ben. For years and years everything's been about me and trying to figure out what's wrong with me, then how to treat my illness." Guilt rolled through her.

"You said your sister was sick too."

"She was, but that was different. When she found out what was wrong, she knew how to treat it. And as long as she took her medication, she was okay. But my condition caused incessant trouble. For years, my parents and I visited doctor after doctor and there were lots of hospital visits—so much time and money spent on finding out what was wrong with me. No one complained. Not even Melissa. But I was probably part of the reason she ran off."

"I ran away too."

"I understand why you don't like being with people who are sick. Even I hate being with me."

265

Sean didn't respond for a long time. "I don't hate being with you." Abruptly he stood and climbed down from the boulder. "We better get back before it's completely dark."

The cold night air seeped through Claire's sweater. She shivered. "Yeah. It's getting cold." She needed to talk to her mother and her sister. Being sick wasn't her fault, but it had been an additional burden on her family. The dark truth laid itself over her shoulders like an icy mist.

It was good that she'd left home. Maybe it was time to become independent and live on her own.

When they reached the RV, Taylor sat in the crook of a tree, strumming her guitar. Willow reclined in one of the chairs beside a table lantern that cast light over her. She looked up from the book she was reading. "Oh, I thought you were Tom."

"Where is he?" Claire asked.

"I don't know. He said he was going to take a walk, but he hasn't come back. He's been gone close to an hour. I'm starting to worry."

"I'm sure he'll be back anytime now." Claire dropped into a camp chair.

Sean picked up a twig and stripped the bark off of it. "Tomorrow, after we stop by the visitor center, do you want to do some looking around? There's a very cool watchtower not far from here, built back in the thirties."

"That sounds interesting." Willow rested the book on her chest.

A park shuttle drove up and stopped. Tom stepped out and gave the driver a wave. He walked into camp, a triumphant smile on his face. "Nice guy. We're not on his route, but he had mercy on this old man and dropped me off here."

"Thank goodness." Willow reached for his hand. "I was about to send out a posse. Where have you been?"

"Rousting out a trip." Tom kissed her fingers. "Because I love you so much."

"What kind of trip?" Taylor asked.

"A rim trip, on the mules." He smiled. "They had a family cancel, and I managed to get us a spot in a group that's going out in the morning."

"Really?" Willow asked "Oh, Tom, that's wonderful. God is blessing us again and again. These kind of things don't just happen."

"*You* might be going, but I'm not. No way." Taylor climbed from the crook of the tree, clutching her guitar. "I'm not riding a mule down a skinny little trail on a cliff side."

"It's not that kind of trip. It's just three hours, and they don't go down into the canyon. The entire ride is along the rim. It'll be fun."

"I don't know if I can ride a mule," Willow said. "My back—"

"You ride your bike." Sean's voice encouraged.

Willow tipped her head to the side. "That's true. I guess I can try."

Claire nodded. "I quit riding my horse, Cinnamon because it was too painful, but I want to go." It would be nice to be on the back of an equine again, even if it was a mule.

Taylor tapped the body of the guitar with her fingertips. "Okay. I'll do it. But if they go down any steep trails, I'm out of there."

"I thought the brochure said you had to be in good health." Willow threw a questioning look at Tom.

"I'm feeling good today, aren't you?" He looked at everyone "Seems to me we've all been doing real good lately. That's what I wrote on the form."

∽◎ ◎∾

The aroma of hay, grain, and manure kindled memories that carried Claire back to the ranch. There had been a time when she and Cinnamon spent days roaming the forests and grasslands covering the property. Those were precious times.

One of the stockmen led a mule out of the barn and toward her. "I've got a nice girl here for you. Her name is Maggie. She's real gentle."

Claire reached out and patted the mule's neck. "You're a pretty girl."

"Do you ride?"

"Yes. I have a horse back home."

"Good. This will be easy for you, then."

Claire stepped in front of the mule and ran a hand down its nose. "We're going to do just fine." She pressed her forehead against the mule's face and breathed in its scent, so much like a horse. When she got home, she was going to take Cinnamon for a ride.

The trail leader gave instructions on riding and safety, then everyone mounted their mules. Tom would have pushed himself over the top of his mule if one of the ranch hands hadn't caught him.

As they moved away from the corrals, hooves clopped along the trail and raised dust that sifted over the riders.

Caught up in the moment, Claire felt no pain. When they approached the canyon rim, the world spun wildly. She grabbed the saddle horn and willed the whirling to stop.

"Just look at that," said Willow. "I could stare at that view all my life and never get tired of it. God astonishes me."

Overcoming her dizziness, Claire smiled and pressed her hat down onto her head so the breeze wouldn't snatch it away. This was a remarkable day. She was riding again, and along the Grand Canyon at that.

Staying close together, the mules plodded along, seemingly uninspired by the view. Riders snapped photographs. Mostly, everyone remained quiet, almost as if they were alone with God and his creation.

Claire was so caught up in the splendor she forgot about anything except the present moment.

When Taylor's mule took a step toward the cliff, she pulled hard on the reins. This happened more than once and the leader repeatedly reminded her that the mule knew the trail well.

Sean had a large mule but his long legs still looked too big for the small animal. He didn't seem to mind. Each time Claire looked at him, he wore a smile.

Every once in a while the lead rider would stop and share a piece of local history or talk about a particular plant or tree. Before they'd started out three hours hadn't seemed like a long ride, but about halfway through, it clearly was. Claire's feet and legs throbbed, and her heart felt tattered and unsteady, but she pushed the suffering out of her mind. Dysautonomia would not win.

When they returned to the barns and corrals, Willow could barely climb off her mule. A ranch hand helped her down. With her palm pressed against her lower back, she slowly straightened. "That was awesome, but I need some pain medication and a bed." She smiled.

Tom moved slower than usual but didn't complain.

Claire leaned over her mule's neck. Getting off wasn't going to be easy. Moving slowly so as not to black out, she lifted her left foot out of the stirrup and raised her leg onto the mule's back. Every inch of her screamed exhaustion, and her leg was a heavy weight when she dragged it over the mule. Hanging on to the saddle horn, she wiggled her right foot out of the stirrup and slid her body off, then leaned against the mule's side for a few moments until she was steady on her feet.

Most of the riders in the group seemed fine, except for Claire, Tom, and Willow. Sean and Taylor had only one complaint—that their legs felt peculiar.

Claire smiled. She knew that feeling. Even when she'd been able to ride often, there were days she left the saddle with wobbly legs. Today they shuddered and threatened to collapse.

The band of friends took a shuttle back to the campground, then hobbled to their site. At the RV everyone sat around the picnic table.

"Thank you, Tom, for arranging that," said Willow. "I'm so glad we went, but I fear it will take a few days to recover."

Taylor studied Willow. "Is it worth it—worth all the pain? We didn't have to ride mules. We could have seen the view without them."

"It's about more than just seeing the view," Claire said. "It's doing what we used to do, being who we used to be ... as much as we can."

"And tasting the pleasure of doing something special," Willow said.

Tom leaned forward, arms on his thighs. "I get why we rode the mules, but let's be honest—we're not who we used to be. We can't measure today against what we did before. If we do that, we come up short. And that sticks in my craw."

"I'm always asking, 'Do I push through, or do I give in to my aches and pains?'" Willow brushed her hair off her face. "I never know if the answer I get is the right one." She looked at each of them. "I've decided there isn't a right or wrong answer. It's different every time. And for me, I want to live the best life I can. It doesn't mean being reckless, but just pushing enough to stay in the game."

"I think I get it." Taylor leaned back in her chair and crossed her legs. "But I couldn't be like that. I'm not brave like you."

"You are," Willow said. "You fight your own battle, and most days you win. Today you rode a mule along the rim of the Grand Canyon, for heaven's sake. And you hate heights."

"I know, but it's not the same. I didn't like the height, but I wasn't really in any danger."

Claire didn't want to talk about any of this. "Why can't we just be thankful about what we got to do?"

"I think you're right, Claire." Willow eased out of her chair. "And right now I need to lie down and think about how much fun I had today." She headed for the steps. When she reached them, she turned and looked at Claire. "You're right, you know. We need to live in the *now* of life. It can't be about how much we suffered yesterday or what we might face tomorrow. It's about today. And today was good."

CHAPTER THIRTY-NINE

Travel from the Grand Canyon to Las Vegas was uneventful. Willow drove most of the way and proved to be competent.

When they arrived at an RV park on the fringes of the city, Claire and the others encouraged Willow to try to park the coach. With Sean's guidance, Willow managed to maneuver the RV into their assigned spot. She turned off the engine. Wearing a triumphant smile, she raised clasped hands over her head, and a cheer went up from the travelers. "So, am I ready?"

"You are." Sean gave her a high-five. "Way to go."

Sean's enthusiasm made Claire wilt inside. He was glad Willow would be taking over as driver. He *wanted* to leave. She should be glad that he was going home, but she couldn't be completely delighted.

He had a life that didn't include her. In spite of her best efforts not to fall for him, she had … hard. And once he left, all she would have was memories.

"I'm proud of you." Tom moved up behind Willow and gave her a hug.

She patted his arm.

"So what …?" Tom stumbled and nearly fell. Gripping the back of the seat, he barely managed to stay upright.

Willow pushed to her feet. "Tom?"

Face pallid, he quaked as he made his way to the sofa. "Just dizzy."

Willow sat beside him and put an arm around his shoulders.

Daisy rested her head on his lap.

"Look at that. Daisy understands."

"Yeah." Tom stroked the dog's head. "Never expected we'd like each other."

"I'll get you some water." Claire filled a glass and handed it to him. "Maybe you should reconsider driving at the track."

Tom took a drink, then looked straight at Claire. "I'm not letting something like a little dizzy spell hold me back. I'm driving."

He could be so stubborn. She wanted to throttle him. Instead, she sat down at the table. After driving all the way from Oregon to Florida and back across the country, they were finally in Las Vegas. And she was going to have fun. Worrying about Tom wasn't fun.

He looked at everyone. "What are you staring at? I'm fine. It's time to call a taxi and get down to the Strip. I'm ready for a good time."

The cab driver dropped them in front of the New York-New York Hotel & Casino. Claire stepped into the warm evening air, feeling as if she were about to be swallowed up by the tumult of sights and sounds. The Strip was jammed with cars jockeying for a place, horns blasting. People crowded the sidewalks, where vendors peddled their wares. Lights and banners shouted at pedestrians.

Shrieks reverberated from the rooftop of the New York-New York building. A roller coaster swept down a tight turn and into a loop, riders screaming in terrified delight.

"Oh man, I want to ride that thing." Tom watched as it disappeared inside the building.

"You're already dizzy," Willow said. "What do you think will happen if you get on something like that?"

"Maybe it'll straighten me out." He grinned.

"Men," Willow uttered, throwing him a fierce look that withered into a halfhearted smile.

Tom kissed her. "You might as well give up. You don't have a vicious bone in your body." He kissed her again.

"I'm starved," Sean said. "I read about a place to eat not far from here that sounds good. Are you up to a short walk?"

"I'm good to go." Tom turned to Willow. "How about you?"

"I'm hungry," Claire said.

"Me too." Taylor picked up her purse and slung it over her shoulder. "And maybe when I'm done eating, I'll find a profitable slot machine." She smiled.

"Okay. Let's get moving." Tom took Willow's hand and they started down the street.

They looked a little wobbly but content. Claire's heart warmed at the sight of them. Maybe one day she'd find someone who teased and laughed with her, who loved her just the way she was.

The restaurant Sean recommended had seating on an outdoor terrace overlooking the strip. He couldn't have picked a better spot. The vitality of the city was infectious.

Once they were served drinks and their dinner orders were taken, Sean settled back in his chair. "So, tomorrow's the big day." He rapped on the tabletop.

"Can't wait." Tom took a drink of lemonade. "I'm ready to tear up the track."

"Tom, be sensible." Willow folded her arms over her chest and eyed him. "You've been dizzy off and on today. And don't deny it. How do you think you're going to drive?"

"I'm gonna get in the driver's seat, turn the key, and put my foot on the gas." His lips lifted in a crooked smile, then he turned and looked at the street. "I've never seen so many *interesting* people."

Taylor's gaze followed a man with more piercings in his face than any person had a right to. "I could think of a better word than 'interesting.'"

Willow leaned toward Tom. "We're not done talking about you driving. You've got to be realistic."

"I'm sorry if you're afraid, but I'm not. And we *are* done talking about it."

The challenge seemed to seep out of Willow. She said nothing more about it, but the rest of the night she and Tom barely spoke to each other.

Claire was weary when she climbed into bed, but she couldn't sleep. All the sights and sounds of the city stayed with her. And her thoughts kept wandering to Tom. Why was he being so hardheaded?

Taylor snored quietly. Claire rolled onto her side with her back toward Taylor. Maybe Tom had some kind of death wish.

No. That couldn't be it. He was enjoying life, especially with Willow.

Sean readjusted his blankets and let out a sigh.

"You awake?" Claire whispered.

"Yeah." He fluffed his pillow. "This bed is the worst."

"I feel bad, but I'm glad you got stuck with it and not me." Claire chuckled.

"Oh—thanks a lot." He kicked his feet out from under the blanket. "It's not your fault. I probably wouldn't sleep anyway."

"Why?"

"Thinking about tomorrow."

"Aren't you afraid, even a little?"

"No. It's going to be a blast."

"You know Tom shouldn't be driving. How can you let him?"

"You think I have control over him? He's his own man. When he sets his mind to something, no one's going to change it—not even Willow."

"But he could kill himself, or someone else."

"Of all people, I'd think you'd understand. He's been counting on it. It'll probably be his only chance."

Claire rolled onto her back and tucked one arm behind her head. "I know. I'm just worried about him."

Sean didn't say anything for a long moment, then asked, "What happened to God? I thought you trusted him."

"I do … but sometimes he allows things we don't want. This could be one of those things. Tom's life is already hard. If something happens to him, what about Willow?"

"Do you have any choice but to trust? Really? You've got to put Tom in God's hands. He loves him more than you do." His voice had taken on a hard edge. "I've been hearing that over and over from Willow lately, and from my mother all my life."

Claire closed her eyes. When had her faith become so weak? *Keep Tom safe. Please.* Until now Claire hadn't realized how much she loved him. She couldn't stand the thought of something awful happening to him.

CHAPTER FORTY

The following morning, Tom was unsteady on his feet but acted as if everything was fine.

Claire forced herself to be quiet about her fears.

He nearly fell while making his way down the RV steps.

Willow's eyes were clouded with worry, but she said nothing. She went through the RV and opened all the screened windows, set out a fresh bowl of water, gave Daisy a kiss between the eyes, and closed her in the RV.

While they waited for the cab, Tom and Willow stood side by side but didn't speak to each other. Once in the cab, Willow sat in front. Taylor and Sean got in the back and, just as Claire was about to climb in, Tom moved past her, slid in, and took her spot. He wasn't going to sit with Willow?

Claire took the remaining spot in the front. She gave Willow an encouraging look and patted her arm. Willow placed a hand over Claire's.

"To the speedway," Tom told the driver.

No one else spoke.

"Hey, cheer up," Tom said. "It's not like we're getting a root canal done or something."

That lightened the mood and soon there were comments about the sights along the way, including the X-Scream ride on top of the Stratosphere. All agreed it was a terrifying ride and one they never wanted to experience. Even Tom admitted it was too much for him.

At the speedway they drove beneath a large overpass and into a huge, empty parking lot. The rumbling sound of racing engines reverberated from the track.

Taylor rolled down her window. "That sound gives me goosebumps."

"This place is huge," Sean said.

"Yeah, impressive," said the driver. "I make all the races I can."

Sean paid the fare while the rest of the group headed for the track.

Claire moved slowly, the throbbing of the cars vibrating in her stomach. She didn't know whether to be frightened or thrilled.

"I can't wait to get behind the wheel," Tom said.

Claire couldn't help but smile. He was one of a kind. And she loved that he was unafraid.

"This is extraordinary," Willow said as a race car flew past.

Tom gave her a kiss. "We need to sign in. I'll be back."

Willow caught his hand. "I'm sorry for being such a shrew."

He kissed the back of her hand. "I'm sorry for being so crabby." He winked at her, then traipsed off toward the office with Sean at his side.

While the guys signed in, the women checked out some of the display cars. Taylor sauntered to a bright-red car sponsored by DuPont. "This one's mine." She leaned against it.

"Let me get a picture." Claire snapped a couple of shots. "You and that car are a perfect match. Sure you don't want to drive?"

"I might look good, but I'm not crazy." She grinned. "At least not crazy enough to get behind the wheel of one of these."

"I like this one." Willow glanced inside a yellow vehicle with Cheerios painted across the hood. "And Cheerios is one of my favorite cereals." She smiled while Claire took more photos.

When the guys came out of the building, they wore driving suits—blue coveralls with a light gray front from the waist up and a Richard Petty logo splashed across the chest. Sean caught Claire's eye and winked.

Her heart galloped, and her face heated up. He was so handsome.

"You look like you're all set," Willow said. "You didn't have any trouble getting approved?"

"No sirree." Tom didn't look directly at her. "No trouble at all."

"They didn't ask about your health?"

"Sure. I told them I'm feeling good, and so is Sean."

"You didn't tell them." Willow's tone accused.

"Anyway, they're going to take us through a class to show us how to drive the course. We'll ride along with a driver, then they drive with us, and then we're on our own." He rubbed her back. "It'll be fine."

"They offer ride-alongs," Sean said. "You're supposed to make reservations, but they're asking if anyone wants to ride with a professional driver.

"No, thanks," Taylor said.

"What would I have to do?" Claire asked.

"A pro does the driving and you just strap yourself in for the ride of your life. You still have to climb in through the window, though. No doors."

"I could do that." Willow's eyes were full of mischief. "What do you think, Tom?"

"I think you'd look real cute in one of those cars." Tom gripped a handrail and his gaze faltered. "And you can do anything you set your mind on."

Willow gently grasped his upper arm. "Are you sure you can drive today?"

He nodded.

"Okay. I trust you." She stepped away. "I think I'll watch from the sidelines."

An announcement for the next group was sounded.

"Gotta go. See you." Tom kissed her.

"See you." Willow hugged him.

When Tom and Sean walked away, anxiety flooded Claire.

This wasn't about driving a car. It was about feeling alive. She couldn't fault them for that.

"Hey, people are up on the roof." Taylor said. "I bet there's a good view up there."

"Let's go see." Willow circled the building looking for an elevator. There was none. "All right—up the stairs we go." She headed up, one slow step at a time.

By the time Claire reached the roof patio, her legs felt rubbery. She needed to sit. And then she saw the track. It looked smaller from the roof. The front straightaway was bordered by spectator stands, then the huge oval track banked and disappeared around turn one. She would be able to watch the cars as they maneuvered through the turns and raced past the stands.

A smattering of small tables and chairs offered a place to sit, and Claire made her way to the closest table and lowered herself onto a plastic chair.

Willow joined her.

Taylor moved to the roof's edge. "I can see Sean. He's getting in one of the cars."

"Already?" Claire joined Taylor. "Oh. He's just a passenger." She blew out a relieved breath.

"This time. Tom's down there too." Taylor pointed. "See? He's with a bunch of other guys, along the wall."

Willow limped toward them.

"Willow, where's your cane?"

"I didn't bring it. Probably should have though." When she reached the edge of the rooftop, she gazed down at the cluster of drivers waiting their turn. "I see him. If only he wasn't so stubborn." She turned to Claire and Taylor and held out her hands. "Time to pray."

They clasped hands and bowed their heads.

"Father, we know you are in charge of our lives," Willow said, "that you hold us in the palm of your hand. But we are weak, and we lack faith. I'm afraid, and I ask you to help me ... us ... to trust you. Fill us with your peace. Please take care of our guys. Let this be a fun experience for them, and don't let any harm come to them. I know you use all things to the betterment of your kingdom, and I am excited to see what you do with this. We thank you for loving us. Amen."

Claire looked up, and they all smiled at one another.

The women remained on the rooftop and watched while each student driver had an opportunity to ride with a professional.

Claire's nerves jumped.

"Oh, there goes Sean," Taylor squealed. "He's the next guy up. And he's getting into a car ... on his own."

"I'm going down." Willow headed for the stairway. "I need to be at the track."

"I'm coming too." Claire caught up to Willow, as did Taylor.

The ladies reached the track just in time to see Sean tear out of the pits and speed down the entrance, quickly building speed. A prickle of apprehension moved through Claire.

Acting as if he had no fear, Sean attacked the course. There was another car already out, and Sean easily passed him on the straightaway, then slowed when rounding the next curve.

"He's amazing." Claire pressed the palms of her hands together, pride building inside.

Sean made several laps. Each seemed faster than the one before. And with each lap he became more aggressive on the corners.

Willow put an arm around Claire's shoulders. "He's a natural."

Claire couldn't take her eyes off of his car as it came around again. The engine roared as he gained speed, and Claire's heart sputtered. *Don't get too confident. Be careful.*

"He's really something. More aggressive than I imagined," Taylor said.

When Sean finished his last lap, Claire ran down to meet him.

He stepped off the track, a broad smile on his face. "That was great!"

"You were wonderful!" Without thought, Claire threw her arms around him.

He hugged her and lifted her off the ground. "I'm ready to go again." He set her down. "What a ride!"

Tom walked up and extended a hand. "Way to go, buddy!" He smiled broadly.

"Thanks." Sean gripped his hand.

"Claire, you really should give this young man some thought," Tom said. "He might be famous one day. You'd be quite a pair."

How could Tom say something like that? Unbelievable. She needed a good comeback. "I'm not someone he's interested in."

Sean stared at her. Before she could say anything else he turned and looked at the track.

"Oh, is that right?" Tom lifted one eyebrow and grinned. He leaned in close and whispered. "He's just scared. Give him a chance."

Claire narrowed her eyes. "Shouldn't you be getting ready?"

"I'm up next." He gave Willow a quick kiss on the cheek and headed for the pits.

A car pulled in, and, with help, Tom climbed through the window and into the driver's seat.

Willow didn't take her eyes off of him. "He's so brave." Her eyes misted.

Sean put an arm around her. "He's going to love it."

"I know." Willow kept her eyes on Tom's car as it pulled up, ready to take off.

Tom gave her a wave and a smile.

Father, keep him safe. Claire stood shoulder to shoulder with Willow.

The engine revved as Tom moved into position.

A pit official raised a flag, then waved it and the car flew onto the track. Tom wasn't holding back. He raced toward the first curve and disappeared around the turn.

"He's good." Taylor pressed the palms of her hands together and made a little hop.

Willow watched turn two, at the other end of the track. "He's great."

Soon Tom's car appeared, and he picked up speed and raced past them.

"Way to go, Tom!" Sean shouted, as the car headed into turn one and slowed before whipping around the corner and moving out of sight.

"He's doing it," Willow said. "He's really doing it."

A few moments later when Tom's car appeared at the second turn, he had slowed down. He didn't speed down the straightaway like before. Instead he headed for the pits.

"Oh no. Something's wrong." Willow moved down the barrier wall toward the pits.

When the car came to a stop, Tom turned off the engine.

Two men approached the car and gave him a hand out.

Tom removed his helmet and smiled as he walked toward Willow.

"Tom, what happened?" Willow hugged him.

"That was awesome! I loved every minute." He settled serious eyes on Willow. "But my depth perception is off. And when I looked at you cheering me on, I knew that what really matters is *us*. I can't afford to be foolish."

Willow circled her arms around his neck and pulled him close. "Oh, Tom. I'm so sorry, and so thankful."

"Don't feel bad. I had the ride of my life. And I have something a lot more important than a fast car right here in my arms." He kissed her. "I wouldn't want to miss any of our adventure together."

Willow wiped away tears. "I love you."

"I love you too."

"Tom, I wish you'd been able to finish your race," Claire said.

He smiled. "I've got a great life." He gave Claire a quick hug. "Be happy, girl. Life is good."

Was it possible he had no regrets? He'd wanted to drive so badly. Was he sincerely content with only two laps?

How could anyone be satisfied while missing out on so much? Claire didn't know, but she longed to discover how.

CHAPTER FORTY-ONE

When they left Las Vegas, after staying two more nights, Sean sat in back on the sofa and Willow drove. Heading west, Tom rode in the front passenger seat, seemingly satisfied to be the copilot.

Her head resting on Sean, Daisy sat between him and Claire. Taylor was at her computer as usual.

Sean would rather be driving. That way he didn't have to carry on a conversation with Claire or Taylor, who seemed filled with enthusiasm about the latest in beauty creams and make up.

Finally conversation dwindled, and Taylor lost herself in her computer, and Claire submerged herself in in a book.

Sean settled back, glad for a quiet ride across the Nevada desert.

"How do you think I'm doing?" Willow called over her shoulder.

"Good," Sean said. "You've got the hang of it."

"I'm feeling confident, like when I was young." She glanced at him in the rearview mirror. "I am a little nervous about Highway 49. It's winding, and there are a lot of drop-offs."

"Just keep your speed down, and you won't need to worry."

"Drop-offs? You mean cliffs?" Taylor peeked over her computer.

"Not yet," Willow said. "Not until we get to Central California. I promise to be extra careful."

Taylor didn't look reassured, but she went back to whatever she'd been doing on her computer.

Willow caught Sean's eye in the mirror again. "I can't convince you to stick around for a while longer? At least to drive that portion of the road?"

Sean chuckled. "You'll be fine. And I already told my mom I'm coming. She'd never forgive me for showing up late."

"You called?" Willow asked.

"No. I sent a text." He hadn't wanted to talk to her, not yet.

"Sean! A text? You should have called her."

He was not getting into this conversation. "She's fine," he said with a note of finality.

Willow said nothing more.

Now that it was nearly time to leave, he wanted to stay. He liked these people. They'd become friends, and the past waited for him in Monterey—issues between him and his parents that needed to be resolved. It wouldn't be fun.

When he'd left three years earlier, he'd gone without a word of explanation. And to make matters worse, he'd contacted them infrequently.

They'd had high hopes for him, and he'd let them down in every way. He hadn't finished college, wasn't married, and had been a drifter since leaving home. And working with his father? He still didn't want any part of that.

"Even if you just told your mother in a text, I bet she can't wait to see you." Willow called over her shoulder.

"Yeah, I'm sure Mom's excited." He blew out a breath. "My dad, well, I figure he's hoping my visit is short."

Claire rested her book in her lap. "Why?"

"I'm sure you're wrong about that," Willow said. "Parents love their children. Can't just turn off love."

"My father wanted me to go into business with him. I refused."

"What does he do?" Claire asked.

"He owns a software company."

"That sounds interesting."

"Maybe to him, but I'm not cut out for that kind of work. Can't convince him, though. He won't listen."

Willow looked at him in the mirror. "I'll be praying for you. Both of you—that you can each hear the other."

"Me too," Claire said. "Don't give up hope."

"Thanks." Even with Willow and Claire praying, Sean doubted there was any hope for him and his parents. Still, he had to try, for his own sanity. The weight of guilt he carried seemed to be getting heavier.

Claire stared at him. "I know they'll be glad to see you. And when they're reminded of what a fine person you are, they'll be supportive of your career choices, whatever you choose to do."

"You're thinking about your parents. Not mine." He still felt the bitterness. It was there, sharp as a thorn wedged in his heart.

"People can change." Her lips lifted in a quiet smile.

Daisy wiggled her way onto Sean's lap and he stroked her side. If only people could be like dogs. They kept on loving no matter what a person did.

His parents would have a meltdown if he brought Claire to meet them. They'd had enough of disability and sickness. And they wanted grandchildren. Claire was sick, and he didn't know if she could even have children.

He let out a dismal sigh. Life could be so unfair. The days ahead without Claire would be dull and lonely.

He glanced at her and imagined what would happen at home if they became a couple. *What would have happened if I'd told her how I feel? If I asked her, would she come with me to Monterey? What if I asked her to never leave me?*

He rested his head on the sofa back, crossed his arms over his chest, and stared at passing cacti through the window above the dining table. His eyes grew heavy and finally he slept.

"Oh, let's stop here! I've heard of this place!"

Willow's voice startled Sean awake. He opened his eyes and peered outside. Nothing but dirt and scrub. "Stop where?"

"Peggy Sue's Diner." Willow slowed and took an exit off the highway. "I'm hungry. Anyone else?"

"A big, juicy burger sounds just about right to me," Tom said.

Sean straightened and looked out the window behind the sofa. Sure enough, a diner sat in the middle of nowhere, surrounded by dirt and an occasional dust devil. In contrast to the arid surroundings, the building was colorful and friendly. It had an arched front entrance painted various shades of pink, blue, and turquoise, with a red banner with the word "diner" on it.

"It's adorable." Claire stood before Willow had completely stopped.

Willow pulled the coach to the side of the roadway in front of the building, and everyone spilled out.

The sun was hot on Sean's shoulders. He looked up and squinted against the brightness of it. He wasn't much of a desert fan. He'd be glad to get back to the coast.

Taylor stretched from side to side, then straightened and studied the building. "I hope the food's better than the design."

Peggy Sue's was even more colorful inside than it was on the outside. The floor tiles were checkered black and pink tiles, and a life-size Betty Boop statuette stood just inside the entrance. She was set up in a replica of a theater ticket booth. Photos of famous artists from the '50s and '60s decorated the walls, and the booths retained the look of the 1950s, when the restaurant had originally been built.

The aroma of onions and grilling burgers made Sean's stomach growl. He hadn't known he was hungry until now.

"This should be good," Tom said, sliding into a booth on the highway side of the building. "I'm gonna get a malt. Haven't had one of those since I can't remember when." He picked up a menu. "I wonder if they have any pie."

"Pie?" Willow asked as she scooted in beside him.

"You know I've never met a pie I didn't like." Tom grinned.

Taylor sat next to Willow, and Claire slid onto the bench across from them. Sean took the space beside her.

"What a fun place." Willow glanced over her shoulder. "Oh look—Elvis."

"Elvis? What?" Sean followed her gaze.

A statue of Elvis Presley playing a guitar stood in the back of the restaurant.

"Is this what a diner was like back when you were young?" Claire asked Willow and Tom.

"Pretty close," Tom said. "I remember my grandfather taking me to a local diner for malts when I was a kid."

A waitress, wearing a dress and apron that looked like it had been taken right out of a classic magazine, took their orders.

Still in a celebratory mood, everyone included a malt with their food, except Sean, who decided on a Coke.

Soon the waitress returned with their drinks. "Enjoy," she told them with a cheery smile. "Your food will be right out."

"Thank you." Willow tasted her malt. "Not long now and we'll be back home."

"I'm not ready for it to be over." Tom used a spoon to dip out a mouthful of his malt. "When we set out, I had my doubts—a group like us making a cross-country trip didn't seem possible. 'Course, Sean came along and gave us a hand."

"God's provision." Willow leaned against Tom and gave Sean a grateful smile.

He smiled back, then looked away. He wasn't who they thought. He'd griped a lot of the way, if not out loud, at least to himself. And now he was bailing before they'd made it home.

But they didn't need him anymore.

The waitress returned with their orders—burgers and fries for Tom and Sean, turkey sandwich for Willow, BLT for Claire and Taylor.

"It's been an outstanding trip, lots of surprises. Hate to see it end." Tom bit into his burger.

Willow picked up a napkin and dabbed a drop of ketchup off his chin. "We've had an awesome time. We've learned a lot. Even fell in love." She planted a kiss on Tom's cheek. "We've become a family … and more." Willow tossed a devilish look at Claire and Sean.

Sean cringed inside. Everyone seemed to think he and Claire belonged together. They didn't. "I'm glad I met you all. I'll be sorry to say goodbye."

"When are you leaving?" Claire asked, voice quieter than usual.

"Before you take the cutoff to Yosemite. I've made reservations for a flight out of Bakersfield into San Jose, then I'll take the shuttle to Monterey." He dipped a fry in ketchup and ate it.

Claire nodded and stirred her malt.

"It won't be the same without you," Willow said.

Tom grasped Sean's arm. "You'll have to come by and visit us."

"I'll do that," Sean said, but it would never happen. These people and this trip would soon be only a memory. Cherished, but a part of his life that he'd put aside. He couldn't spend a lot of time with people like this, no matter how good and kind they might be. It was too painful to care about people who suffered every day.

Taylor leaned on the table. "What was your favorite part of the trip?"

Claire took a bite of her sandwich and chewed slowly, averting her eyes, as if she were afraid of being called on.

Willow forked a bite of salad and chewed thoughtfully. "I know I should say Savannah, because I saw my daughter and grandson, and I so loved our time together. But even more than that—Florida and swimming with the dolphins. It was the most extraordinary experience of my life."

"What about us?" Tom asked.

"Well, that is where we spent our honeymoon." Willow laughed.

"True." Tom smiled. "We'll go back one day." He slurped some of his malt.

"I wanted it to be Nashville," said Taylor. "But that was a disaster." She smiled. "It should be Florida, but it's not. It's Salina, Kansas."

Sean picked up his hamburger. "Salina?"

She steepled her fingers on the table in front of her. "It was horrible having a manic meltdown. But when you all stuck with me when I was at my worst, I felt … loved, more than I can remember. It changed everything." Her eyes filled with tears. "You guys changed everything. I never told you thank you. You saved my life."

Willow reached across the table and took her hand. "We love you, dear."

Taylor swiped away a tear. "I love you too."

"Claire, what was your favorite part of the trip?" Sean asked with more urgency than he'd intended.

She set her sandwich on the plate, took a breath, then said, "I loved all of it. I'm still sick, but I think I'm stronger than when I left home. I haven't accomplished anything extra special or discovered what God wants for me, but I believe he'll show me at the right time. And I did things I never imagined I would. My favorite part was swimming with the dolphins too." She closed her eyes for a moment. "I remember feeling free and whole and healthy. It was magical. The trip was worth it just for that."

That day on the white sands of Florida *had* been magical. He'd almost believed that he and Claire could have a life together. He'd been carried away by the beauty and exhilaration of the sea, dolphins, blue skies, and a beautiful woman. But it had been a momentary delusion. No one could live in a place like that forever.

"What about you, Sean?" Claire asked. "What was your favorite part?"

"All of it. I liked every bit." He took a bite of his burger.

Willow laid both palms flat on the table and sat taller, as if something important had just struck her. "I think God would say to us that no one can steal our joy, because it comes from the Lord. He gives it to us. And he is our strength." She turned her gentle smile on Sean. "*He* is our strength. And is always with us."

Why had she singled him out? He wasn't the one who was sick.

He was fine. Just fine.

CHAPTER FORTY-TWO

When the RV approached the Bakersfield airport, Sean stood and hefted his bag. "Just drop me out front."

Willow pulled into the unloading zone and turned off the engine. She swiveled around in her seat. "Well, this is it."

Trying to ignore the heaviness in his heart, Sean stepped out of the RV and onto the sidewalk in front of the small municipal airport. His life was about to change … again.

Tom clapped a hand on his shoulder. "It's been a pleasure. Stay in touch."

"I will. I'm glad we met."

"Me too. I know I was a bear a lot of the time, but God's been good to me. And he's looking out for you too." Tom gave Sean's shoulder a squeeze.

Willow stepped up to him and gave him a hug. "I don't know what I'm going to do without you. You're like a son." She took his face in her hands. "You take care of yourself. Remember us." She hugged him again, then wiped away tears, stepped back, and stood with Tom.

"I know things started off rough, but I'm glad we're friends," Taylor said, then stepped aside.

"Come here." Sean pulled her into a hug. "You were the best back-seat driver I've ever had." He grinned.

"Glad to be of help." She smiled back.

Daisy stuck her nose out of the RV.

"Ah, Daisy. I almost didn't say goodbye." Sean patted her head. "You've been a good friend, girl. You take care of Willow and Tom."

In answer, Daisy wagged her stub of a tail, along with her hind end.

Sean turned to the last of his companions. "It's been quite a journey, Claire." Staring into her trusting, blue eyes, he felt lost. What could he say? She was more than just someone he'd met along the way. She was a treasure. "I'm glad we met. I won't forget you.

You're one of a kind."

"You too." Her eyes glistened.

"I'm going to miss you." Sean barely managed to get the words out. He was afraid to hug her—he might not let go. He shifted his bag on his shoulder. "Have a great trip home. Enjoy Yosemite." He turned and walked into the terminal.

What would life look like without his traveling friends? They'd begun to feel like a permanent part of his life. He kept walking.

He needed to get home. Begin again.

ৎ৵ও ৫৵৹

Traffic through Santa Cruz was heavy, but the bus driver maneuvered along the highway as if he was driving a sports car. He'd obviously driven this stretch of road many times.

Taylor would have flipped out.

Sean smiled. Soon they left the city behind, and Sean settled back in his seat. The shuttle would have been more comfortable ... if he'd remembered to call.

When the highway dipped down along the ocean beach, he leaned against the window and gazed at the waves hitting the shoreline. The man sitting next to him smelled of stale cigars, ruining any chance of him catching a whiff of the sea.

As they headed farther south, mist closed in around the bus and the temperature dropped. He was glad when cigar man got off in Watsonville, but a woman wearing heavy perfume replaced him.

Sean looked into the fog and longed for the journey to end. When he'd called his mother from the airport, she'd sounded anxious, but promised to pick him up at the bus station. It had been so long since he'd been home that he didn't know what to expect.

The last time he'd seen her she'd been thin and frail and looked like the life had gone out of her. Benjamin had been everything to her, and then, at fifteen, he was gone.

Sean had stayed home, gone to school, and considered working for his father, but finally had to leave. Even though Benjamin had died, it felt like he was still there in the house—sick and suffering.

The affliction went on long after he'd been buried.

The bus wound south on the coastal road, and bushes and wind-twisted cypress pressed in on the highway. The fog cleared momentarily, as if to show off the jagged rocks and foaming sea below.

He'd nearly forgotten how beautiful it was.

He dozed off and startled awake when the driver announced the stop for Monterey.

They left the highway and rolled toward the depot.

Sean's stomach quailed. What would he say to the parents he'd abandoned? Would his father be there to meet the bus? He hoped not.

When the coach pulled into the station, his mother's white SUV waited. It still looked new.

Sean grabbed his bag from under the seat, and made his way toward the front, then stepped off.

His mom stood by the terminal, arms folded across her chest. Her hair was shorter, and she'd lost that traumatized look she'd carried with her for so long. She looked rested … and pretty.

She held up a hand in a tentative wave, then walked toward him. "Oh, Sean. Welcome home. " Then, as if unable to restrain herself, she hugged him and hung on for a long moment before slowly let go. She stepped back and gazed at his face. "You look wonderful." Her blue eyes were gentle and a soft smile rested on her lips. "You always were handsome."

"You're looking good too."

She glanced down at herself. "I'm getting fat."

"No. You look wonderful. Did you cut your hair?"

"I started wearing it short last year, and I colored it. Do you like it?" She showed no trace of anger.

Had she forgiven him? "Yeah, I do. It suits you."

She draped an arm around his waist. "Come on. Let's go home. I'm making your favorite meal."

"Enchiladas?"

She nodded. "And ice cream with strawberries for dessert."

Sean gave her a sideways hug and squeezed. "Thanks, Mom." Why was she being so affectionate? He didn't deserve it.

Later, she'd probably let him know how furious and hurt she'd been all this time. Later.

She leaned against him, and they strolled toward her car.

As she pulled the vehicle against the sidewalk in front of the house, an ache welled up inside Sean. The modest bungalow looked mostly the same. Maybe a bit tidier. It felt like home, and thoughts of his early childhood washed over him. Those had been good days, but they hadn't lasted long.

Only months after Benjamin's birth, things started to go wrong. He was in and out of the hospital for months before the shattering diagnosis of cystic fibrosis was given. A pallor settled over the home and everything and everyone in it. Sean was only six, and at first he didn't understand that his life would never be the same. But he soon learned.

He was afraid. Afraid for Ben. Afraid of the suffering. Afraid his brother would die. And afraid he wouldn't. Afraid he'd languish in his misery forever.

Before Benjamin, life had been fun, filled with activities and joy. After the diagnosis, all that went away, replaced by his parents' worried expressions, whispered conversations, and trips to the hospital.

His mother looked at him. "Sean? Are you all right?"

"Yeah. It's just been a while."

"It has." She studied the house. "We thought about selling, but I just couldn't, especially not after you left. The house seemed like my only connection to my boys."

Her boys?

Sean stared into her deep-blue eyes. "I apologize for taking off like I did. I just couldn't stay."

"I understand. Sometimes I feel like that, like I want to run away." She pressed a palm to his cheek. "Come on. Let's go in. I made sun tea this morning."

Sean stepped inside. As always, the room was decorated in good taste, with a plush sofa, mahogany accessories, and a matching bookcase. The carpet was soft and luxurious beneath his feet.

Memories darkened the space.

He quickly moved out to the back patio. The tiles had been replaced with new stonework, and the yard was lush, bordered by an orchestra of colors, textures, and fragrances. Honeysuckle and roses scented the air.

His mother stepped out and onto the patio, a glass of tea in each hand. She handed him one, moved to the patio table, and sat down.

"Thanks." Seann took a sip. "The yard's not how I remember it."

"I love working in the garden. And now I have time. When Benjamin was sick, things like the garden were neglected. After he was gone, I didn't have the energy ... not for a long while."

"I remember." Sean couldn't keep the bitterness out of his voice.

"It was terrible. And you were neglected the same way this garden was. I wish we'd given you a better childhood. If I had the chance to do it again, I would. Only I don't know what I would have done differently."

The remorse in her voice tore at Sean. He wanted to stop her, but he needed to hear. Needed to know that she had cared.

"Ben was sick so much of the time and needed so much from us. It seemed like all I could do was take care of him. I was just worn out."

Sean's anger ebbed. "You did the best you could. I know that ... but the other kid—me—was lonely."

She reached across the space between them and took his hand. "I hope we can spend time together now. Get to know each other better."

"I don't know how long I'll be staying."

Hurt and regret touched his mother's eyes.

A car door at the neighbors' closed. "Where's Dad?"

"He wanted to meet you at the bus, but he got hung up at work."

He nodded. His father wouldn't be as forgiving as his mother. When Sean was a kid, it was his father who seemed the most distant and angry. Sean wasn't ready to face him, not yet. "Do you mind if I take your car and go down to the bay?"

"No, of course not." She pushed to her feet. "I need to get busy with dinner anyway."

"What time should I be back?"

293

"Six o'clock sound all right?"

"Sounds good. I'm never late for enchiladas."

She pressed the keys into his hand. "The steering pulls a little to the right."

"Okay. I'll be careful."

CHAPTER FORTY-THREE

Sean left the house and drove the streets that ran along the bayside. The smell of sea and brine swept through the open car window, and he breathed deeply. If only he could soak in its purity, it would quiet his spirit.

There weren't many people on the beach, so he pulled off, locked the car, and followed a trail leading to the sand. He strolled along the upper part of the beach and climbed rocks that bordered shallow embankments.

He and Benjamin had played here.

Sometimes they'd pretend Ben would one day get well and be strong. They dreamed of having their own business, right here in Monterey Bay. They'd take visitors out sightseeing or fishing and get rich doing it. He smiled at the naiveté of those young boys.

Squalling seagulls fought over a tidbit left in the sand. The more pompous pelicans sat and watched the bickering, occasionally clacking their bills in disapproval.

Sean moved out onto the sand and moseyed along the beach, memories assailing him. Benjamin had fought hard to live, and God hadn't been fair. Why would he take someone like Ben?

He'd been the kind of kid who always hoped for the best, enjoyed life no matter what came his way, and gave of himself to others. Ben was the kind of person who grew up to make a difference in the world. He should have had his chance.

If one of them needed to die, it should have been Sean.

He settled on a rock sitting along the foot of an embankment. It felt satisfying to be here, but was it where he belonged? If he stayed, what would he do? Go to work for his father? The idea made him squirm. Sitting at a desk and overseeing the minutia of the computer world was the last thing he wanted to do.

Shoving his hands into his pockets, Sean strode back up the beach to the car. He climbed in and stared at the waves as they washed inland. He should leave. Now. Drive to the bus station, get a ticket, and go on his way. He didn't need his father's judgment or anger. He'd had enough of that.

He started the engine, gripped the steering wheel, and pulled onto the road. Maybe he could catch up with the RV at Yosemite. Tom had said they planned to spend a couple of weeks there.

Claire's charming face came to mind.

She'd wanted him to work things out with his parents, to confront his past. She was right. It was like her to do the brave thing.

And now it was time for Sean to stop running, to begin healing. Time to face his father.

When he got home, he dredged up courage, feeling as if Claire, Willow, Tom, and Taylor walked into the house with him, offering their strength.

His mother was in the kitchen.

"Smells good." He gave her a quick hug.

"It's nearly ready." She nodded toward the backyard. "Your father's outside."

"Oh. I didn't see his car." Sean took a shallow breath.

"He always parks in the garage."

No reason to put off the inevitable. Sean headed for the patio. He stepped outside and closed the sliding door behind him.

His father looked up right away, then stood and faced Sean. He stared at Sean, hazel eyes wary. "Son."

He was heavier than when Sean had last seen him, his hair mostly gray now. "Dad."

"It's been a while." He moved toward Sean, reached out, and shook his hand. "Good to see you." He picked up his empty glass. "Can I get you something to drink?"

"Nah. I'm fine." Sean sat on a cushioned patio chair. "How was work?"

"Good." His dad refilled his glass from a pitcher of tea and sat. "I meant to meet you at the bus depot, but I got hung up at work."

"That's all right. I didn't expect you to be there." Sean kept his voice emotionless and turned his focus to a cluster of marigolds growing at the edge of the garden.

His father leaned forward, arms propped on his thighs. "What happened to your motorcycle?"

"I hit an antelope and lived to tell about it, but the bike didn't make it." Sean almost smiled. "I was out in Eastern Oregon when it happened."

"Shame. That was a nice bike."

"Yeah." Sean felt a flash of anger. As usual, his father only thought about the material possession involved, not the danger to his son.

The patio door slid open, and his mother stepped out. "Only a few more minutes and dinner will be ready." She sat beside his dad and took his hand, gazing at Sean as if she were trying to memorize his features.

"What have you been up to?" his father asked.

"Traveling mostly. Working here and there. The last few months I've been driving an RV for a group of people who made a cross-country trip."

"Why'd they need a driver?"

"They're disabled."

He compressed his lips, but didn't respond. "Do you have any plans?"

"I've got a few ideas."

Sean's father nodded slowly. "Any chance you'll stick around here?"

Here it came. His father wanted him to stay and work for him. "Probably not. And I'm *not* working for you, so don't even ask."

"I wasn't going to." His father didn't sound defensive. "Not that I wouldn't like it, but I know how you feel." He rubbed his palms together. "I want you to know I regret what happened … before you left. I never should have pushed you like I did. I wasn't thinking straight in those days … after Benjamin. I just wanted you to stay."

"We both did." His mother rested a hand on his father's shoulder. "We've prayed that one day you'd come home and we'd sit out here and talk … the way a family should." Tears brimmed in her eyes and she let them fall. "Your father and I have learned a lot since you left. We're back in church, and it's not just for show. We love the Lord. We hope you will too one day."

"I might not always live in a way that pleases God but I believe. I thought you did too ... all those years were a lie?"

"Not exactly." His mom brushed away the tears. "There was a time when we did embrace the Lord and his grace. But when the days got hard, we lost our way. Instead of telling anyone, we pretended we were fine."

"I guess I knew that." Sean's heart felt as if it were being held in a vise. He'd done that too.

But he wasn't like that anymore. Claire, Willow, and Tom had shown him what a living faith looked like. They were strong and trusted even when there seemed to be no hope. Not in a phony way, but transparently—imperfect, yet growing and never giving up.

Sean's father rested his arms on his thighs and clasped his hands. "Everything that was happening with Ben ..." He shook his head. "I was mad at God and couldn't trust him. I didn't even know if I believed he existed anymore."

Sean relaxed his jaw and took a breath, but he didn't want to release the resentment.

His dad had been cruel, unavailable.

Sean straightened his back. "I didn't know."

"We didn't want you to. And I knew you didn't want to stick around after Ben died. Why would you? This place was like a tomb. Your life here hadn't exactly been cheery. Your mother and I were no help. We barely spoke, not to each other and not to you." He glanced at her. "We've been working on that too."

Sean hadn't expected transparency or mercy from his parents. He was prepared for the usual harshness and walls.

Now what?

The hostility encasing his heart began to crack, and he couldn't hold back the truth. "I was angry—at everyone. All I wanted was to be a *regular* family. But I knew it would never happen, that it was foolish to even hope for."

"We could have done better." His dad furrowed his brow and stared at his hands.

"I don't think any parent knows what to do when one of their children is dying." More tears spilled onto his mother's cheeks, and she wiped them away. "Everything was about Benjamin, not because we didn't love you, but we just didn't have any more to give … not after all the treatments and the trips to the hospital, nearly losing him again and again, and waiting for the day he would be gone. We failed you, Sean. We're so sorry. Please forgive us."

The last of the wall around Sean's heart came down. "It wasn't just you. It was me too." Guilt pervaded Sean like a dark stain that reached inside and colored his soul. "I was sick of Ben being sick. Sick of him taking all your time. I wanted him … I wanted him to … die. I wanted it to be over." He rubbed his forehead, fighting to hold back tears. "He always loved me, though I was the worst brother ever. And after he died, I realized how much I loved him and wanted him to live, only I couldn't tell him, because he was gone."

His mother pulled Sean into her arms and smoothed his hair the way she once had when he was a child. "You were just a boy. You loved your brother, but it crushes a person's spirit to always be the one who comes last."

Sean hung onto his mother, and then his father's arms came around him. "I didn't really want him to die. I just wanted life to be about something other than sickness and death. I wanted it be about living as a *real* family."

His mother tightened her hold. "We let you down. And there's nothing we can do to give those days back to you. Can you forgive us?"

"I forgive you." Sean sobbed. "I forgive you."

His mother lifted his chin until his eyes met hers. "You and me and your father, we are a family. And Benjamin will always be part of us. He's not here with us, but I know he would tell us to be unafraid, to love, and to live with our arms outstretched."

"We won't hold you back, son," his father said. "Whatever it is that you feel you're supposed to do, we want that for you." He squeezed Sean's shoulder.

"I want to stay for a while," Sean said.

But what would his father say if he knew Sean loved a girl who was sick, a girl who could die, a girl that might suck the life out of him, just the way Benjamin had?

CHAPTER FORTY-FOUR

The RV rounded a tight corner and Claire grabbed hold of the edge of the sofa. She glanced over her shoulder at the ravine that dropped away below them and thanked God they weren't driving on that side of the road.

Taylor threw an anxious look at Claire. "Every place we go there are cliffs."

Claire's stomach tumbled and she prayed Willow knew how to drive a road like this.

"Not too far now," Willow called back.

"How far is not *too* far?"

"Maybe another twenty miles," Tom said.

"Twenty miles? Of this? I can't stay on this road even one more mile." Taylor's words quavered.

"There's no place to turn off." Tom's voice was harsh, his words clipped. "Willow's doing a good job. Relax. Enjoy the view."

Tom had a right to be irritated. Taylor had been a backseat driver for the last six thousand miles, but if he'd used more tact, it would be easier on all of them.

"It's beautiful countryside." Willow gazed out over the mountains.

"Keep your eyes on the road," Taylor said.

Willow laughed. "We're fine. The road is plenty wide enough and it's in good shape. And even if it wasn't, we're in the Lord's hands." She smiled at Taylor in the rearview mirror.

Taylor covered her eyes. "I hate these kinds of roads."

"I don't like them either," Claire said. "Maybe we can try to enjoy the beauty together." Was Taylor on the verge of a serious meltdown? When they turned onto a new highway and drove into a town called Groveland, Claire was quick to say, "This is a cool-looking place."

"Yeah. Cute." Taylor sounded calmer.

Claire let out a long breath. She was tired of traveling, and sightseeing held little appeal. Without Sean, everything seemed less interesting. She just wanted the trip to be over.

"Maybe we can pull off and get something to eat," Tom said.

"I can make sandwiches," Claire said.

Tom groaned. "I've had enough sandwiches to last me a lifetime. Let's eat out."

"I'm with you. I want to get out of this rig," Taylor said.

"That looks like a good place." Tom pointed at a large wood-sided building. "Iron Door Saloon."

Willow looked at the building. "Do you really want to eat in a saloon?"

"The sign says it's a grill too." Taylor gave her a cheesy smile. "I'd *really* like to get off this RV."

Willow let out a sigh. "All right. Let me find a spot."

After Willow parked, Tom followed her out the driver's side door while Taylor and Claire took the steps. The four of them stood in front of the building and silently studied it.

Tom leaned in close to a sign on the door. "Says here it was built in 1863. It's been here a while."

Claire's gaze roamed over the murals painted across the front of the building. There were pictures of the rugged Yosemite mountains, a bear, and a cowboy on his horse. Her sour mood ebbed. "This might be a fun place to visit. Let's go in."

Pictures of local history hung on the walls, along with mounted trophies of deer, moose, caribou, and buffalo. Strangely enough, the ceiling had dollar bills stuck to it. Did they ever fall off?

It was evident the owners had worked hard to maintain the building's historical essence. A heavy wooden bar with a massive mirror above it ran along one side of the saloon. Seating was mostly wooden tables and chairs.

Tom dropped into a chair. "Looks like we've stumbled onto some of the local flavor." He smiled and picked up a small menu. "I'm ready for a good steak."

"Sean would have liked this place." The base of her throat ached as Claire took a seat across from Tom.

Willow glanced around. "Yes. I think he would."

A young man with sandy-brown hair and gray-blue eyes walked up to their table. He was wearing blue jeans and cowboy boots. "Afternoon. I'm Jonathan. Can I get you something to drink?" His eyes lingered on Taylor. "Haven't seen you around. Where you all from?"

"Oregon," Willow said, "but we came the long way around—across the country and now back again."

"That's pretty far, all right. How long have you been traveling?"

"We left Oregon in April."

Jonathan gave a low whistle. "That's a while—four months. You homesick yet?"

Tom opened his menu. "I'd be glad to just keep on driving."

"That sounds like fun." Jonathan opened up a writing pad. "I'm filling in, helping out my sister. But I'll do my best to get your order right and not spill anything on you." He smiled and a dimple appeared in his left cheek. "Drinks?"

Taylor kept her nose in her menu. She looked flushed. "Just water."

"Me too," Claire said.

"Water for all of us," Willow said.

"Okay. Water it is." Jonathan walked away.

"He's a cutie." Willow winked at Taylor.

"I didn't notice." She continued to study her menu.

When Jonathan returned with their drinks and took their orders, Taylor barely glanced at him.

While they waited for their food, Claire picked up a card resting among the cluster of condiments in the center of the table. "Hey, Taylor, they have live music here, and karaoke nights, and open mic nights."

"Really?" Taylor took a drink of water. "Too bad we'll be staying up at Yosemite."

"There's no reason to hurry up there," Willow said. "We can stay here for a few days. I'd like to explore some of the shops in town, and there's a museum. I love museums. There must be a campground near here. We could stay for a couple of nights."

Tom frowned. "I really want to head up to Yosemite. We're so close."

"We'll get there," Willow said. "But first we're going to become acquainted with this charming town and some of its people. And maybe Taylor will get her chance to sing."

As it turned out, there was an RV park close by with spaces available. Finished with their meal, they headed to the location and got a spot. After a short rest, another camper kindly gave the travelers a ride into town. Tom and Willow went off to explore a museum while Claire and Taylor wandered through some of the shops. They ended up back at the Iron Door Saloon.

"It's hot and I'm thirsty. Might as well go in." Taylor pushed on the door and stepped into the cool interior. "They have some gifts here. You might find something for your family."

"I'll take a look." Claire headed for the gift displays, and her feet complained about each step.

Taylor wandered to the bar, where Jonathan was quick to join her.

Claire tried to keep her mind on finding gifts for her folks, but she couldn't help but notice that Taylor's cheeks were flushed. The entire trip, she'd not shown interest in a man. Why Jonathan?

Taylor laughed at something he said.

He placed a sheet of paper on the bar in front of her and handed her a pen.

She wrote on it.

Whatever happened with Taylor was none of Claire's business, so she turned back to the earrings on display in front of her. She found a pair for Autumn and a coffee mug for her father by the time Taylor came over wearing a curious smile.

"What are you so happy about?"

"I'm going to do it."

"Do what?"

"Perform. Right here. Tonight. It's open mic night."

"You are?" Claire hugged her. "I'm thrilled for you." But inside she quailed. What if something like the disaster in Nashville happened again? "Are you ready?"

"I think so. Jonathan said they like to have all kinds of

303

performers." She glanced back at the bar.

"Oh, he did, did he?" Claire grinned. Her gaze went to Jonathan. "He seems nice, and he's good-looking."

"I hope you don't mind, but he invited me to go out to a ranch where he works ... this afternoon."

"No, I don't mind." Claire studied Taylor. "Are you sure it's all right, though? You barely know him."

"He works with troubled teens who live at the ranch. His sister is the cook here, and she's coming with us." She watched Jonathan. "If it's all right with you, I'm going to hang out for a while."

Claire knew a brush-off when she saw one. "No problem. So you want me to meet you back here tonight?"

"Oh, I'll be back in plenty of time. Jonathan will drop me off at the RV." With a wave she hurried away.

Claire set the cup and earrings back on the display shelf. Shopping didn't feel like fun anymore. She headed for the door and stepped out into the heat.

How far was it to the RV park? Her head felt like a bomb had gone off inside. She needed to lie down.

She wandered along the street. Where were Willow and Tom? She said it was a small museum. Claire found a bench in the shade, sat down, and dialed a number on her cell phone.

"Hello." Her mother's voice sounded so good.

"Hi, Mom. It's Claire. It's time for me to come home."

CHAPTER FORTY-FIVE

Claire applied a pale lipstick, then stood back and looked at her image in the mirror. Not bad.

Taylor peered into the RV's bathroom. "Does my hair look all right?"

"It's gorgeous, like always," Claire said. "You have perfect hair—thick and long, with just enough curl. People pay a lot of money to get hair like yours." She lifted her own locks. "Mine's limp and lifeless."

Taylor turned and faced Claire. "Are you kidding? It's beautiful."

"Okay, then, we both look great." It was her life that felt limp, not her hair. It had been that way since Sean left.

Taylor applied lipstick, then stood back and smoothed her white, blousy shirt over her hips. "I wish it wasn't so hot. I'd wear my jean jacket."

"How did things go this afternoon?"

"Good. Jonathan's a really nice guy."

"What's the ranch like?"

"Big. Jonathan said they have twenty-five hundred acres. It's a working ranch, only they have more teenagers than ranch hands. The kids have chores and get ranching experience, along with counseling and relationship-building."

Willow poked her head in the door. "Time to go, ladies." She focused on Taylor. "You look beautiful."

Taylor placed a hand on her hip and tipped slightly to the side. "Really?"

"Yes. And you know it."

"Looks don't count if I sing like a frog."

Willow grasped both of Taylor's hands. "You have a lovely voice and fabulous songs. I have no doubt you'll do well. But we've got to get there."

Taylor grabbed her guitar and stepped out of the RV.

Willow clasped a leash onto Daisy's collar. "I hope they don't mind having a dog in the place, but it wouldn't be right if she missed out." She gave Daisy a pat and headed for the door.

Claire followed.

When they reached the saloon, Jonathan met them at the entrance, glanced at Daisy, but didn't say a word about her. Instead, he focused on Taylor. "You look great. Can't wait to hear you sing."

"Don't expect too much."

Jonathan didn't seem to hear her. "I saved us a spot." He led them to a table up front. Before Taylor could sit, he pulled out a chair for her.

The place was packed. Where had everyone come from?

Moving among the din of voices, waitresses carried trays of food and drinks. Country music spilled from an old-fashioned jukebox. No one complained about Daisy, but several people oohed and aahed over her.

Jonathan placed Taylor's guitar on the stage, then returned. He leaned close to her and whispered something in her ear.

She laughed. They seemed awfully friendly for having just met. Did he know yet about her being bipolar?

A man dressed in shorts and flip-flops walked onto the stage. He looked like he belonged on a California beach. He cracked a few jokes, then introduced the first entertainer—Jack, a comedian and a regular that the crowd cheered for.

Jack soon had everyone laughing so hard they were holding their stomachs. He had a gift for seeing everyday events with a new eye and sharing them in a way that was hilarious.

Claire couldn't remember laughing so hard in recent history. Every once in a while, she glanced at Taylor, who also seemed to be having a good time. Claire prayed all would go well. Another Nashville might crush Taylor.

A second comedian wasn't as funny as Chuck, and received less than enthusiastic applause when he stepped off the stage.

The man in the flip-flops returned. "Let's change things up a bit with a little music. We have a new talent in town. A real pretty gal from Oregon, who, I've been told, sings like a bird. You're going to love her. Welcome Taylor Reaves!" He raised his hands and clapped, as did the audience.

Taylor tossed a panicked look at Claire. "I'm on."

"You're ready." Claire smiled encouragement. Taylor *was* ready. If she only knew that.

Taylor popped out of her seat and walked to the stage. Her guitar waited for her, where Jonathan had left it propped against the stage wall. She picked it up, slung it over her shoulder, and moved to the microphone.

Willow grabbed hold of Claire's hand. "Here she goes."

Claire took a deep breath. *Come on, Taylor. You can do it.*

Taylor grabbed the microphone stand. "Thank you. The song I'm about to sing is especially close to my heart. It's all about suffering." She grinned. "Well, it *is* country."

The crowd laughed.

"And it's also about friendship and love and hope. It's my life." She moved back a step and strummed the guitar, then looked up and moved toward the microphone.

Claire held her breath.

When Taylor's rich alto filled the room, joy and pride filled Claire.

Tonight Taylor's voice was fuller, more powerful and tender all at the same time. In song, she told the story of a little girl who watched her father's back as he walked away from her and her mama. She sang about the dark days when there seemed to be nothing to live for, then the light that showed her a new way.

Tears filled Claire's eyes, and when they spilled over, she tried to stop them. The song was beautiful—Taylor was beautiful. If only her sister had heard this, had known Taylor, had discovered there was hope.

When Taylor finished, people stood and the room erupted with applause, cheers, and whistles.

Taylor broke into a broad smile and held her guitar above her head, then bowed and walked off the stage.

Willow met her and gave her a big hug before she even reached the table.

Claire pulled Taylor into her arms, fresh tears streaming down her cheeks. "I loved it. It was wonderful."

"Maybe you could make it in Nashville, after all." Tom patted her back.

"I figured you were good, but I had no idea," Jonathan said. "Just think, I'll be able to say I knew you when …"

Taylor laughed. "You're getting ahead of me. All I did was sing one song in front of a crowd in a saloon." Her eyes sparkled with delight. "But it felt pretty great."

Over the next few days Taylor spent most of her time with Jonathan while Claire joined Willow and Tom on multiple tours of Yosemite.

The national park was everything she'd imagined—massive waterfalls, green meadows, powerful granite mountains, and giant trees. There were also a lot of winding cliff roads, which meant it was just as well that Taylor wasn't with them.

The morning of the fourth day, Claire sat at the table eating a bowl of cereal. It was time to tell everyone she was heading home. She'd already purchased her bus ticket. Now that she'd decided to go, she could hardly wait to see her family and Cinnamon. "Any plans today?"

"I'm going up to the ranch," Taylor said. "They're having some sort of horseback riding thing going on." She shrugged. "I barely know how to ride, but I guess it doesn't matter."

"We're meeting with some new friends, Ed and Sarah," Willow said. "They want to tell us more about a traveling ministry they're involved in. It sounds exciting. They travel to churches all over the West Coast and help out in any way that's needed."

Claire nodded. "That sounds great." Her mouth went dry, and her heart skittered. "I'm going to take the bus back to Oregon tomorrow. I'm not sure what I'm going to do there, but I need to go."

"You might have more opportunities for writing and illustrating," Taylor said. "You're good. You ought to keep working on it."

"It's really just a hobby. I seriously doubt anything will ever come of it." Claire could barely even acknowledge to herself that she would love it if someone thought enough of her stories to publish them. But hoping for something like that was foolish.

Tom sat across the table from Claire. "We can take you home."

"I've already got my ticket. And I know you're not ready to leave yet. I'll be fine. It's not that far."

"The rest of the trip won't be the same without you."

Willow hugged Claire around the neck. "I really wish you'd change your mind. Please stay."

Taylor frowned. "We're finally getting along, and now you're leaving? It's just a couple of more weeks."

"I need to go. But we'll stay in touch." Claire held back tears.

Tom glanced at Willow. "We've decided to team up with the church group. I'm still healthy enough, and Willow's a good driver, so now's our time."

"That sounds perfect for you guys. I'm happy for you."

Willow settled a gentle look on Claire. "We'll be stopping by your place whenever we can."

Claire's heart squeezed. She could hardly imagine daily life without these dear people being a part of it. They were family now. "I'll be counting on that."

"Since everyone's making announcements, I might as well throw mine in," Taylor said. "I'll be sticking around here. I'm going to work at the ranch where Jonathan works."

"Really? What will you be doing there?" Willow asked.

"Mostly just general labor to begin with, but I'll be bunking with some of the girls. It could work into something meaningful. I feel like I belong there … with the kids. Turns out I get along with messed-up teens. Who knew?" She grinned.

Willow beamed approval. "You're going to be wonderful with those kids. The Lord knew all along."

"What about your music?" Claire asked.

"I don't think I'm cut out to be a performer. I'd rather keep things light and fun. I'm sure there will be plenty of opportunities to play out at the ranch."

"I'm really happy for you." And Claire was. "Instead of singing, you're working with kids. Maybe that means I will become a writer after all."

"Weird to be going our separate ways," Tom said. "I'm used to us hanging out together."

Claire let out a sigh. "Yeah. It's going to be hard to go back to the way things were."

"Trust me, they won't be the same." Willow gave one of her motherly looks. "You've changed."

Claire tried to smile. She wanted to believe Willow.

CHAPTER FORTY-SIX

Claire checked her bags, then bought a pack of gum from a candy machine. A bus pulled into the depot, and dread rose inside her chest. Was she doing the right thing?

"That's you." Taylor grabbed her arm. "I have to say this before you go." She took a breath. "When we first met I thought you were a loser. I was the loser." She grinned. "Only not so much these days. Thanks to you."

Claire hugged her. "You're a good friend."

"Come here, young lady." Tom pulled Claire into a hug. "I can't believe you're leaving us." He held her away from him. "If I had a daughter, I'd want her to be just like you."

"Thanks, Tom." She studied his face, lined by the years. "You're a great second dad." She kissed his cheek. "Take care of yourself, and make sure to take just enough risks, but not too many."

"Aye aye, captain." He saluted her.

"I'll keep an eye on him." Willow took hold of Claire's hands. "You are a precious young woman. God has great things in store for you. And I can't wait to see what they are."

"I hope I don't have to wait too long to find out."

"All in the proper time. You'll see." She kissed Claire on the cheek and hugged her. "I love you, sweetie. We'll bring the rest of your things when we get home."

"Thank you." Claire wiped away tears. "I'd better get on the bus before it leaves without me." She carried her cane but didn't use it.

The driver loaded her bags. Then, with her legs feeling heavier than usual, Claire climbed the steps and moved to the back of the bus. She found a seat next to a window. When the bus pulled away, she waved and didn't even try to hold back her tears.

She told herself she wasn't leaving her life behind, though it felt like it. But she had a family waiting for her in Oregon. And if Willow was right, a new adventure.

The hours dragged, but Claire's spirits lifted as the bus traveled north. Heavy forests and rolling hills dressed in sunbaked grasses welcomed her. Familiar landmarks eased her sadness. The closer to home, the more she struggled to remain seated. She bounced her legs and hummed quietly, envisioning the coming reunion.

When the bus pulled into the depot, she spotted her parents right away, grabbed her backpack, and made her way down the aisle. Claire eased down the bus steps.

Her mother waited on the sidewalk, wearing a big smile, arms open. When Claire took the last step her mother pulled her into a tight hug. "It's so good to see you."

"Mom." Claire held onto her for a long moment, then stepped into her father's waiting embrace.

"I've missed you." He smoothed her hair off her face and kissed her forehead.

"I missed you too." Claire couldn't stop smiling. Coming home had been the right thing to do.

She and her parents set out for the ranch while her mother peppered her with questions. The excitement and adventures of the trip spilled out—one story after another. The memories grew fonder and burrowed deeper with the telling.

Her father turned into their driveway, and Claire breathed in the smell of late summer—a second cutting of hay and ripening fruit. She'd forgotten how much she loved the ranch. "I can't wait to see Cinnamon. How is she?"

"Good." Her mother smiled at her over her shoulder. "I'm sure she knows you're coming home. She's been pacing the corral fence and watching the driveway since yesterday."

Her father cleared his throat. "She's been out in the pasture with the other horses, but we brought her down and put her in the corral for you."

"I can't wait to ride her. I'm going to take her out tomorrow."

"Riding? Do you think that's a good idea?" Her mother looked at her with a furrowed brow.

"Maybe not, but I'm doing it anyway. I managed to ride a mule at the Grand Canyon, didn't I? And I've been having more good days than I used to."

Claire's father winked at her in the rearview mirror.

That evening Claire slid beneath cool sheets in her own bed for the first time in months, tired but content. A summer breeze and the sound of crickets drifted through her bedroom window.

She still didn't know what lay before her, but fear of the unknown no longer held her in its grip. Retelling the stories of her journey reminded her of all the things she'd done that she'd never imagined she could do.

God had helped her along the way. That wouldn't stop now just because she was home.

Maybe this is what Willow had meant when she talked about being thankful in any circumstance. The pain in Claire's body remained, but it didn't torment her. Maybe it was the eagerness for the coming days.

⁂

She woke before sunrise, when the early morning light touched the sky. Stiff and weak, she rolled onto her side and sat up. With a careful stretch, she smiled. It was a new day.

Aided by her cane, she hobbled into the kitchen. No one was up, so she put coffee on and went outside.

It was too early for autumn, but she could almost taste it in the air. Her eyes fell upon Cinnamon.

Last night's reunion had been too short, so she headed for the corral. "Good morning, girl."

The horse put her head over the fence and nickered.

"How are you?" Claire ran a hand down Cinnamon's face and breathed in the musty fragrance. "I was hoping we could ride today, but we might have to wait until tomorrow. I'm pretty sore from all the hours on the bus yesterday."

The screen door thudded closed, and Claire's mom stepped out on the porch, a coffee mug in each hand.

Claire leaned on the wooden fence. Tomorrow she would ride Cinnamon. And if she couldn't? Well, it would be the day after, then. No matter what, she was riding. She was going to learn to live each

Bonnie Leon

day as it came.

Her mom headed toward her. "Thought you might like some coffee." She gave a mug to Claire. "Would you like to join us for church this morning? I could use some help in the Sunday school class."

"I think I'm up to that."

"Wonderful. The kids will love having you back. They've been asking about you."

"You're making that up. I stopped teaching a year ago."

"Well, some of them remember you."

"That's nice to know." Claire leaned against the fence and took in the surrounding hills, blanketed in summer-scorched grass. "I'd forgotten how beautiful it is here."

Her mother's gaze roamed across the landscape. "We are blessed."

"It sure feels good to be home."

Her mother draped an around Claire's shoulders and gave her a squeeze. "And so good to have you here."

They headed back to the house.

Her mom glanced at a big oak tree near the garden. "Your father and I had a headstone made for Melissa. It's under the oak where you two used to swing."

An ache swelled in Claire's chest. "I wish we'd been closer. Maybe I could have helped her. Sometimes, when you're in a dark place, it's hard to see any light at all."

"When you were young, you two were such good friends. But Melissa changed. She withdrew from us."

"Did she? Or did we push her away? Was it easier to just let go?"

Sorrow touched her mother's eyes.

Claire shouldn't have said anything. She leaned against her mother. "How about some breakfast?"

They walked into the house, and the smell of frying bacon greeted them. Her father's way of saying, "Welcome home."

Later that morning, Claire shared one of her stories with the Sunday school class. It was about some odd-looking stones who learned how precious they were to God. The tale flowed and the kids liked it so much they asked for another. She promised to have another story ready for the following Sunday.

It didn't take long for Claire to fall into step with ranch life, though it was different than before. She rode Cinnamon often and helped in the garden. There were painful consequences for her activities, but they were worth it. On the roughest days, she'd recall her adventures with Tom, Willow, Taylor, and Sean. The memories were sweet and gave her strength. She frequently heard Willow's gentle voice offering guidance. Often it drove her to the Bible where she found answers to her questions and comfort for her sorrows.

The next afternoon, she and her mother were picking cantaloupe when Claire came across a huge pumpkin. "How did this get mixed up with the cantaloupe?"

"Probably a pesky bird dropped a seed, or the wind blew it in. I think we should designate this one as the jack-o'-lantern for Halloween." Claire's mother studied it. "This is going to be a monster." She set a cantaloupe in a wheelbarrow. "Let's take a break."

After getting glasses of lemonade, they settled into chairs on the patio. Tall, golden grasses in the field danced in the breeze. It cooled Claire's skin. "The days are getting shorter and cooler. I can feel it in my body."

"Maybe this year will be better than last. You're stronger than you were last summer." Her mother studied her. "You've changed, Claire."

"Have I?"

"You're determined, more resolute, more content. And you're engaged with the world. Before you left, you'd pulled inside yourself, shutting out most everything."

"I didn't see it then, but you're right. Sometimes on the trip I felt more confident, more resilient. But the rest of the time I thought I couldn't do *anything*." She took a drink of lemonade. "I can't help it but sometimes I still long for the old me, the one before I got sick. I want to do everything I used to be able to do. Like ride Cinnamon full out instead of holding her back, to tear through a forest trail on my dirt bike." Using her index finger, she caught a droplet of water tracing a line down the outside of her glass. "But I feel freer than I did before leaving. And I'm trying to be okay with who I am. I've got to get used to my life the way it is now." She gazed at an ancient oak with leaves scattered at its feet. "I still don't understand the ways of God, but I know I can trust him. At least, I feel that way on a good day." She grinned. "I haven't arrived yet. But I have more peace than I did before, and I think that's what I want more than anything."

Her mother reached across the table and grabbed a hold of Claire's hand. "I know it's not easy for you."

"It's not. Every day I have to fight. This is the only life I have, and I'm determined to keep pushing so I can keep living, not just existing. But I'm afraid that if I ever get completely comfortable with who I am, then I've given up on who I can become. And I can't let that happen."

CHAPTER FORTY-SEVEN

During her first several weeks home, Claire hadn't been able to bring herself to visit her sister's memorial. She wasn't ready to come face to face with Melissa's death. But this afternoon after picking one of the last batch of summer roses, she knew it was time and took the bouquet and made her way to the old oak.

Her father had left the tire swing just as it had been. The headstone wasn't elaborate, but a picture of her sister had been imprinted in the granite. Claire stared at the image for a long while.

Melissa had been so beautiful. Her laugh resonated through Claire's mind. It had always made her think of deep-throated wind chimes. On the days of light, Melissa loved life and always had a knack for finding fun.

Claire's eyes moved to the inscription.

Melissa Murray, beloved daughter
May 05, 1996 — June 11, 2015
Untamed – Forever in our hearts – Always in our thoughts

With an ache at the base of her throat, Claire sat on a bench her father had built. Her sister's life had been too short. She should still be here. *I didn't understand. I'm sorry. I should have been a better sister.*

Claire remained there a long while, crying, reminiscing, and praying, then left lighter of spirit. Melissa would have forgiven her.

Her legs ached, but she walked to Cinnamon's corral anyway. Leaning on the fence, she waited, knowing the mare would trot across the enclosure and nuzzle her. When Cinnamon reached her head over the fence, Claire looked into her big brown eyes. "How you doing, girl?" She rested her hand on the horse's velvety soft lips. "Do you know how beautiful you are?"

The horse nickered as if she understood.

Claire combed the horse's mane with her fingers. "Do you want me to let you into the pasture? I'll bet you do."

The sound of an engine carried up the gravel driveway.

Who was here? Claire looked over her shoulder.

A motorcycle rolled into view.

Claire turned and faced the road.

Whoever was on the bike headed toward her and stopped about ten feet away.

Claire's heart rate picked up.

Sean?

But it couldn't be. He was in Monterey.

The man removed his helmet.

It was him.

The world tilted and Claire grabbed hold of the fence.

Sean smiled and dismounted, then walked toward her. "Hey. How are you?"

"I'm good."

An awkward pause hovered between them.

"What are you doing here?" That sounded rude.

"Just in the neighborhood." He tucked his helmet under one arm. "Actually, I've been missing you. Hope you don't mind my dropping by."

Missing me? "No. I don't mind at all." Claire was so glad to see him she wanted to leap into his arms. "How did you find me?"

"I stopped off in Groveland. I had hoped you were still there. Tom told me where you lived." He turned to the paddock. "I take it this is Cinnamon." He ran a hand over the horse's neck. "She's a beauty."

"She is. You'll be happy to hear that we've been riding together."

"Really?" He smiled, his hazel eyes teasing. "I knew you would."

"I figured if I could ride a mule, I could ride her." Claire glanced toward the house. "Would you like to sit and have something to drink?"

"Sounds good. It's hot here, worse than I expected."

"Yeah. This time of year the days are still pretty warm."

They walked to the house, her mind in a frenzy. Why was he here? He said he'd missed her. But he'd driven all the way from California. He could have called.

The back door opened and her mother stepped out.

"Mom, I want you to meet Sean Sullivan. You remember … I told you about him. He drove the RV for us."

"The hitchhiker? Why, yes. How nice to meet you." She reached out and shook Sean's hand. "I'll get us some iced tea. Have a seat." She nodded at the patio table.

Sean and Claire sat.

Sean rocked his feet, heel to toe. "Nice place. I can see why you love it here."

"It's home."

Her mother reappeared with glasses and a pitcher of tea.

The three of them chatted. Claire's mother asked all sorts of questions, but the one Claire wanted answered most—why was Sean here?

When there was a break in the conversation, Sean said, "Claire, do you want to go for a ride? I'd like to show you something."

"On your motorcycle?"

"Yeah. I'm a good driver. Are you feeling good enough to go?" He glanced at her mother, hesitation in his eyes.

"I'm feeling okay."

"You two go," her mother said. "I'll get the pork chops ready for the barbecue. Will you join us for dinner, Sean?"

"I'd like that." He stood. "Do you have a helmet? You said you used to ride."

"I rode dirt bikes. But I've got a helmet." She tried not to limp as she walked to the shop. She grabbed the helmet from its peg on the wall and hurried back. "What are you going to show me?" She pulled on the helmet. "I live here, so I ought to know more about this area than you."

"You'll see." His smile was full of mischief.

Claire climbed on the bike behind Sean and put her feet on the pegs.

He glanced back. "Ready?"

"Uh-huh."

"You better hang on. I'd hate it if you fell off." He started the engine, and it pulsed beneath them.

Claire put her arms around his waist. The closeness was unnerving.

Sean headed for the road. When they reached the highway, he turned south and roared down the pavement.

Claire hung on tighter as the countryside flew past. She rested her head against his back, at first to keep the wind and bugs out of her face, but soon it felt like she belonged there. It was exhilarating to roar down the country highway.

It was perfect.

Sean drove through town, expertly threading his way through traffic, then he broke free and headed west.

The wind and sun were like a warm bath washing away her pain, fear, and sorrow.

"How you doing back there?" Sean hollered.

"Fantastic." Claire laughed.

"Good." He picked up speed. He'd gone only about five miles out of town when he pulled up in front of a shop of some kind. He turned off the engine and took off his helmet. "We're here."

Claire removed her helmet and climbed off the bike. "Here where?" All she could see was a shop and a small house a couple of hundred feet to the left of it and back from the road. Did he need parts or something?

He turned and looked at the building. "What do you think?"

"About what? The shop?"

"Yeah. The shop." He grinned.

"Sean, what are you trying to say?"

He looked at her, his expression no longer teasing, but serious. "Claire Murray, ever since we said goodbye at the airport in Bakersfield, you're all I've thought about."

"I've been thinking about you too." Claire's heart pounded in her chest, only this time it didn't have anything to do with her illness.

"I spent a lot of time in Monterey walking the beaches, praying, and talking to my parents. I had a lot to work out. I don't understand everything that happened while I was home or in the years before, not yet, but what I do know is that I'm the one who is disabled— emotionally."

Claire's gaze didn't waver. "I know."

"You knew all the time that I was the one who needed the most help?"

"I don't know about most, but you were in trouble. It took me a while to see it, but I knew something was really wrong." She placed her palm against his chest. "Sometimes it's the wounds in a person's heart that are the hardest to overcome."

"I get that now. I haven't been able to love or trust anyone, especially not myself, for a long time. My brother's illness and his dying scarred me more than I knew. I blamed my parents. I even blamed Benjamin. But none of it had to do with them. It was me."

Her heart breaking for Sean, Claire caressed his cheek. "Don't be so hard on yourself. You were just a kid when you were going through that."

He scuffed the ground with the toe of his boot. "When Ben died I knew it should have been me."

"No," Claire whispered.

"I stayed angry and bitter all these years, closed myself off to love—closed myself off to you." He looked at her in a way no man ever had. He saw her, not her illness.

"I love you, Claire. I've been afraid to say it, but I do." He took her hand and pressed his lips to it.

"I bought this place for you, for us. I found it online a few weeks ago and signed the papers yesterday. There's the shop, and the house. And twenty acres of land too. It's a good place for a new beginning." His hands gently took hold of her arms. "I want to make a new start— for us." His eyes held hers.

"What about my illness? I'm still sick. That hasn't changed and probably never will." She turned away from him. "I'd be like Ben, dragging you down."

"No. That's not true. And I don't care about your illness." He stepped around her and faced her. "That didn't come out right. What I mean is I love you no matter what. And I can't stop loving you. I don't want to stop. All I want is to share your life, the good and the bad." He pulled her to him. "I love you just the way you are."

Claire thought her heart would burst. "I love you too. I prayed God would bring someone into my life, someone who loves me just as I am." She took his face in her hands. "I hoped it was you, but I was too afraid—"

"Don't be afraid. Trust me. Trust God." Sean pulled her closer.

Was he going to kiss her?

His eyes went to her mouth.

He *was*.

"I've never kissed a man before." Her voice quaked.

He smiled. "Well then, we'd better make the first an outstanding one." He tenderly held her face in his hands and pressed a kiss to one corner of her lips and then the other.

Claire thought she might faint.

He brushed his lips over the fullness of her mouth, a whisper of a kiss. "I love you so much." He pressed his lips more earnestly.

Claire draped her arms around his neck and returned the kiss. He covered her mouth with his.

Claire was trembling so hard, she feared her legs would go out from under her.

Their faces parted ever so slightly.

"Sean Sullivan, that was perfect." She smiled, trying to keep her tremulous lips still. "But it's not enough. I need another one." She caressed his lips with hers and whispered, "I love you."

"I love you more," he whispered against her mouth.

They smiled at one another, then laughed, and fell into one another's embrace. They stayed like that for a long while, Claire rejoicing in Sean's love … the Father's gift.

And then they looked at the old building.

"It's not much," Sean said. "But I've always liked working on motorcycles. I know I can make a go of it."

"Maybe I can help."

"You know how to work on bikes?"

"Actually, yes, a little. I used to fix my dirt bike, back when I rode." Claire leaned against Sean. "And I might be able to make a little money by writing. Willow and Taylor like my stories. They think I should get them published."

"That would be amazing." He pressed a kiss to her forehead. "Whatever happens, we'll do it together." He tightened his hold on her. "I want to spend my life with you." He looked out over the pasture. "Who knows? Maybe one day there will be children racing around this field or helping me in the shop."

"But—"

"No buts. Whatever happens, we can do it with God's help. And he can do anything."

Claire rested her head against his chest, her heart and spirit full.

"Yes, anything is possible."

The End

Bio

Bonnie Leon is the author of more than twenty novels, including the best-selling *The Journey of Eleven Moons.*

On June 11, 1991, a log truck hit the van she was driving, and her world changed. The accident left her unable to work. After months of rehabilitation, she was told by physicians that she would never return to a normal life. Facing a daunting fight to reclaim a sense of normalcy, and in search of personal value, she discovered writing. She has been creating stories ever since. Through chronic pain and disability, she found new purpose.

Bonnie is familiar with the challenges of disability beyond her personal experience. Her sister endured the debilitating illnesses of lupus, multiple sclerosis, and bipolar disorder. And her daughter is grappling with the chronic progressive disorder of syringomyelia.

As often as possible, Bonnie speaks for women's groups, teaches at writing seminars, and mentors young writers. She also administers an online support group for those living with chronic pain and disability and is a participating member of the Syringomyelia and Chiari Network. (www.togetherwearestronger.org)

Married to her teenage sweetheart, she is the mother of three grown children and has eight grandchildren. Bonnie and her husband, Greg, live in the mountains of southern Oregon.

Acknowledgments

I've longed to write *To Dance with Dolphins* for a long while but have had to wait. I'm trusting that God's timing is perfect.

I live with disability and chronic pain, and through the years I've learned a good deal about living and loving in an altered state. But this story needed to be about more than my personal experience. I reached out, and so many exceptional people came alongside to ignite this tale.

Though neither my sister Leslie nor I knew it at the time, her personal struggle opened my eyes to truth. She lived with lupus, multiple sclerosis, and bipolar disorder. Her fight for significance was not always triumphant, but there were many bright moments, and in the end she prevailed.

Dear daughter Sarah, you are a beautiful picture of courage. Even when the light of hope fades, you smile and stand strong against the coming storm.

And to my oldest daughter, Kristina, you are a blessing. No matter the time or day, you will be here when I need help, especially on my worst days. Your kindness makes it possible for me to write.

Kyleah Kohl, I owe you a great deal. Your sweet spirit and personal experience with dysautonomia helped bring Claire Murray to life in this story. Thank you, Kyleah, for trusting me with this very private part of your life. And I owe your mother, Deanna, a great big hug for sharing you with me.

I have many friends who live with disability. Their insights, personal experiences, and encouragement brought greater depth to this story. Thank you, April McGowan, Ollie Gamble, Patti Iverson, Jane Squires, Judy Gann, Connie Francis, Natalie Valenzuela Royston, John Edward Blake, Brandon Ketcham, Jane Lindemann, and Renee Charon. You have blessed me.

Special appreciation goes to my dear friend Kathy Steeves, who lives with MS. I am thankful for your prayers and for the example of your tenderness toward God and others. You inspire me to be a better person.

I could never complete a book without my critique buddies. Once again, thank you, Ann Shorey, Judy Gann, and Sarah Sundin. I appreciate you all. I owe you for hanging with me through this project.

Thank you, Andrea Cox. You are tough, and we didn't always agree, but in the end your hard work made this book better.

And special thanks go to Faith Ogard and Allisia Wyson, who took part in an online contest to name Willow's dog, Daisy. I love the name you came up with. It's perfect.

Wendy Lawton, thank you for believing in this book. I have not forgotten the first time we discussed this story. Your enthusiasm has stayed with me through the years and helped me hang on to the dream until it became reality.

Sherrie Ashcraft, I am grateful for your faithfulness, oversight of my work, and your prayers.

Nicole Miller, you've done it again. I think this is my all-time favorite cover. It is stunning, and you are amazing.

Christina Tarabochia, along with your other roles at Ashberry Lane Publishing, you are the hardest-working editor I've ever known. You don't give up. You don't settle. You keep working until a book shines. The words *thank you* are not enough to express my gratitude. You're the best!

Did you enjoy this book? If so, please sign up for the Ashberry Lane newsletter at www.ashberrylane.com. Don't miss future Heartfelt Tales of Faith. Also, we'd love for you to share your opinion of *To Dance with Dolphins*, if you wouldn't mind leaving a quick, honest review on one of the many online sites.

Thank you!

Enjoy another Ashberry Lane book from Bonnie Leon!

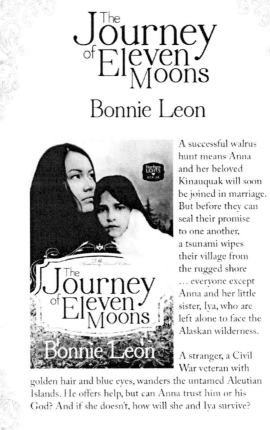

A successful walrus hunt means Anna and her beloved Kinauquak will soon be joined in marriage. But before they can seal their promise to one another, a tsunami wipes their village from the rugged shore … everyone except Anna and her little sister, Iya, who are left alone to face the Alaskan wilderness.

A stranger, a Civil War veteran with golden hair and blue eyes, wanders the untamed Aleutian Islands. He offers help, but can Anna trust him or his God? And if she doesn't, how will she and Iya survive?

Daughter OF THE Cimarron

SAMUEL HALL

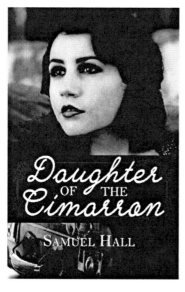

Divorcing a cheating husband means disgracing her family, but Claire Devoe can't take it anymore. Forced to provide for herself, she travels the Midwest with a sales crew. Can she trust the God who didn't save her first marriage to lead her through the maze of new love and overwhelming expectations? The long twilight of the Great Depression—with its debt, disgrace, drought, and despair—becomes the crucible that remakes her life.

ASHBERRY LANE

ASHBERRYLANE.COM

Like
THERE'S NO
Tomorrow

Scottish widower Ian MacLean is plagued by a mischievous grannie, bitter regrets, and an ache for something he'll never have again. His only hope for freedom is to bring his grannie's sister home from America. But first, he'll have to convince her young companion, Emily Chapman, to let the woman go.

Emily devotes herself to foster youth and her beloved Aunt Grace. Caring for others quiets a secret fear she keeps close to her heart. But when Ian appears, wanting to whisk Grace off to Scotland, everything Emily holds dear is at risk.

CAMILLE EIDE

ASHBERRY
LANE

ASHBERRYLANE.COM

Like a Love Song

CAMILLE EIDE

When she finally surrenders her heart, will it be too late?

Susan Quinn, a social worker turned surrogate mom to foster teens, fights to save the group home she's worked hard to build. But now, she faces a dwindling staff, foreclosure, and old heartaches that won't stay buried. Her only hope lies with the last person she'd ever turn to—a brawny handyman with a guitar, a questionable past, and a God he keeps calling Father.

ASHBERRY LANE

ASHBERRYLANE.COM

BROKEN *Wings*

THE Thistle SERIES
BOOK ONE

DIANNE PRICE

He lives to fly—until a piece of flak changes his life forever.

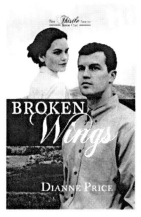

A tragic childhood has turned American Air Forces Colonel Rob Savage into an outwardly indifferent loner who is afraid to give his heart to anyone. RAF nurse Maggie McGrath has always dreamed of falling in love and settling down in a thatched cottage to raise a croftful of bairns, but the war has taken her far from Innisbraw, her tiny Scots island home.

Hitler's bloody quest to conquer Europe seems far away when Rob and Maggie are sent to an infirmary on Innisbraw to begin his rehabilitation from disabling injuries. Yet they find themselves caught in a battle between Rob's past, God's plan, and the evil some islanders harbor in their souls.

Which will triumph?

ASHBERRY
LANE
ASHBERRYLANE.COM

On the Threshold

Sherrie Ashcraft &
Christina Berry Tarabochia

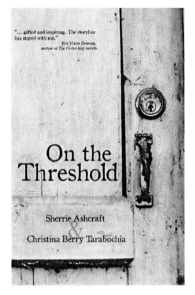

"... gifted and inspiring. The storyline has stayed with me."
Eva Marie Everson, author of The Cedar Key novels

On the Threshold

Sherrie Ashcraft
&
Christina Berry Tarabochia

Suzanne ~
a mother with a
long-held secret

Tony ~
a police officer with
something to prove

Beth ~
a daughter with a
storybook future

When all they love
is lost, what's worth
living for?

ASHBERRY
LANE
ASHBERRYLANE.COM

CPSIA information can be obtained at www.ICGtesting.com
Printed in the USA
LVOW11s1618150915

454264LV00003B/706/P